PRAISE FOR AVA MILES

Nora Roberts Land
"Ava's story is witty and charming."
—Barbara Freethy #1 *NYT* bestselling author

Selected by *USA Today* as one of the Best Books of the year alongside Nora Roberts' *Dark Witch* and Julia Quinn's *Sum of all Kisses*.

"If you like Nora Roberts type books, this is a must-read."
—Readers' Favorite

Country Heaven
"If ever there was a contemporary romance that rated a 10 on a scale of 1 to 5 for me, this one is it!"
—The Romance Reviews

"*Country Heaven* made me laugh and cry...I could not stop flipping the pages. I can't wait to read the next book in this series." —Fresh Fiction

Country Heaven Cookbook
"Delicious, simple recipes... Comfort food, at its best."
—Fire Up The Oven Blog

The Bridge to a Better Life
Selected by *USA Today* as one of the Best Books of the Summer.

"Miles offers a story of grief, healing and rediscovered love." —USA Today

"I've read Susan Mallery and Debbie Macomber...but never have I been so moved by the books Ava Miles writes." —Booktalk with Eileen Reviews

The Gate to Everything
"The constant love...bring a sensual, dynamic tension to this appealing story." —Publisher's Weekly

More Praise For Ava

The Chocolate Garden
"On par with Nicholas Sparks' love stories."
—Jennifer's Corner Blog

"A must-read...a bit of fairy magic...a shelf full of happiness." —Fab Fantasy Fiction

The Promise of Rainbows
"This is a story about grace, faith and the power of both..."
—The Book Nympho

French Roast
"Ms. Miles draws from her experience as an apprentice chef...and it shows...I loved {the} authenticity of the food references, and the recipes...looked divine." —BlogCritics

The Holiday Serenade
"This story is all romance, steam, and humor with a touch of the holiday spirit..." —The Book Nympho

The Town Square
"Ms. Miles' words melted into each page until the world receded around me..." —Tome Tender

The Park of Sunset Dreams
"Ava has done it again. I love the whole community of Dare Valley..." —Travel Through The Pages Blog

The Goddess Guides Series
"Miles' series is an **exquisite exploration** of internal discomfort and courage, allowing you to reclaim your divine soul and fully express your womanhood."
—Dr. Shawne Duperon, Project Forgive Founder, Nobel Peace Prize Nominee

"The Goddess Guides are a **world changer**. Well done, Ava." —International Bestseller Kate Perry aka Kathia Zolfaghari, Artist & Activist

Also by Ava Miles

Fiction

The Merriams Series

Wild Irish Rose

Love Among Lavender

The Love Letter Series

Letters Across An Open Sea

Along Waters of Sunshine and Shadow

The Dare Valley Series

Nora Roberts Land

French Roast

The Grand Opening

The Holiday Serenade

The Town Square

The Park of Sunset Dreams

The Perfect Ingredient

The Bridge to a Better Life

The Calendar of New Beginnings

Home Sweet Love

The Moonlight Serenade

The Sky of Endless Blue

Daring Brides

The Dare River Series

Country Heaven

Country Heaven Song Book

Country Heaven Cookbook

The Chocolate Garden
The Chocolate Garden:
A Magical Tale (Children's Book)
Fireflies and Magnolias
The Promise of Rainbows
The Fountain of Infinite Wishes
The Patchwork Quilt of Happiness

Dare Valley Meets Paris Billionaire Mini-Series

The Billionaire's Gamble
The Billionaire's Courtship
The Billionaire's Secret
The Billionaire's Return

The Goddess Guides to Being a Woman

Goddesses Decide
Goddesses Deserve The G's
Goddesses Love Cock
Goddesses Cry and Say Motherfucker
Goddesses Don't Do Drama
Goddesses Are Sexy
Goddesses Eat
Goddesses Are Happy
Goddesses Face Fear

Other Non-Fiction

The Happiness Corner: Reflections So Far
Home Baked Happiness

Love Among Lavender

The Merriams

Ava Miles

ISBN-13: 978-1-949092-09-7
www.avamiles.com
Ava Miles

To all the people who always told me the truth—it truly is the most prized of fragrances.

And to my divine entourage, who continues to show me even happier, more expansive visions of my life.

ACKNOWLEDGEMENTS

After researching master perfumers and the perfume industry, I wanted to give special thanks to Roja Dove. Like Tim McGraw for COUNTRY HEAVEN, Roja's vision and artistry made LOVE AMONG LAVENDER even more magical. Until him, I didn't realize perfume was about more than scent; it was about us as people and our character; a fragrance that sums us up in a powerful transmission of notes. Not only am I going to pay more attention to what I smell and what it tells me, but I'm going to see every encounter with scent as a moment of sheer majesty. Thank you, Roja, from the deepest part of my heart.

Making perfume is a lot like looking for true love.

Some scents completely overwhelm you or lose their luster the moment they touch your skin.

Others fade the longer you wear them, best forgotten anyway.

The perfect scent is a balance of different notes...

That's the kind people stop you on the street about, the one that everyone wants to have.

When you find that scent, you'd best wear it the rest of your natural life.

Clara Merriam Hale
Budding Matchmaker Extraordinaire

CHAPTER 1

BEAU MASTERS NEVER TOOK A MEETING WITHOUT HIS BUSIness manager.

And yet, here Caitlyn was, alone with the wholesome superstar of country music. She was going to hyperventilate. *Pull it together. Forget he's the world's most compelling man and the key to your success. This is business.*

When Beau had called her two days ago at her new perfume headquarters in Provence, France, asking her to meet him at his office in Nashville, she'd done a happy dance all the way onto the corporate jet.

"Should we wait for your mother?" She asked to be polite, sure, but also to cover herself. Based on the short phone conversation she'd had with his mother, Mary Ellen Walker was a difficult woman to please. She was also notorious for being the gatekeeper to Beau Masters. From what Caitlyn had read about him, and she'd done her research, his mother—*mom*ager—had handled *everything* for him since he was first discovered at the tender age of sixteen. A music scout had overheard him singing at a funeral of all places, and he'd put out a string of number one hits since his first single, "Home Bound."

A shadow crossed his face, and he shifted in his chair. Even in jeans and a simple white button-down shirt he commanded attention. "She won't be joining us today. Usually I stick in my lane—writing the songs, doing the concerts, meeting with fans, smiling in promos—but your proposal really captivated me."

Captivated? "It did?" she asked, trying not to gape. "That makes me so happy."

His smile punched through like the sun through a patch of clouds. That earnest, white-toothed smile was the perfect companion to his boy-next-door looks. Some might think it a tad crooked, what with the way his bottom lip curved, but she personally thought that slight twist of the lip made him more appealing. When he smiled, you smiled. It was cause and effect, like her scientist sister would say.

"I know I have a reputation for keeping my head out of the business side and all. Getting discovered so young kinda set me and Mama down a certain road. She ran a hardware store with my daddy, and she's always said I don't have a lick of business sense in me, like him. Maybe you'll be able to teach me some things if we reach an agreement. It's clear from your proposal—and how you carry yourself—that you're real smart."

Beau looked at her, and she couldn't look away. Not that she wanted to. His eyes, a mix of blue and gray, seemed to see into her soul.

"Thank you for that," she said, sitting up a little straighter in her chair. "I'm sure you're being modest, but you can ask me anything about business."

Did her *anything* sound a little breathless? God, he really was so handsome. Her eyes dipped to his square jaw. It was manly enough to take a punch if he was ever in a bar brawl defending a woman's honor, which he had been, according to media reports. He'd even been caught on camera chasing down a purse-snatcher. Beau didn't just sing about being a good man.

He was one.

She knew she was grinning back at him like an idiot. What she should be doing was making the most captivating pitch of her life. She wanted this man—this famous singer—to be the face of her new perfume. A perfume for women. It wasn't the conventional way of marketing perfume, but she knew in her gut it would work. Look at that smile, after all? It seemed to promise Beau was the best friend—or boyfriend—you could ever have.

Get your head in the game, Merriam.

She was a senior executive, for heaven's sake, not some teenager on a date. Her brother had approved the funding for her pet project for the beauty and skincare branch of their family corporation, Merriam Enterprises, and she intended to prove herself.

"Let me tell you a little more about what I have in mind," she said, leaning back in her chair, trying to match his relaxed pose. Only she leaned back too far in her enthusiasm and felt her chair tip backward.

Beau shot out of his chair like a cannon and caught her before she could fall all the way. He loomed over her for a second, his mouth twitching, his scent a feast for the senses. Something fresh yet manly.

"These ergonomic chairs might be comfy but they buckle under the slightest pressure." Like her in his presence, it seemed. Well, that was a problem easily fixed. If she convinced him to be her spokesperson, they wouldn't have to see each other again until the marketing plans rolled out. She would be safe in that throng. Commercials and photo shoots were always a hot mess.

"So, as I was starting to say before my chair interrupted me..."

His smile deepened, and she reined in her need to sigh like a schoolgirl.

"As you read in my proposal, my team at Merriam Cosmetics and Skincare is about to create the world's best *organic* perfume, one that uses ingredients found in nature to enhance a woman's natural beauty and allure. I don't like the way the cosmetics game is usually played. Companies often market makeup by making women think they're not good enough. That they need to look like someone else. Be someone else. I want to help them feel beautiful as they are."

"I couldn't agree more," he said. "I figure natural is the way we came in, so why change it."

Feeling she'd finally found her stride, Caitlyn nodded and leaned forward slightly—careful not to jostle the chair—as if she were about to confide a secret. "Exactly. My research suggests you're the perfect spokesperson to convince women they want to buy it and wear it. You're aware of your appeal, I imagine. Women believe you when you talk because you're honest."

His smile slipped. "Honesty has always been a hallmark of my life."

Amen, she almost said, but he looked discomposed. Maybe embarrassed? "Then there's your appeal to the male audience. You're a man's man. Men want to be like you. You're one of those good guys everyone wants to have over for a barbecue. When you tell a guy to buy something special for the woman in their life, they'll do it. You sing about treasuring a woman in so many of your songs, and that appeals to both purchasing audiences."

Of course, the phrase he used was *my woman*, and the way he sang it was downright swoon-worthy.

"That's mighty kind of you to say, Caitlyn, but I'm just a regular guy who's been blessed with a nice voice and a platform to sing great songs about the things that matter to me."

"*This* is why you're so compelling. You're real." She'd worked with other celebrities to promote their products. Many of them had egos as large as their paychecks, but Beau Masters seemed true to his image. Personally, she wanted to thank God and kiss the ground or something.

There was no wizard behind the cloth. Beau was simply an incredibly handsome, sweet, nice guy with mega talent.

You need to stop before you embarrass yourself.

"That's why I wanted to come to you with my new perfume—" She paused for a second, wondering if she could call him Beau, then decided not to push her luck. "You're everything I hope to say with this product because to me it's about more than perfume. Plus, I know you've been looking for something to promote."

"My mother has," he informed her.

And she wasn't here. Curious and curiouser. "Well, Mr. Masters, look no further for something awesome."

"It's Beau, Caitlyn, just Beau."

His Southern accent reminded her of cold mint juleps that went down easy on a hot day. A woman could get tipsy on that voice. Mercy, what did her voice sound like, she wondered? A barking frog? "Well, Beau, I think our perfume is the perfect product for you and your brand."

"I'd love to hear what you think my brand is." His lips twitched again. Was he finding her amusing? Who could blame him? She was acting a little starstruck. Not her usual.

"As I told my brother, who decides on new business initiatives, you're the world's most compelling man. Women trust you. I don't fully know you, and *I* trust you."

"That's mighty kind of you to say," he said, his cheeks flushing a touch.

Adorable. "You're nice, earnest, and easy on the eyes with a voice like an angel." She wasn't going to blab about the mint juleps. Way too weird. "It's no wonder people have paid you to sing at funerals since you were seven. What better voice to send off a loved one?"

"It was good money, and when Daddy died, I wanted to help Mama in my own way." He flushed deeper. "I can't believe your brother's still talking to you after you said all of that. Isn't he upset you don't think he's the most compelling man? Unless you're married, of course."

"I'm not," she said way too quickly. "This brother, Quinn—I have several—doesn't want to be nice or earnest. He's more of a bossy type."

"I see." He picked up his glass of regular old tap water. Not fizzy or spring water at some exacting temperature. He was a celebrity, but he didn't expect anyone to cater to him—nor did he cater to himself. "Tell me a little more about your family. Do you all work for the business?"

He would like the family angle. Before hitting it big, he'd helped his mama with the hardware store after school, or so she'd read. They'd sold it after the release of his first big album, *Score*. "There are seven of us, and all of us have worked in the company. My oldest brother, Connor, is the president. Quinn is the second. Ah...are you sure you want to hear this? We have a big family."

"I like big families, so yes, please tell me about everyone." He leaned forward, sipping more water, his light eyes steady on her face. "It's important to me to know who I'd be working with."

She snorted. "Oh, you won't be working with them. Unless you want to, of course."

He laughed. "I didn't mean that. Hearing about your family helps me get a better sense about you. Families... define a person."

The way his voice dimmed was akin to a stink bomb being released in a classroom. Again, she wondered what had happened between him and his mother. Had they fought? Heck, she could understand family squabbles. Her brothers knew how to drive her batty.

"Trevor and J.T. are next. They're twins and have this incredible ability to read each other's minds. Like in *X-Men*."

"I love those films," he said.

"Me too!" *Easy, tiger. Settle down. This isn't speed dating.* "Trevor works with Merriam Oil & Gas, and J.T.

used to have an executive position there too, but he stepped down to protect the family from his ex-wife." Usually she wouldn't speak about it, but she thought he'd understand.

"Let me guess," he said, his mouth bunching like his water had gone sour. "She wanted money."

"Yes, but only to make him suffer," she said, nodding. "The good news is he's finally clear of her, and now he's doing something else for the family. Our great-grandfather, Emmits Merriam, who started the company after striking oil in Oklahoma, loved art. J.T. got the bug. He's opening an art museum at the university Grandpa Emmits founded in Dare Valley, Colorado."

"Education is important," Beau said, pouring himself some more water. "I'm glad your family values that. I made sure to get my GED since I left school early. I wanted to support my mama after all she did for me."

She knew the story, but this was the Beau in his songs. The one who took care of the people important to him. The world needed more men like him. "My mom and her dad were both college professors, so believe me, education was big growing up. But I digress."

"You're talking to a Southerner, Caitlyn. Digressing is what we do for breakfast, lunch, and dinner. It's why we call these interactions 'visits' instead of 'meetings.'"

How quaint. She needed to get her Southern on. They had such a pleasant, colorful way of saying things. "I'm glad you're cool with digressing because I talk a lot. Drives my brothers crazy. Except for Flynn, who's up next. Okay, well, I *mostly* don't drive him nuts. He's right after me in birth order, and we hang a lot since we've both made New York City our home base."

"I wouldn't have taken you for a city girl," he said, leaning back in his chair in that loose-limbed way of his.

"Don't get me wrong. I grew up in Napa back in the day, and it's all farmland. I love it. There's nothing like walking through the vines at night as the sun is coming down. And when the fog rolls in..." She took a moment to grab her water and down some. Man, she was thirsty from jet lag. "You get the idea. It's beautiful and so picturesque your heart soars in your chest."

He smiled at her. "You could write a song for me, talking like that."

And here she'd thought she was done swooning. "Why, thank you, but I think I'll stick to my new perfume. Anyway, when I knew I wanted to focus on fashion and cosmetics for the company, the Big Apple was the ideal choice. Back then, Paris didn't occur to me as an option, or I would have gone there. I spend my time between New York and L.A. for work, but Paris is my true love. No better city in the world in my humble opinion. We're creating the perfume in France specifically because it's the perfume capital."

"So what does Flynn do for the company?"

"He's the tech guy. If you need a tech app or a management software tool... Heck, if you need someone to combat a virus, Flynn is your man, although he's itching for a change. But again—"

"You digress," he finished for her. "If my count is right, there's one sibling left."

"Yes, that's Michaela. She wasn't named after that TV show, *Dr. Quinn, Medicine Woman*, although she gets that all the time. Makes her want to jump off the roof. Doesn't help that she's Dr. Michaela. She got her Ph.D. in Food Science, and she's crazy smart. Treks the Amazon and other places looking for the next superfood or life-saving mushroom, vine, or flower. Not the illegal kind, mind you."

"I got the picture," he said, chuckling. "Y'all sound like quite a family, and I like the way you support the family business."

Y'all. She loved that word and the easy way he said it. Southerners were awesome at taking two words and crunching them into one. "We do our best. My mom is awesome. She's from this Irish-American neighborhood in Chicago, and no one can kick ass—oops, butt—like her. She didn't come from money like my dad—who's really great, although super focused like my older brothers. Doesn't matter that he's retired now. All right, that's my family. What else can I tell you?"

Again, one of his killer lopsided smiles. "Can I smell this incredible perfume of yours?"

"Not yet," she practically sang it out to sugar the truth. "We're just starting our blending process in Provence. I have *the* most incredible perfume maker on the planet working with me. He combines ancient Egyptian techniques with modern French ones."

Beau's brows shot up at that, but she'd expected it. Quinn hadn't gotten the Egyptian angle in the beginning either.

"The Egyptians set the world on fire with their perfumes. I mean, they were the groundbreakers way back when. They're so good that ancient perfume discovered in Egyptian tombs still retains its smell. Four *thousand* years after it was made."

"That is pretty incredible," Beau said. "I like things that last and are made thoughtfully. Today, everything seems to be made so cheaply and poorly because it's more cost-effective. Chaps my hide."

"Exactly! That's why I thought we needed something unique. Master blenders are like the rarest of diamonds, and this guy I've brought on has the background and the vision to make this work. He's a true artist. Combining the ancient ways with the modern French style for perfume, the current gold standard, will take it to a whole new level. Plus, we're using flowers and other ingredients from organic farms, and that's really important to people these days. Besides, I like the notion of using the pure essence of flowers in our perfume. The less pesticides, the better. Although scents don't only come from flowers, of course."

"Good point," he said, leaning forward again. "Pure essence," he said, rolling the words over his tongue. "That's a lot like honesty, it seems to me."

There was that word again. *Honesty*. It mattered to him. "Yes, perfume is like wine in many ways. It doesn't lie, so to speak. Take it out of the casks too early, you're going to taste it. Store it improperly, you'll want to spit it out. With perfume, it's much the same, I'm learning. Add too much of one thing, and it overwhelms everything else. It's an incredible art."

"Sounds like it," he said in that sexy drawl. "I support a lot of farmers through concerts and fundraisers. I like to joke that if I hadn't wanted to sing so badly, I probably would be planting seeds in the spring and driving through my fields in a John Deere tractor come fall, harvesting my crops. I value what farmers do. They work hard for their living and aren't appreciated enough, if you ask me."

She wanted to applaud. "You'd love the farm I bought in Provence. It's mostly lavender—my favorite scent—but it has other flowers we'll likely use for the perfume. A fragrance has so many scents blended together, and we'll be searching for the highest quality organic ingredients. We'll be working with other farmers around the world, I expect, but you should see the way they pick flowers in Provence. It's all done by hand. Some of the women bring their young children to work with them. I've seen their new babies lying on a blanket or in a basket as they pick the May roses or jasmine. The families take lunch together. It's magic."

"Sounds like quite a sight. Families need to eat together more."

"We always did growing up," she piped in.

"I imagine it's a nice change for a mother. Raising children can't be... Never mind."

She wondered why he'd cut himself off. When he didn't finish the thought, she said, "That's why I think you're a perfect fit for this. You understand the story I'm trying to tell. Farmers sow seeds for flowers every year— well, not all flowers because some are already rooted, but you get the idea. They have to believe those tiny little specks they're sowing will bloom into something beautiful. That takes a lot of faith, if you ask me, especially in our culture of instant gratification."

His blue-gray eyes scanned her face, and she tried to stay still under his intense regard even as her heartbeat kicked up. She'd known he was handsome, but in person, it was insane.

"I couldn't have said it better, Caitlyn. In fact, the reason I decided to meet you was because you said in your proposal, and I quote, 'perfume connects us to our roots. To the land, to people we've never met, and lastly to ourselves. In those special notes of fragrance, we begin to understand who we are and what we want to project in the world.'"

Her hand dropped off her chair, her body tingling. "You memorized all that?"

"It struck me here," he said, bringing his hand to his heart in the sweetest, most earnest gesture she'd ever seen. "Hard. My new album is about roots. The ones we know. The ones we think we know. Even the ones we're afraid of."

She couldn't imagine Beau Masters being afraid of anything. But of course, he would be. He was just as human as the rest of them. "I think I'm going to love this new album."

"I'm just starting to write it, but what you said... It got me to thinking. Heck, it was almost like you read my mind."

"Kindred spirits," she breathed out loud.

Before she could kick herself for being too forward,

and *so* unprofessional, he nodded. Holding her gaze, he said, "Exactly. Tell me more about my contribution."

She wanted to high-five him. And possibly hyperventilate. "We'd want to use one of your songs in our marketing. Something that fits the perfume and the story we're telling. It sounds like you'll have something—"

"On my upcoming album," he finished for her.

"That would be awesome. We'd want both TV and print advertisements as well."

His brows winged up. "That's not the favorite part of my career, let me tell you. Now, I dress up okay for photos, but in the beginning I was a mess."

"You were discovered young," she said. "Trust me, you did better than I did back then. I didn't find my groove fashion-wise until I moved to New York after college. Before that, I was known to wear plaid pants with a striped shirt because I loved the way the lines intersected. My brother Flynn likes to pull out the pictures to remind me."

He leaned toward her as if confessing a secret. "Well, I could barely tie a tie, and it really didn't look great with Levi's and work boots. My mama thought... Her opinions figured in strongly, I suppose. Dressing me like a simple man seems to work the best."

He was wrong. He'd look good in anything. "You're being modest. And I haven't seen any photos of you wearing a tie, although I imagine you likely bust one out for church."

He laughed. "We still dress up pretty formal for church in these here parts. I always say you've gotta stop trying to do something you're not good at after a while, so I stopped trying to dress up. I'm more comfortable in jeans and a work shirt. Although I do get a little tired of being so buttoned up and boring all the time."

Boring? He was talking crazy. Sure, she'd never seen him wearing the tight jeans and blingy belt buckles favored by some country singers, and the only hat he'd ever been photographed in was a baseball cap, but simple worked for him. He was as wholesome as apple pie and just as tempting. Not that she could say so.

"Your style works, trust me. What else can I tell you?" She wondered if it would be crass to talk compensation yet. Her initial offer had been included in her pitch.

"Why do you really think I'd be a good fit for this? Be completely honest with me."

Her specialty. His fixation. "Because you care about people, and the women who see these ads are going to pick up on that. Maybe they don't feel good about themselves, especially after a long day of worrying, working, and taking care of the kids, but you're going to assure them that they should. That they *matter*. That they deserve to feel sexy and fabulous just as they are."

He made a humming sound that sounded like a note from a cello.

"Women need to hear more of those messages. If you let all the media get to you, you're going to feel like you can't ever be pretty enough or skinny enough or smart enough." She stopped, realizing she'd gotten way too personal. This was about women in general. Not her in particular.

"Is that how you feel, Caitlyn?" He covered his mouth with his hand, studying her.

Damn. "Sometimes. That's part of the reason I want *you* to be our spokesperson, not a glamorous actress or model. I want to tell a different story, make a social statement or two, and I think you're just the man to do it with me."

Okay, that was really personal, but it was also honest. She wasn't just making a perfume. She was making a stand for women, one she'd already made for herself. Once again, she thanked Jace the Jerk. They'd been dating for a few months, on their way to serious, when he'd offered to pay for a boob job, saying she'd look so much better, *sexier*, with bigger breasts. If she hadn't been so hurt, pissed off, and generally insulted by his offer, she might not have pushed forward with this venture. Starting anything new was risky, and perfume was an established market. But she had a new angle, and she was going to ride this train to success. She was a Merriam, after all. They never did half measures.

"I think I'd like to be that guy too, Caitlyn." Beau lowered his fist and smiled. "Talking to people through my music is important to me. I can envision this campaign working the same way."

"Yes! Awesome!" Terrible business words, but God help her, she was *excited*.

"I'd really like to do this with you," he said, slapping his knee as if to punctuate it. "But I'm going to need a few things."

"Brass tacks time. Being a Merriam, I love this part. Tell me."

"I'd like to come stay at the farm in France with you for a spell. Get to know the land and the people involved in this venture. Like your perfume guy. Connect to the roots, you know. Smell the air."

"The air smells like nothing you've ever experienced."

"I can't wait. Also, I'd feel a mite more comfortable seeing what kind of perfume you come up with before signing the contract. You understand."

Her brother Quinn wouldn't like that, but she couldn't deny it made sense. "That's to your credit. Some celebrities don't care what they hock so long as they get paid. Oops, did I say that out loud?"

"It's refreshing," he assured her. "I have lots of people wanting me to 'hock' things, but few care to tell me why I should in a way that works for me. Your proposal was one of the best I've read—and yes, I do read them even though Mama handles that side of things—which is why I pushed to meet with you myself."

"Great!"

He leaned forward almost conspiratorially, and she followed suit.

"Between us, my mama doesn't get this roots thing. In fact, she's not happy about the theme for my upcoming album."

"Family!" She waved her hands in the air dramatically. "They love you, but sometimes they just won't let you fly."

"Nice to have someone get that," he said. "Usually she's fully behind me, but..."

"You're growing up." She winced, gesturing to his big body. "Not that you're not grown up or anything. You just turned thirty, after all. I only meant that sometimes parents want to keep thinking of us as dependent children. It's a comfort and a pain in the ass."

"Did you say 'kindred spirits' earlier?"

She could die right now, she decided. She'd never had a kindred spirit outside of her family before, she realized. What a happy surprise. Michaela was never going to believe her.

"I figure once I get the lay of the land and smell this incredible perfume you're planning, we'll be good to go."

She tapped her feet under the table.

"You have happy feet," he said, grinning.

"What?"

"Musicians always hear the beat." Then he winked at her, and what a wink. Pure charm. "Caitlyn, it's been a pleasure."

When he extended his hand, she clasped it. He held it, his touch warm and friendly. But his eyes were shining, and she felt like the center of his world.

She'd picked the perfect spokesperson! This perfume was going to be the hit she'd envisioned. That thought was followed by another—she'd never been so attracted to a man, inside and out, as she was to Beau Masters. Did he feel the same way, or was she letting her imagination get away from her?

"Thanks again for the meeting," he said. "I'm really looking forward to this."

"Me too!"

"And thanks for telling me your story," he added, walking her to the door.

His hand was gentle against the small of her back. "What story?" Her brain had gone blank at his touch. First, kindred spirits and now this...

"Roots, Caitlyn." He opened the door to the suite, leaning his shoulder against the frame. "Roots."

"Yes! Roots. Well, I have to get back to France. Poor me, right? See you, Beau."

"All right now," he said as she walked backward. "Have a safe trip back."

She probably looked like an idiot, but she couldn't bring herself to turn her back on him. The way he stood, all tall and manly against the door, made her mouth water.

"I'll be in touch when my schedule opens up," he said, "and I can pop over to the farm in France."

Her right foot came out of her heel, and her ankle wobbled. She bent down to straighten her lucky Manolo Blahnik pumps, the shoes she'd been wearing when Quinn had agreed to fund her perfume venture. Suddenly a masculine hand took her arm to steady her. Those long, tapered fingers trailed down to her ankle, helping her back into the shoe. Warmth followed them.

Oh. My. God.

She raised her chin, and Beau Masters was inches away from her on bended knee. There were gold flames in his blue-gray eyes, she saw. His scent washed over her again, all woodsy and male.

"Ah... thank you. I must be the clumsiest person on the planet."

"I don't think so." He ran a finger over the lace pattern

on her arch. "These are some shoes."

"They have flowers on them. I thought it fitting since perfume—"

"Comes from flowers," he finished for her.

He was finishing her sentences again. She was in trouble. "Yes. Well, thanks for being my Prince Charming, but this Cinderella has a plane to catch."

She didn't, not really—the private jet would leave whenever she was ready to leave—but if she didn't get away from him now, she was going to do something stupid.

"Any time, Cinderella." He took her elbow gently, and together they stood.

He didn't remove his hand. She didn't want him to.

They stared at each other, and she couldn't bring herself to look away. She wanted to keep talking with him, keep looking at him, keep being with him.

Her brother Trevor had told her that he'd fallen for his now-wife Becca after only a brief encounter. The idea seemed ludicrous, the kind of thing that only happened in storybooks and rom coms, and yet her mom and dad had a similar story about love at first sight. The Merriams weren't conventional in other ways, so why should they be when it came to love?

"Maybe..." Beau trailed off, his voice husky.

She froze, feeling the vibration in that single word. Was he going to ask her out? Her brain exploded. Could she say yes as a professional?

How could she tell him no, feeling like this?

He made an unidentifiable sound and then looked away from her. "Ah, maybe you could...send me some pictures of the farm. The process. Even...a video or two of you making the perfume with the master blender. Your business ideas. I'd...ah...like that."

It felt like her heart had dropped to the soles of her feet. He was asking her to *text* him about business? She was so dumb. "Of course. Sure."

He started walking her toward the elevator, his hand still wrapped around her arm like a delicious hot pack for muscles needing TLC.

"Your door is open." She gestured to his suite.

Chuckling, he kept walking with her. "I guess I'm forgetful."

"And I'm clumsy. What a pair." *Keep it light, Caitlyn.*

"You're too sure of yourself to be clumsy," he said, surprising her.

He punched the down button, but his hold on her hadn't relaxed. Hot tingles coursed out from where the pads of his fingers touched her skin. She firmed her ankles so they wouldn't buckle in her shoes again.

"I really should get going."

He rubbed her arm. Just once. "I wish..."

Her whole heart leapt in that pause, but the elevator door opened, and the moment was lost.

"Never mind," he said softly.

"I'll send you some pictures," she said, taking a step toward the elevator.

Except...he didn't seem to be letting her go. She was so confused. Was he interested, or was she completely misreading him?

"Don't forget about that video."

"I won't." She gently pulled on his grip despite her soul-deep desire to stay put.

"Oh, sorry. I didn't realize I still had you." That compelling smile of his almost sent her to her knees in sheer bliss. She needed to get on that elevator before she did something she'd regret.

The elevator started to shut. He lurched forward and stopped it with the hand that held her arm. She already missed its warmth.

"I'm keeping you." His low-pitched voice made her belly tighten, like he was singing a song just for her.

I wish. "No, I'm keeping you." She forced herself into the elevator and punched the lobby button. "Bye, Beau."

He raised a lone hand in the air, almost a wave. "Bye, Caitlyn."

Her throat was tight. It made no sense, but she suddenly felt deeply sad. Bereft, even. Like she was saying goodbye to someone she didn't want to be without. They watched each other as the door closed, and she memorized the way his crooked smile smoothed out, the way his eyes seemed to stare into her soul. When the elevator started to descend, she took a few steps back until she hit the back wall.

She felt like the door had closed on something that might have been beautiful.

CHAPTER 2

ROOTS.

Beau sank into the chair Caitlyn had sat in, feeling oddly uprooted from their meeting. No, not a meeting. That was the wrong word for something so magical and unexpected.

Her warmth still burned his hand, and he rubbed his palms together, not wanting that heat to dissipate. What a woman! Sure, he'd known she was special from her proposal. Being a singer, he knew the power of words and the union they created between the person delivering them and the one receiving them. Usually he was the one delivering, so when someone moved him with words—especially not in a song, his normal medium—he paid attention. Caitlyn had riveted him with her talk of roots and seeds. Of the importance of knowing where something came from. It was as if she'd opened the book of his soul. Now he knew her voice too, the way she clipped her vowels and consonants, talking as fast as a speeding car at times. Suddenly he heard guitar and fiddle, and lyrics started to form in his mind.

She was more than a breath of fresh air. She was a hurricane coming in off the Gulf.

Finally!

He'd been suffering the worst writer's block of his life. After a recent songwriting retreat with fellow country singers, Rye Crenshaw and Jake Lassiter, he'd come home with nothing but the theme for his new album—roots—and a heap of balled-up paper. He had a contract for a new album and no songs, and he was behind for the first time in his career.

Meeting Caitlyn had shaken things up for him. He felt more like himself than he had in a good long while.

He sat back in the chair, humming, and allowed himself to think of her. When she'd walked in, the sight of her in that blue dress and the tan legs beneath it had nearly rendered him speechless.

More guitar, louder now, filtered into his mind.

The cloth of that sexy blue dress moved with her as if storm winds stirred around her. She was young and beautiful, and she spoke with the full force of her heart. Caitlyn had shaken him out of his writer's block, and he wasn't so foolish as to ignore a sign like that. He already knew he could fall in love with this woman if he let himself, although he hadn't seen it coming until he'd sunk to the ground before her.

This time a harmonica wailed in his mind. *When she came out of her shoe and I bent down to help, her arch seemed like a long road I'd traveled, one I'd been on too long alone.*

The words were the refrain for a lifetime, and he knew it.

He'd gone steady early in high school, and then stardom had come knocking, and women had started to throw themselves at him willy-nilly. At sixteen, he'd had women press their panties into his hand at a fan meet and greet...and offer him sexual congress more apt to that Christian Grey guy than a guy like him, who really only wanted to go steady and do some serious loving out in the woods. Some were his age, some thirty years older.

The more they'd pursued him, the more he'd withdrawn. He'd even asked for his mama's help in protecting him from the predators, and for a time, he'd been so busy, he hadn't dated at all. Setups from friends later on hadn't gone much better. Every woman he met wanted Beau Masters the country star. Not plain ol' Beau. His mama had started to vet them even, wanting to make sure they weren't pursuing him for his money or fame. He'd bided his time, knowing the right woman would show up when the stars aligned. Someone he would both admire and want.

It felt like there'd been an outright meteor shower with Caitlyn. And what had he done? He'd stopped himself from asking her out. If he was honest with himself, his mama's advice had caught him up short. *True love doesn't happen overnight, Beau*, his mama would say. *Songs are one thing, life is another. Time always reveals a person's character, and with your success, Beau, best wait and not put yourself in a bad situation. I rushed into marrying your daddy, and look what happened.* Besides which, he'd been raised to do things the *Southern gentleman's way.* A gentleman took his time—he showed a woman he respected her before he asked for a kiss or even a date.

Although his mama was sometimes a mite bit too pushy, he mostly agreed. In fact, given how powerful his feelings were, he didn't want to screw anything up. The slow approach was the way to go, but he certainly wasn't about to let this opportunity slip through his hands. He pulled out his phone and texted her.

Hey Caitlyn! Thanks again for coming today. I'm really glad to have met you. You're a breath of fresh air and lovely to boot.

He read what he'd sent and cringed. *This* was the best Beau Masters, award-winning songwriter, could come up with? He sucked at serenading women.

His phone beeped, and he read her reply with sweaty palms.

Hey back! Great to meet you too, Beau. Made my day. I'm so excited about the perfume. Talk soon. Your kindred spirit. Hope that's not too weird.

He smiled slowly. He needed to look at his schedule and see when he could make that trip to the farm. He wrote: *No, I like it. Your KS.*

Golly molly, he might as well be in grade school again, scribbling hearts on her notebook. But then she sent him a smiley face, and his heart lit up. Okay, maybe he hadn't made a fool of himself. Besides, she *liked* his nice guy side. Not that he'd ever let anyone see a glimpse of darkness in him.

His father had been a bad enough man for both of them. A drunk. A philanderer. A brute. But while Beau took pride in being nothing like his daddy, it was easier to defeat the devil you knew. After choosing the theme for his album, he'd decided it was time to face his own roots. Where had his daddy's people come from back in the day? He knew next to nothing about Walt Masters and his Masters ancestors. His mama never talked about them, and to hear her tell it, they were all dead.

Which was why he'd sent his daddy's baby tooth to a private genetic testing company. Dr. Clarridge had called earlier, while Caitlyn was still visiting. Shifting in his chair, his stomach doing flip-flops, he called the doctor back.

"Dr. Clarridge," her crisp voice answered.

"It's Beau Masters, returning your call."

"Oh, hello, Beau," she said. "Thanks for getting back to me so fast. I'm sure you have a million things going on. Listen, I know you had some trouble locating a sample of DNA from your father."

"I got lucky with the boxes I found in the attic. Until then, I hadn't thought my grandmother was a sentimental

woman. It surprised me to see she'd kept his baby book."
A lock of soft, brown hair and Walt's first lost tooth
tucked into a small envelope with a tooth fairy on it—the
evidence of the sweet boy he'd been had shocked Beau, so
different than the man he remembered.

"That's just it, Beau," she said. "While the baby tooth
contained enough DNA for testing, the sample you gave
me isn't from your father, I'm afraid."

He wandered into his private office, not believing
what he was hearing. "It has to be, Dr. Clarridge," Beau
said.

"It's not," she said, her voice gently certain. "We ran
the tests twice to be sure. Maybe it's someone else's."

"The whole book is devoted to my father. There were
no other children."

A fist clenched his gut, and he picked up the baby
book still on his desk and opened it. The photos from his
daddy's childhood and young adulthood had come from
the same box. Beau didn't see much of himself in the man
they showed. The resemblance was so absent, he'd pur-
chased a magnifying glass to better study the old photos
and compare them to childhood photos of himself. He
looked so much more like his mama. Their eyes were the
same stormy blue. Their noses had the same slope, level-
ing out into full lips. She was all over his face.

The lack of resemblance was even starker because
he'd had to reacquaint himself with his daddy's face after embarking on this search for roots. Growing up, his
mother had removed all traces of Walt Masters from their
home, saying he was a man best laid to rest forever. She'd
raised Beau to be his opposite, hammering into him an
ever-growing list of never and always: never swear, always be grateful; never shout, always listen; never drink,
always keep a cool head; never lie, always tell the truth.
And on it went. No wonder he had a reputation for being
the squeakiest clean music star in the country.

"Beau, I'm sorry, but the DNA in your sample doesn't match. Maybe you should look through his things again."

"There were no more boxes."

"Well, if you find something else that would make a good sample, send it along," Dr. Clarridge said. "With him being gone so long, we don't have a lot of options, you know. We can give you a comprehensive report about you, of course. Perhaps your mother can fill in some of the information about your father in the absence of a sample."

He could ask Mama. Except she never spoke of his daddy. Hadn't since the day of his funeral. After the funeral luncheon, she'd taken down all of his pictures and boxed up his clothes and keepsakes for Goodwill. That's why Beau had sung at funerals, he'd realized recently. Mama hadn't wanted a fuss, so there had been no music to accompany Walt's passing. Somehow Beau had wanted other people to have a better send-off.

"Thank you, Dr. Clarridge," he said, his heartbeat a crescendo in his chest. "Write up what you can from mine."

"I'll be in touch when I'm finished. Goodbye, Beau."

He sank into his office chair, studying that single photo in Walt Masters' baby book, the page he'd thought would unlock the story of his Masters genetics and ancestry. He picked up a photo of his daddy as a young boy from the mess of photos on his desk. If the tooth wasn't his daddy's, how had it gotten into the book?

Something was wrong here. His eyes lowered to the mess of photos on the desk, finding a photo of himself at around the same age his daddy had been in the picture. Everything went silent in his mind.

A burn started in his stomach.

Conventional wisdom said babies favored their fathers when they were born out of some evolutionary compulsion, almost as if a man needed to see for his own two eyes that a child was his before all the modern tests came on the scene.

Beau looked *nothing* like his daddy. Never had. Not in all the years he'd been alive.

Was Walt Masters really his daddy?

But how could it be otherwise? His mama was a churchgoing woman. She wouldn't have...

He threaded his hands into his hair as agony throbbed there, pressing at his skull. His elbows banged onto the desk, but he ignored the pain.

It can't be. It can't be. It can't be.

He lowered his hands and took in all the photos of him and his daddy scattered over his desk. The truth couldn't be hidden any longer. The tooth sample said that Walt Masters wasn't his daddy—and these photos told the same story.

His mother was the only person who could put his questions to rest.

He raced to her house in Belle Meade, just south of his office downtown. His mama loved the neighborhood, from the endless lawns to the tasteful mansions, which she considered an appropriate fit for her newfound money and status, both of which she'd gained from working hard managing his career. Not to his taste, and even less so today as he stepped out of his Ford pickup truck and walked to her front door.

He'd blasted the air conditioner, but his T-shirt was still damp from nerves and sweat. Mind spinning, he rang the bell. She would be home from the hairdresser.

"Beau!" Her blond highlights were woven into long, straight caramel hair. People commented they looked like mama and son all the time. It struck him that no one had ever said so about him and his father. Not even after he'd died. As a child, Beau had thought it a politesse because his daddy had been such a notorious bounder.

"I need to talk to you," he said, stepping inside the house.

"Bertha just made sweet tea," his mama said. "How about we have some in the sunroom? Bertha! Bring some of that tea in for my boy here. Now, tell me about your meeting with the Merriam heiress. If you hadn't pushed, I never would have let you take it alone."

Leave it to his mother to call someone an heiress. He'd never have used that word to describe Caitlyn Merriam. "It was great. I told her I wanted to do it, assuming they put together a wonderful scent like I expect they will."

He was growing nauseated as they stood in the foyer. How was he supposed to ask her this? She was his mama, the woman who'd raised him single-handedly after Daddy had died, working two jobs to keep them afloat, and then helped him launch his career.

He owed her everything.

"You should have discussed that with me first, honey," she told him, pushing him toward the sunroom like she was wont to do even for a little woman. "That's my job. You didn't sign a contract yet, did you?"

"No, Mama, I know you're better at business than me, but I'm not that dumb."

Bertha appeared with the pitcher of tea and two glasses the moment they sat down. His mama waved her off, but not before Beau gave her a smile and a "thank you."

"I still don't like this idea, Beau. People complain all the time about women wearing perfume in church and just about every product line out there is pushing unscented. So many people have allergies, you know. Besides, it's a French perfume, and your people are more made-in-the-U.S.A. types even though so few products are anymore."

She was pouring him tea like she had a million times, and he just couldn't take it anymore.

"*Stop.*" His voice sounded like it did when he was at the end of a tour, worn out. Done.

She put her hand to his forehead. "What's wrong with you? Are you coming down with something, honey? You look downright pale. I'll have Bertha fix you up a juice. Straighten you out right away."

He took her hands. Looked her straight in the eye. When he did that with someone, he could always tell if they were being truthful. "Mama. I have to ask you something."

"Well, spit it out, boy. You look like you're a tick about to pop."

"Was Walt Masters my daddy?"

He felt her hands jerk in his grip. Saw the shadows enter her eyes, chased by a fear he hadn't seen in his mama since the day their landlord had upped the rent on them, hoping to steal the hardware store out from under them after Walt died. The fool man had insisted a woman couldn't run a business alone, but Beau's mama had proved otherwise.

"*What?*" She yanked her hands out of his. "Are you crazy? Stop talking like this, Beau. This new album has sent you straight off the deep end. I told you nothing good would come of looking into the past. If I'd known I still had those boxes in the attic, I would have tossed them in the trash."

He had his answer, and he had to fight the gorge rising in his throat. He watched her hands shake as she drained the tea she'd poured for him. "Mom, there was a baby tooth in Daddy's baby book. I sent it in for genetic testing. It came back—"

"*You did what?*" She launched herself at him, shoving him hard in the chest. "Why would you do a fool thing like that? How dare you imply—"

"Because I wanted to know my roots! You never talk about him. All my life it's felt like he's this horrible shadow I can't shake. I don't know nothing about him except that you raised me to be nothing like him." His voice broke.

"Of course I never talk about him. Why would I talk about a drunk, a liar, and a cheat? Beau, I tried to protect you from all that. The stories would make you ill. They... Listen, sugar, of course he's your daddy. The lab must have gotten—"

"Then why don't I look anything like him?" He clenched his fists at his sides as his volume rose. "Please, Mama. Tell me the truth. For once, tell me about him. I want to understand how the lab could have gotten this so wrong when they do everything so scientific. Please." *I want to believe you.*

"I will not talk about him beyond what I said, Beauregard."

The sound of his full name rocked him back, and she grabbed his shoulders and shook him. "You're more a man than Walt Masters ever was. I made sure of that, raising you right. That's all you need to know."

She was breathing harshly, like Cousin Alice with emphysema. "Mama, if you were unhappy with Daddy and found someone else to—"

Her open palm crashed against his jaw. "How *dare* you!"

His chest turned to stone. "He's not my daddy, Mama. Tell me who is."

Those eyes—so similar to his own—turned hard. He remembered this woman. She was the one he remembered from childhood, the one who'd shouted at her "clumsy" husband who came home from the bar reeking of cigarette smoke and took a six-pack of beer to his green Barcalounger, ratcheting up the TV volume to blasting for his evening game shows.

"You would condemn me?" Brimstone was smoking in her eyes now. "After everything I've done for you?"

He felt his chest split open from the pain. "I would never condemn you, Mama. Never." He would have to make sense of her choices and the woman he'd thought he knew later. "I only want the truth. Who is my real daddy?"

She laughed, harsh as a window shattering from an errant baseball. "*No.*"

He blinked. "No? Mama, please. You owe me the truth."

"I owe you nothing. You owe me, boy."

He stared at her as her harsh tone crashed over him.

"Beau, I told you nothing good would come of this new album." She stormed to the edge of the room. "Roots! There's nothing but heartache and pain there. Look around you. Do you see this house and all we've built? Your career? You walk down the street, and people admire you for the man you are. This is what happens when you keep looking forward. The past will swallow you up whole. I won't let you do that, Beau. I've worked too hard to get you where you are."

"Mama, I've worked plenty hard myself."

Her hand sliced through the air. "You will stop this nonsense right this minute and find a more decent topic for your album. And you'll tell that Merriam woman you won't be doing her French perfume. Her proposal was a bad influence. I shouldn't have let you talk me into not being there. I see that now. Beau, I won't have this roots nonsense continuing. You heed your mama. I've always known what's best, haven't I?"

His jaw tightened. "I'm not sixteen anymore, Mama. Maybe I need to take a more active role in the business side."

"But you hate that part, and it's my forte," she continued, picking up her phone. She kept talking to him as she placed a call. "I have the perfect product in mind, honey. It's more in keeping with your nice-guy image. And if you want to do a cologne, a new proposal just came in—"

"Put the phone down, Mama."

"Yes, hello, this is Mary Ellen Walker, Beau Masters' mama and manager. Well, aren't you a sweetheart to say so. Yes, I talked to Beau about your offer, and we'd like to—"

He grabbed the phone out of her hand and clicked off the call.

She faced him down with fisted hands at her sides, eyes blazing.

"How dare you interrupt my call like that! I raised you better."

His mouth curved, bitterness burning his lips. "If that isn't the nice guy you like, so be it. Now, tell me who my real daddy is."

She lunged for the phone. "I will not!"

"You're really not going to tell me?" He evaded her as she reached out for the phone again.

"No. I won't. When you're ready to apologize for making me so upset, we'll forget all about this little incident and talk about some 'appropriate' ideas for your new album. You're behind in the songwriting as it is, Beauregard."

That infernal name again. Anger shot through him. "Because I didn't have the material I needed to write something real. I knew something was wrong. I've always known."

Her brows shot to her hairline. "Don't raise your voice to me."

"Mama, I can't write anymore because I don't have the truth." He held out his hand in a silent plea. "I need the truth."

"Well, you won't get it from me," she said, her eyes turning predatory. "Enough of that... If you're having trouble writing, honey, I'll find a songwriter for your new album. We'll ensure they're the kind of songs you do best."

When she put her head against his chest, his heart thundered like a summer storm. He didn't want her to touch him. Least of all manage him like this.

"No, Mama." His voice carried across the room.

They locked eyes. "I won't have you ruin everything we've created over this. It's *nothing*."

"If it's *nothing*, then why are you acting like this? Mama, this isn't nothing. It's everything." His whole life was rotten to the core, and he'd been too dazzled by the shiny outside to realize it.

"Asking these questions will serve no one," she said, pushing her hair back behind her ear. "You'll be nothing if you keep going down this road. I love you too much to let you."

"It's my career, Mama," he said, planting his feet. "And my life."

"Try doing anything without me," she said. "See how far you get. Heck, son, you don't even have a bank account or credit card I'm not on."

She'd always paid his bills and taken care of money things. It had made sense before. Now it made his insides liquefy. "I can change that."

"Come on, honey," she said, patting his chest. "Let's not fight anymore. We're both talking crazy. Mama will handle things. Like I always have."

"You can't handle this, Mama," he said. "I'm doing this album, and I'm doing the perfume too."

He turned and walked out of the room. She wasn't the person he'd always thought her to be. Walt Masters wasn't his daddy.

What did that mean for him?

"Where are you going?" she asked, hurrying after him. "Beau!"

He kept walking.

"Honey, think. You need to stay here with your mama. Get over these crazy ideas."

Crazy ideas. Leave it to her to act all Southern in a moment like this.

"I'm making my album, Mama." He pivoted and faced her in the foyer, the one he'd consented to remodel for her at an exorbitant price. "You best think on that while I'm gone."

"Beau, wait! Don't think I won't find you. When you're acting this crazy—"

He slammed the door behind him, praying her new-found sense of breeding would prevent her from making a scene for the neighbors in her front yard. Wrenching open the truck's door, he pulled out his phone. Started memorizing numbers. Caitlyn Merriam was at the top of his call list.

He needed to get a new phone, one his mother couldn't track.

He needed to take her off his bank accounts and credit cards, grab his passport, and his song notes.

Then he needed to get the heck out of town.

CHAPTER 3

CAITLYN HELD THE PLANE.

How could she do otherwise after receiving Beau's text? From a new number, no less. *This is your KS. Mind if I come along to France early? What's your flight number? I'll buy myself a ticket and see you there.*

She'd knocked over an entire display of boots after reading that. She'd found the perfect pair of teal cowboy boots embroidered with flowers at a famous shop downtown. After righting the fallen boots, she'd texted him right back, doing a little happy-dance shimmy as her fingers flew across the phone. *Awesome! You're kidding. What a surprise.*

Sending off more texts directing him to her private jet area at Nashville International Airport, she headed to the cashier and finished her purchase. He was coming with her! Holy hell.

Maybe he'd regretted leaving things unfinished and unspoken. She was going to have to figure out a way to ask him. They could have a forthright talk about keeping things separate on the business and personal front.

The first person she texted was Michaela: *Beau Masters is coming to France with me.*

She'd already updated her sister and Flynn on their

meeting minus the whole kismet moments where she'd felt like she'd fallen through a wormhole into an alternate reality, one where she and Beau really could fall in love. But maybe she didn't need to be so circumspect. His text seemed to suggest he'd fallen through the wormhole too.

Were they still crazy if it was a shared insanity?

Her sister responded: *No effing way. Did you throw him over your shoulder or something? Way to make things happen, Caity girl. Keep me posted.*

But when Beau set foot in the cabin, where she eagerly awaited him in one of the cushy white leather seats, he didn't look happy to see her. In fact, he looked like downright blue.

She started to wonder if she'd misread the situation. Again. His trademark smile looked like a poor reflection of itself, and even his shoulders were stooped. Maybe something else had happened to prompt this quick turnaround.

"Hey!" His voice was as flat as the tire on an old bicycle. "Bet you didn't expect to see me so soon."

She jumped out of her seat, noting his single leather duffel scuffed from age. So he was coming only for a few days. Had she expected more? Yeah, she'd hoped this was some grand romantic gesture. No denying it.

"No, this is great. I'm so happy you could come this soon. But I'm a little embarrassed. I have mixed feelings about using the company planes. I love the ease and the quiet, but when it's just little old me... You're saving me from a heap of guilt."

"Then I'm happy to be of service," he said as Joris, their flight attendant, stepped out of the cockpit.

"Welcome aboard, Mr. Masters. Can I take your bag?"

"I can stow it myself if you show me where," Beau said, stepping farther into the cabin.

Joris simply nodded and opened one of the roomy compartments. That man was the epitome of calm, but then again he was accustomed to her oldest brothers, Quinn and Connor, who used the company planes more than the rest of them. She loved her brothers to bits, but they could be downright difficult sometimes.

Beau chuckled darkly as he stowed his bag in the compartment. "You went boot shopping."

"It's Nashville," she said, swinging her hands at her sides, nerves racing over her skin.

"Next time you're in town, I'll take you to my favorite place. They have some boots in the back that would blow your mind."

Next time? That sounded more promising, but again, she cautioned herself. She didn't want to presume. "I can't wait. Come sit. Joris, tell Frank we can take off whenever he's ready."

"You've got it, Caitlyn," Joris said. "Can I get you something to drink, Mr. Masters?"

"Beau, and water's just—" Before he could finish, some emotion flashed in his gaze. "No, wait," he called. "How about..."

He closed his eyes like he was working on the biggest decision of his life, and she held her breath. What in the world?

Those stormy eyes were dark gray when he opened them again. "Vodka. With a lime if you have it, Joris."

Her mouth dropped open. One piece of info had been consistent across all of the articles she'd read about Beau: he never drank. Everyone knew he stayed away from the sauce since his dad had been a drunk. Should she ask him outright what was going on? No, she'd let him tell her if he chose. She still couldn't be sure he was here for business or personal or both. He should set the boundaries.

"Surprised?" he asked her, coming down the aisle toward her. "Me too, but the reasons don't.... Never mind."

She didn't take offense—he was using 'never mind' almost like she and Michaela used 'whatever' when they didn't want to finish a thought. Rather than press him, she nodded and said, "I'm celebrating our meeting with champagne. Come sit. It's about a twelve-hour flight to Cannes. Then about a forty-minute drive to the farm-house. Ah... Our perfume maker is staying in the small guesthouse, so you'll have to bunk in the main house with me. Ibrahim—that's his name—insisted even though I won't be staying there full-time, and—"

"Will that make you uncomfortable?"

"Not at all." She waved her hand, hoping he couldn't tell she was even now fantasizing about what might happen in that house. "It's a big house and we're both adults. Professionals."

"Exactly. I'm glad you feel that way. I want to be where the action is. Please don't make a fuss. I just need a bed. Although when I first moved to Nashville, I slept on the floor in my sleeping bag. I can do that again, I suppose, but I'm not a spring chicken."

"If you're no spring chicken, then I'm in trouble. I'm two years older."

"Are you? I wouldn't have guessed." His mouth twitched again. "You look pretty spry to me."

There he went again, making another comment that had her wondering what he was thinking. And feeling. "Thank you. Seriously though, the farmhouse isn't luxurious or any-thing. If you'd prefer something else—"

"Nah, I get fidgety if anything is too luxurious. I figure they have something to hide."

"Then this plane must be making you incredibly ner-vous," she joked.

That teased a genuine smile out of him. "The company is keeping me pretty calm. Thanks for letting me come along, Caitlyn. I...needed to get out of town."

"I wondered when I saw you. Bad day, huh?"

"Meeting you was the best part so far," he said, trying to smile. "But the part that came afterward was pretty awful.

Since we're to be company, you should know that I had a horrible fight with my mother, and I need to clear my head."

Was the fight over him wanting to be the spokesperson for her perfume? "You mentioned she wasn't as eager for you to work with me. Was it over—?"

"The antecedents were much bigger," he said, his face darkening. "Again, thanks for letting me come along. I figure it's the best thing for me right now. Everything is...messed up. I'll stay out of your way. Sorry if I'm imposing. Maybe I should—"

"Stop," she said gently, and compassion drove her to take his hand even though she knew it was unprofessional. But he surprised her by curling his fingers around hers. They exchanged a look, and she said, "Kindred spirits help each other in moments like this."

He sighed, and her belly stopped jumping. "Thank you. I've never had a kindred spirit until today."

Her heart soared. "Outside of my family, I haven't either."

He squeezed her hand, and she returned the gesture. She was starting to believe she'd read him correctly after all. He was interested, only he was preoccupied by this argument with his mother, and it was vexing him something fierce.

"Family fights are the worst. We had an epic row recently, my two oldest brothers against the rest of us siblings. My mom had to come in and mediate, which translated into her whacking them both on the backs of the heads, reminding them of what's important, and then telling them to make nice."

"She sounds like a mighty fine lady."

"She is," Caitlyn said. "I can call her if you need her. Maybe she can become a family interventionist in her retirement."

His laugh was harsh. "I'd need to hire her full-time right now."

Joris cleared his throat, arriving with Beau's drink.

Caitlyn almost snatched her hand back out of reflex, but Joris was discreet. He wasn't going to tattle to Quinn that he'd caught her holding hands with her celebrity spokesperson. If her brother found out, he'd call her out on it for sure, reminding her of all the reasons it was unprofessional. Like she didn't already know.

But Beau was the one who pulled away, and when he eased his hand from hers, she felt oddly bereft again.

"Thanks, Joris," Beau said, gripping the crystal tumbler with both hands.

"Frank says we'll be taking off in fifteen."

She made her mouth move. "Great, Joris. Thanks."

Joris made himself scarce, which was a good thing since Beau's face had tightened into a mask of agony. He was staring at that glass as if it were a gateway to hell.

"Tastes just like water, right?" he asked. "I thought if I was going to try alcohol, vodka would be best. I can't stand the smell of whiskey."

His jaw clenched, and she wondered if his father had been a whiskey drinker.

"You don't have to drink it, you know," she felt compelled to say.

"It's always been on the 'never' list, but that list needs to be blown to kingdom come." He met her eyes, and in them she could see storm clouds. "Never mind me. I'm acting a little..."

Crazy? Somehow she knew that was the word he'd stopped himself from saying. Should she caution him against drinking to drown his sorrows? God, they barely knew each other, and she wasn't sure what to do.

"How about a toast then? That always lifts my spirits." She extended her champagne flute. "To new friends and grand adventures."

His knuckles were white as he lifted the glass to touch hers. "To truth."

Whoa. She nodded, awash in the emotion radiating

from him. He hadn't just fought with his mother, she could tell, but a rift had opened up between them. That kind of thing could tear a person's heart in two. Taking a sip of her champagne, she felt the bubbles touch her lips. Man, she loved that feeling. Joy in a glass, she liked to say. But Beau was feeling anything but joy, and it was painful to watch.

He was staring at the glass still, and then he drew it to his mouth slowly. Took a tepid sip. Pulled a face. And then set it down on the table between them with a *thunk*. He shook himself.

"Not to your liking?" she asked hesitantly.

He wiped his mouth with his free hand. "I'm acting a little..."

Again, she knew he wanted to say crazy. "Want to try some of my champagne?"

"No, I'm good," he said, a brick wall in his tone.

"Do you want to talk about your fight with your mother?"

He waved out as if to say *no way*, the gesture going awry and knocking the vodka glass off the side of the table. She caught it, but the liquid sloshed down the middle of her dress and the table.

"Oh, crap, I'm so sorry," he said, already wiping the table with the edge of his T-shirt. "Your dress."

"Let me find some paper towels." She unbuckled her seatbelt and rose to go to the galley in the rear of the plane. "It will dry in a jiffy."

Joris, who'd buckled in for takeoff, looked up from his magazine. She rolled her eyes as she grabbed a couple of napkins. "You know me. Klutz." Oddly, she wanted to protect Beau.

"We have towels in the bathroom," Joris reminded her.

"This is fine." She headed back to the main cabin only to find Beau standing in the aisle, hands clenched at his sides.

"Again, I'm so sorry." He looked at her middle and then back up, his perusal oddly sheepish. "A pity. Your dress looked real nice up until I ruined it."

"It's not ruined." He'd liked her dress? She'd tried on three before choosing it this morning.

He dug into his other pocket and handed her something. A handkerchief.

"For your dress. Those napkins will leave a trail."

His initials were embroidered in the corner in baby blue thread, and they were...

She wasn't going to be able to use them in a marketing campaign.

"You laughing at my initials?" he asked, his mouth curving.

"No, of course not."

He snorted, and it transformed his fractious energy. "You have a terrible poker face, Caitlyn."

How embarrassing. "I do and I am sorry. I also have a juvenile sense of humor."

He laughed harshly. "Nothing wrong with it that I can tell. My initials are funny, and so much more than I knew until now. BM. My mama..."

She waited when he broke off, his jaw clenching.

"She wanted me to change my last name, Masters, to her maiden name when I decided to be a singer. That's when she changed her own name back. Huh. I'd forgotten that."

His eyes took on a far-off quality, and again she waited, totally on eggshells.

"She said I ought to take her name since she'd mostly raised me by herself. And she joked about seeing those initials flashing in neon lights on stage. She said it might remind people they needed to go to the bathroom during my set."

"Or the doctor," she said, trying to bring him back. "I'm sorry. I shouldn't joke."

"No, I'm glad you can. I kind of need it right now. You know...it's funny, but I always kept this handkerchief from my nana so I'd remember where I'm from. Who I am. She was my...daddy's mother."

"Roots," she said. This was somehow tied to his new album, the one he'd told her about in the meeting.

"A good joke. My initials. Perhaps I should change my name, after all."

She was horrified. "Don't you dare! I love Masters."

His stormy eyes locked onto hers. "You do? Why? It's just a name."

"No, it's not. It's your name. Besides, it sounds elegant."

"I thought so too." He covered the hand holding the handkerchief. "Keep it. A memento, if you like."

Oh, how could she refuse him when he gazed at her that way? "Thank you. I'll treasure it."

"And be sure to send me the dry-cleaning bill for the dress."

Was he crazy? She was courting him to work for her. "Don't give it another thought. Come sit down again." She had to take his arm, which was rigid with tension. "We'll be taking off any moment now."

They buckled back in, and she stored her champagne flute in one of the holders under the oval-shaped windows, then added the vodka glass. One thing she didn't put away was the handkerchief. After using it to wipe off her dress, she kept it tucked in her palm, the cotton soft against her skin.

"I'm terrible company right now," he said as they took off. "Maybe I shouldn't have done this."

She laid her hand over his forearm. "Don't be silly. You be exactly what you need to be right now. Besides, you made me feel better, spilling the glass like you did. I mean, now I'm not the only clumsy one around."

He met her eyes, and the right side of his mouth tipped up. "You aren't clumsy."

"Why don't you close your eyes and take a nap? I know I always feel better after I've gotten some rest."

He blew air out of his nose rather like a horse might, indicating that while he was too polite to say so, he thought her suggestion pure bullshit. She closed her eyes, hoping to help him along, but kept her hand on his arm. Before long, the façade worked—on her—and she succumbed to sleep.

Murmuring woke her, and she opened her eyes and stretched only to see Joris walking back down the aisle. Beau was watching her, and she smiled at him. It was so wonderful to wake up to him sitting right across from her. It felt *right*. The setting sun lit the left side of his face, highlighting the strong curve of his cheekbone and jaw. *Oh, boy*.

"You caught me staring, and I probably should apologize, but you look so beautiful when you sleep I couldn't help myself."

Her heart grew warm inside her chest. "Only when I'm asleep?" The words slipped out, but she didn't have time to regret them.

"No, Caitlyn," he said, his body more relaxed now. "You darn near take my breath away all the time. Is it too bold to say so?"

She shook her head. "No, so long as we keep comments like that separate from our business relationship. I'll be honest—I'm glad you called it out there. I was waiting for the right moment. Making and selling this perfume is my dream come true. I've shifted my duties at work to devote myself to it full-time. And having you involved? Priceless. I don't want this thing between us—whatever this is—to mess that up."

He nodded. "Of course. I don't want to make you uncomfortable."

"Kindred spirits, remember?"

She held out her hand again, and he took it, his clasp

strong and steady. "I have some things to work out on this trip, but I'll be a gentleman, I promise you."

Oh, she loved the gallantry in that comment. He spoke so differently than most people she knew. Then again, she didn't associate too much with Southerners, given where she lived, but even she knew they talked about being gentlemen in a way no one else in the country did. "Like I told you, just be what you need to be. You don't have to pretend to be something else."

He swallowed thickly at that.

"In fact, I really like the man you are."

He turned his head and looked out the window. "I appreciate you saying that. I'm going to ask you to remind me of that if I need it. All right?"

What in the world did he mean by that? "Of course. You can count on me."

"I know I can," he said, squeezing her hand. "Despite appearances, Caitlyn, you can count on me too."

"You wouldn't be here if I thought otherwise," she told him.

The plane flew through a wall of clouds and popped out into that magical open space above them where blue sky stretched to infinity. They both turned their heads as the sun's vibrant rays filled the cabin.

"You know," she said, "since childhood, this view has been one of my favorites. My mom told me when I was six years old that this vantage point is a reminder that the sun is always shining, even when we can't see it."

His mouth curved, and he turned his head toward her, leaning across the table between them to touch her face with his free hand. "When I look at you, I see sunshine in your eyes."

She knew she loved him in that moment, but the feeling was too new and scary for her to acknowledge it. Even to herself.

Instead, she unbuckled her seatbelt and shifted to

the seat next to him. Leaning her head against his strong shoulder, she felt his arm come around her. They watched the view together in silence, and she discovered words were unnecessary, a feeling she'd only heard described before by people in love.

She held the handkerchief he'd given her the rest of the trip.

CHAPTER 4

THE FRENCH COUNTRYSIDE AWOKE BEAU'S SENSES IN A WAY he'd never expected, what with its rolling green hills, rich orange earth, and acres of fragrant flowers.

The late August sun was hot, scorching even, but Beau had convinced Caitlyn to roll down the windows as they cruised through what he'd call backroads in the car that had picked them up from the airport. Perhaps it was his feelings for her, but despite his grief, the world seemed more light than dark. His nose couldn't make out many of the scents around him yet, but he knew the difference between the floral ones and the downright earthy ones.

He'd never been to France. But this...

He'd never expected this. Much like the beautiful woman holding his hand.

The manicured rows of lavender captivated him, the various shades of purple blending into blue depending on the way the sun tilted in the sky. The organization of the land spoke of deep caring, knowledge, and precision—all things he valued in his own career and life.

When they turned off the main road, Caitlyn bounced in her seat. "This is our road. These are our fields. Oh, I'm so happy to be back. I know I just bought it, but I feel like I'm coming home."

She'd told him she'd struggled to find land to purchase around the perfume capital of France, Grasse. Generations of well-established families and perfume houses seemed to own the entire area, from Chanel to Fragonard. Looking a touch farther afield, she'd found a hundred acres still in Provence, a farm that grew mostly lavender, which she intended to use in the perfume, but also other flowers like jasmine and rose. Even better, there was an old lavender distillery on the property, and the overseer came with the land, something she'd explained was customary in France.

"I can't wait for you to meet Ibrahim, of course. The Bisset family, our overseers, are the third generation to farm this land, and they do so with a rhythm that only comes with time and dedication."

"I'm looking forward to it too," he said, his chest filled with awe for the nature around him, the explosion of colors saturating his vision.

"I know you're tired," she said, pressing her hand to her heart, "but if you're up for it, I'd love to show you some of the fields close to the house. They're all lavender. We even have a tractor, a blue one. I convinced Jean Pierre to teach me how to drive it. He wasn't sure at first, but I'm very persuasive."

Was she ever.

They pulled up in front of a two-story stone house, golden in the late afternoon light, with bright blue shutters. The slanted roof was composed of orange terracotta tiles. Rustic, he thought, liking it immediately. The guesthouse stood to the far right, only a short distance away, and beyond it was a pergola covered with green branches and purple blooms, the stone pillars framing a sturdy wooden table with chairs boasting a breathtaking view of the lavender fields and the rolling hills beyond.

He felt himself breathe, easily and freely. Yes, he might be able to sort out the broken pieces of his life here.

And the air...redolent with spice—like nothing he'd ever experienced.

"Isn't it beautiful?" she asked. "Oh, I could pinch myself. And it's mine. Come in."

The driver, a stoic man named Claude, hastened to the back of the car to take their bags. Beau barely stopped himself from grabbing his own bag as the man passed him. Having people tote his luggage made him uncomfortable.

Masculine laughter spilled out from an open window, and Caitlyn froze in place.

"No way!" she said. "He couldn't have..."

Then she was running toward the front door, hot on the heels of Claude. Beau followed at a slower pace, his lips hitching up. She was always racing off like her pants were on fire. Her boundless energy was infectious, even after the long journey.

"Flynn!" she yelled as she disappeared in the house.

"Caity girl!" a man answered from inside.

Beau heard her give a girlish shriek as he stepped into the house. The walls were stone here too, decorated with bright geometric rugs, bold draped cloths, and vibrant paintings of single-interest flowers, women walking in lavender fields, and one of a sea with waves crashing against it. The eclectic look wasn't his taste, but he liked it nonetheless.

"Beau! Come meet my crazy brother. And Ibrahim. We're down the hall in the library."

He noted the wide stone stairs that led to the second floor. The exposed beams in the ceiling looked ancient, roughened by years of bearing weight and soaking in sunlight from the massive upstairs windows. Plants were spilling out of massive clay pots everywhere. He walked down the hall, his boots causing a pleasant staccato to his ears.

He heard Caitlyn's delighted chatter mixed with two masculine voices, one very exotic.

Past the dining room and a large kitchen, he found them at the back. He stood in the doorway, nearly blinded by the light in the room. Facing west, it boasted a view of more lavender fields. His nose twitched at a spicy scent. Yeah, he'd been right to come here.

"Beau!" Caitlyn ran forward and dragged him toward the two men standing in the middle of a conversation area with a green leather sofa and contrasting cream-upholstered chairs. "This is Flynn, my brother. He was in Prague. Don't ask why. Decided to fly in spontaneously and meet you when Michaela texted him I was bringing you along."

Her brother had wanted to meet him, eh? He studied the man, noting his sandy blond hair and casual outfit of gray cotton pants with a white cotton shirt. The easy style was a feint—Beau noted the man's assessing gaze. Flynn was being a good brother, he expected, coming to make sure he was on the up and up. Even if he didn't know about their connection yet, the brother likely sensed there was something beyond professional interest about the last-minute trip. Beau didn't mind—he rather appreciated she had someone looking out for her.

"Hey, Flynn," he said, extending out his hand to the man. "I'm Beau Masters." He tripped over his last name and noted how the sound of it just wasn't the same anymore.

"Good to meet you." Flynn's handshake was firm, and he looked Beau directly in the eye, man to man. "So this is the world's most compelling man. I can check meeting him off my bucket list."

Caitlyn groaned, but Beau felt his mouth twitch. Clearly her brother wasn't above giving him crap, but he knew it was a test.

"You might save your ink," he said, arching his brow. "If I'm the world's most compelling man, the world is in trouble."

Caitlyn swatted him. "That's not true. Flynn, stop teasing him. He's not used to us Merriams yet. Now, let me introduce you to the world's most amazing perfume blender, Ibrahim Magdy."

Beau turned to shake the man's hand, noting his tall, elegant build and tailored suit and jacket. Although Ibrahim gave off an air of sophistication, what with his thick salt-and-pepper hair, high cheekbones, and formal posture, his brown eyes were friendly. Warm, even. If Beau had to guess his age, he'd peg him in his early fifties.

His mouth formed a pencil-thin smile as he took Beau's hand. "Appears the world is in trouble with both of us," he said conspiratorially, his vowels and consonants musical and smooth. Beau wouldn't be weird and say he loved the man's accent, but he did. It was completely different than anything he'd ever heard, slow like a Southern drawl, yet not honeyed.

"Caitlyn sees the best in people," Beau said, gesturing to Flynn. "I imagine she says you're the best brother in the world."

Flynn laughed. "Do you say that, Caity girl?" He yanked on her long hair playfully, and she pushed him in the chest.

"Stop that. I'll kick you out, Flynnie boy, I swear I will."

He held up his hands. "No more pranks or nicknames. We have an august guest. I'll be on my best behavior, I promise."

Like hell, Beau thought. "Nothing august here except the month. In fact, I should go help Claude. Where do you want me bunking? Like I said, I don't want to be in the way."

"You can take the room across from me, Beau," Flynn offered at once.

Of course, he could. He nodded, fighting a smile.

"Ibrahim recommended the room facing east for me, but I simply loathe mornings," Flynn said, playfully shielding his eyes. "Supposedly, morning is one of the best times to smell the fields, after the air has cooled and the flowers have rested. Right, Ibrahim?"

That intrigued Beau. There were optimal times for such things?

"Exactly," Ibrahim said. "Since you're here, Mr. Masters, I assume you've agreed to be the spokesperson for this incredible perfume Caitlyn envisions. Of course, I also hope to make a men's fragrance."

"Oh, Quinn will agree after we rock the first one, trust me," Caitlyn said.

"I sure do like the story she wants to tell with it, Ibrahim," Beau said, smiling at Caitlyn, who beamed back at him. "I've been thinking a lot about roots myself." He'd pushed his pain under the surface in the midst of his flight from Nashville, but he could feel it waiting, hot and insistent. Before long, he would have to reckon with it and everything he'd learned.

"It's important to know where you come from," Ibrahim said, "but a man—or woman—must at some point become his own person, setting all that aside."

Beau gave him another look. Those dark brown eyes were studying him avidly, as if the man was trying to understand what made him tick. Beau had good instincts about people, and he knew they could be friends.

"I couldn't have said it better, especially being the middle kid in our family," Caitlyn said, making Flynn groan. "Can't you see why I love Ibrahim? Every time he says something, it makes you think. I'm going to head up to my room and freshen up. Beau, I'll show you to your room."

"You run along," Flynn said. "I'll make Beau comfortable. Oh, speaking of which, Uncle Arthur and Aunt Clara are still interested in visiting you here. Maybe now would be a good time. I bet they'd *love* to meet Beau."

She gave her brother a look that could have shriveled some of those flowers outside. Flynn stared right back.

They were carrying on a sort of silent conversation, rich with subtext.

"Why, thank you, Flynn," she finally said, her voice tart like lemon pie. "You're just a doll."

Ibrahim wandered to the door. "I'll head back to the guesthouse and do a little more work. Caitlyn, Jean Pierre learned your brother and Beau would be coming when I walked the fields earlier looking for inspiration. He was so excited to have you return he invited us all to his house for dinner. I said I would pass the invitation along. You know Provençal hospitality. Are you up for it after your trip?"

She glanced over at the grandfather clock, saying, "It's four o'clock now. If I take a nap, I should be right as rain. Beau?"

He was tired and a part of him wanted to lick his wounds, but he wasn't the kind of man to turn down hospitality, especially from strangers. "We Southerners are known for our hospitality, so I understand what an honor it is. Of course. What can I bring?"

Flynn slapped him on the back, leading him to the door where Ibrahim stood. "You can pick a bouquet of flowers for the missus."

"Don't listen to him," Caitlyn said, trailing in their wake. "He'll have you standing on your head and juggling if you listen to him."

"You made twenty dollars doing that," Flynn said as they walked down the hall.

"I'll see you later," Ibrahim said, heading in the opposite direction.

"Wait until you see Ibrahim's lab," Caitlyn said. "I'll show it to you tomorrow. Right now, I need a shower and some water. God, I'm thirsty."

"Jet lag is a bitch," Flynn said. "Go on. I'll take care of Beau."

She gave him another look, giving him the opportunity

to speak his mind if he had any objection, then smiled at him and veered off toward the kitchen. Flynn gestured to the stairs, and Beau headed up, sensing a talk. Caitlyn's brother tromped behind him, the beat of his fancy leather shoes adding further punctuation to his tough-guy routine. Beau kept his footsteps quieter, communicating through sound that he wasn't a threat.

At the third door on the right, Flynn gestured to the doorway. The first sight Beau saw upon stepping inside was his leather bag sitting on a maroon rug in front of a large bed with a curved wooden headboard. Sure enough, through the windows, lavender stretched as far as the eye could see, a carpet of blues and purples.

He turned to face Flynn as the man followed him into the room and quietly closed the door behind him.

"You can trust me with your sister," he said before Flynn could speak. "Being a gentleman isn't just important to me. It's who I am. But I appreciate you're the kind of man to make sure. I know some singers have a bad reputation with women, but I'm not one of them. I respect Caitlyn and would never make her uncomfortable."

"And they say Southerners aren't direct," Flynn said, resting against the door. "I'm glad you understand why I dropped in, and I thank you for being honest."

"It's a value I can't live without," he said, his mama flashing in his mind. She was the one who'd taught him the importance of honesty, yet she'd lied to him his whole life. He still couldn't make sense of it.

"I admire that. But if you hurt her, you'll answer to me and the rest of our brothers, and believe me, I'm the nicest of the lot." He flashed a vicious smile and Beau almost laughed. Flynn wouldn't be nice in a fight. He knew it.

"Yankees haven't cornered the market on honesty," he said, his drawl purposely exaggerated. "I'm only getting the lay of the land here."

"Is that all?" Flynn asked.

Had he given away his deeper affection for Caitlyn? He figured it was likely. Well, best clear the air either way. "Originally, yes, that's what I'd planned. But then I met your sister, and she got to me. Right here." He tapped his heart. "She's pretty wonderful, and I seem to be falling for her. But I can tell that's not news to you."

He pushed off the door. "I'm a perceptive guy, and I noticed how you looked at her in the library. She *is* wonderful and trusting, with a heart like an eager puppy. She's been hurt by 'nice guys' before."

The words echoed in the room, the stone walls adding their own acoustics.

"I won't hurt her." He'd keep all his junk to himself and enjoy his time here with her. After that, he didn't know. Couldn't think that far ahead. He was still trying to take in the fact that he really wasn't Beau Masters. He was only Beau, a man with no last name, with only half of his roots known.

"Glad we're clear. Still, I find it interesting you could take off like this given your schedule. Most celebrities don't have that luxury."

So he suspected something? Well, good for him, but Beau wasn't sharing. "I'm a lucky guy, what can I say."

Flynn opened the door. "Nice talk. Get some rest. These Provençal dinners can go a few hours. I'm hoping Jean Pierre will be kind to us and let us beg off early since we all flew in today."

*****

The evening passed in a blur. Jean Pierre and his wife, Anais, were kind, and their two young children charmed everyone. Yet the excitement of coming here, to this magical place, had started to wear off. The doubts and anxiety crept back in, especially when he was introduced to Jean Pierre's father and grandfather, both of whom had worked this land in their heyday. The signs of their family likeness were stamped into their faces, from their aquiline noses to their strong brow bones. These men knew who they were, where they belonged. Four generations graced this table, and Beau couldn't stop thinking about the father he didn't know. How his mama had asked him to change his last name to her maiden name prior to his first record, erasing Masters forever, without explaining why.

Jet lag led into depression, much like the pastis to wine during dinner, which he left untouched. He'd only reached for vodka out of desperation, and while Walt Masters wasn't truly his father and those genes weren't in his blood, he wasn't going to use alcohol as a crutch. He hoped he was still a better man than that.

Much of the conversation slipped into rapid-fire French. He was the only person who didn't speak it, something he hadn't considered in the mad rush to come here. The whole table laughed at stories Beau couldn't fully grasp. Caitlyn tried to translate, seated as she was beside him, but he finally whispered for her to cease because her eyes were drooping like his. Besides, while the language barrier made him feel like more of an outsider, he nonetheless enjoyed listening to the music this foreign language made. Its melodic feast surrounded him as he stared out at the moon-touched fields, the purple flowers now shaded in midnight blue and white.

He fed his body, noting tastes that were as unfamiliar—yet delightful—as the smells around him. Anais had told them what they were eating, but he'd forgotten, only remembering her comment that the recipes had been in their family for many generations. Again, their connection to history stirred up the agony inside him. The pain was pressing out, and he knew it couldn't be held back any longer.

Finally, he excused himself, deciding it best to play the American card and beg off after the main course was removed. When Caitlyn offered to walk him back, he declined, saying he could walk back alone. It would be good for him even if everyone but Ibrahim expressed it was rather far. He didn't bend, noting he would find it easily once he started walking west. After all, they'd left the lights on in the farmhouse, and the fields were a flat plain. Caitlyn's face seemed strained, but she patted his arm, sensing he needed to be alone. Anais watched him warily—no doubt it was highly irregular to leave mid-meal—and he was sorry he'd hurt her feelings by leaving early.

The formal leave-taking with the Bisset males was awkward. He'd never had a man kiss him on the cheeks, three times no less. And his emotional state was such that it pained him when Jean Pierre's father and grandfather both gave him a hearty embrace. His real father had never embraced him.

And if his mother had her way, he never would.

When he was halfway back to the farmhouse, the lights shining brightly, a beacon of home, he could contain the pain no longer. He sank to one knee, fisted his hands in the soil to steady himself, and faced a lifetime of lies in the lavender-scented moonlight.

He'd spent so long trying not to be something that he didn't know what he really was in truth. He'd been given a list of nevers and always by a woman he could no longer trust. So, what did belong to him?

It was time to find out who, in fact, he was and what was true for him, even if that meant jumping into a sea of indeterminate depth.

CHAPTER 5

WHEN CAITLYN AND FLYNN ARRIVED HOME AFTER BIDding Ibrahim goodnight in the driveway, she took to the stairs immediately. Beau's light was still on.

The door was open. Her scan was perfunctory. She knew he wasn't there.

"Boy wonder still out?" Flynn asked from behind her.

"You don't think he got lost, do you?" She'd worried about him leaving, not only because of the distance he'd need to cross to return to the farmhouse but because of the condition he'd been in. They were both tired, of course, but there was more to it than that. He'd seemed broken down somehow.

"He seemed to be sure he could find his way back," Flynn said, putting a hand on her shoulder and rubbing it for comfort. "I know you're worried but taking to the fields to find him isn't the way."

And it wasn't like she could drive the car through the fields either. "It's been an hour since he left or thereabouts."

"Anais knew you were exhausted, so she took pity on us. No cheese or brandy after dessert... We got away early."

She was grateful for it. The other woman had given

her a look as if to say, "Go after him." "I'm going to sit outside and wait for him. It's nice out and the lavender keeps the bugs away, thank God. I could probably spot him in the fields in the moonlight."

Flynn chuckled. "If you spot him, he'll have seen the house. Okay, I know when you're going to be stubborn. Go wait for him then. I'm going to bed. Love you."

She turned as he brushed a soft kiss on her cheek. "Love you too. Sleep tight."

"Always," he said. "But if he's not back in another hour, come wake me up, and we'll figure out what to do."

God, she hoped they wouldn't need a search party. "Thanks, Flynn."

"I've always got your back."

She left him and walked back down the stairs, only stopping to pick up her shawl again in case her arms got chilled. The night was cool as she stepped out of the house, but in an inviting way.

A few chairs were clustered under the portico by the fields. Curling up in one of them, she settled the shawl over her like a blanket. A powerful calm stole over her as she scanned the fields in the direction of the Bisset house. Moonlight spilled over the land, making the lavender spikes look like a princess' magical silver wand. She inhaled the air, and the spice and perfume filled her nose. Yes, this felt like home.

He would come this way, and she would be here for him.

She didn't have to wait long. His lone dark silhouette appeared, and her heart filled with new emotion. Happiness. Longing. Compassion. His shoulders looked slumped, even in the moonlight. He was a man downtrodden with troubles, and she planned to do her part to lighten them.

When he reached the end of the lavender fields, she stood. "Beau," she called out.

He jumped and held out his hands. "Goodness, Caitlyn. You scared the life out of me. What are you doing out here?"

"Waiting for you," she said, coming toward him, her shawl wrapped around her. "I was worried when you weren't back yet."

His face seemed to go slack, the dark shadows slipping away as he stepped closer. "You didn't need to do that, but I thank you. Seeing you here in the moonlight makes everything better."

And yet, his burdens still weighed on him. She could hear it in his voice. "Want to sit a spell?" she asked, reaching out a hand to him. "Maybe tell me what's got you so worked up. I know you already said it's about a fight with your mother, but if you want to share more, I'm a good listener."

He lifted her hand, turning it over in the moonlight as if in wonder. "I know you are, but you're tired."

"So are you," she whispered. "Talk to me, Beau."

An agonized sound crested out, and he lowered their joined hands. "Come, let's sit then. If I had a jacket, I'd wrap it around you."

"I have my shawl," she said as they walked back to the chairs under the portico. "Besides, the temperature is perfect, not too hot, not too cool."

"Yeah." He sank into the chair next to hers after angling it closer, still holding her hand. "Have you ever had someone lie to you about something so important it sliced you cleanly in two?"

She curled toward him, gripping his hand, and said honestly, "No."

"I'm glad for you," he said, rubbing his thumb over the back of her hand. "It's...the worst. Disappointing. Shocking. Cruel even. I've lived mostly a good life, Caitlyn, and it's hard to wrap my mind around why someone would do this, especially... I don't want to talk about the particulars yet. It's still too raw."

"That's okay," she said, wishing she could reach out and touch his cheek. "You take all the time you need. In the meantime, I'll just hold your hand and be your friend."

He snorted. "You're more than my friend, and we both know it. But until I feel a little more solid in myself, I'm not going to act on that. I told your brother he could trust me with you. Caitlyn, I don't want to mess things up with you, and right now, I'm struggling with who I am."

Who he was? He was Beau Masters, one of the kindest and sweetest men she'd ever known—a man she'd already fallen for. Had his mother lied to him? Was that what the fight had been about? Or had they had a disagreement over the liar himself? Regardless of the answers, this man was hurting, and because she cared for him, she found she was hurting too, for him.

"Oh, Beau," she said, uncurling from her chair. "First, I told you I trust you. Second, I understand not wanting to mess up whatever this is between us. I don't either. But you should know, I'm here for you. I wish I could help you more."

He raised her hand and kissed the back of it. "You're sitting here in the moonlight, listening to me ramble on. You are helping, honey. More than you know."

The endearment gave her the courage she needed to touch his face, and his eyes brightened, the white light from the moon sparking in them like a bright star winking in the night sky. "You're hurting and tired. Rest. Sit with things. Find me if you need company. I hate hearing you don't know who you are."

"Perhaps it's overdue. This is what my album is about, after all. Time to face the music, as they say. I just didn't expect it would go like this."

Roots, he'd said. And lies apparently. She'd have to be patient until he wanted to fill in the rest of the puzzle for her, not her strong suit. "Let's just sit then."

He settled their joined hands against his chest. "Tell me something more about yourself. Anything."

She said the first thing that popped into her head. "I love lavender."

"Why?" he asked, closing his eyes.

"It's calming and smells nice. Did you know it's one of the top essential oils? From a business perspective, it's a winner."

"I sense there's more to it than that."

She inhaled deeply, noting how the fragrance wasn't as strong now with the fields resting. "I don't know really. I've just always loved the smell."

His lips turned up. "And now you have entire fields of them. I liked walking among them in the moonlight. I think I'm going to find a place to sit and write some songs. The fields feel right to me somehow, the plants growing as nature intended but ordered all the same. I like the order just now."

"I don't," she said, sinking deeper into the chair. "I like a little mess and chaos every once in a while. We had to keep things pretty orderly growing up. Clean rooms. Made beds. Dishes immediately in the dishwasher kind of thing. One of the best days of my life was when I got to my dorm and realized I didn't have to keep it clean."

He chuckled, the sound dark and husky in the quiet night. "You know what one of my best days was?"

"What?"

"When I wrote my first song. I was twelve, and I heard it while I was fishing on the river outside of town."

The slow rise and fall of his chest was soothing to her. She could imagine her hand on his chest when they were in bed together, and she had to tell herself to slow down. "What was it about?"

He sang:

River take me with you.
Take me where I want to go.
To lands far away.
Help me see new skies.

Meet new friends.
Explore new worlds.

The power of his voice stole over her. She'd never heard him sing in person except at two of the concerts she'd attended with Michaela years ago. Sitting here, an audience of one, she didn't feel like he was a famous country singer, only a man singing softly to the woman he cared about. "I love it."

A soft laugh escaped from him, and she looked over. His eyes were still closed. "Not my most descriptive or musically complex, but to that boy... That song meant the world. On that day, I dove into the river, so to speak, and knew I'd go places."

No wonder he'd become famous so young. He'd already decided to do something bigger, be bigger.

"Now I'm sitting in the French countryside holding hands with you on this beautiful night. Talk about an adventure."

His eyes opened, and he caressed the line of her cheekbone. His touch was soft, but it left a wake of sweet warmth. She raised her hand to keep his fingers on her cheek. She wanted him to go on touching her forever. Sweetly. Softly.

"When I've imagined courting a woman, this is what I thought it would be like."

That made her smile. "Are you courting me, Beau?"

Again, his mouth tipped up. "You bet I am, honey."

CHAPTER 6

WALKING THE FIELDS, BEAU HAD STRUGGLED WITH PAIN-ful truths. Holding hands with Caitlyn, talking with her, he only needed to be. It felt good to share stories of moments that had been true for him, like that first song by the river. It reminded him that his mama's lie hadn't tainted everything.

"I don't think I've ever been courted before," she said, curling back into the chair like she was wont to do. He'd noticed she liked to tuck her feet under her when they were on the airplane. The pose was sweet and oddly innocent, but he couldn't wait until they knew each other better so he could suggest she curl up on his lap instead. Having her hand rest on his chest was enough for now, but it wouldn't be in time. He told himself to be patient. He had a lot to work out. She deserved to have a solid man courting her.

"I'm not surprised," he said, wanting to laugh when her face bunched up at his teasing. "It's not because of you. You're the most beautiful woman I've ever met. Certainly one of the sweetest."

"Thank you very much," she said, squeezing his hand for good measure. "I was about to leave you and head inside."

"Courting is a lost art," he said, kissing the back of her hand again. "People are always rushing to the finish line. Isn't that why you want your perfume to make women feel like they matter?"

Her lips twitched. "You remembered."

"'Course I do," he said. "And you need to feel like you matter. To me. As a woman. That's the art of courting, honey." Suddenly he remembered something she'd said during her pitch—in an odd moment of vulnerability, she'd talked about not feeling good enough. He'd seen the uncertainty in her eyes. Courting was something he would have done for any woman he liked, but he knew it would resonate with Caitlyn's soul.

She sat up again. The woman never sat still long. "I want you to know you matter to me too. I guess I'm also courting you."

He couldn't help but chuckle. "Where I'm from, it's the men that do the courting. Part of being a Southern gentleman. But I'll accept your courting all the same."

She settled back down in her chair. Only time would tell how long she'd stay there. "Good, because you don't have much choice about it."

"I like the fire in you," he said. "I felt it in your proposal. Your words. You have passion. As an artist—and a man—I respect that." He wouldn't tell her he looked forward to exploring it. Not yet.

"Do you have a courting book, or do you just make up your game plan on the fly?" she asked.

He had to think about it a moment. His mama's instructions came to mind, but he didn't want to abide by her list any longer. He wanted, needed, one of his own. "Don't worry none. I have some ideas, but the more I get to know you, the better I can tailor it to you. Your likes. Your interests. I'm looking forward to learning more about you. Tell me something else about you. Unless you're too tired."

She sat up again, and he found himself smiling. "I could stay up all night talking with you. Something about me... I love ice cream. Chocolate. Vanilla. Salted caramel. You name it. Not the fruit ones as much, though. We had an ice cream truck that would come to the edge of our driveway at four o'clock on Wednesdays in the summertime. I always ran out first to see him."

He could well imagine it. Her little legs running down a dusty country road. Had she had pigtails or braids?

"His name was Pedro, and he was the kindest man. Grandfather of thirteen, I believe. His dream had been to make ice cream, and when he retired from banking in San Francisco, he got himself a food truck. I could never decide on one flavor, so he'd use one of the plastic trays he kept for banana splits to give me a flight of ice cream. I adored him for it. One of the saddest days of my life was when my mom told me he'd had a heart attack in his truck. I cried every time I ate ice cream for almost a year afterward, thinking about him. Now I smile. He was living his dream, just like I'm living mine. I think he'd be proud of me."

He delivered another kiss to her hand, this time inside her palm. "He would be, yes. We should find some ice cream around here. Celebrate his memory."

"Ice cream isn't French," she said, "but I figure we'll find something. I'm glad I thought about him. Some people make an impact."

And some people tore you apart, Beau thought. He'd never imagined it would be his mother. His mood dipped, and not even the soft warmth of Caitlyn's hand in his could ease it. This time he sat up and kissed her hand again. "Come on. We both need some shut-eye."

Pulling her gently from her chair, he stood there studying her in the moonlight. Her long hair was curling at the ends, right above the rise of her breasts. Temptation stole over him. To touch her. To kiss her.

He reminded himself again there was plenty of time.

"Thank you for waiting up for me," he said, caressing her cheek again. "No woman has ever done that before."

She curled her face into his palm, and the trusting nature of the gesture moved him. "It was my pleasure. Thank you for singing your song. It was nice to hear your voice. In the quiet, with the lavender all around us...I think it's the best song I've ever heard."

He thought of the songs he'd written, and the ones he had yet to write. How many of his fans could appreciate such a simple song? She was special that way, appreciating the dreams he'd had as a boy. He needed to figure out how many of those dreams still belonged to him. "You're beautiful and sweet, and I... Caitlyn, I'm glad you were the first person I thought of when I knew I needed to get out of town." The truth of that stole over him. He'd somehow known to come to her.

"Kindred spirits, remember?" She squeezed his hand again.

Yes, he thought, but looking down at her with the moonlight washing over her face, he knew what else he wanted her to be.

His woman.

CHAPTER 7

A THUNK SHOOK CAITLYN AWAKE THE NEXT MORNING, and she opened her eyes to see Flynn sitting on the side of her bed, a breakfast tray in hand.

"Mornin', sunshine. The Frenchwoman you hired to cook, Katrine, was fretting about you coming down for breakfast since it's almost ten o'clock. She made a second batch of *pain de campagne* this morning just for you. And I got up to check on you and heard you and Beau talking on the portico. Glad he found his way back. You two looked awfully cozy. Of course, he didn't say much when he surfaced from his room this morning."

Cozy was a good word for it. She'd gone to bed with a smile on her face. "Coffee. Stat."

Flynn plunged the French press down and poured her coffee. The roasted beans smelled like nirvana, and she grabbed a slice of the rustic country bread still warm from the oven. "Yes, my queen."

She snorted, inhaling the roasted scent of coffee as she lifted her cup. "You're so funny." The first taste of coffee made her eyes flutter shut. "God, I needed this."

"Are you dating him?" her brother asked, tsking his tongue. "You know the speech I'm supposed to give here."

"We've already had the business and personal talk,"

she said, smacking him on the arm. "Give me a little credit."

"I give you all the credit, but you're my sister. I get to be a little protective," Flynn said. "Speaking of credit, I like Ibrahim a lot. You did good finding him. Did you know he speaks eight languages fluently? Doesn't that blow your mind?"

"We Americans are lucky if we know two languages." She laughed. "My Spanish still isn't much beyond *gracias* and *cerveza.*"

"And you don't even like beer," he said, grabbing a slice of bread and dripping honey onto it with the serving spoon. "I'm going to take off this morning, but I meant what I said about Uncle Arthur and Aunt Clara. They're eager to visit, and you might enjoy having them here."

She released an audible sigh. "I don't need chaperones, but maybe you're right. Aunt Clara is excited about my new perfume venture, and they've been talking about coming over. Let me settle in here a few more days with Ibrahim—and Beau. Besides, they only just returned from Ireland."

"I still can't believe Trevor and Becca are already married," Flynn said, chortling. "Dad and Michaela had to hustle to make it there before the minister arrived."

Trevor and Becca had married mere days after Caitlyn's mom, Assumpta Merriam, had arrived in Ireland and called for a summit to settle the nastiness between Connor and Quinn and the rest of the siblings. Most of the family had already been in town, so the couple had decided there was no better time to exchange their vows.

"What a sight it was," Caitlyn said, smiling. "Them marrying in the front hall of her bed and breakfast, the wild Irish Sea visible from the windows. Have you heard from him?"

Even though they were honeymooning at Becca's inn, The Wild Irish Rose, Trevor had insisted neither he nor his new bride would be taking calls for the immediate future.

He made a face. "No, he's still got his 'honeymoon' message on. I believe it says something like, 'Just married the woman of my dreams. Leave a message unless it's life and death. If it is, hang up and call either the police or Connor Merriam of Merriam Enterprises.'"

"Haha," she said. "I need to call to hear the message."

"It's one for the ages. Damn, I'm happy for him. I want to be happy for you. You're still beaming moonbeams."

She knew what he meant. Every cell of her body seemed filled with light. "I'm really glad you came, Flynn," she said. "You have moments of being sweet."

He popped the last piece of bread in his mouth. "And you need to get your butt going. Final words from your brother..."

She took a healthy sip of her coffee.

"I know it's not my business, but you're my sister. While this guy seems nice, he's got something major going on. Dating him might be... Just be careful, okay? I don't want you hurt again."

"I've thought about this a lot, Flynn, and the reason the whole mess with Jace the Jerk hurt so much was that I let him undercut my confidence. Whatever's going on with Beau is about him, not me. He said something about an epic fight with his mother and bone-cutting betrayal."

"Shit." Flynn stood. "That sucks if they're close."

While she still didn't have the full picture, she felt safe to say, "They are. She mostly raised him by herself after his dad died young, and she's been his manager since he launched his music career."

"Growing pains perhaps? I looked him up. He turned thirty last month. That messes with the mind."

Flynn was nearly the same age. "Messing with yours, is it? You have until November to get it on right. What do you want to do to celebrate the big 3-0, by the way? The family wants to throw you a party, but if you want to make it a destination thing, I'm sure I can get away. Michaela too. Trevor, not so much." But he would, she expected, for Flynn's big birthday. "Not sure if it's even worth asking Quinn or Connor. They're workaholics."

"And that's not how I want to be," he said. "I'll give it some thought, but I'll be honest—I've been thinking life, the universe, and everything. Big birthdays are the worst. They dredge up all sorts of uncomfortable questions." He grimaced and took her coffee out of her hands, taking a sip. "How did you get through it?"

"Other than the sad state of my personal life, I thought my life was going pretty well. I knew I'd figure out my next big thing, and I decided patience was better than beating my head against the wall."

"And now you own a flower farm in Provence and will be launching a new perfume. It's because perfume doesn't change a woman's sex appeal, right? Only enhances what's there?"

Bingo. She stared at him. "Flynn Merriam, sometimes you surprise the hell out of me."

"I'm good at interpreting other people's motivations. It's figuring out my own life direction that's a problem for me."

She pushed the tray aside and rolled out of bed. "Are you heading back to Prague?"

He kissed her cheek. "Nope. Copenhagen. There's a lovely Danish model I met in Prague. Let me say she doesn't wear any makeup. The sexiest women I know let their natural beauty shine."

"It's why I love France," she said. "But you're always meeting models. It's like you're a model magnet. Maybe it's time for a change."

He shook his head. "Like I always say, they're terrific. Beautiful. Accomplished. Low-maintenance. They have their own careers. Like to travel. Most aren't looking for commitment. That's what I want right now."

"Nothing wrong with that," she said, "so long as you're on the same page."

"Okay, I'm out of here. Claude is probably outside by now. If you need anything, I'm only a short plane ride away. Because you sure as hell wouldn't call Quinn."

Their brother was in London, also a short plane ride away. "Unless I was dying, and he was closer than you."

"Does he know yet that you did some things out of order?"

She'd bought the land and hired Ibrahim before securing Beau. Somehow Quinn had thought she needed Beau first and then the rest, but she'd thought, correctly it seemed, that she'd have a better chance of getting Beau interested if she had something to show him. "This way was better."

She just wished Beau had already signed a contract. Quinn was going to ask, and she owed him an update after her Nashville trip.

"I told Ibrahim goodbye," he said, treading to the door. "If I don't see Beau on my way out—"

"I'll give him your brotherly regard." She raced across the room to hug him again. "You really are the best. Keep me posted on where you are."

"Have fun creating this perfume. From talking to Ibrahim, it's going to be a fascinating experience. Savor it."

"I plan to."

He waved and then he was gone. She headed to the bathroom and dressed. The heat was already making its presence known in the house despite the stone walls, which kept it cooler. But the air smelled like the most perfect lingerie sachet tucked back inside a wardrobe drawer, and she stretched her hands overhead to take it all in.

Today was going to be a great day.

When she finally found Beau, he was stretched out on the grass in the backyard, Chou-Chou, the three-week-old baby goat, grazing on the short verdant grass beside him. He had on a button-down shirt and jeans with his cowboy boots. Her mouth went dry at the sight. But God, in this heat, he had to be roasting. She was glad to be wearing a simple yellow cotton dress.

"You found a friend, I see," she said, smiling at the scene.

He opened his eyes, and she watched as they roved over her dress. "And you look like the sun itself today. I was hoping I didn't wear you out, keeping you up talking like I did."

Their eyes met and held, and she was aware of the breeze rustling the edge of her dress where he'd looked moments ago. "No, I loved every minute of it."

"Me too. Have you met Chou-Chou? Katrine managed to communicate to me that he's one of the Bisset goats."

"Yes," she said, "but he lost his mama in the birthing and wanders off through the fields, crying like he's looking for her."

He looked off. "That's mighty sad. Katrine mentioned bringing over some kind of cheese too, but I couldn't understand the rest. I hate not being able to communicate with everyone."

The white goat had the most adorable brown spots and tiny feet. It gave a hearty *bah* and headed right for her. She petted its small pointy head and short horns. "He's a Rove goat, special to the region. The milk produces the most delicious cheese called Rove Brousse. Jean Pierre's grandfather still makes it at ninety-two."

"I was sorry I couldn't communicate with them too," he said, rolling onto his side. "Seemed like nice people."

"They know you don't speak French." She sat down beside him, the sun hot on her skin.

He hadn't shaved, and it was strange to see those usually clean-shaven cheeks a little scruffy. Downright sexy, really.

He laughed when Chou-Chou nuzzled his face. "Hey, now. Keep to the grass. Heck, he probably doesn't understand me either."

Unfortunately, he was right. She spoke to the animal in French and it gave an answering *bah*. "You'll find your way with each other, like you will with everyone else. Traveling always leads to interesting connections. Even when you don't speak the same language. I can't tell you how many times I've had to talk with my hands, hoping to get something across. I've found a simple smile sometimes says it all. Trust me, you have a really terrific smile."

"So do you, honey."

She couldn't help but shiver and smile all at once. He laid his head back on the grass, settling onto his back. Chou-Chou stepped over him, and she would have laughed had Beau's sigh not been so loud. "I'll tell you what—I'm grateful to be here. It's hot like this at home, but back in Nashville, it's humid as all get-out. It's cool in the shade here. And the fields are captivating, always flashing some new shade of purple or blue, depending on the way you look at them."

"It is beautiful, isn't it? I live in an apartment in Manhattan, and I love it, but this... I could get used to it."

"Me too, even with all the French things. I think I ate more bread than Katrine was expecting. I thought they ate omelets here. I think I offended her when I asked."

She laughed. "Breakfast is usually just bread and jam, or honey, with tea or coffee."

"The coffee was great once she showed me how to push that lever down. I'm all thumbs with this stuff. Took me darn near twenty minutes to figure out how to turn the shower on this morning."

"Oh, I forgot. Yes, trying to figure out how to flush the toilet or turn on the water can take forever if you're not used to it. But seriously, are you feeling better after our talk last night?"

"Being with you livens me up," he said, "and so does this little fella apparently. I'm...grateful for the respite, Caitlyn. I'm glad we're courting."

If she had her choice, she'd keep sitting on the grass with him, the lavender swaying in the breeze, until the sun set. That was courting in her mind. "Me too, Beau." She let her hand rest on his arm. "Now, I need to go find Ibrahim. I can't believe I slept in so late."

"We didn't head in until after two," he said, running his fingertips over her hand.

No, and they could have talked all night. They'd made their way to the house with slow steps, wanting more time to whisper in the moonlight and hold hands.

"I really do need to find Ibrahim," she said, aware of her need to remind herself this was not a vacation. "I promised him we would talk about themes and vision and such for the new perfume."

He sat up, laughing as Chou-Chou took the opportunity to nuzzle his face. "Silly beast. I'd love to join you, if you don't mind. There's something in the way Ibrahim talks about things... He sees scents like I see music. It might help me with the new album."

Yes, she could see how he would make that connection. "Perhaps another kindred spirit," she said with a small smile.

"Can I have more than one?" His gaze settled on her face and then dipped to the curve of her lips.

Her heart started racing. Was he going to kiss her? Last night, he'd only squeezed her hand before heading to his room.

"I'd be pretty lucky to find one besides you," he continued, raising her hand to his lips and kissing it softly. "Come on. If we don't get moving, we'll linger here all day like I'd like to."

She smoothed back the lock of hair that had fallen on his forehead. "Yes, Ibrahim probably has been up for hours." And she was here to work.

Beau let go of her hand and pushed to standing, sending Chou-Chou off with a nice rubdown. They started toward the guesthouse.

"If it's not too nosy, is there a Mrs. Magdy?" Beau asked. "I mean, it would be hard to be away from your woman, I'd think."

Your woman. She loved being independent, but somehow the way he said that—and the way he sang it too—made her envision two people belonging to each other. Because in her world, he'd be her man as much as she'd be his woman.

"She passed away six months ago, he told me. I hadn't known that when I offered him the job." But she'd understood why he'd be open to a change after such a loss.

"Sounds like he needed to get away from the past too," Beau said, opening the front door for her.

The house was much cooler, and together they walked down the hallway to Ibrahim's so-called lab. The door was open, sunlight and Raï music spilling out. The drums and reed flute wove together in a sinuous melody, dancing. Beau stopped short, putting a hand on her arm.

"What is that music?" His tone was wistful.

She made a humming sound. "It's Raï." God, she loved it.

His laugh was short, almost serious. "Honey, that ain't Rye Crenshaw. He's a friend, so I'd know if he made music like that."

Rye Crenshaw was a friend? It figured that he'd know other country music stars, but she had a fan girl moment before she managed to snap herself out of it. "Not R-y-e. R-a-ï. It's what I'd called Bedouin music."

"Huh?"

"From North Africa. You know, Bedouins. People who lived mostly in the desert, although I think Raï technically comes from Algeria."

"It does, but the music goes back much further," Ibrahim said, appearing in the doorway. "Some call it Arab rhythm and blues. Others folk music. I listen to it when I'm working with Oriental scents, ones known for their warmth and sensuality. Myrrh. Sandalwood. Frankincense. Cedar wood. Agar wood. Come inside. I'll show you."

Caitlyn moved to follow Ibrahim, who'd slipped back inside, but Beau's hand was still on her arm. On his face was what she could only term wonder.

"What is it?"

"I could hear the baseline with that flute," he said, his ear cocked. "There's a violin. Wait. Is that accordion? Caitlyn, how have I never heard this music before?"

She shrugged. "I don't know. I've always liked it, but I have eclectic taste in music."

He lifted her hand and put it on his chest, flattening her palm there. "Hear the drum? It's like a heartbeat. My God, it's...beautiful."

She became aware of her own heartbeat. It was tripping inside her chest from touching him, and suddenly she was aware their heartbeats had the same cadence. *Kismet*, she thought. Their eyes met.

She knew in that moment she'd fallen for him the rest of the way.

CHAPTER 8

THE MUSIC.

The sound of it had blown his heart clear up to his throat. In his chest was an open and empty space, vibrating with the sound he imagined the earth made out in the lavender fields at night. The drum was primal. The flute filled with longing. This was the music of something lost, of the quest to find it again.

It was the music for the journey he was on, he realized. To find his roots.

Caitlyn's touch to his forehead brought him back. Her green eyes seemed as vibrant as the verdant green hills they'd traveled through just yesterday. Everything was foreign to him here, from the language to the scents, *except this woman*. From the very beginning he'd *known* her. She was his kindred spirit. What he was feeling for her, stronger and more urgent each moment they spent together, was his only surety right now.

Somehow it made sense to be somewhere completely unfamiliar. His own person had become unfamiliar to him.

This was where he would retill the soil of his life and start anew.

"I'm glad you're here with me for this moment," he

said, raising her hand to his lips and kissing the back of it.

God, he wanted to kiss her, his body beating with the music. This woman...

He wanted her to be his.

His gaze fell to her full lips, a touch rosier from being out in the sun. Outside, he'd stopped himself from kissing her, wanting to court her, learn her, tantalize her even. Her skin was pink, he realized, making him wish he could cool her down by running an ice cube over it, one he'd plucked out of his own water glass.

Good ol' Beau wasn't supposed to have such thoughts this early, certainly not act on them.

But good ol' Beau didn't exist anymore, a small voice inside whispered. He was gone, buried under a lifetime of secrets and lies.

He closed the distance between them and put his hand on her back, lowering his head, already wondering how her lips would taste. He imagined a field of strawberries.

"Not here," she whispered, nodding to the doorway, a frown twisting that luscious mouth.

He took a few steps back, realizing he'd almost embarrassed her in front of a colleague. "Sorry."

"No, I want to kiss you too," she whispered, following him and running her fingers over his lips in a single pass, much like lighting a match over the striking surface of a matchbook. The trail of fire she left in her wake made him step away from her again. He had to. He inhaled a few deep breaths to settle himself, ones filled with scents of musk, exotic and alluring, like the woman before him.

"Then later," he whispered back.

Her mouth tipped up, and then she was dashing toward the doorway. "Tell me about your playlists, Ibrahim. I know Beau would love to hear more. I love that you listen to different music depending on which scents you're working on."

By the time Beau reached the doorway, he was calmer.

A wave of scent as powerful as a single tide washed over him, notes of earth and wood dancing with each other. "Yes, I'd love to hear more about all of it. My goodness, your lab... I never..."

Ibrahim was standing behind a long glass table filled with bell-shaped jars, a weighing scale, and a myriad of tiny glass beakers in a wooden ring stand. His notebook lay open before him, covered in intricate handwriting in midnight blue ink. The waist-to-ceiling glass shelves mounted on the wall behind him were filled with an awe-worthy number of labeled apothecary bottles.

"Are all those scents?" he asked. Upon closer inspection, he caught a few labels: *orange blossom, amber, musk, jasmine.*

Ibrahim gave his signature pencil-thin smile. "Yes, and that's only a fraction of the ones available. Scents are like stars. There are millions out there. Today we hope to discover what constellation we want to be in. Sit down. Please."

He had an inviting way with words, and Beau pulled out a white metal chair for Caitlyn first and then himself across from Ibrahim at the glass table. As they got settled, Beau noted a refrigerated glass cabinet to the right filled with more apothecary bottles as well as another lined with funnels, stirring rods, and what looked like the regular old hot plate he'd cooked on in his first low-rent apartment in Nashville. A fan's motor permeated his consciousness over the meandering notes of the music, and he knew it to be practical. The scents in here must need somewhere to escape so as not to become overwhelming.

"This is quite a lab," he said, his hands on his knees as he took it all in.

"Caitlyn was kind enough to allow me to outfit it as I wished, and it was easy to have everything I needed shipped here. Thank you again."

She leaned forward in her chair, arms waving enthusiastically. "Are you kidding? I feel like I'm back in high school chemistry, which I didn't do so well in by the way."

Beau tucked that little tidbit away, wanting to record every detail he could about this woman who captivated him so.

"Don't worry," the older man said. "There won't be a test. We're among friends here. Since you asked about my playlists, I listen to opera when I handle floral scents. Verdi seemed to capture spring itself in his music. Do you know it, Beau?"

He choked out a laugh. "I was born in a small town in Arkansas known more for its strawberries and peaches than its music beyond country." But that wasn't an excuse now. "I've always thought opera..." He didn't want to call it hoity-toity.

"Was for a certain class?" Ibrahim raised a brow. "According to what I've read, the same is said of country music. I doubt that's fair."

Caitlyn covered her mouth to smother her laughter, and Beau couldn't blame her. If they'd been alone, he would have tickled her ribs to bring out that laugh of hers. "You've got me there. Not everyone who listens to country is a redneck or good ol' boy."

"You'll have to educate me on those stereotypes. They're unfamiliar to me, I'm afraid."

He laughed, trying to imagine Ibrahim in a small country town. "Perhaps later. I'd like to hear more about your playlists. So, you've told us about the musks and the florals. What other kinds of scents do you work with?"

"The last of the four main categories on the modern fragrance wheel are called fresh notes."

"Sharper scents like lime and citrus, right?" Caitlyn asked.

"Exactly."

"So what music is for them?" she pressed.

"Cuban music," he said. "The kind that reminds me of nights in Havana back when Ernest Hemingway, Rita Hayworth, Frank Sinatra, and others used to go there."

Beau was embarrassed that he didn't know who the lady was on that list. "I wonder what country music would be good for."

"I'd say the florals," Caitlyn said. "It makes me think of a couple walking through the country holding hands."

Her eyes strayed toward his, and he knew she was thinking about how they'd done the same last night.

"Or cuddling up with your man in front of a warm fire after the kids go to bed." Her voice went soft.

He turned his head sharply. She was referencing one of his songs.

He couldn't help but sing the lyrics:

After tucking the little ones in bed and kissing them goodnight,
All I want to do tonight is cuddle up next to you,
The warmth of the firelight and the touch of your hands dancing over my skin.

It was as if he'd written the words for her before they'd met. His gut tightened, thinking about running his hands over her. *Slow down, boy.*

She must have caught the look on his face because her eyes widened, and a blush shimmered on her cheeks. "Of course, country music is about lots more than that," she hastened to say. "Tornados, dogs dying... You know. Life."

Sad images, but all too real to the people he'd known growing up. "I haven't done a tornado yet."

She coughed loudly, her cheeks turning pinker—a pale rose of a color. "Best get on that then. Maybe for the new album..."

Maybe, indeed. A tornado wreaked havoc, ripping up everything in its wake. Disassembling an entire house.

He understood its power now. "Yes. I just might. Sorry, Ibrahim, we're... What do you call it, Caitlyn? Digressing?"

"Exactly." She beamed a smile. "Please continue, Ibrahim."

The man hadn't moved a muscle during their exchange. "If I may suggest, I thought we'd talk more about your vision for the perfume, and then we can start matching some scents."

"Like shoe shopping," she said, bouncing in her seat. "I hope you don't mind my vernacular. I love perfume, but some of the technical stuff is so out of my league. I mean, the math and all that."

"There's math?" Beau asked.

"A plentiful amount, I'm afraid. It's maddening. You add a certain amount of one note, and then you must balance it with another and so on."

"Notes?" Beau asked. "Sorry, I didn't read up on any of this." In fact, he didn't have much of an excuse for being here. He only knew that he wanted to be. "Maybe I should leave you two—"

"Don't be silly," Caitlyn said when he started to rise. "You need assurance our product will be worthy of your name before you sign a contract. I'll do whatever it takes to get your John Hancock."

He heard the steel in her voice. She was a businesswoman to her core. "Thank you for understanding. Please go on, Ibrahim."

"Notes are single scents such as lavender or bergamot or cinnamon."

They could put cinnamon in a perfume? He'd always slapped on his aftershave without thinking much about such things. Growing up, he'd used plain old Stetson from the local drugstore until he'd made it big and had the money to shop in a department store. He'd always been drawn to Acqua di Parma, Blu Mediterraneo. The scent had made him think of white-sand beaches and far-off places, but his mother had vetoed the idea and chosen Ryan Williams For Men, saying he should be able to say he wore an all-American scent if asked in an interview.

His anger resurfaced. Something so small, and still she'd managed to get her way. And he'd allowed it.

But damn her.

"To make a perfume or a cologne, you need to blend three levels. Some call it the top, middle, and base notes, but I prefer head, heart, and bottom. Makes it feel more personal somehow."

"Also translates nicely to the body," Caitlyn said. "I've come across some incredible blogs on essential oils and how they affect certain parts of the body like the head and heart and what some practitioners of Eastern medicine call the root. Like peppermint being great for mental clarity while rose opens the heart. And then there's ylang ylang for the root center."

Ibrahim rose and opened the glass cabinet behind him. "You already have a passion for perfume, Caitlyn, and a pure understanding. Smell is one of our five senses, and some say the least used. And yet, the body is processing scents throughout the day. The smell of garbage makes us cringe. A newborn baby's smell makes us fill with more love than we knew we had inside us. A pine tree's smell can bring us peace."

Now this was something Beau could understand. He appreciated the way smells told a story, and often used them to create a wider sensory array in his music. Fresh-baked pies. Fresh-cut grass. He knew the people hearing those lyrics could conjure those smells up in their heads and find them pleasing and relatable.

Caitlyn put her hand over her heart. "And then there are the memories they bring up, right? Like when I smell my Grandma Anna's red leather gloves, the ones my mom gave me after she died. They hold a slight trace of Chanel No. 5, and it makes me both miss her and feel she's still with me, all at once."

A beautiful, haunting image. Beau might have to ask her later if he could use it in a song. When they'd bagged up his father's clothes for Goodwill, all he recalled noticing was the smell of Wild Turkey and stale cigarettes.

"A classic perfume, that one, and one of my wife's favorites," Ibrahim said, taking out a few bottles. "Did you know the modern perfume industry began in Grasse, France, because the leather makers were trying to disguise the hideous tanning scents that smelled up the town? Some creative person had the idea to sprinkle the leather products in floral waters, and a pair of scented gloves ended up with Catherine de Medici, who investigated the scent and wanted more of it."

Beau couldn't fathom anything in France smelling bad, but he reckoned it had its places like everywhere else.

"I'll bet Egypt's fascination with perfume started very differently," Caitlyn said, leaning forward when Ibrahim set three bottles in front of them, their labels disguised by the angle.

"Egyptians had a complex relationship with perfumes," he said, pulling out the stoppers. "Perhaps we'll go into that another time. First, I want you to smell these notes and tell me what they conjure for you. Don't look at the labels."

Caitlyn bent her head to sniff the first one. "And you said there wouldn't be a test."

"It's not a test," Ibrahim said. "Just tell me what associations it has for you, if any, or how it makes you feel. All you need is a quick inhale. If you breathe in too much, you'll saturate the olfactory sensory neurons in your nose."

Caitlyn passed Beau the bottle, and their fingers brushed, making their gazes fly briefly to each other. "Ibrahim's too modest to say so, but master perfumers have to be able to distinguish four thousand individual notes."

"You're kidding," Beau said, leaning forward to sniff.

"I know!" Caitlyn slapped her hand on her forehead. "Unreal, right?"

"What's the verdict?" Ibrahim asked, resuming his seat.

"Lemon, I think." Caitlyn made a humming sound as Beau set the little bottle back on the table. "Reminds me of the lemon meringue pie my mom makes on the Fourth of July."

Beau closed his eyes and let his mind replay the smell over and over, like he'd do with a musical note. "It reminds me of that yummy soup in this Thai restaurant in Las Vegas on the Strip. Lemongrass."

Ibrahim's brow winged up. "Very good, Beau. Lemon and lemongrass are often confused."

"Not by him," Caitlyn said, rolling her eyes. "Okay, I'm going to win the next one."

Beau rubbed her arm. "It's not a contest."

"I'm one of seven kids," she responded. "Trust me, *everything* is a contest." She brought the next bottle to her nose, sniffed, then passed it to him. This time he knew she was brushing their fingers together intentionally and flashed her a quick smile. "All right, I have my guess."

Beau inhaled shallowly again. This scent was dark. Musky. Masculine.

"Cedar," she called out like a star student might in class. "Beau?"

That didn't sound right to him. He let the scent settle in his nose. "I'd say sandalwood. Like the oil my massage therapist uses on me."

"Correct." Ibrahim stoppered the two bottles they'd finished and set them aside. "Try this one," he said, nodding to the third.

Caitlyn's frown was epic, and he gave her a nudge.

"Hey, this is supposed to be fun."

She stuck her tongue out at him, making him and Ibrahim laugh, and then inhaled the final note. "You go first this time."

Leaning forward, Beau breathed it in. Something herbal. Again, he thought of food. Focaccia bread from the Italian place around the corner from his office downtown. "Rosemary."

She glared at him, all flirting gone. "I agree. We have rosemary all over our place in Napa. I'd recognize it anywhere."

"Excellent," Ibrahim said. "But where do you feel the note? Head, heart, or bottom?"

Caitlyn blew out a breath, and he could all but hear her wheels grinding. Who would have expected she could be so competitive? Then again, she was from a family of serious businesspeople, and this was her new venture. He could be this serious about his music and then some.

"For me, it's all heart because it makes me think of home," Caitlyn said, "but if I were being scientific, I'd guess it's a bottom note because it's from the earth."

Did he have a memory? "Nothing specific comes to mind for me on this one. Other than focaccia bread, which you may laugh at."

Ibrahim put the stopper in the last one. "No, that's perfect. What does focaccia make you feel?"

"If I were writing a song, I'd say it reminded me of grandmotherly Italian women serving sustenance with a side of comfort and wisdom."

"Jeez, I'm getting killed here." Caitlyn covered her ears. "A master perfumer and a famous country singer known for his stories. I have nothing to add to this discussion."

She was joking, but there was a thread of seriousness to it.

"Stop that," Beau said, touching her arm. "You're way

too hard on yourself. Neither of us would even be here if it weren't for your vision."

"I agree," Ibrahim said. Shifting his gaze back to Beau, he said, "You should use that line in a song about the grandmothers. It evokes all sorts of emotions in the heart. And yes, rosemary is a heart note."

Incredible. There was so much more to perfume making than he'd considered. It truly was an art. "How long does it take you to make a perfume?"

The man's quiet laughter seemed to ruffle the air like a gentle breeze. "How long does it take you to write a song?"

"Lately?" He laughed. "As long as it takes."

"Precisely." Ibrahim drew the three bottles together. "Here we have a fragrance, right? Three simple notes. Head. Heart. Bottom."

Caitlyn popped up. "Great! I'll call marketing." When she sank back in her chair, she was smiling again. "Why do I get the sense we're about to get to the math part?"

"Yes, it's maddening, isn't it?" Ibrahim said, pushing the bottles aside. "We must create a certain equation of scent, one that blends well together and tells the story we'd like to share with the wearer, the public at large. Some scents are volatile on their own, for example, lavender, but that's also what makes their scent last longer."

"Oh, great! Leave it to me to find the most volatile scent and say, heck, yeah, let's make a new perfume out of it." She made a shooting gun motion with her hand to her head.

"Ah, but that's part of the magic of making and wearing perfume," Ibrahim said. "Paired with another note like, say, jasmine, it's rounded out or balanced."

"Huh," Beau thought out loud. "This is fascinating. It sounds a little like making music. It's all about creating a perfect blend."

Blend. That word again. Who'd imagined music and

perfume had so much in common? He wished he had a notebook. Just from talking with Caitlyn and Ibrahim, he was feeling juiced up on ideas for song lyrics.

"I think you're what Caitlyn calls a kindred spirit, Ibrahim," he added. "She thought you might be."

Ibrahim gave a slow smile. "Kindred spirit. I like that. Now, Caitlyn, tell me more about your vision. When creating a perfume, we want a theme or a character, if you like. I know you want something that connects a woman to her roots. Something that helps her remember her sensuality."

Sensuality. Suddenly the musky scents in the room seemed to vibrate inside Beau's nostrils, that one word punching those olfactory neurons Ibrahim had mentioned. Belly-deep awareness of Caitlyn gushed over him—the slight pink tint of her skin from the late morning sun, the lines of her bare calves in her flat gold sandals, the warmth of her. He wondered what she smelled like. He hadn't paid attention before.

He would not make that mistake again.

"Yes, I want all those things," she said, a far-off look in her eyes, "but I don't want women to feel they need to change anything about themselves to wear our perfume. I want them to feel they matter. They're important. They're *enough*, just as they are. The perfume should be a celebration of that. I'm still searching for the right name for the perfume, but that's where I'm headed, Ibrahim."

Beau tucked all of this away, her words adding further confirmation to the realization he'd come to last night. This woman, his woman, not only wanted courting. She needed it.

"A wonderful start," he said. "My late wife used to say perfume transcended time and place. A million lifetimes exist in one small bottle. Lives you hope to live and perhaps ones you already have: a young girl on the brink of womanhood, a woman at a crossroads, and one who has chosen her path."

"Oh. My. God. Yes!" Caitlyn leaned forward. "I wish I could have met your wife. She sounds awesome."

Emotion glinted in his brown eyes. "She believed in helping women too. Your vision is one of the reasons I took this job. I thought she'd like knowing I was continuing her work with women."

He'd loved her. That much was plain as day. Beau hoped he'd earn the man's confidence before he returned to Nashville. He would be honored to hear his story and learn about his loss. "What was her name?" Beau asked.

"Rania," he answered, his voice as soft and husky, like the sandalwood they'd sampled.

The room seemed to vibrate from the sound of her name. Only two beats, but the power of his feelings for her was evident. Beau could have ended a song that way.

"A beautiful name." Caitlyn sighed. "I'm sorry I never asked whether you had children."

Ibrahim smiled sadly. "No, we often had to remind ourselves we were blessed enough with our love for each other."

Beau had an appreciation for words, and Ibrahim had a lovely way of using them. He might have said so, but the other man shook his head slightly, as if dispelling a haze, and said, "Now, let's talk about which scents best fit this vision."

He was clearly eager to change the subject, and the look in Caitlyn's eyes indicated she knew it. Honored it.

"Before we jump to scents," she said, "I'd like to hear what Beau thinks about all of this. Any characteristics you'd like to see in this perfume?"

As the drums in the music picked up, blending with a chorus in a tongue as foreign as his current circumstances, Beau said, "A fragrance that doesn't sour over time or fade on your skin. Or overwhelm others with its strength or bitterness. Of course, you're the master, Ibrahim, and

I'm sure your perfumes wouldn't do that."

He couldn't help but think of his mother. Once he'd considered her to be the most admirable person in his acquaintance. Strong. Supportive. Honest.

But she'd lied to him. He'd always thought his mama had hated his daddy for his infidelity, but she'd cheated too. She'd broken her vows, things she'd always taught Beau to value and honor.

"You remember to be a good boy, Beau," she used to tell him. "Not like your father. Always look and act like a good Southern gentleman. Don't sass your teachers. Only speak when spoken to. Make sure you use your pleases and thank yous."

Damn her, he thought. *Damn her and her always and don'ts.*

Ibrahim's all-knowing gaze pinned him to his chair. "A fragrance of truth, so to speak, to oneself and to others."

He cleared his throat. "Yes."

The older man nodded after a long moment, like a beat of silence in the middle of a song. "Truth is the most prized of fragrances. It will be so."

Caitlyn looked from Ibrahim to Beau and then threw up her hands. "I thought you two would get along, but whew! It's like you already have a secret language. Watching you two is like watching my twin brothers, Trevor and J.T."

Ibrahim smiled again. "Like Beau said, 'kindred spirits.'"

His life was crazy, Beau realized, as the song ended on a crescendo of drumbeat and fiery hand-clapping. Like the silent space inside his heart, he felt bereft of all sound. To him, sound was life. Even silence had a sound to him.

"I have more than enough to work with now," Ibrahim said, his smile wry. "Thank you both."

"No, thank you, Ibrahim." Caitlyn was standing up, but Beau seemed glued to the chair. Ibrahim's words and the music, which was finally fading, had filled him to bursting, and yet he still felt a strange hollowness inside.

He thought about the truth he was seeking. The quest for self-knowledge—for a sense of who he was now that he could no longer define himself by who he did not want to be. Walt Masters: alcoholic, cheat, liar, and deadbeat. The words should have been engraved on the man's tombstone, but instead Beau's mother had carved them into his heart.

Perhaps this was the best news he'd ever received. Unless his real father was just as bad as Walt, he didn't have a genetic predisposition to become a bad guy.

Maybe it was time for him to explore the things Old Beau had been told to eschew to find the truth of himself.

CHAPTER 9

CAITLYN WATCHED BEAU WALK OFF AS IF HIS HEAD WERE IN the clouds.

She understood. Her mind felt like a melon that had fallen from the counter and split wide open.

She returned her gaze to Ibrahim. "Are your smelling sessions always this...intense?" she asked.

He gave his small, mysterious smile. "With every smelling session, we're going to uncover more of your secrets. It'll help us flesh out your vision for this fragrance and the notes to match it."

Secrets? Her short laugh turned into a snort.

He waved his index finger like a metronome. "I know what you're thinking, but we all have secrets, Caitlyn. I'm talking about the ones deep inside us, the ones we don't want to admit to ourselves, which nonetheless govern our actions and shape our worldview."

"You're like the Perfume Jedi," she breathed out. "Except I'm not that deep and mysterious. What you see is what you get." Her jazz hands were supposed to make him laugh, but he just continued to gaze at her. Could she tell him how unsettling that was? "I'm serious, Ibrahim."

"I know you are," he said, "but you undervalue yourself. I will ask you now: why lavender fields?"

"Beau already asked me this. It's my favorite scent. One of the most popular essential oils."

His narrowed eyes pinned her to the chair. "And..."

She floundered for more of an answer as he walked over to his phone and punched some buttons. The first strands of a violin filtered into the room, followed by a flute. Then a soprano burst of Italian piped through the speakers with all the ebullience of Mother Earth in spring, unstoppable and captivating. "Your florals playlist."

"You didn't answer my question." He came back to the table, but they remained standing.

Well, she'd heard he was eccentric but brilliant, hadn't she? She wanted to make a special perfume, something that made a difference. If it required her to do a little soul-searching, well, who was she to say no?

"Lavender is calming to the spirit. Puts us in our Zen place." She wanted to high-five herself. "And heck, it came with this farmhouse, right?"

"Your zest for life is as refreshing and unmistakable, Caitlyn, as a note of orange blossom. But you often answer serious questions with humor. I wonder why."

Thunk. The sound seemed to come from inside her, vibrating through her entire being. Was that her heart? "Have you always seen through people like a Jedi or are all master perfumers like you?"

"See what I mean?" He came around the table and put his hand companionably on her shoulder. "Beau is also asking questions. Seeking answers. As am I. Perhaps we will all find them together."

He was leading her to the door. "What answers are you seeking, Ibrahim? You have a greater handle on life than most people I've met."

His chest seemed to rise with his inhalation, different than when he was testing perfume notes. "Who I am without my beloved Rania. How I want my life to be now. How I can forget her scent and the pain of losing her."

Well, shit. Her mouth fell open. Talk about baring your soul. Is that what he wanted her to do? That was... scary. "You must have loved her very much."

"I did. We were lucky to find each other young. Eighteen if you can imagine it. Fresh at university, me at Givaudan Perfumery School in Grasse and her at the Sorbonne in Paris. Train rides every weekend became our letter writing, every kilometer a love sonnet to each other."

How romantic. Goodness, but he talked like no one she'd ever met.

"She's the only woman I've ever loved. I never imagined that I might continue to gray and age without her. Sometimes I find her absence completely intolerable, like life has no meaning without her skin next to mine day and night. The fields of lavender were supposed to drown out amber, her favorite scent. And yet, I still smell it and her all the time here."

"Because scent is a memory," she said, her heart flooding with compassion for him.

His smile turned wry. "We perfumers are an odd lot. Half artist. Half scientist. Fueled by a seemingly insane passion: to blend together the perfect notes to evoke deep, pure emotion, mood, memory even. Sometimes I think we must be mad to undertake such a quest, and yet it is all I long to do. Now for your perfume homework, as you like to call it."

"All right," she said, rolling her eyes dramatically until he smiled. "Give it to me."

He handed her a small, rolled piece of paper the uninitiated might have mistaken for a hand-rolled cigarette.

"Read it when you return to your room. When you feel you have the answers, you'll share them with me."

The paper seemed to burn in her palm when she took it from him. "Are you going to do the same with Beau?" His growing investment in this venture and their growing

connection ensured he'd follow through with the contract, right? She trusted his word, but Flynn was right.
Quinn was going to have her for lunch when he found out
she'd taken certain...ahem...liberties with his conditions.

"If he's open to it, I suppose. Do you have any reser-
vations about me starting to brainstorm and daydream a
little for our men's perfume?"

She didn't have the funding for that yet, something he
knew. But that wasn't what he was asking. "So long as you
feel it's not burdensome to your current tasks."

"Ah, *cherie,* daydreaming is never burdensome. I'll
see you at dinner. Katrine told me she was making lamb."

She walked to the door but stopped in the threshold
and turned back to him. "Ibrahim, deep down I don't
know why lavender. I only knew it had to *be* lavender."

He smiled that signature smile of his. "See, the true
answer is coming already."

***

Up in her room, Caitlyn unrolled the small piece of
paper. The finest of linen, she realized, with a textured
edge. Of course Ibrahim would use such paper. But the
words stole her breath:

The source of a great woman is...

Her first thought was "family." "Teachers" followed in
short order. She took the paper over to her scent journal,
one she'd found at her favorite stationery store in Paris,
and wrote the prompt and her answers on the first empty
page. Once she'd done so, she reached for more answers,
but her mind stayed stubbornly blank.

Her phone caught her eye, and she saw Michaela had
sent her a text. She abandoned the journal and picked it
up.

*How's perfume making? More importantly, how's
Beau? Flynn said he passed the pervert and entitled celebrity test. Being a fan, I'm relieved.*

Chuckling, she responded: *Flynn was sweet to put on his protective brother hat. Beau is wonderful, but perfume making is hard.*

How was that for honesty? She'd understood how linked emotion and perfume were, but this process was more personal than she'd expected. Intimate even. She had an aha moment and wrote it down.

Perfume blends and lays on your skin in a way makeup doesn't.

She sat back. Had she gotten in over her head? No, if this was the process, she'd give it her all. It was the Merriam way.

Enthused again, she opened her work email and saw Quinn's message asking for an update along with an easy salvo questioning the expediency of having Beau Masters visit the farm so quickly. Apparently Flynn or Michaela had let it slip, not that it was a secret. She wasn't even a little surprised by his final question before signing off: *Do you have a contract for legal to look over?*

Said contract was sitting on the scuffed-up desk she'd appropriated as her personal workspace near the window. Well, how was she going to answer? If Quinn knew Beau hadn't signed yet, he could balk. Maybe stop production even. That wouldn't do.

Beau *would* sign. His word meant something. Plus, he believed in this perfume, and he also believed in her. That was everything.

But Quinn wouldn't see it that way until the bird was in hand, so she needed to delay. She wrote him a flowery message about the beauty of the fields, Ibrahim's incredible artistry, and then said: *I have the contract right in front of me.*

Technically, it was true, but she felt a little guilty. It wasn't the first time she'd had to equivocate with Quinn. He had a rock for brains sometimes. Clear steps. Clear rules. He was a great vice president, but horrible at improvising.

Sometimes you had to trust your gut and take a risk, especially when you knew it was worth it.

Beau was definitely worth it.

Still, she hated fudging the truth, so she called Flynn to soothe her conscience. "I just stretched the truth about Beau's contract," she said when he answered. "Am I going to go to some business hell or something?"

"Hello to you too," he said, laughing. "Nah, I think you're okay. Business hell is for people like the Enron and Madoff jerks. You know, the ones who steal from old ladies and long-time pensioners. What did you say exactly?"

She laid it all out, and he didn't interrupt her once. That was Flynn, and she loved his ability to listen. Quinn and Connor didn't have the patience for it, hence their Big Bad Wolf status.

"Well, we figured he'd ask. Although I didn't talk to Beau for long, he doesn't seem like the sort who'd go back on his word. Plus, he cares about you. But Quinn isn't trusting. You'd think living in London would have taught him the power of a gentleman's handshake."

"Right!" And Beau certainly was a gentleman. "Why didn't I think of that? Should I write Quinn back? Wait. No, stupid idea."

"What you said. So, how is the man you currently have eyes for?"

"We're getting to know each other better." Flynn might laugh if she said courting. "It's not all lust and stuff."

Flynn laughed, the jerk. "Lust and stuff? Yes, I know you need that body-mind connection."

"You make me sound like a square."

"Never. Look, I did talk to Aunt Clara and mentioned you needing a chaperone."

"And here I was thinking you're a good listener. When I talked to her about coming, it was for the sheer pleasure of having her and Uncle Arthur visit. I distinctly remember telling you I don't need a chaperone."

"That woman needs a hobby," he said. "Do you know how many scarves and sweaters she's already knitted for Christmas? It's driving Uncle Arthur crazy."

Caitlyn glanced at her knitting project tucked on the bedside table. Pathetic. She hadn't had much time to devote to it lately. Her perfume homework and this new enterprise had dominated her thoughts these last few weeks.

"Fine, I'll call them. If they want to come, I'd love to see them. But I don't. Need. A. Chaperone." Or a matchmaker, as her aunt and uncle seemed to consider themselves. Beau had almost kissed her today, which suggested they were doing fine on their own.

Her eyes darted to the unsigned contract on the desk. Was she screwing everything up? Oh, crap, she wasn't sure. When she was with Beau, all she wanted to do was cuddle up next to him and feel his arms go around her. Staring at his unsigned contract was another matter. It gave her heartburn.

"Yeah, yeah, I hear you," Flynn said. "You've got Ibrahim if you need a buffer from Country Boy. Not that it sounds like you do. But be sure, Caitlyn. You have a lot riding on this, and with him still unsigned..."

"I know, I know." She gave a little shriek because it felt good. "What time is it in Colorado right now?"

"I need to get you a world clock," he said. "You suck at navigating time zones. They're seven hours behind you."

She did the math. "Too early to call. I'll give it a few hours. How are you, by the way? Is your model still proving entertaining?"

"As a Vegas floor show," he said. "We had the most divine meal last night followed by some—"

"Please! You know my rule. I'm happy to hear about your *peccadillos* if you need advice. Otherwise, you're my brother. Yuck."

"You're such a prude," Flynn said. "See ya, Caity girl."

He hung up, and she found herself tapping her foot on the stone floor. Prude? That got her back up. She was feeling a little insecure these days after Jace the Jerk. The only person she'd told about the whole boob-job thing was Michaela. She'd sworn her to secrecy, fearing Flynn and Trevor and J.T. might decide to visit Jace the Jerk themselves. She wasn't so sure about Quinn and Connor. They loved her, but would they step away from their laptops and conference room meetings long enough to defend her honor? Something inside her felt squirrelly at the thought. It reminded her too much of her dad and how much he used to work.

Suddenly she had a flash of her dad pressing some strongly scented present into her hands.

He'd just come back from Provence. Wait! Seriously? Yes, he had, she recalled. Her birthday had been coming up, and although her mom had usually been the one to buy the gifts, he'd thought of her on his trip. When he worked twenty hours a day. The paper box had contained three beautifully wrapped lavender soaps. A set, he'd said. The region was famous for its lavender. She'd wrapped her arms around him, the love and gratitude as strong as the scent enveloping her.

She decided to text him, something she normally didn't do.

Hey Dad! Hope you're doing great. Miss you! Listen, I don't know if I properly thanked you for buying me those lavender soaps for my sixteenth birthday. Teenager, right? But I'm here at the farmhouse with the lavender fields all around me, and I just remembered how sweet that present was so thanks. Love you!

She'd only used those soaps on special occasions, never wanting them to run out. But they had, she recalled. She could see the last, thin piece in her hands in the shower on the day of her graduation from Stanford. As it had disappeared in her hands, transforming into soap bubbles, her throat had backed up, and she'd actually cried at the loss of them.

God, Ibrahim had been right all along. She *did* have a reason for buying a lavender farm. It reminded her of an unexpected sweet gesture from a man she loved deeply but still didn't completely know or understand.

Whoa.

She sank down on the bed. This perfume stuff was really freaky. And emotional. And heavier than expected. Heck, she needed a tissue right now, just thinking about all that. If it was affecting her so much, it would affect other women, right?

That's what she really wanted.

It struck her that she could use some emotional buffers, what with Ibrahim stirring up her memories and Beau stirring up everything else. Aunt Clara and Uncle Arthur might keep her from going to the dark side. She almost laughed at the thought.

Working for a few hours, answering emails and checking in with her skincare people, righted the balance inside her. Of course, she could do this perfume thing. If swimming in some uncomfortable emotional waters was necessary, she'd do it along with her homework. Wasn't falling in love a little emotional?

When the afternoon sunlight started to wane, she shut her laptop and called her aunt and uncle. Aunt Clara picked up on FaceTime right away. Uncle Arthur was grumbling at the kitchen table, his unshaven face half visible.

"Hello, dear," Aunt Clara said. "We just finished breakfast. Flynn texted me you were going to call. How's everything there? Your pictures of the lavender fields have got my feet itching to travel. Please say you're open to a visit. I'm not sure I can hold Arthur back much longer."

Her uncle's snort made her laugh. "Hold me back? Woman, we were just in Ireland. I know you want to see all these flowers before they fade, but seriously, I'm too old to be a jet setter."

"Eighty is the new forty," her aunt said, not missing a beat. "Besides, you have no hobbies. And traveling keeps one young."

"You look younger and younger," Caitlyn said, happy to see her aunt still had the newlywed glow. "Both of you. And yes, please come visit. You'll love Ibrahim, my perfume master. Our celebrity spokesperson, Beau Masters, is here too."

"I've seen some of his videos, dear," Aunt Clara said, fanning herself. "He's a hottie."

"Seemed a bit uptight to me," Uncle Arthur said. "Too buttoned-up for my tastes."

Her aunt swatted him. "Oh, stop fussing. He's a clean-cut young man. I remember you looking pretty much the same way in New York in the late fifties when we first met."

"I had *panache* back then, Clara. Good Lord, if you're going to tell a story that old, get it right."

"*Panache,* was it? I thought that was all me, dear. Oh, never mind. Well, Caitlyn, I'll give Hargreaves the good news, and we'll be on our way as soon as we can. Open-ended visit like we did with Trevor?"

"Sounds perfect. I'll make sure everything is ready. Uncle Arthur, you'll love the food. After all, you financed a French restaurant in Dare Valley."

"It's a burr in my saddle," he said, "the way Brian tries to feed me snails swimming in some white wine butter sauce. I'm going on record, Caitlyn. When we come to visit, I won't eat anything that slides across the ground."

Her aunt's mirth made her sway on the chair, and Caitlyn found it hard not to laugh out loud. "Point made. You have my word. Oh, I'm so happy you'll be coming," she said, meaning every word. Now that she'd actually made the call, she knew it had been the right thing to do. "There's so much to share."

"Yes," her aunt said, her laughter fading and tears sparkling in her blue eyes. "Isn't it wonderful? See you soon, dear."

They said goodbye, and she felt that odd tension in her chest again. Emotion, she realized, from Aunt Clara's watery response. She knew how precious this new lot in life was to her aunt. Until recently, Aunt Clara had been estranged from Caitlyn's father. A horrible argument had torn them apart, so much so that none of them had even met their aunt until recently. Shawn Merriam was uncompromising, and he'd run the Merriam business like his predecessors—with grit, fearlessness, and hard work. That was the man he'd been pretty much twenty-four seven for as long as she remembered. Still was, perhaps, despite being retired. It was the kind of man she feared her older brothers, Quinn and Connor, were becoming.

Her dad's text seemed to punctuate her thoughts.

Lavender soaps? You have a good memory. You're welcome, I guess. It was a long time ago, Caity girl.

She shook her head in bemusement, holding on to that rare glimpse of a softer side of her dad, the man who'd bought her the lavender soaps... In her heart of hearts, she wished she could see that side of him more often.

She walked over to the window, looking out across the endless blue and purple stalks swaying in the fields. This time she inhaled deeply, letting the scent fill her olfactory neurons until it caused a corresponding reaction in her heart. She finally came to the full truth.

For her, lavender smelled like a father's love.

CHAPTER 10

SITTING AT THE EDGE OF A LAVENDER FIELD STRUMMING HIS guitar wasn't a bad way to handle his roiling emotions. Like rocks in a waterfall, Beau couldn't stem the force—he needed to allow the thoughts and fears and worries to sweep over him.

His mother had cheated on her husband.

The thought seemed stuck in his mind like a sand burr in one's shoe. Had she done it more than once? His gut flipped over. Did she know who his real father was? God almighty. Is that why she'd remained silent?

It struck him that perhaps Walt Masters had always known the truth. Maybe that was why he'd drunk so much, why he'd always seemed so hateful to his son.

He had so many questions, so many doubts. How could he find any peace if he didn't know the truth?

Truth.

Who would have imagined that such a thing could be found in a perfume? And yet, he believed Ibrahim could do it. Beau had only just met the man, but he felt like he'd known him forever. Surely, he had a poet's soul.

His phone buzzed in his pocket. Only five people had his new number, and he was delighted to see it was his friend, Rye Crenshaw.

He switched his guitar to one hand and answered. "Well, ain't this a happy surprise. How's the family?"

"Tory's pregnant again, so the family is just about as dandy as you can get."

"Congratulations! I'm so happy for y'all."

"You couldn't possibly be happier than I am. Man, I get choked up thinking about it. Every time I see her, I stroke her belly. Driving her a little crazy with that, but she gets it. She's over the moon too. Boone is still too young to understand, but I still point at her belly and say, 'baby,' and he laughs."

The image lifted a smile on Beau's face. "I didn't know you when you were the bad boy of country music, but you sure are a bona fide family man now." A couple of years ago, Rye and his sister, Tammy, had asked him to take part in their annual country music concert to raise money for abused women. They'd hit it off straight away and become the closest of friends.

"Indeed I am, and proud of it."

There was an audible pause, and Beau knew his friend hadn't only called to share his news. "Best tell me why you're really calling."

"You a mind reader now? I'm a bit reluctant to be an errand boy, but your mama has been stirring up trouble. She called me last night, saying you'd up and disappeared. She was worried you might have done something crazy. When I didn't play along, she told me to give you a message."

His guitar slipped from his hands and thudded to the soft earth. "What is it?"

He heard the sound an angry wolf might make when cornered, and then Rye said, "She wanted you to know she's going to sign you to the Ryan Williams' cologne if you don't resurface."

His mama had never threatened him before. His stomach turned queasy. He picked the guitar back up, needing the comfort of it. "I'm sorry she involved you," he finally said.

"Me too, especially since I had to bite my tongue after she delivered that doozy. Bubba, what's going on? I'm not a busybody, but when a mama threatens her son, trouble's afoot. I speak from experience, all past, thank God."

"I don't know as I should say it...I haven't told anybody."

"Are we friends or not? Heck, there isn't anything I haven't done, so you needn't be worried I'd ever throw a stone, not that I'm worried you did something stupid. You're the most honest-to-goodness guy around."

If that didn't make him wince, he didn't know what would. "Fine, it's just..."

He wanted to cuss again, he realized. Something strong and foul and real. Good Beau never swore. But sometimes, in a frustrating moment, he wanted to let loose. Like now.

"*Shit*..." The word felt odd on his tongue. "Hell, Rye, I... My dad isn't my real dad. I just found out."

Rye gave a loud whoosh before saying, "Jesus, Beau, that's... Shit is right. You only found out now?"

"Yeah." He proceeded to tell his friend the whole story, clenching his hand around the top of his guitar the whole time, the strings cutting into his palm.

"No wonder you skipped town. I'm sorry for you, Bubba. How do you feel about it?"

"Rootless," he said. "It's funny. This album was supposed to figure all that out."

"Perhaps it will," his friend said. "No one said turning up rocks was fun."

"No, they didn't. Turning thirty gave me the push to look at all this, and now... I don't know shit about myself, my mama, or my real daddy."

"Funny how some part of us knows when we're ready to face up to the darkness. Listen, I've had my own share of upheaval with my family. Let yourself feel whatever you need to feel. And, hell, Beau, maybe it's time for you to let yourself go a little."

"I'd been thinking along those lines."

"Good, because I don't normally recommend this as a matter of course, but maybe Beau Masters needs to get his bad boy on."

"What do you mean?" he choked out.

"Do what you want for a change without anyone's input or say-so. You hear what I'm saying, Beau?"

He coughed to clear the emotion in his throat. "Yes, thanks for that. I have been trying so hard to be this perfect guy for so long. Sometimes it's exhausting." Being a gentleman with Caitlyn was different, though. That was clear as glass to him.

"Sainthood must be, I think. I'm not saying you need to go all crazy, but maybe running wild would do you good."

"As a reformed bad boy of country music, where would you suggest I start?"

Rye laughed. "I always loved me a good Stetson. I could pull the brim down over my forehead and no one could see my face. It was my kind of rebellion, I expect, after my own mama kept insisting that I smile in the face of lies and bad manners. I got pretty fed up with that."

Beau would buy a black Stetson. He'd always admired men who could wear a killer cowboy hat. They had an attitude he didn't possess. Bold, brash, confident. "Now that you mention it, I'm kinda sick of looking like a nice guy all the time." Damn—yes, damn—button-down cotton shirts. "I always looked ready to go to church, and starched shirts makes my neck itch. What else did you do?"

"I liked monster trucks for a time. Tory turned me away from it, but it was fun while it lasted."

Monster trucks didn't interest him, but maybe a motorcycle? He'd always liked the look of them. He'd have to consider buying one when he returned to Nashville.

"I probably shouldn't talk about all my drinking and women chasing, what with being a married man and all. I'm not saying you need to give that a go, but if you need a night out to kick the dust up, then you do it. Although, hell, do the French even have good bars?"

Beau looked around at the endless beauty of the lavender fields. "Not where I'm staying. It's peaceful here. Farmland as far as the eye can see." Exactly what he needed right now if he was being honest. Any running wild he did would have to be his way—which likely wouldn't involve any bars.

"The biggest thing, Bubba, if I may... Whatever you do, don't lose sight of what's important to you."

Talk about honesty. First Ibrahim and now Rye. "I appreciate you saying so. I should let you go. Thanks for calling, Rye. Congrats on the baby. Sorry again about putting you in the middle of something."

"Your mama is lucky I'm reformed, or I would have given her a piece of my mind. You call if you need anything. If I can help, I will."

"I know that. Thanks, Rye."

"Take care of yourself, Beau."

The call ended, and Beau heard the bleating of a goat in the distance. He looked over and saw Chou-Chou trotting down a row of lavender straight toward him, his mouth tipped into what could have been confused for a smile.

"Hey, buddy," he said, scratching the little fella under the ears when it butted him with its pointy head. "Since you don't understand English, what I'm about to say won't upset you none. My friend just called, and I'm pissed. My mama is pulling some real...shit."

His mama would threaten to wash his mouth out with soap, hearing him talk like that. Oddly, the thought made him happy, like popping the cork on something bottled up too long. *Take that, Mama.*

"Shit, shit, shit."

"Baa," answered Chou-Chou.

"How about damn? Dammit. Damn you." He thought of his mother, and his blood turned to lava in his veins. "Damn you, Mama. Damn you." He heard some music in his mind. Guitar. But it was angry, and no words accompanied it. Yet.

His chest was as tight as an overstretched tarp over a fishing boat, and Chou-Chou leaned his head against him as if sensing his distress.

"I'm swearing with a foreign goat for a witness," he mused as a hot breeze blew over them. God, it was almost a country music lyric. Not a dog for him, but a goat. He stood up. "Enough time for pity later. I have some shopping to do, Chou-Chou. Come on, let's head on back to the house."

The goat trailed behind him, his little legs kicking up the same dust Beau's boots unearthed. The sight struck him. Rootless earth got carried away by the wind. It needed an anchor to stay on the ground. He glanced at the farmhouse, a bold punctuation in a sea of purple. Once again, it struck him that Caitlyn helped ground him.

He hadn't expected to feel grounded in a place called Provence.

But he did.

Now it was time for more truth. He called Dr. Clarridge when he reached the edge of the field. When she answered, he said, "Doc, you might have already figured this out, but that baby tooth I gave you was from the man I thought to be my real father." He cleared his throat. "Seems he's not. Is there any way for you to tell me more about my ancestry or my real daddy's genes?"

"That news must have been deeply distressing for you, Beau," Dr. Clarridge said. "But to answer your question, yes, I can isolate out what your sample contains to approximate your paternal side better, but it's not going to be significant without a sample from your mother."

He had to press his hand to his gut to draw a breath. "That's impossible." His mama had made that point effectively.

"Well... You might also consider whether you're interested in finding other biological relatives."

What? He felt lightheaded at the idea. "That's possible?"

"We can upload your DNA to several databases and see if anyone is a match. I can't promise we'd find your real father or even any relations. Uploading raw DNA is still a new phenomenon, but you might be surprised. It's a serious decision, Beau."

"Don't I know it." He tipped his head back, the blue sky too bright for his eyes. "Let's do it. I want answers, and if this can provide them..." He cautioned himself that he didn't have to reach out to any relation Dr. Clarridge might find. If it turned out his real father was as bad as Walt, he could take the genetic information and leave the rest in the past, much like he'd planned to do with Walt after this search.

"I'll be back in touch soon," Dr. Clarridge said. "Goodbye, Beau."

"Bye, Doc."

He closed his eyes, pinching the bridge of his nose. She might be able to find his people. Could he have half brothers and sisters? An entire family tree he didn't know about?

His mind wandered back to his mama. Would she really commit him to the Ryan Williams deal in his absence? He didn't think she'd dare. If he called her about it, he'd be giving her what she wanted. A bad boy would ignore her, and that was what he planned to do.

"Beau!"

Caitlyn was striding across the lawn toward him. The sun played off her brown hair, bringing out different shades of brown and red. The easy sway of her hips drew his mind away from his troubles, but it was the wide smile on her face that shoved them off for good.

"Hey!" He pocketed his phone, Chou-Chou at his side.

"You seem to have a new friend," she said. "I hope you're ready to make a couple more. My Aunt Clara and Uncle Arthur are coming to visit. They're eighty-year-old newlyweds. You're going to love them."

More family? Was this her way of slowing them down?

Of course, he hadn't even kissed her yet, so they could hardly go much slower. Maybe she was just excited to see her family. At the thought of kissing her, his eyes lifted to her lips. Was it too soon? Would it be weird with a goat around? Plus, he was all sweaty and dusty from being in the fields. She'd want a more romantic moment for their first kiss, wouldn't she? She deserved it. Yes, there was plenty of time for a proper kiss.

"Would you be interested in a stroll in the fields after dinner tonight?"

The smell of her, fresh, floral, and little musky, reached him. He took her hand. *You're the lavender holding my earth in place.*

"I'd love that," she said, smiling. "Are you okay though? You seem upset again."

He thought of his troubles—ones he wouldn't dump in her lap. Touching the line of her cheek, he couldn't hold them in his mind.

"I'm better now," he answered, the truth as clear as day.

Being with her was the only thing that made sense.

CHAPTER 11

THE BLACK COWBOY HAT SHOULD HAVE ALERTED CAITLYN that something was amiss when it arrived two days later.

Except Beau looked so hot in the Stetson—like the Marlboro ads of old—that all the spit had dried up in her mouth when he'd walked into the kitchen with it on, fresh from the shower. Speechless, she'd actually given him a thumbs-up. She'd hoped he'd wear it when they took their stroll after dinner, something they did like clockwork, holding hands as they walked through the rows of lavender as the moon was rising, sharing stories about themselves.

The hat was practical too. It kept the hot Provence sun off his head, after all, and the hours he was spending playing guitar in the fields had started to show on his suntanned face. He hadn't shaved for two days either, and my, oh, my, a little scruff looked sexy on him. She kept wondering how it would feel against her skin when he finally kissed her, something their strolls hadn't produced yet. Apparently this whole courting thing went at a snail's pace.

It wasn't until the next morning she realized he was intentionally changing his image. She noticed the ripped seam at the shoulder of his new white T-shirt and offered to sew it for him. He flinched for a moment and then sputtered out a laugh, except it was more like a car backfiring. "*This* is intentional, Caitlyn."

Since when did Beau Masters wear ripped clothing? Later she noticed he'd tucked his T-shirt into his jeans, a thick hand-tooled leather belt visible at his waist.

Weren't these external signs of whatever internal turmoil was plaguing him? He hadn't told her more about them—"courting isn't counseling," he'd said on their first after-dinner stroll—and she'd respected his privacy, telling herself it was enough to hold his hand and hear stories about his favorite fishing spot as a boy or his favorite music teacher who'd seen promise in him.

While she worked during the day on business matters, he worked in the fields on his new songs. So far, the new album was giving him fits. If she didn't know better, she'd say he was trying out for a country version of Don Quixote. Except she didn't know if Don Quixote had ever played the guitar in lavender fields. Tipped windmills, sure. And Beau's companion wasn't Sancho Panza, but Chou-Chou, the trusty goat.

She shouldn't worry about him, but his color seemed a touch gray sometimes under his burgeoning sun-kissed skin, like a sour bottom note under a heavy heart note.

"He's working things out," Ibrahim said from behind her. He'd caught her watching Beau as he ambled off into the fields after breakfast, Chou-Chou at his heels.

She turned to look at him. "He's upset," she said, stating the obvious.

He laughed. "Aren't we all? He can only find the answers he's looking for alone. No one can reach inside us and pull out what's festering. Can't turn straw into gold."

She made a rude noise before she thought better of it. "Ibrahim, I figured out why I chose lavender. My dad bought me some lavender soap when I turned sixteen."

"*Hmm.*"

"*Hmm?* Is that all you're going to say? You said I'd remember when I was ready."

He patted her arm. "And so the process of discovery has begun. For us all. Oh, the perfume we're making."

She watched him leave the main room, most likely to his laboratory. These men were going to drive her crazy! Thank God, her aunt and uncle were due to arrive today.

A few hours later, Claude pulled into the circular driveway. The sunlight made her wish for sunglasses, the lavender swaying like hot purple straw in the fields.

The door popped open, and Hargreaves exited the passenger's seat. Aunt Clara's butler since the late 1960s, he didn't look his eighty years. Good breeding and clean living, she'd heard him say. He gave her a warm but in-scrutable smile.

"Good afternoon, Miss Caitlyn," he said, extending his hand to help Aunt Clara out of the car.

"Hargreaves! How many times do I have to tell you to drop the whole 'miss' thing?" Caitlyn asked.

"As many times as you'd like, Miss," he answered.

Aunt Clara threw out her arms, almost hitting Hargreaves, who stepped back quickly. "Caitlyn, my darling!"

She was one half Auntie Mame, one half something all her own. All of it was welcome. They needed a little life in this house—a little vibrant volatility to match the lavender in the fields. Hugging her, Caitlyn said, "Aunt Clara! I'm so happy you're here."

"What about me?" Uncle Arthur barked, exiting the car and slamming the door before Hargreaves could close it. "My bones are protesting all these long trips to see you Merriam kids. Why can't you live in Dare Valley like J.T.?"

"Because my brother has a purpose for living there while I prefer to be here." She gestured to the farmhouse. "Isn't it gorgeous?"

"Breathtaking," her aunt sighed, wrapping an arm around her waist. "My heavens, Hargreaves and I should have lived here years ago instead of that drab funeral home in Manhattan."

Her Park Avenue home *had* been very drab, or so Trevor and J.T. had said. Caitlyn had never been there. "You're better off in Dare Valley with your new husband over there. How's it going, Uncle Arthur? You up to a third honeymoon in a year?"

"You bet your sweet *derrière*, as the French would say," he said, kissing her briskly on the cheek. "I suppose this isn't such a bad place. Hell if you had allergies though."

"Then you're safe," Aunt Clara said. "His bark is so bad hay fever would never dare bother him."

Her uncle snorted. "My bark is much worse than my bite. As you know, dear. So who's this country singer you've shacked up with? Flynn told me to keep an eye on him, although he says he's mostly a good egg."

She swatted him. "Oh, stop! I haven't shacked up with anybody."

Her aunt said, "Too bad, dear. He's rather handsome if a little stiff."

"You'll like Beau. He's a nice guy." Certainly, he didn't seem stiff anymore, wearing a black Stetson and ripped T-shirts every day.

"I've listened to some of his music," Aunt Clara said as they walked to the house. "Those songs of his are downright sweet."

"I gave up being sweet in 1958 when I went to the Big Apple to make my way in the world," Uncle Arthur said. "Sweet will get your ass kicked."

Her aunt rolled her eyes. "You weren't sweet, that was for sure, but I've always been more attracted to serious and intense. Like you are now."

"Hah! Did you hear that, Hargreaves?" Her uncle was following them with Hargreaves just behind.

"I'm trying not to listen, sir," Hargreaves said, causing them all to laugh.

"Claude, if you'll bring in the bags," she called before they crossed the threshold.

"Oh, look at the bold way you decorated this place," Aunt Clara said. "Arthur, we may need to tear down some of the walls in our house and replace them with stone ones. This is brilliant."

"I'll get the sledgehammer out when we return, my love," her uncle said, not missing a beat. "So where are you stashing us old folks?"

She pointed to the staircase. "You'll be on the second floor with all of us."

Her uncle tapped the stone floor. "At least stone doesn't squeak like wood. I won't hear you sneaking around at night, Caitlyn, if you have a mind to."

Caitlyn flushed.

"Arthur! Behave yourself." Aunt Clara patted her back. "Don't mind him. He's cross from the traveling. If you show us our rooms, I'll put him down for a nap."

"Is that what we're calling it?" her uncle asked.

She swatted him again. "Then we'll dress for dinner and have some champagne. Wait! It's rosé here in Provence."

"I have a sparkling rosé you'll go nuts over," Caitlyn said.

"So long as Hargreaves carries you up to our room if you overindulge," Uncle Arthur said. "You'd break my back."

Hargreaves said, "I'll make sure to keep up my regimen of dumbbells and pushups while we're here, Madam, in case the need should arise."

Hargreaves shared a smirk with Uncle Arthur. Oh, how nice to see. How they managed it, all of them living together, she didn't know. But her aunt had said she couldn't do without Hargreaves, and from what little

Caitlyn had seen of him, she understood. He was a butler who took care of things. And he had the kind of insightfulness only possible for someone who'd spent a lifetime anticipating others' needs.

"I thought I'd come out of my lab and introduce myself," she heard Ibrahim say. "Caitlyn has been telling me all about you. Ibrahim Magdy at your service."

"Clara Merriam Hale." Her aunt was already moving toward him. "Oh, my, it's wonderful to meet you. Flynn told me I was going to adore talking to you. My love for perfume started with my grandmother. She wore Arpège, and the day she let me dot some on my wrist and behind my ears from that black Art Deco bottle, I felt all grown up. My, how I loved that perfume."

"A classic," Ibrahim said, raising her aunt's hand and kissing the back of it. "With sixty-two notes, only a woman confident in herself can wear it."

If the gallant hand-kissing hadn't already taken Caitlyn aback, his words certainly would have. "Did you say sixty-two?" she asked. According to the research she'd done on perfumes, that number was way over the top.

"Yes, *cherie*." Turning to her uncle, he said, "And you must be the legendary Arthur Hale. Flynn told me about the newspaper you founded in the United States. That you won a Pulitzer. It's an honor to meet someone who devoted himself to printing the truth and expressing thought-provoking opinions. I looked up some of your articles online. You have a way with facts and words, Mr. Hale."

"Arthur, please," he said, shaking the man's hand. "Caitlyn tells us a master perfumer must be able to distinguish close to four thousand distinct scents. How is that even possible?"

"We are all born with gifts, are we not? And you must be Hargreaves. It's a pleasure to meet you."

Hargreaves bowed. "And you, sir."

Ibrahim's nostrils flared, something Caitlyn was starting to notice.

"Eau Sauvage by Dior," he said. "An elegant choice."

"Madam gifted it to me when I first went into service with her, and it's suited me all these years."

"Good God, Hargreaves!" Uncle Arthur said. "You wear perfume too?"

The butler's mouth twitched. "Cologne, sir, although it's technically not from Cologne."

"Like crémant not being real champagne," Caitlyn said.

"Hello!" Beau's voice boomed, and then he came striding into the house, that sexy black Stetson sitting on his head like he was born to wear it. It struck Caitlyn that he was changing right before her eyes, shifting in his very bones—the pieces that made him what and who he was.

"I'm Beau Masters. Hope y'all had an easy trip over."

He set his guitar on the side table in the entryway. Caitlyn introduced everyone, her eyes flickering to his jeans. There was a new rip there with an added layer of grime, almost as though he'd been kneeling in the dirt. He smelled of sweat and lavender, and darn it, she felt herself growing warm in response.

"I listened to some of your music coming over," Aunt Clara was saying. "Very touching."

"Thank you, ma'am," he said, his drawl pronounced. "I'm shooting for more than 'touching' with this new album."

"Your outfit is new, is it not?" Aunt Clara asked, her eyes narrowing as she swept her gaze up and down his body.

"Turns out I secretly wanted to dress like a cowboy," he said with a wink.

When had he discovered this? He hadn't said a word about it on their walks. Right now, she was starting to feel like he was only sharing a version of Beau caught in time, one from ages past: the five-year-old who'd fallen in love with caramel apples at the state fair and tried to make them himself the next Halloween—a complete disaster; or the ten-year-old who'd snuck into the town's drive-through to see *The Matrix*, something his mom had thought inappropriate for him. The current man, the hurting one, was trying to remain a mystery. Did he think her affection would change if he shared his struggle?

"Back where I came from," her uncle said, "only cattle rustlers looked like you do now."

Beau extended his hand, and they shook. "Cattle rustler, eh? That might be the best compliment I've ever had. Caitlyn tells me y'all are newly married. I think that's wonderful."

"It is," her aunt said, her skin glowing. "We were lucky to find each other again. He broke my heart in 1960, and it never quite mended."

Uncle Arthur winked. "I was a ruffian if not a rustler."

"I might use that in a song," Beau said. "It's a nice lyric."

"By all means," Uncle Arthur said. "This is Hargreaves. Clara won't travel without him."

"Sir, it's good to meet you," Hargreaves said. "I see you're playing a Fender Telecaster."

Beau tipped his cowboy hat back, surprise flashing in his blue eyes. "You know guitars?"

Uncle Arthur said, "Is there anything you don't know, Hargreaves?"

His smile was inscrutable, and Caitlyn wondered again what had led a man like him, one with so many talents, to spend his life as a butler. "Every day with you introduces me to a treasure trove of things yet unknown, sir."

Her uncle snorted. "Good Lord, I'm starting to think we all need naps. Caitlyn, dear, lead the way. Gentlemen, we'll see you later at dinner."

She started up the stairs with the trio but found herself looking back over her shoulder. Gentlemen, her uncle had said. Such an old term, like courting, and yet one she was growing all too familiar with from the man standing at the bottom, his head tipped up, following their progress. If the shiver down her spine was any indication, Beau was looking at her legs. She wanted more than hand holding and watching.

"He's as compelling as you said, dear," Aunt Clara whispered. "I have to admit...I like his new mode of dress." She fanned herself.

"I rather do too," she said, turning left down the hall.

Her uncle laughed. "I'll tear up some of my shirts if it makes you so hot and bothered, Clara."

"It will make them harder to launder, sir," Hargreaves deadpanned.

Everyone laughed together, the sound releasing some of the tension that had built up in the house these last days.

"Oh, I'm so glad you've come," she said, stopping to hug her aunt as they arrived at the door to their guest room. She hugged her uncle for good measure. Hargreaves only lifted his brow when she jokingly moved to embrace him.

Aunt Clara waved a hand. "We are too, dear. I'm quite certain you don't need a chaperone, but..."

Uncle Arthur put his arm around her. "Clara, I know that you're thinking, and I need a few more days to be sure."

Caitlyn glanced at Hargreaves, who seemed to be fighting a smile. "Sure of what?"

Her aunt gave her a knowing look. "That you need matchmakers, dear."

"Aunt, I think—"

"It's a good thing we've arrived, and not a moment too soon." She patted her on the cheek for good measure. "You'll be shacking up with him in no time."

"*Clara.*"

"No, Arthur, it was as obvious as the nose on your face. Hargreaves, tell me I'm right."

He stood there in his butler's outfit of black trousers, black tie, and white shirt, all ironed to perfection, and said, "Yes, Madam, I would concur."

Caitlyn stomped her foot. "Stop this. I asked you to visit because I wanted to see you, not because I need matchmaking."

"You're both *watching* each other, dear. Like two bonfires whose flames haven't mingled yet."

She thought about Ibrahim's comment about missing the press of his wife's skin. "We're courting."

"I'm liking the boy better all the time," her uncle said.

"You both need a push," her aunt said with a firm shake of her head.

No kidding.

Aunt Clara smiled grandly, her blue eyes sparkling. "Don't worry, dear. I've been known to give a good push in my day. Make sure to wake us for dinner so we don't oversleep. Tonight is going to be monumental."

Caitlyn couldn't wait to see what her aunt cooked up.

CHAPTER 12

CAITLYN'S ELDERLY RELATIVES WEREN'T AT ALL WHAT BEAU had expected.

Talk about piss and vinegar. Spry. Saucy. The butler was still a foreign concept to him, but the man seemed nice enough. He even knew about guitars, and that spoke to good taste.

Not that playing his own guitar was helping him much. For the past three days, pretty much all he'd done was play with Chou-Chou, his constant companion. The baby goat seemed to like his music, so at least he had one fan. When his rage at his mama surfaced, he'd play hard enough to feel the bite of the strings on the pads of his fingers. The goat would sometimes start to bleat along with him. God, what a pair they made.

He'd broken five strings but hadn't streamed together five honest-to-goodness verses. None of his old lyrics suited him, except what he'd written about Caitlyn. The old songs sounded too sweet, too "touching," Caitlyn's aunt had said—false.

He'd decided to seek help from the one person he suspected might be able to push him in the right direction. That deserty Bedouin music, Raï, was audible as Beau walked down the hallway to Ibrahim's lab. He'd looked it up, deeply curious, only to discover it was a music known for shaking things up, speaking truths some felt were best left unsaid. No wonder it spoke to his heart.

He knocked on the doorframe since Ibrahim's back was to him. The man turned from his perusal of the apothecary bottles.

"Beau! Come in."

"Hope I'm not interrupting," he said, taking off his hat out of respect. This lab had a sacredness to it despite its clean, clinical look. "I did some reading on Raï music, and no wonder you love it. It's the music of truth."

Ibrahim gestured to one of the metal chairs in front of his glass table, and they both took a seat. "I've been listening to more of your songs. You sing about matters of the heart. Family. Love. Hometowns. Why is it you're so stuck right now?"

"Is it that obvious?"

Gesturing to Beau's clothing, Ibrahim smiled. "If I hadn't noticed it before, your evolving look would give you away. You're like a silkworm struggling in the cocoon. The process is messy now, but it will end in new wings."

With any other man, this conversation would have been weird. But Caitlyn was right to call Ibrahim her Perfume Jedi. He was like Obi-Wan Kenobi and Yoda rolled into one. "My concern is how long the struggle will last. I have songs to write. Issues...to sort out." A woman to court. "How do you cut through the struggle?"

"The silkworm only incubates for three weeks before emerging. We humans follow a sometimes less predictable schedule. But there's no silk without the process, and that's where the magic is."

Something about the way Ibrahim said that reminded him he wasn't the only one in the midst of a struggle. "You miss your wife a lot, don't you?"

He pressed both hands to the glass table. "Yes, terribly. Like I told Caitlyn, it's one of the reasons I took this position. I thought I could escape her scent and all the memories it evokes. It was agony to think I *wanted* to escape for a while. Why would I wish to escape the happiest memories of my life? But pain is a funny beast. It makes us run, howl, and push back from the very things that once nourished our soul. Loss makes us forget our truth for a time."

Beau's throat clogged up with emotion like a backed-up pipe. "I came here to escape, but you're right. It's like the emotional suitcase followed me."

"There's no escaping our inner hurts." He folded his hands. "I thought I'd get started on the men's fragrance. I'd like your help if you're open to it."

"I'm not sure you want to base a fragrance off anything I have to say. I'm just a regular ol' guy. Nothing flashy."

Except that was Old Beau talking. This one was arresting conversations among Caitlyn and her family with his torn shirts and jeans and cowboy hat.

"Like Caitlyn, you underestimate yourself. I have a phrase for you to finish. Take as long as you need to find the answer that sits well with your soul, something you'd feel comfortable singing in a song perhaps. I'll suggest some more exercises as we go along, just like I've been doing with Caitlyn for the perfume. And if you don't mind, I'd like to stop in on you and Chou-Chou and listen to your guitar sessions."

"Not much to hear musically. I pretty much stink to high heaven right now." His audience was a baby goat, after all.

"And yet, the guitar notes are much like the notes in a perfume. Hearing them played in the fields while the hot sun beats down, the air redolent with lavender... How could I miss the chance?"

When he put it that way... "The view will be better than the show."

"Again, you underestimate yourself. Here is your homework, as Caitlyn calls it." He scrawled something on a small piece of paper, his hand cupping it for privacy, then rolled it up and passed it to Beau.

Taking it, he said, "Thank you. Is there anything I can do for you, Ibrahim? You've been more than generous with me. I mean, Caitlyn's party wasn't the only one I crashed. I'm sorry I haven't thanked you for putting up with me."

Ibrahim made an unintelligible sound, rather like a scent note Beau couldn't distinguish. "Let me think on it. And Beau, you aren't crashing anything. You're a welcome addition to this perfume we're making. I'll see you at dinner shortly. I hear Katrine has another masterpiece in store."

The flavors in her cooking had surprised him, but each dish had been a treat to his taste buds. "Thanks, Ibrahim." As he left the room, the strains of music followed him—a haunting vocal in a language he didn't understand...except somehow he did. The longing in the singer's voice grabbed the throat, and the striking drumbeat bespoke of the continuity of life. One person's pain didn't put a halt to the world—although for that person, it likely felt as if it should.

Loss makes us forget our truth, Ibrahim had told him.

He needed to consider that. When he let himself back into the farmhouse, he unrolled the paper in his palm. He stopped short as he read it.

A good man is...

That was it? That was easy. Old Beau had this one down pat. A good man was someone you could count on, someone who kept his word, someone who did the right thing.

But was he that man really? Or had he been playing a part his whole life, shoehorned into a role he'd never auditioned for?

"Beau!"

He jerked around in surprise to see Caitlyn standing in the doorway to the kitchen in one of her short-sleeved cotton dresses, this one the color of pink bows at Easter.

"What are you doing?" she asked.

Curling his hand around the paper, he shoved it in his back pocket. "Nothing much."

"Did Ibrahim give you homework too? I told him it would be up to you."

So they'd spoken about him? "I'm happy to do it. Hoping it might fuel my songwriting. Chou-Chou is a darlin', but he's no collaborator." And yet, sometimes when the baby goat bleated in time with his guitar, he swore the poor thing was grieving for his mama.

Shit. No wonder they got along. He was grieving for his mama too, the woman he'd thought she was, the one he was scared she wasn't.

"He's really taken to you," Caitlyn said. "Ah...would you have time to help me with the final touches for dinner? I sent Katrine home to her family. I just woke Aunt Clara and Uncle Arthur, and they'll be down shortly. Hargreaves was already up and reading a new mystery. He loves to read on vacation."

Beau looked down at himself. This wasn't the proper dress for a dinner with Caitlyn's elderly relations. He'd have to wear something more in keeping with the Old Beau. Appearances. First impressions. His mama had always told him they were important.

But hadn't they already met him like he was now? Would getting gussied up affect their opinion of him, and if it did, was he interested in what they thought? He'd been raised to think of others' opinions before his own. What the hell good had it done? He was tempted to remain dressed as he was, a shocking yet exciting thought.

"Of course, I can help." Still, old habits died hard, and he found himself saying, "I should probably shower and change. I imagine I smell after being outside all day. Sorry." Damn Old Beau.

Great, now he was cursing himself. But why in the hell had Old Beau sucked up to people? Worried so much about others' good opinion?

His mama was the one who'd felt that way, of course, and he realized why. She'd wanted everyone to think she was lily-white.

"I don't think you smell bad," Caitlyn said, drawing him out of his reverie. "I mean, I have a scent journal now. Smells are just smells." She leaned closer and sniffed, as delicate as a butterfly fluttering its wings after landing on a flower. "Earth. Lavender, of course. Sweat. Salt. Metal. Maybe from your guitar strings? A touch of pine."

Not pine, but the cedar in his body wash. He hated to tell her because she was so competitive. "Probably goat too. Chou-Chou likes to cuddle."

She laughed, a delighted sound. "You two are so sweet together."

Sweet? He was starting to hate that word. "Do you think I'm too sweet?" he dared to ask.

She was silent a moment, and her eyes drifted to his mouth. "Sometimes. Lately, I'm certain of it."

The room seemed to vibrate with tension. Being her kindred spirit, he knew she was referring to kissing, something he'd had to reel himself back from every time he was with her. Why did he think being a gentleman meant *not* kissing the woman he wanted? Wanting that didn't make him a bad man. Another lie he was done with.

"I was waiting for the perfect time to do this." He took hold of Caitlyn by the upper arms. They were dotted with freckles, he noted as he drew her against his body.

Her big green eyes zeroed in on his face. "Hang perfect."

"My sentiments exactly," he said, and he pressed his lips to her slightly parted ones.

Shock ran through her body like a tremor in the earth. But her lips softened, and she tilted her head to the right, bringing their mouths more flush. He tasted something tangy on her lips and sucked her bottom lip into his mouth. She groaned, shrugging free of his hold, only to twine her arms around his back. Their bodies pressed together, from chest to belly, and he put a little distance between them at the base. Too forward for a first kiss. But that was Old Beau, and the new man breaking free inside of him wanted to feel the soft openness of her hips nestled against his hardness and his thighs.

He cupped her lower back, right above the sweet rise of her butt, and pressed them together. He groaned this time, the feel of her softness as sweet as the first song he wrote. Her hand tickled its way up his spine, and her fingers tangled in his hair, cradling his skull in a way that made him want to lift her leg around him and press her into the stone wall.

A lifetime of restraint shattered.

He moved her backward the few steps to the kitchen wall, his hand sweeping under her bare knee and lifting her thigh until it was angled around his waist. Her dress rucked up, and he slid his fingers up the soft skin there. God, he'd been fantasizing about her legs, looking at them every chance he could get. She moaned. His loins seized up, and he tugged her closer, fitting her tighter to his body.

Their mouths changed angles again. Her mouth parted, giving him the access he'd been waiting for. His tongue thrust in, impatient from the wait. She jerked in his arms, and his hand came around to caress her butt, all convention dissolving inside him. She was beautiful and ripe and everything he'd ever wanted to touch and then some. The soft swell of her cheeks had him straining against her, and he put his mouth to her neck, needing to taste her there.

"We should probably..." She grabbed his head and brought it back to her mouth for a starving, openmouthed kiss of teeth, tongues, and wet heat. Then she lurched back and pushed at his chest. He staggered back a couple steps, and it was enough space for her to hustle around him.

She planted herself on the other side of the wooden butcher's table, a boundary if ever he saw one. Her brown hair was mussed, her rosy lip gloss smudged. Old Beau would have apologized. New Beau only grinned.

"That was well worth the wait and then some," he found the cheek to say.

She patted her hair back into place, although it didn't do the job. He could still see his mark on her and that gave him a primal delight. When a man wanted a woman like he wanted her, his mark should be on her.

Narrowing her eyes, she said, "I was about to renegotiate our courting."

A new emotion coursed through him, one he didn't recognize at first. It was daring. "Were you now? Come here, honey. I think I want to renegotiate too, for another kiss."

She plopped her hands on her waist, studying him in the quiet kitchen. The sun was fading into the fields, the blues and purples of sunset blending with the stalks of lavender swaying in the still-hot breeze. "I realized today you're managing me, only showing me pieces of you from the past, not the man with the ripped shirt and jeans in the here and now. You didn't have a chip on your shoulder before."

He shrugged. She wasn't wrong, but that chip wasn't anything compared with the burden he'd shouldered his whole damn life.

"My entire world could be ending, and it doesn't change the fact that I want you."

"That's... It warms and unhinges me all at once," she

said, dropping her hands to her sides. "Beau, I want you to share what's really going on. All the way."

"I told you I was working some things out," he said softly. "Give me time."

"Are you really not going to tell me after we kissed like *that*? It felt like losing a lifetime of good sense."

"I know, and I realized it doesn't make me any less a gentleman." He held out his hands and then let them fall to his sides.

She only blinked at him. If she were a boat, the wind had left her sails. "Of course it doesn't. Why would you even think that?"

"Stories I can't tell you just yet." He stared at her, noting the fading red imprint of his mouth on her neck.

How was he supposed to tell her he was a bastard? The son of two cheating, lying, no-good people. He couldn't tell her that yet, not when he still didn't know what it meant for him.

"Caitlyn, let me be. Please."

Her neck cracked when she nodded. "Fine. Go on up and shower. Or don't. Your call."

The resulting quiet seemed louder than the cacophony of one of his concerts.

"Go on. I can set up dinner." She turned her back on him, walking to the oven and checking on the clay crock inside.

Leaving like this would break both their hearts. He went up behind her and put his hands around her waist, kissing her gently on the back of her neck. She stilled but didn't move away. "Be down in a bit."

He kissed her again, lingering over the scented skin of her neck—fragrant with lavender—before stepping away and walking out of the kitchen.

CHAPTER 13

CLARA SURVEYED THE SAD STATE OF THEIR DINNER PARTY. Good heavens, she'd come in the nick of time. Caitlyn's usual happy chatter had dried up, and she sat mostly silent at the head of the table. And this Beau Masters fellow, sitting next to Ibrahim, was a monosyllabic rock of silence, nothing like the charming man she'd watched on YouTube. What in the world was going on? Caitlyn's response was clear. She'd been hurt, Clara sensed. When Beau had pulled out Caitlyn's chair, she'd barely looked at him, which had made him glower even more.

Hargreaves was lucky he'd declined to join them, preferring to keep a separation between himself and his employers at dinnertime. She was going to have to pull a few horses by the teeth to turn things around.

"Caitlyn, dear, everything is so tasty. I especially love the bread. It's with olives, isn't it?"

"Yes, it's called *fougasse*, Aunt."

Ibrahim—what a fascinating man—smiled thinly across the table from her and Arthur. "Caitlyn, do I remember you telling me this morning that it's the Provençal version of focaccia? You asked Katrine to make it special, isn't that right?"

Beau seemed to sit up straighter in his seat, Clara noted. Why? Oh, this dinner was filled with enough subtext to tantalize a diplomat. It felt like an undertow threatening to drag them all under after tossing them around some.

"Yes, Ibrahim, that's right." Caitlyn forced a smile—a brittle look that didn't suit her—and lifted her glass of sparkling rosé, taking two healthy swallows.

The perfumer lifted a slice of the bread and sniffed. "Funny how my mind wants to tell me there's rosemary in this bread. Beau mentioned the other day how the scent of rosemary makes him think about focaccia bread and Italian grandmothers."

"You Italian, Beau?" Arthur asked. "You certainly have the olive skin, but Masters doesn't strike me as Italian. Your mother's side, perhaps?"

The young man visibly paled under that golden skin. "Not Italian... At least not that I know of, sir." He looked down at his plate but not before Clara noted the tension in his face. His jaw had locked down like a security gate in a bank robbery.

Arthur slapped an inch of butter on his bread, something the French just didn't do. But would he know that? No. Would he care? Definitely not. And she wasn't going to tell him.

"Masters," Arthur said. "It's a good name. Anglo-Scottish origin, isn't it?"

"I wouldn't know, sir." The young man kept his head down, his words barely intelligible between his Southern drawl and soft tone.

Clara had been surprised to see he hadn't changed for dinner. The rip in his dirty white T-shirt looked shadowed in the low light of the dining room chandelier. Clara had thought it best to eat inside since Arthur was a bit punchy from travel.

"Masters *is* actually of Italian origin, I believe," Ibrahim said. "From the Latin, magister, meaning one who is in charge. I imagine it was usually applied to a trade, but I like to think it also means a man who is in charge of himself, his life."

Beau's head shot up at that, and his blue eyes seemed to glitter. Then his mouth twisted, and he reached a hand out for his wine glass. He hadn't drunk any so far, and they were halfway through the meal.

Caitlyn gripped the edge of the table with her right hand, Clara saw, from her seat next to her. "*Beau?*" her niece called.

"To all the Masters," he said, lifting his glass in a toast.

His voice was as rough as jagged fingernails. Not a happy toast then. But Clara and the others raised their glasses with him. All except for Caitlyn. She kept her green eyes on him, staring at him with what Clara could only term unflinching compassion.

His throat moved as he drank. One gulp. Two. At the third, Caitlyn stopped breathing. Clara reached for her left hand under the table, and the young woman clenched it.

"Always liked the pink stuff," Arthur said, his brows smashed together. "What about you, Beau?"

"It's...good," his gravelly voice said.

"You know, pink champagne cocktails were all the rage in the late 1950s, right, Clara? After that nauseating Cary Grant movie came out."

She knew he was hoping for a diversion, so she played along. "*An Affair to Remember* was a beautiful love story, you old poop."

He winked. "Caitlyn, which chick flicks make your generation go all crazy?"

"What?" she asked.

She tore her eyes from Beau for a moment, until the man surged to his feet. "You'll have to excuse me. I think I got too much sun today."

His chair scraped on the floor, and they all watched

him walk out of the dining room. Caitlyn stood up, her
eyes trailing him out of the room.

"I'd leave him be, Caitlyn," Ibrahim said quietly.

"I hate waiting, especially after..." She sat down heavily. "I'm sorry, Aunt Clara. Uncle Arthur. I should have
told you."

"Told us what, dear?" she asked. "That your man is
going through some crisis? Like his torn-up clothes didn't
advertise that."

"At least he left his cowboy hat off at the dinner table,"
Arthur said. "Shows he hasn't lost all civility."

Ibrahim raised his napkin, but not before Clara caught
his smile.

"Civility, Arthur?" Clara could have poked him.
"Sometimes you are too pompous for words."

He laughed. "My dear, to the Beau Masters you
showed me in those darn videos, civility *is* important.
Wouldn't you agree, Ibrahim?"

He'd only just met the man, and here he was, already
cultivating allies. The legendary Arthur Hale at work.

"Absolutely," Ibrahim said. "Shall we continue dinner
or call it a night? I know you must be tired from your trav-
els. You needn't stand on any ceremony for me. I won't
speak for Caitlyn."

Her niece's mind wasn't with them. Clara wasn't sure
she'd heard a word they'd said. But if they adjourned
now, all Caitlyn would do was fret. Maybe she'd even be
tempted to go after Beau. Ibrahim had been here longer,
so she'd honor his advice. If he thought Beau needed to
be left alone, then she'd do her best to help that happen.

She glanced at Arthur and raised her left brow a half-
inch, their silent way of communicating concurrence. He
raised his in return. She nodded. My, how she loved the
nonverbal communication between husband and wife.

"We're staying," she said. "The dinner is delicious,
and the company quite fascinating. So, Ibrahim, please

tell me more about how you became a master of perfume."

As he told her, she kept one eye on her niece, who pushed around her food in utter dejection.

She and Arthur were going to have their hands full with this matchmaking.

CHAPTER 14

THE NEARLY HALF-MOON CAST AN ALMOST SNOWY GLOW OVER the fields as Beau stormed toward what he now called his sitting spot.

He had such a spot at his home in Dare River outside Nashville, under a gnarly oak tree. The one here was on a small rise in what seemed the middle of the lavender. It always calmed him, the spicy scent seeming to seep through the very pores of his over-sensitized skin. When he arrived at his spot, he discovered Chou-Chou snoring softly on the ground. Did the animal have no home to go to itself, being orphaned? He sat down next to the baby goat, who stirred and nuzzled closer. His mama had died giving life to him, but where in the hell was his father? Did papa goats care nothing for their sons?

"We aren't too different, are we, Chou-Chou?" He rubbed the goat under his soft ears, staring out at the farmhouse nestled across the fields. Only one light was on, and it was Caitlyn's.

He'd been a complete jerk, excusing himself from the middle of dinner. Part of him had also cheered his audacity. Before, he'd never had the courage—no, the infernal gall—to contemplate such a breach in etiquette. But Caitlyn had ignored his attempt to be the gentleman and seat her, and then there'd been all that talk about his last name.

Truth was he was too binged up for polite company, and his toast to all the Masters had tasted like acid in his mouth. Except, miracle of miracles, that girly pink champagne—what was it called? Rosé—had turned from acid to sweet ambrosia. He'd liked it, and that had scared him. If he liked it, he might keep drinking it, might become an alcoholic like his...

That man wasn't his daddy anymore. Never had been. Beau wasn't destined to become an alcoholic. Of course, maybe his real father was an alcoholic too.

Maybe he was even worse than Walt Masters.

The thought brought chill bumps to his skin, and he dug his boots in the soft earth to ground himself. Like Caitlyn, the land brought him a sense of peace. Always had. Wasn't that why he'd bought a large place in the country instead of moving to Belle Meade next to his mama? She'd wanted to keep him close so she could look after him, she'd said. At least he'd had the sense to set some boundaries.

God, the apron strings now seemed like those of a puppet.

The sounds of a lonely harmonica filtered into his mind, followed by his voice singing *those apron strings didn't look like puppet strings, but now they must be cut.* Then the guitar kicked in, adding to the sadness of the song. *She wants me close, but right now I can't let her.*

Mama has to go.

The mama I knew is gone.

His eyes welled with tears, and he wanted to blame them on the spice in the night air, a blatant lie. He was ashamed to realize he was capable of lying, what with all his talk of honesty. Perhaps he and Mama were alike, after all.

The harmonica filtered back into his mind, lonely, sad,

resolute. Two notes played to convey almost a *waa-waaa* sound. Despair in a sound. But it worked. Maybe instead of trying so hard to write about roots, he had to write about his despair in discovering he had none. That his entire life was rooted in lies.

Caitlyn's light was still burning, and inside his heart something new and powerful burned for her. He wanted her like he'd wanted his first guitar: a small-bodied Rogue Starter Acoustic Guitar in midnight blue. His mama had thought it too bold, but he'd stopped by the music shop in their small town and stared at it in the window for six months before getting up the courage to buy it with money he'd earned cutting grass. He'd refused to return it—a singular moment of defiance—and she'd not spoken to him at supper for over a week, one of her tactics for expressing displeasure. He still loved that guitar the best even though it was now the least expensive and tuned in his collection. A lot of hope and dreams had gone into that guitar, and he'd made some pretty good music with it. Perhaps not the most complex or technical—he was a better musician now—but it had been true.

Where was that truth now? What was true now?

He knew one unassailable truth: he wanted that woman in the house. It was late, and there were a million reasons why Old Beau wouldn't have bothered her tonight, following some line about gentlemanly manners and etiquette, but he was tired of it.

She didn't want him to be a gentleman. She wanted him to be real with her. To keep her, he'd have to tell her the truth and trust she cared enough about him to want the real man, the one who was struggling right now.

Picking up Chou-Chou, he walked back to the house as Caitlyn's light went out. The baby goat deserved a better home than the lonely fields, and he was going to see to it. No different than a dog really. He'd make the poor thing a bed under the portico behind the house. The baby goat didn't stir, and Beau appreciated its trust in him.

After seeing to Chou-Chou, he patted his tiny head again and let himself into the house. Moving quietly, he let his eyes adjust. If Caitlyn didn't answer his knock, he'd go to bed. Talk to her in the morning. But if she was restless like he was, unable to sleep... They hadn't taken their usual stroll after dinner.

His knock was quietly percussive, a demanding drumbeat delivered from the pads of his fingers. Silence. Then he made the same sound again, knowing repetition might capture her hearing. *No, honey, you aren't hearing things. Come answer the door.*

It swung open, and he could make out the shape of her body from the soft moonlight spilling through the windows in her room and the hallway.

"I've been a total ass, and I'm sorry." Old and New Beau both agreed on that. "I know you just went to bed, but if you're up for a walk in the fields with me, I'd like to make up for my bad behavior earlier and tell you things you've wanted to know."

Her sigh was all the more audible in the near darkness, his other senses picking up on it in addition to the spicy scent coming off her skin. A little lavender mingled with something Oriental. Myrrh? Yes, it was perfect for a goddess.

"Everything?"

The earlier pique was back in her voice, and he smiled. "I like that you hold my feet to the fire. Maybe I should buy you a matchbook."

"Or a torch," she said, followed by a rude sound.

He opened his arms. "Burn me down, honey." Maybe he'd rise from the ashes like a phoenix.

"You and Ibrahim... I've never been around two people who speak in such riddles."

Riddles, was it? He thought Ibrahim a master of

wisdom, but perhaps that was the artist in him talking. "I like how Ibrahim talks."

"I mostly do too, but both of you know how to tie my mind up into knots. Fine. I'll take a quick walk with you—not a stroll—but if I don't like what I'm hearing, I'm leaving you in the fields. Hear me?"

"Clear as crystal, honey," he said. He liked this other side of her. She was a nice girl, but she had teeth when she needed them. Maybe it's what he'd needed in a woman all along.

She stepped into the hallway, her silhouette stealing his breath. Her dark robe wafted behind her as she walked ahead of him toward the stairs. In this light, he couldn't see if her legs were bare. Man, he had a thing for her bare legs. Those cotton dresses and the way they pushed up the slightest trace of her cleavage drove him wild too.

He waited until they'd walked a fair distance from the house to say, "I found Chou-Chou sleeping in our sitting spot in the fields, so I brought him closer to the house so he wouldn't be alone out there."

"That was nice of you," she said, stopping between rows of lavender. "But I didn't come out here to talk about your confidant, Chou-Chou."

He tipped his head back at the midnight sky. Cloudless and filled with moonlight, it made him more aware of the murky feeling that had engulfed him these last few days. He could envy that sky. He would get this out.

"This turning thirty business had me thinking about roots, like I've told you. I decided to do one of those genetic tests. I'd always worried I would end up being like my father, that I'd inherited his bad genes, so to speak. It's why I never drank before. It's why I always tried so hard to be a good man. Turns out...Walt Masters isn't my father."

Her mouth parted, and her face seemed to crumple. "Oh, Beau."

He cleared his voice. "All those years I struggled not to become like my father, the bad boy who'd died drunk and wrapped himself around a tree on a country road. The man who lied, cheated, and betrayed my mama, or so she told me. Instead, it looks like my mama and Walt were suited. She broke their marriage vows, and she lied to me about that man being my father this whole time. When I think about that, I start to see red."

"No one can blame you for being angry," she said, taking his hand. "No wonder you needed to get out of town. Beau, I'm so sorry I gave you a hard time. This is a very personal matter, and we've just met..."

"And yet we were kindred spirits from that first moment," he said. "Don't give it another thought. Caitlyn, truth is, I feel torn up inside. My mama was always telling me not to be like my daddy. It's formed the framework of my whole damn life. Only that man wasn't my daddy, and when I asked her who was, she wouldn't tell me. That's when I called you and asked to come here. I...couldn't stand to be near her another moment, listening to her lies and filth. Because Caitlyn, I'm beginning to wonder if she even knows who my daddy really is."

She flinched, and a jolt ran up his arms and traveled straight to his heart.

"Maybe that's why she didn't tell me, and do you know what that makes her? God, that's harsh, but I can't help but think it after everything. My whole life has been a lie. God, I didn't want to dump all this on you. I wanted to be a better version of myself for you."

"Hey, we're kindred spirits, remember?" she said softly. "I'm glad you finally trusted me. I can't imagine how awful you feel right now, but *you're* not a lie. You are a good man, Beau Masters, and you got there on your own. Do you understand? You made yourself."

"No, I was so afraid of my daddy's shadow growing up that I let my mama form me to be his opposite. Maybe if

I hadn't hit so big so young, it would have turned out different. I used to think it was a blessing I had her around to guide me and make sure I didn't get into trouble like many young singers do."

"I can't imagine that," she said. "The bottom line is your mom tried to make you into something you weren't. Someone tried to do that to me recently. It was awful."

He nodded. "She did everything in reaction to him. His presence was so strong, even after he died, that sometimes I felt like he was haunting us."

"If he was everything you said, I can't say I blame her for cheating on him," she said, her voice gentle.

"I told her that when I confronted her. Said I wouldn't judge her. And she gave me nothing, honey. *Nothing.* Since then, I've felt uprooted. I'm not Walt Masters' son. I don't ever have to fear I'll turn out like him if I drink or cuss or act a little wild with a woman. Like I'd like to do with you." Something eased in his heart as he thought about laying her down in the lavender and filling her, hearing her sigh and quake under him. "I've walked a fine line my whole life. Denied myself things I wanted. I'm done with that."

"Hence these new changes," she said, her thumbs stroking the backs of his hands. "I understand now."

"I'm tired of everyone looking to me to be the good guy, Caitlyn. I realize I've acted a little strange these last few days, but I need to find out what I'm like when I'm not doing what other people expect of me."

"Then you've come to the right place," she said, squeezing his hand. "According to Ibrahim, we're all on a journey of discovery. Even me."

That he knew. She was growing more powerful among the lavender. He raised her hand to his mouth and kissed it. Felt the shaky earth inside him settle.

"So far, you're the best part of this journey. From the moment I saw you, I wanted to kiss those rosy lips of yours. Run my hands through your dark hair. Feel it against my bare chest."

Her sharp intake of breath could have awoken the sleeping lavender around them.

He continued, coasting like a man who'd crested a mountain and was on the way back downhill after a rough ride, "Your eyes are the sunshine. I told you that. But I haven't told you about your smile."

Taking a closer look into her moonlit face, he could see tears in her eyes. It gave him the courage to touch those lips, the ones that lifted into the first genuine smile she'd given him since this afternoon.

"Your smile lights me up inside, like a lightning bug. And your laugh... It hits me low in my belly, making me want to tumble you to the ground and put my hands on you. In the midst of all this chaos inside me, you are the one thing I feel certain about, the one thing that I know is true. Honey, I trust you all the way now, and for a man who's been cut up by a betrayal beyond his imagining, that's a hell of a feeling."

"Oh, Beau," she said, and that soft tone drifted toward him like the first flowers of spring, lush with promise and beautiful after so long a wait. "Since you trusted me, I'm going to trust you. I need to tell you what that kiss in the kitchen was like for me."

She'd said it was like losing a lifetime of good sense, but he needed to hear more. "Honey, I'm all ears."

"I haven't kissed a lot of guys," she said. "You might even laugh if I told you how many."

"Then I'm more than honored," he said, his voice darkening in accord with the shadowed land underneath his feet.

This woman. This moment. He was going to be changed by it.

She turned her body to the side and gestured to the fields. "I've grown up in a family that works hard and has been successful at it. My parents always warned us about people wanting us because we had a lot of money. Unfortunately, one of my brothers got caught by someone like that, and he paid dearly for it. I was in my mid-twenties then, and it made me even more cautious."

"I can understand all that," he said, shifting on his feet. "Women like that have chased me too. I've grown cautious."

"But on the rare occasion I've liked someone, and I mean really liked them...I've never been swept away like I was when I first met you. Or today. Beau, that wasn't a normal first kiss for me. You know the polite kind after a first date where it's more a passing glance over the lips."

He appreciated her honesty, even if it was disarming. "It wasn't normal for me either."

"I mean...I wanted to make love with you." She stalked away a few steps. "We were in the kitchen, for heaven's sake. Hargreaves or my aunt or uncle could have walked in. Do you have any idea how vulnerable that makes me feel? How out of control? Especially when you weren't telling me what was going on with you. Do you understand what I'm telling you?"

Funny how her emotions were clear to him when his own were so muddy. "You're scared of what I make you feel."

"Exactly! I thought you were this good guy who sang these sweet songs, the perfect boyfriend. And I wanted him. This other guy, the one with the ripped T-shirts and jeans who has a chip on his shoulder... He doesn't talk to me really about what's going on inside him, and he scares me a little. Even if he is the one who swept me away in the kitchen today, who I wanted more than anything. Oh, hell! I'm not making any sense."

She marched away a few more steps, her hands fisted at her sides, the moonlight cresting over her knuckles. He understood her frustration. Heck, he shared it.

"You're right. I'm changing, and it's messy. But one good thing about kissing you today... I realized kissing you like that—so soon—didn't make me less of a gentleman."

"I didn't fully understand it when you said that before. Now I do."

"Caitlyn, I'm not dithering about what I want anymore. I *want* to kiss you again and sweep you away. I want to do more than stroll with you after dinnertime. Will you go out with me tomorrow night? I'd like to take you to dinner and treat you good. Like you deserve. Hell, I might even shave off this days-old scruff." Although he'd decided he kind of liked it.

"Don't shave it," she said, smiling in the moonlight. "I rather like it."

Kindred spirits, he thought, taking a step closer toward her, his boots sinking into the soft dirt. It gave under his feet, and somehow he understood it was well nourished. The land had plenty to give because it was appreciated, celebrated even. Like she wanted to be. Like she deserved to be.

"Tell me how to make our first date the best you've ever had," he said, laying his hands on her upper arms. "I figure since our first kiss was the best kiss of both our lives, we need to keep climbing."

She touched his face, and the caress was a kind of benediction. "I only want you to be you."

His chest locked in place. "And if I don't know who that is anymore?"

"You do. Deep down. Even if you've forgotten. Beau Masters is the kind of man who makes a bed for an orphaned baby goat."

He snorted. "Have you ever thought that Beau Masters is a pussy?"

He said it as if it were someone else. Old Beau.

"No," she said, her head jerking back, her hand falling away. "We need men like that. Ones who aren't just interested in busting things up or putting things down. We need men who will stand up for something. Even an orphaned baby goat."

"Jeez, Caitlyn, I don't know how I can live up to that." *I don't know if I want to anymore.*

"But you've done it your whole life," she protested. "Beau, I researched everything I could about you. Do you think I would have asked you to be the spokesperson for the biggest venture of my life so far if I felt you were in any way unworthy?"

The weight of it all settled onto his shoulders, a familiar yoke, yet no less constricting. "I'm not an image, honey. I'm a flesh-and-blood man. Don't put all your hopes and dreams on me. No one person can carry them."

Hadn't his mother toppled off her pedestal, destroying the house he'd built on her?

"I'm not putting them on you, Beau," she said, her voice soft as a whisper. "I'm counting on your help is all."

That mollified him some. "I'm asking you again. Will you go to dinner with me tomorrow night?"

In that one moment, he learned struggle could have a sound, and he made himself promise to recreate it in a song. It was a harsh breath followed by soft agonized *hm*. Then silence. "Yes, because I believe more in you than you do right now."

It was the answer he'd hoped for, but he wasn't sure he liked her line of reasoning. "Come to dinner with me because you want me. Not because you want to fix me."

"I wouldn't be that foolish," she said. "Besides, the Beau I believe you to be is pretty wonderful. Why else would I have let you kiss me like that in the kitchen?"

"Would you let me kiss you now in the fields?" he boldly asked.

She put her finger to the mouth he was staring at. "Given how swept away we got earlier..."

He traced her cheek. "While I may be revising my

gentlemanly ways, you can still trust me with yourself. I'm not going to make love to you until you're ready. But make no mistake, Caitlyn, I do want to make love to you."

Her brilliant gaze flew to his, and he could have sworn he heard the whisper of a gasp.

"It's more than want. It's…how I need music. Something I can't live without."

"That's how I feel too," she said. "But before we kiss like that again, I need to be sure, Beau. It's a big step and not one I take lightly."

He remembered she'd said their earlier kiss had made her want him, as a woman wants a man. "I understand what you mean."

"But a sweet goodnight kiss?" Her mouth curved, and he gave in to the urge to trace those delicious lips of hers. "I think we can handle that."

Caitlyn hadn't turned away from him or the heaviness he was carrying. She trusted him as much as he trusted her—which allowed him to trust himself. It was a safe port in a storm right now.

Lowering his head, he whispered a breath from her mouth, "You're the most beautiful woman I've ever seen. Inside and out." Then he kissed her softly, learning the way her mouth curved and fitted to his. Somehow the softness of their touch had the same power as the earlier force of their kiss in the kitchen, and he marveled at that discovery too. "Kissing you is pure pleasure, honey."

She made a sweet sound low in her throat and then patted his chest, her fingertips lingering before they pulled away. "Will you hold my hand back to the house?"

He held out his hand, and she curled her smaller fingers around his. As they started back to the house, the soft ground gave way under their footsteps, but it held firm in the end. The same way they were holding on to each other, he thought.

CHAPTER 15

MAKING A DATE, USUALLY A RARE AND NERVE-RACKING AF-fair anyway, turned out to be even more overwhelming in a country where Beau didn't speak the language.

He'd agonized all morning, looking up nearby restaurants on Yelp, especially ones with English menus. When he'd settled on what one reviewer had called a sleepy French bistro only forty-plus minutes away in Cannes, he'd called to make a reservation only to have the attendant hang up on him after saying in a very thick accent that he couldn't understand *monsieur*. Heck, Beau couldn't understand the man either.

Even worse, he didn't have any clothing good enough for his first night with the most beautiful woman in the world. He needed a new outfit and a reservation. Now. Should he ask Ibrahim to help? He balked. The man was working. No, he'd figure something out.

Heading down the stairs finally—he'd purposely delayed his breakfast—he ran into Clara and Hargreaves. They were standing in the foyer speaking in whispered tones.

"Good morning, Beau," she said when she caught sight of him.

Hargreaves turned as well and bowed slightly at the

waist. Old Beau had been schooled in manners since he was a boy, but this was a type of civility he'd never get used to.

"Good mornin', Mrs. Hale," he said, taking off his cowboy hat. "Hargreaves."

"It's Clara."

"Clara. I feel I owe you and your husband an apology for my abrupt leave-taking last night. I acted like a right jackass."

"You seem to have a lot on your mind these days," the older woman said. Beau noticed she had on a cream knee-length dress that made his outfit of a dirty ripped shirt and jeans seem out of place. "Caitlyn tells me you two are going on a date tonight. You can't imagine how delighted I was to hear the news. I'm lending you Hargreaves for the day to ensure everything goes off without a hitch. He speaks French and is well versed in bringing together all kinds of social engagements."

Desperation prompted him to say, "Do you read minds, Clara? My drawl hasn't been helping me with making a reservation."

"I'd be happy to handle that, sir," Hargreaves said. "Shall we confer while you have your breakfast? Madam, I'll see you later."

"Have fun, you two. I'm going to pull Arthur away from his paper and take him for a walk before the sun gets too warm."

"Tell him he can borrow my cowboy hat if he has a mind," Beau called, watching her dash up the stairs, looking much younger than a woman near eighty.

"That, Beau, would be a sight," she said before disappearing from view.

Hargreaves fell in beside Beau when he started walking to the kitchen. "Ms. Caitlyn is with Ibrahim, I believe. In case you were wondering about being overheard, sir."

He could 'sir' just about anyone, but he'd never taken

to the address for himself. "Beau is just fine. I don't stand much on ceremony."

The man's inscrutable face didn't move, and Beau wondered if he was like one of those guards with the tall black hats in front of the queen's palace in London he'd seen in that spicy Fergie video for "London Bridge."

"I'm embarrassed to admit I don't have the proper attire for a dinner out with a beautiful woman, and I can't order anything online fast enough."

"I have arranged for a car today in case you needed to run errands," Hargreaves said as they entered the kitchen.

Just how long had Mrs. Hale—Clara—been planning on assisting him?

"Thank you," he said, slicing himself a piece of country bread. Every morning it lay on the counter, waiting, and every moment he smelled it, all he could think of was home. He wondered if Ibrahim could bottle this scent.

"Shall we leave in a quarter hour, sir, for your shopping?" the butler asked.

"That would be great." He had no idea how long it would take, but they were miles out from the nearest town. "It's Beau, though."

The man gave him a slight smile—"Yes, sir."—and then bowed slightly and left.

Beau decided to stop pushing. The man could call him whatever he chose.

The drive to the nearby town Hargreaves had suggested was a quiet affair. Uncomfortable with being driven but resigned—if Hargreaves refused to call him by his given name, he certainly wasn't going to allow him to drive—Beau was surprised to hear his phone ring. Checking it, he saw it was Rye.

"Hey, man," he said when he answered. "You still celebrating?"

"Every chance," Rye said. "Look, Bubba, it's late here, but I thought I'd take a chance and call you. Seems people think I'm some kind of conduit. Your mama must have said something."

"I'm sorry," he said. "All of my people...report to my mama."

"I can help with that. Tommy Penders from your record label called me. He wants you to call him right away. He's concerned about your new album. Says he needs to hear some songs. I told him I thought your theme of roots was going to speak to a lot of people. Mentioned we'd had a songwriting retreat. It pacified him some, but he's still itching. I think your mama's got him all worked up."

Probably because she was worked up, worried about what he might write about her. "I'll call him. Rye, I'm really sorry you're in the middle of things. If you do have a trustworthy person in mind to handle some calls, I'd be obliged."

"I can't think of anyone better than Clayton." Rye's brother-in-law was a smart and no-nonsense manager. From what time he'd spent with the two of them together, it was clear their working relationship was different from the one Beau had with his mama. Rye led the way—Clayton only cleared it for him.

"If you'll text me his number, I'll call him."

"You'd best not call Penders from your phone," Rye said. "Have Clayton set it up for you. That man knows how to keep a person's privacy intact."

He was relieved. Tommy and his mama were tight, and the exec wouldn't blink twice about giving her Beau's new number even if asked to keep it to himself. "Thanks."

"Hang in there, Bubba. Every shitstorm eventually runs out of shit."

He laughed. "Wish I could sing that."

"Me too," Rye said, "but I'm reformed. You, however, might need to speak the words if you feel them. I'd say that's good music, the kind you feel strongly about."

"The kind of lyrics pinging around in my head these

days would make a churchgoer drop to his or her knees and pray for my soul." He looked up to see if Hargreaves was watching, but the man was a silent force in the front of the car. Something told him that the butler was the soul of discretion.

"Your audience shouldn't dictate what you sing about," Rye said. "Take it from someone who learned the hard way. You can't bottle up your own truth."

Rye couldn't know how apt his phrasing was. "You should meet the master perfumer here."

"I hear perfume and all I smell are strongly scented women. They always made me wonder what they're hiding. You know that old phrase—I shouldn't say it—whores in church." Rye's laughter had a pleased edge to it, as if he were a kid who'd gotten away with swearing. "God, sometimes I miss speaking so plainly. Perhaps I need to open up my inner spigot a little too. All right, Bubba, I gotta get on. Time to feed Boone."

"I wondered why you were up so late," Beau said.

"Getting a little time with the missus," he said, a wink in his voice. "Gotta get an early start with our boy around. I'll holler at Clayton in a bit. Have everything ready for you to call Penders back. My recollection is he doesn't like to wait."

No, he didn't. The man jumped on everything. Heck, he'd signed Beau, a complete unknown, after hearing him sing "Amazing Grace" at his granny's funeral. "Thanks. See ya."

The call ended, and for the rest of the ride into town, he contemplated his troubles. Reminded himself of his blessings. Caitlyn was at the top of the list. He wasn't going to let the past color the excitement of today.

The small town they pulled into was lined with sandstone shops two or three stories high, dotted with a profusion of pink, blue, purple, white, and red flower boxes with hanging vines. People were strolling in the narrow streets, some arm in arm. A couple of women strode along with an air of authority, if he had to use a phrase, their long, sleek hair trailing behind like cloaks of confidence.

But as they left the car, Beau's attention was captured by a lone man walking toward them—or rather the man's navy suit. Normally seeing a man in a suit made Beau's skin itch. Something about the way this man wore his threads was different. He was like those women they'd passed earlier. Confident. Bold. He wore that fine suit like an old gunslinger might have worn chaps. His white shirt didn't look scratchy from starch, but soft and comfortable. A yellow tie with a path of navy lines was mimicked in a similar cloth artfully folded in the man's breast pocket. He moved smoothly past Beau, and because he was so attuned to smell, Beau picked up woodsy notes of oakmoss and leather, if he had to guess.

"I want *that*," he heard himself say out loud.

"A very smart suit, sir," Hargreaves said. "I had thought we were merely shopping for a shirt and trousers. I see we have more to purchase than I thought. If you will give me a moment."

Beau watched as Hargreaves took off after the man in brisk strides. He didn't understand whatever he said that made the man halt and turn, but he did so, an almost disgruntled expression on his face. The two conferred, and finally the man laughed. Rich, baritone notes much like his cologne. They exchanged a few lines of brusque French, then he sauntered off. This time Beau noticed his shoes. They were a rich caramel, somehow a perfect contract to the navy suit.

As Hargreaves returned, he found himself floundering. He'd left his cowboy hat in the car, and thank God. He'd have looked even more like a fish out of water than he did now.

"I have learned of a couple of shops I believe will see to your needs, sir," Hargreaves said. "If you will follow me."

Beau wanted to ask what the man had laughed about. He couldn't imagine Hargreaves making fun of him. They walked slowly, turning at this street and then another. Beau only followed. The square was filled with the scents of fresh baked bread, roasted meat, and jasmine from flowers planted in the large containers flanking a few restaurants with open seating. Then the sharp, pungent scent of coffee hit his nose, and he inhaled deeply.

"I hope you'll let me take you to lunch after this, Hargreaves," he said, nodding to a woman who smiled as she passed him, almost in amusement. "I must look like the worst kind of tourist to them."

"We're about to remedy that, sir."

He hadn't expected Hargreaves to answer. At the next street, Hargreaves stopped in front of a store window showing two men's suit jackets, one in a deep maroon that reminded Beau of the last shade of sunset while the other was in a rich cream he'd dot on cherry pie.

"Here we are, sir," Hargreaves said, opening the door.

Beau stopped short. Was he being crazy? Seeing some guy in a suit and wanting to look like that? His mother wasn't the only one who'd encouraged him to stick to the down-home look. Tommy Penders had done the same, hadn't he? "I don't know if I can pull this off."

But New Beau said: *You don't know who you really are. Why not find out?*

Maybe his real father had a penchant for nice-looking suits, ones that made a man look confident, elegant even. He'd have never imagined wanting to look like that, but he wanted to present himself as a man who knew how to treat a woman, and he'd bet that Frenchman did. He wouldn't blunder over a restaurant menu or order the wrong bottle of wine. And he certainly wouldn't balk from kissing a woman he wanted.

"Like I told my mistress when she was very young,

fashion is a matter of the heart. Come, let's see what yours is telling you."

A matter of the heart. He was still reeling from that statement when the female shopkeeper called out to him. She left the severe-looking man behind the counter, striding forward in a bold red dress, uneven at the edges. It looked like someone had been drunk when designing it, and yet, the cuts were too precise. They were intentional and somehow perfect in their imperfection.

Then she smiled at him, a kind smile that lit up her brown eyes. It was the same kind of encouraging smile a few of his schoolteachers had given him when he'd wanted to ask another question about a subject—everything from why beavers dammed up a river to why geese traveled in a V— but was afraid of other students poking fun at him for being an egghead.

Then she spoke, and her soft, foreign words went straight into his soul.

Hargreaves translated, "She says 'Come inside. There's much to discover, and you look like a man ready to discover it.'"

The words echoed his conversation with Caitlyn last night, which seemed like a sign. As he stepped over the threshold, the suited man behind the counter came out to join the woman in the red dress. Hargreaves listened to him for a moment and then introduced the man as her husband. Beau understood that look now. The suited man was protective of his woman.

No other customers or employees were in the shop, so Beau took the leap and told them, via Hargreaves, about the changes he'd been making in his life. About the good-old-boy style he'd grown beyond like a dried-up house-plant that had run its course. Hell, he'd been dressing the same since he'd made it big at sixteen, he realized—like he was still in high school.

Somehow it was easier to put his feelings into words,

knowing they couldn't understand him. He found himself sharing how he'd torn his clothes, looking for something different inside him. A new image for the musician he was, yes, but also for the man. They needed to be one and the same.

She'd raised an eyebrow then and said, "*Musicien*," which he understood. Her nod communicated a new piece of the puzzle of him.

Hargreaves continued to provide rapid-fire translations.

"What kind?" the woman asked.

"Country," he answered.

Another mysterious sound came from her, and she looked him up and down again. "Any Italian in your blood? Your coloring and those eyelashes make me think Rome."

"No, Spanish," her husband corrected. "Madrid. That nose..."

His heart started pounding. "Not that I know of."

The questions that followed, translated in Hargreaves' voice, seemed to open up the hollow area in his heart.

What is it you wish to say now?

What do you want people to know of you when they see you on the street?

He found himself thinking of that damn cocoon Ibrahim had mentioned. He responded: he wanted people to know he was more than he seemed. That he still had goodness but he'd been touched by shadows, ones he couldn't make sense of yet. She loved that answer and spun away to a wall of stacked golden-colored drawers under their displays, pulling out shirts and jackets.

What kinds of colors grab your attention and captivate you?

He looked to the window display, saying, "I would never have imagined liking that maroon in the window, but it's arresting, isn't it? I figure I'm an open canvas."

When Hargreaves translated, "Music to my ears," Beau laughed.

They got down to the nitty-gritty then, everything from linen to the finest cotton he'd ever felt, so soft and breathable it could have passed for a second skin. He went on instinct, nodding his head when he liked something and shaking it when he didn't. Hargreaves continued translating, and then the husband asked him a question that floored him:

What have you been waiting your whole life to say as a man?

Is this how the French chose their clothes? Good Lord, no wonder their outfits suited them so well, as if every inch of fabric they'd chosen aligned with their attributes and traits. It was much like Ibrahim talking about how a person picked a scent. It had to be individual, unique, something that expressed their very nature. A matter of the heart, as Hargreaves had said.

He discovered a new truth about himself. He was a man who was as comfortable wearing torn clothes as he was these fine threads. He liked being country *and* confident.

He was proud of the man he was becoming.

"Hargreaves," he said, feeling himself standing taller every minute. "Would you ask them what their names are and give them mine? Please."

They were helping him unearth a new aspect of himself, and it only seemed right that they should do so on a first-name basis.

"Colette," she said with a warm smile.

"Étienne," her husband replied, his cheekbones sitting high as if he spent most of his days assessing what looked best on people from atop a mountain.

"Beau," he said. "Beau Masters."

Hargreaves introduced himself as well, his smile welcoming. A new camaraderie was born, and then Étienne went to another set of shelves and brought out trousers. Some matched the jackets Beau favored, but a few others were in direct opposition, almost as different as the sound of a piano from a trio of spoons. But Beau knew two very different things could make music together, and after Colette held a few combinations up against him, a hairsbreadth away from his body, he was ushered into a dressing room.

They quickly fell into a pattern. He'd try something on and then make an appearance. The husband and wife sometimes smiled in tandem. Other times, they argued about whether or not the outfit worked, but even in their passionate exchanges, Beau noticed how they touched each other. A finger to the cheek as they spoke or the slight caress of the hand. They spoke a language all their own and weren't afraid to let others see it.

He lost count of how many combinations he tried on, but they seemed to settle on four outfits in the end. He'd decided early on to disregard the price tags; it wasn't like he spent much money on himself. Besides, he wouldn't scrimp on a good pair of boots. Why would he with this? He'd never gone on his very own tailored shopping spree before.

The black velvet jacket was one of his favorites, along with a fine white shirt that felt like silk against his skin. Colette told him he could wear it with jeans, and then she laughed, saying she'd noticed he looked very good in jeans when he was standing outside their shop. She blew a kiss to her husband, and said, "No men wear jeans quite like the Americans. You should definitely keep that part for your new look."

Eyeing himself in the mirror, he could rather see himself wearing that fine shirt open at the collar with a leather belt and torn jeans. His boots would add pure country.

Sometimes country, sometimes confident, he heard

in his head, along with the heavy strings of guitar followed by a fiddle. More makings of a new song. Hot damn.

"Would you like to wear something new out of the store?" Colette asked him. "Not that I don't like what you came in with."

He looked down at his torn clothes. Yes, he liked the look, but somewhere in the middle of trying on all of these new textures and colors, he'd realized he'd torn his clothes because he'd been torn up inside. But he was mending, wasn't he? He was finding out more about his essence, as Ibrahim would say.

"I'd like that very much, Colette."

After dressing in his new threads, he emerged to find his purchases boxed up neatly according to type, so he could find what he wanted. He told Colette about his date with the most beautiful woman in the world tonight. She asked if he'd chosen a place yet, and he looked at Hargreaves, who seemed to shrug. "If you have a better place, I'm sure we'll love it."

Colette made the reservation herself for two at eight o'clock, saying her friend who owned the restaurant would take good care of them. Then she asked him about shoes, pointedly looking down at his boots.

"Do you sell shoes?" he asked.

"No, but we have a shop we'd recommend," she said. "You can pick up your purchases later. I will come with you and tell Louis about what you've bought today. He will transform your feet in no time."

Colette strode ahead of them as they walked to the new shop, her sandy blond hair waving down her back, a scent of something complex and yet floral trailing in her wake. Did everyone wear perfume here, their own special calling card? None of it was overwhelming. He needed something that fit him. Ibrahim would know.

Louis welcomed Colette warmly with three kisses on

her cheeks and then turned to nod at Beau and Hargreaves as she explained the situation in fast, musical French. The man glanced down at Beau's boots, his mouth tipping up to the right, before he met his eyes. Louis was in his fifties, and his outfit—a cream jacket, blue shirt, and pink and cream tie and pocket square—seemed to announce him as a man who liked cool breezes and even cooler drinks, like a mint julep, if he'd been visiting the States. Beau liked him instantly when he said, "Every man wishes to be a cowboy, but so few pull it off."

He replied by opening his arms. "And here I was thinking I envied a man who could wear a fine suit so confidently."

With that, a bond was struck. Colette told them she'd see them soon, and then Louis started walking around Beau. Feeling sized up, he let the man take his time. He was like Ibrahim, looking for the intangible things that made one person distinct from another. Beau realized he did the same with people in his songs, looking for the story of them, why they acted like they did, what was important to them.

Soon he was taking off his boots, laughing at the dust from the lavender fields. He explained it to Louis, who was intrigued to learn of the perfume farm. "A great work of art, a perfume."

Beau asked him, "Why?" curious to hear his answer.

"It lasts longer than a set of clothes one wears for a day, and so must say more about someone and for a longer time," was Louis' reply.

Before suggesting any shoes to Beau, Louis offered them an afternoon coffee, calling for them from a place down the street. A young man arrived with a tray and three small cups. Beau thanked the boy and savored every inch of his coffee, and they sat, Louis and Hargreaves speaking for a spell before turning back to him.

After the small break, a happy luxury that reminded

Beau of something small-town shopkeepers might do at home, he started trying on different shoes. No surprise, he selected a pair the color of Halloween caramels straight away, followed by four more pairs in suitable colors and styles. Again, he discarded his boots to pull on the caramel shoes. The boots didn't really work with his new outfit. He almost laughed at himself, but he was having too much fun to feel embarrassed.

As Louis checked him out, two Frenchmen walked past the shop. One had on a green jacket with a navy scarf tied around his neck. Beau had never seen a man wear a scarf like that. His trousers were the color of sand while his friend wore a tan suit punctuated by a purple shirt and pocket square. They had that air about them. Bold. Confident.

He turned to Louis. "What makes a Frenchman his own man?"

When the shopkeeper hesitated, Beau thought he'd phrased it badly. But then Louis ripped off a tag, and said, "How he holds himself, what he laughs about, how he makes love to a woman, how generous he is with his children, how great of a friend he is. Oh, so many things— all done with dignity."

Dignity. Another simple word, yet laden with meanings as deep as a country swamp. Louis' description was one he could chew on, especially the part about making love to a woman. Although the act was meant to be special, he'd never considered it as a reflection of his character, his essence. But when he thought about Caitlyn, and how special he wanted to make her feel, he thought he understood what the man meant.

"Thank you, Louis," he said, managing to grab one of the shopping bags before Hargreaves could pick them both up.

The butler gave him a look, only the subtle lift of a brow, but Beau gestured to the other bag on the counter, the one he'd left for him. Because Hargreaves had dignity too, and Beau would not deprive him of it.

As he stepped out into the hot sunny street, he felt a foot taller. Walking back toward Colette and Étienne's shop, he caught a few people staring at him, more out of curiosity and appreciation, he thought, than because he didn't belong. His chest felt broader, and he held his shoulders back without thinking about it. A proud posture, he realized.

A tall brunette in a navy sheath dress and three-inch heels smiled at him as she approached them, walking in the opposite direction. Caitlyn would wear something like that, he thought. He smiled at the woman, and she said something in French.

Hargreaves waited a beat before saying, "She said you looked very elegant, sir."

He beamed the rest of the way to the shop. Colette and Étienne greeted them warmly with perfunctory kisses. Again, it was weird to have a man kiss his cheeks, but he wanted to honor the custom. It was like a man hug, he told himself, only French.

Colette looked at his shoes with a knowing smile. "If your woman doesn't appreciate you after tonight, come back here. I have a sister who would love to go out with a man with as many facets as you have."

His head jerked back. Facets? Somehow the word was perfect for what he was discovering about himself. He was so much more than that one-dimensional guy trying to fit the constraints of a square hole. "Thank you both. So very much. You have made my day." He wished he could do more to thank them but didn't know what that would be, so he and Hargreaves picked up the bags and left the couple standing in the doorway, holding hands. Somehow that last look felt like a chocolate mint after a satisfying meal. Sweet. Satisfying. They were in love. Worked together. Challenged each other. Grew together.

He wondered if he and Caitlyn might do the same. For the first time since all of this had begun, he found himself looking toward the future.

"I'd like to do something more, Hargreaves," he found himself saying. "As a thank you to them."

Which begged another question: how would he thank Hargreaves? He would have to ask Clara.

"I can arrange for a summer bouquet of the region's flowers, sir, if you'd like. I believe Madam Colette would like them, and it wouldn't be too personal a gift."

He didn't believe Étienne would be jealous, and flowers did seem to please most women. "That would be wonderful, Hargreaves. In fact, I'd like to get some flowers for Caitlyn before we leave town. Would that be all right?"

"As you wish, sir," Hargreaves said. "There's a flower stand in the square if I recall."

There was indeed, and Beau was overwhelmed by the selection at first. But New Beau was finding his wings. Caitlyn had mentioned she didn't care for roses, he remembered. They had more than enough lavender, and anyway, it wasn't a flower. There were happy-faced flowers the shopkeeper told Hargreaves were asters, although they looked like purple daisies to him. They reminded him of Caitlyn's playful side, but they didn't feel bold enough for her. She was trying to make a statement, after all, and she'd launched this whole enterprise herself.

His gaze settled on a large wine-colored flower with a million petals, anchored by a thick dark stalk. "What are those?"

"Dahlias, sir," Hargreaves said.

They were bold. Arresting. Strong. Everything Caitlyn was and more. He signaled to the shopkeeper. "I'll take them all."

"An excellent choice, sir," Hargreaves said.

When they settled back in the car after stowing the packages, he slumped in the back seat. If he was this tired, he couldn't imagine how the older man felt. "Do you want me to drive?"

"I'll be fine, sir," he said after a pause, and Beau felt the eggshells of Hargreaves' dignity underneath his new shoes. He needed to be careful, he reminded himself. This man had many facets too.

When he checked his phone, he discovered a text from Clayton with instructions for how to call Tommy without it being traced to his phone. Not wanting to put it off, he followed the process right away and called his office. His assistant answered, and Tommy picked up a few minutes later. "Beau! So glad you got my message. Boy, your mama has been looking everywhere for you. Rye Crenshaw must be going soft. I never thought he might spirit a man away."

"Rye? Soft? Come on, Tommy, maybe you're the one who needs to get out of town for a while." He didn't know how much his mama had told the man. "I can't recommend it enough. Turns out, it's great for songwriting."

"Good to hear, Beau. That's a relief. Your mama said this whole roots theme was borrowing all sorts of trouble. I thought it might be wise if you shared what you have so far. Maybe we can help guide you a little."

Beau pulled on his bottom lip with his teeth, weighing his options. "After doing ten platinum and Grammy-winning albums with me, you're a touch more concerned than I'd expect, Tommy. What in the *world* has my mama been telling you? You know she can be a mite high-strung sometimes."

Actually, he didn't know what Tommy thought of his mama. He'd assumed everyone liked her, but it had been just that. An assumption.

"I'm only looking out for your best interests, Beau, like always. You know you're the star of our label."

"My new album is going to blow your mind," he said, beginning to believe it. "Just today, I heard the makings of another song in my head."

"What's it called?"

He decided it was time to trust the music he was hearing, regardless of how different it was from his usual style. It only popped up when it was broadcast from his heart. The rest of the lyrics would come. "Sometimes Country, Sometimes Confident."

"Interesting," Tommy said. "Got any of your heart-breaking love songs yet? You know how your female fans love those."

They were, in fact, some of his biggest downloads. Caitlyn flashed into his mind. There was so much to say. Hot kisses. Moonlight-drenched lavender. Playing it safe. Wanting to cast aside all good sense. "I'm still working on that, but it's going to be a doozy, I promise."

"Good," he said. "Your mama mentioned this new endorsement you're entertaining. *A French perfume?* Beau, I never knew you swung that way."

He straightened in the car. The homosexual slur was base and uncalled for. "Not that there's anything wrong with anyone's sexual orientation, Tommy, but you couldn't be more uninformed. I'm sure my mama didn't describe the full proposal. It's actually very in tune with my new album. It's about the roots of a person and who they are. It's about everything farmers and country people talk about—one of my strong bases, you know. The land. The people who make something from it. It might have roots in France, but it's universal, Tommy, and it's going to be a wild success." He'd leave out the part about helping women feel their worth. Tommy sure as hell wouldn't get that.

"Still, your mama's instincts might be right. You'd do best with American brands, ones where the flag is visible. Ball Park hot dogs. Chevy trucks."

"You know why I don't want to do a truck commercial, Tommy." Not after the man he'd thought was his daddy had died in a crash.

That he had to remind the man sickened him. How much poison had his mama pumped into him?

"Of course. It slipped my mind, Beau. But there are lots of other American products. If you're keen to do a fragrance, for God's sake, do a cologne. Your mama says the Ryan Williams people are real keen to have you after she met with them."

He frowned. Had she gone to them herself or had she been sitting on their proposal for some time, waiting for the right moment? "The interest is flattering, but this one is hitting me in all the right places. You can pass that message along for me."

"But you haven't *signed* yet, right?" Tommy pressed. "Your mama says they don't even have the perfume ready? Plus, what company uses a man to advertise a woman's fragrance? Not even Dior or Chanel do that. This company sounds like they're new laundry hanging out to dry."

He realized he was gripping the knee of his new slacks. "*This company* is a multi-billion-dollar conglomerate run by the Merriam family, whose ancestor struck oil in Oklahoma, Tommy. They aren't some fly-by-night upstart."

"Be that as it may, the label has concerns about you doing this perfume, Beau. We're inclined to see things your mama's way. It doesn't suit the image we've spent almost fifteen years creating with you, an image your fans love, I might add."

His mama had been working it, no doubt. Beau would have to do some high-stepping when he returned to Nashville to convince them to see things his way. He thought of Caitlyn. Should he tell her he was getting pushback? No, it would only worry her, and he'd have his way in the end. He was one of the label's top stars. "You're going to pull rank on my endorsements now? I don't believe that kind of oversight is in my contract. I've worked hard enough to make this kind of decision on my own."

"You sound mighty defensive, Beau. You've always entrusted the business side of things to us and your mama. She said this new album was making you touchy. Maybe you should come home. Be around the people who care about you and your career."

He glanced out the window at the organized fields of farmland. If he hadn't known where he was, he'd might have thought he was traveling through his own state of Tennessee. The world felt small in that moment, but he'd sprung his trap and he wasn't about to amble back into it.

"Tommy, you trusted me with the other albums, and it paid off for you and the label. I'm grateful for all your support. But this new album is very personal to me, and like I told my mama, I really need to have some space to write the songs that will touch people. In the absence of that creative control, I won't be happy. Do you understand? I don't feel like I'm asking a lot. It's my name on the album, after all. The same goes for any products I endorse."

The three beats of silence on the other end were oddly in time with the rotations of the tires on the road. Round and around we go, Beau thought, waiting to see how Tommy would play it.

"Well, all righty, boy. Don't get yourself all hot and bothered. Ol' Tommy was just trying to look out for ya like I have since you were a kid. But if you have a handle on things, great. I'll sleep better tonight. Only you might call your mama. She's more than a touch worried about you."

"Like I said, she's sometimes high-strung. I just turned thirty, Tommy. Time to cut some apron strings."

More silence. "Every mama likes a mama's boy, I suppose. All right, Beau, I'll anxiously look forward to the first batch of songs when they're ready. Do you think you could have one ready in a couple weeks? My cardiologist would thank you. He hates seeing my blood pressure shoot up. We can talk about this perfume more when you return to Nashville."

His attempts to stir up Beau's guilt would have worked on Old Beau, but he felt immune to them. "I'm sure I'll be able to send you some songs. Only you know how hard it is to tell time in the country, right? No clocks out here other than the sundial."

"That's a good one, Beau. We'll talk soon."

Tommy would discover otherwise when he realized he didn't have his direct number. *Thank you, Clayton.* "You take care of yourself, you hear."

He ended the call. Kicked out his feet. Thought of his mama and all the trouble she was stirring up. Should he call her? No, she'd only wheedle and cajole and crush his newfound creativity. Their last conversation had suggested she'd come at him with a two-by-four. He couldn't allow that. He had songs to write.

A woman to woo.

"Is there anything else I can help with, sir?" Hargreaves asked. "If there is, all you need do is ask."

He caught the man's inscrutable look in the mirror. His gaze kept flicking between Beau and the road. "Thank you, Hargreaves. You know, I don't know much about butler stuff, but back where I'm from, one good turn is served with another. I'd really like to do something for you. You mentioned liking music. Is there anything I can do for you?"

"Thank you, sir, but no. It's an honor to be of service to you."

"Don't misunderstand this question, but why? You just met me, and it's not like I've put my best foot forward."

"You might be trying on new shoes, Mr. Masters, but you're important to the Merriam family, whom I've served for over sixty years now. Of course, I'm also coming to know you as a person. Would you like me to turn up the music, sir?"

He knew it for a purposeful change in topic. "Find

something that suits you. I'm finding I like new types of music. Do you know Raï, Hargreaves?"

"Well, of course, sir," he replied. "It's world-famous."

And yet, he'd needed Ibrahim to introduce him to it. "Sometimes the world feels big, and sometimes it feels small." A good song lyric, he reckoned.

"Indeed, sir."

Beau's ears cocked when he heard the guitar. Hargreaves raised the volume of the music, and he sat forward. Sharp. Fast. Almost metallic in sound. "Hargreaves, what kind of guitar is this?"

"Flamenco, sir, one of my passions. Do you like it?"

"Yes." It had the same commanding appeal that Raï did. "You recognized my guitar by sight the other day. Do you play?"

"I learned flamenco guitar as a teenager before I entered service," he said. "It ruffled my father. One of the few things that did."

A personal comment from the warm but reserved man. It felt like a victory in a day filled with them. "I'd love to hear you play sometime."

"Thank you, sir. I'll leave this station on if it suits you."

No promise then. "Please." He settled back and closed his eyes before saying, "Where is this type of guitar from, Hargreaves?"

"Spain, sir."

He remembered Colette and Étienne arguing about whether he had a little Italian or Spanish blood. He almost wished for a mirror. They'd talked about his nose, his eyelashes, his brow. Was his face so foreign then? What secrets did it hold, ones he had yet to plumb? Would they ever be known to him? God, he hoped Dr. Clarridge struck gold and found his people, even though the thought made his diaphragm clench.

He felt a black cloud descending on him again,

the angry, sometimes soulful flamenco guitar a perfect accompaniment.

He still did not know who he was, but today he'd claimed more for himself. Facets. He liked that word.

When they arrived, Arthur and Clara emerged from the house, hand in hand, looking like a much older version of the passionate shopkeepers from the village. He left the flowers in the back of the car, hoping to get a bead on Caitlyn's whereabouts. They should be a surprise.

When he emerged, Clara clucked her tongue and said, "Goodness, Beau! You look like a new man. Very chic."

The makings of New Beau felt well seeded in this moment. "Thank you. It was quite a day."

"I'd say. Hargreaves, you outdid yourself."

"Mr. Masters did most of the work, Madam."

Clara shot an elbow into Arthur's side.

"Now you won't get kicked out of the restaurant," Arthur said. "I had a horrible vision of the *maître d'* ruining Caitlyn's evening."

"Where is she?" he asked.

"Finishing up some work and getting ready for your date. You were later than she expected."

He pointed to the trunk before retrieving the bouquet. "We did more shopping than I expected. Hargreaves, let me help you with the bags."

"I'll take care of them, sir." He stood there in his black suit, a study in dignity. Beau knew enough about people to understand it would be a slight to reject him.

Nodding, he said, "Then thank you. Arthur, I didn't see you this morning to apologize—"

"Clara told me." He waved a hand. "You treat Caitlyn well, and we're good. The flowers are a smart beginning. If you need any more help getting back on track, so to speak, find me. I've been known to say the right thing in a tough moment. Not that I'm suggesting you're having one or anything."

Beau suspected those sharp blue eyes didn't miss much. "I appreciate that, but I'm cresting out of it. I guess I'll go put these flowers in water and get ready. Check on Chou-Chou."

"Your baby goat cried like crazy today in the fields, missing you," Clara said. "I finally had to bring him back to the bed you made him and sit with him for a while."

His heart clutched, hearing that. The poor fella. Beau guessed it was official. He was friends with a goat.

"Perhaps a drink before you two head out?" Clara asked, trailing her hand down a strand of pearls around her throat.

He'd liked the rosé last night. Perhaps it was time to try a drink in a more celebratory fashion. What better occasion than his first date with Caitlyn? "Deal."

Heading inside, he strode to the kitchen, realizing he was starved. He stowed the flowers in an earthen pitcher and hid it in one of the cabinets. Then he scrounged up a snack. He was munching on bread and cheese when he heard footsteps behind him. He turned to see Ibrahim smiling that pencil-thin smile of his.

"I see your outing was fruitful," he said, pulling something from his breast pocket.

"You look like the men I saw in the village, I realize. Confident. Put together. I'm still a work in process." He thought of his new song title again. "Sometimes Country, Sometimes Confident." Yep, he was going to write the heck out of it.

Handing Beau a small vial, Ibrahim said, "You're closer than you think. Don't rush the experimentation process. It's the most fun part of any process, perfume notwithstanding. I blended this for you today when I heard about your evening with Caitlyn."

Gratitude filled his chest. "You're a mind reader," he said, patting the man on the shoulder. "I was going to ask for your help in this department."

"You mentioned wearing cologne before, but I hadn't detected any since you arrived."

"My mother chose the brand," he confessed, staring at the blue vial. "She overrode my wishes, something I've realized I've been letting her do for some time."

"A real man must make his own choices to be happy," Ibrahim said. "This isn't your lasting scent. But it's your 'now' scent."

Beau opened the bottle. A blast of citrus followed by something fresh and woodsy, then a final note of mystery. "I couldn't possibly guess all these scents, Ibrahim, but I like them."

The man walked to the door. "An explosive burst of citrus at the front. The volatility of lime can be surprisingly cleansing. Then notes of the land, pine, and a touch of cedar to comfort the nose. For the base notes, I chose myrrh and frankincense, scents to remind a man he's more than he yet knows. Enjoy your evening, Beau."

Before he could ask more questions—or even thank him or ask him to join them for a drink—Ibrahim had disappeared. The Perfume Jedi had struck true and sure. Beau inhaled the fragrance again.

They were the perfect notes for the man he was becoming.

CHAPTER 16

BIG BROTHERS HAD A WAY OF DRAGGING DOWN DATE EXcitement.

Still, when Quinn texted her *legal hasn't received the contract yet*, she knew it was her own fault. She needed to respond but didn't know how. Thankfully, she knew whom to ask.

Flynn picked up right away. "Yo."

"Thank God, you answered," she said, slumping in relief. "Quinn just asked where the contract was for legal, and I need to hold him off a little longer." Hopefully not too much longer.

"You're wired," he said. "You slept with Beau."

Yikes! "Not yet, moron."

"But you're thinking about it." He could have sawed logs with that sigh. "This is big for you, Caity girl. I feel a return trip to Provence coming on."

"No, stay where you are. I have everything under control." She was so full of shit. She'd been stewing all day, especially after hearing Beau and Hargreaves had gone clothes shopping. Shopping! Uncle Arthur hadn't helped, saying if Hargreaves didn't work his magic, they were going to get kicked out of the restaurant before they were seated for violating the dress code.

"I'll hold off," her brother said, "but only because I trust Uncle Arthur and Aunt Clara. Now, what to do about Quinn. How about this? Have Beau sign a nondisclosure agreement and send that to legal. As a business move, it's solid. After all, Beau has been involved in your creative sessions for the fragrance, right?"

"He's not going to tell anyone anything." But Flynn was right. She needed something to show Quinn, and an NDA would be better than nothing. "All right, I'll write something up. Do I give it to him before or after our date?" She lowered her head and knocked it on her desktop. *Here, Beau, let's have a good time, but first, can you sign a trustworthiness contract?*

"He'll understand if he's a good guy and a true professional, Caitlyn. You need to keep the business stuff separate, and the other stuff? Well, you be smart about that. Don't rush into anything."

"I should be writing this down." She snorted and then sobered. "Flynn, have you ever kissed anyone who immediately made you want to go all the way?"

"Well, nearly everyone, but I don't think you're just talking about sex. You're talking about soul-kissing, aren't you?" he asked.

She released a slow stream of breath, her diaphragm tight. "Yes, I suppose you could call it that."

"I've heard of it, sure. Never had one yet if I'm being honest."

"What would you do if you did?"

"Not sure. Run like hell? Marry her the same night? Emotion has a way of informing a decision in the moment. Caitlyn, you need to be careful here. Beau is going through something. Remember how Jace the Jerk turned out?"

"Better than you."

"Then I'll keep quiet. Look, you know how Quinn works, so to prevent ulcers, let me recommend getting a contract in place as quickly as possible," Flynn said, heaviness in his voice. "Think of it as a business appetizer."

"Funny." She gripped the windowsill. "Thanks, Flynn. For talking this through and for being my brother."

"Ah... Now I might just make a return trip to see you and pull your hair."

"Jerk!" She said it half-heartedly. He hadn't pulled her hair in years and usually only did it in good fun. "I need to draw up this NDA and then dress for my date. Beau went shopping for it."

"Really? That's big for a guy. Sorry if that sounds sexist."

She didn't mention Beau had torn all his serviceable clothes. Would he have gone shopping if he'd had something suitable to wear? A new thought twisted her gut—Jace the Jerk hadn't liked her for her. He'd taken her shopping for clothes because he hadn't thought her clothes suitable or sexy. She hadn't realized until the boob job offer that nothing about her had been suitable to him. He'd had a Pygmalion complex. God, she wasn't treating Beau the same way, was she? Now that he'd told her everything, she could see why he was torn up. She had faith that he'd find his way back to the truth at the core of him.

"You get a pass on that comment. Now I really have to go. Where are you, anyway?"

"Bologna," he said, "having dinner later with a beautiful Italian model who's in between major fashion shoots."

"Italy. You and J.T. Well, have fun."

"You have fun and be smart. Love ya."

"Love ya too," she said, ending the call.

Then she got out her laptop and hand-tailored the nondisclosure agreement. Usually she'd have legal draw it up, but she had a good template to work with and knew how to massage it. Pleased with the language, she printed it out and set it aside. She'd ask him to sign tomorrow. Keep things separate. At peace with her decision, she changed into an emerald green cotton dress with an asymmetrical neckline that fell to mid-calf. Still comfortable but a little dressier. When she looked in the mirror, she felt sexy, truly sexy for the first time in a long while—since before Jace the Jerk.

When she came down the stairs for her date, her heart in her throat with nerves, she heard the rumble of conversation in the main room and followed it. Beau stood next to her aunt, a glass of sparkling rosé in his hand.

Holy mother of God. He looked...beautiful in a plum-colored jacket, white shirt open at the collar, and dark gray trousers. She couldn't take her eyes off him. And he even had a pocket square! The dove gray fabric was a touch lighter than his trousers, and his shoes... My God, were those Italian? Her study finally landed on his face, and she detected a very sexy air of confidence.

He was transformed.

Someone cleared their throat, and she glanced away to see Uncle Arthur walking toward her.

"Don't you look a sight for these old eyes," he said, kissing her cheek. "I wish your great-grandfather were here to see you. Grandpa Emmits would be so proud."

Her eyes watered. "Oh, you dear man. You're going to make my mascara run."

"Then stop wearing it," he teased. "Come on. Beau seems to have found something decent to wear, hasn't he?"

"I'd say," she murmured as her uncle took her elbow. "Good evening, everybody."

Her aunt kissed her cheek. "You look lovely, dear. That dress is fabulous. Paris?"

"Milan," she said absently, her gaze locking with Beau's. "You...look incredible. I've seen some makeovers, but you look like a guest on *Queer Eye for the Straight Guy.*"

He'd changed so much a ripple of anxiety went

through her belly. Although she was happy he'd found confidence, it struck her that the man she'd met in his office was barely discernible in this handsome, well-dressed man before her. For Beau, she was happy, and even for herself—but what did this mean for her perfume? This suit-wearing man didn't resemble the earnest singer she'd known women would listen to about her perfume. The thought made her feel awful, and her heart clenched.

"Don't be silly, dear," Aunt Clara said. "He had Hargreaves to help, and a lovely French couple who owns a quaint shop nearby."

"I left more of Old Beau in the village," Beau said, kissing her cheek sweetly. "Did you know I'd never worn a full suit and tie except when I was singing at funerals for money? Until today, I sure as hell had never worn Italian shoes. But I'm finding I really like this new facet of myself. Sometimes country only gets a man so far."

She went with honesty since he valued it. "But I still need that Beau Masters for my perfume," she said, infusing her voice with a teasing tone although she didn't feel like laughing. "You'll still bring him out sometimes, right?"

He only shrugged.

Shrugged? She couldn't breathe suddenly. She wasn't sure what to do.

This beautifully dressed man looked like he should be selling cigars, not perfume.

Aunt Clara put a drink in her hand. "Have some bubbles, dear."

She was thinking a whiskey might need to come next. Suddenly it no longer felt like that NDA could wait. She needed something from him. Some assurance that this would work out as they'd discussed. Oh, how she hated feeling this insecure.

"Thank you," she said to her aunt, trying to smile. "Beau, can we speak privately for a moment?"

"Of course," he said, his gaze sharp on her face.

Her aunt and uncle shared a look. "Arthur and I will go find another bottle," Aunt Clara said.

After they'd left, she faced him. "I know the timing isn't great, but we need to talk about a little business item. I understand your feelings on signing the contract right now, but I'd like you to sign a nondisclosure agreement. After all, you are staying here and participating in our planning sessions."

His blue-gray eyes blinked, and then his mouth snapped shut. "You're bringing this up now? Before our date?"

She made herself nod. "Our legal department is by the book, and as the head of this project, I need to follow protocol." She put her glass down on a side table. "I got some pressure about the contract today, and while I want to honor your feelings on that score, I need to give my team something."

"Of course. I didn't think about putting you in a bad position. If I could sign the contract right now, I would, but it's still a little premature on my end."

She wanted to ask why, but before she could decide how to phrase it, he said, "I'm happy to sign an NDA. My reticence was only because you caught me off guard." Setting his glass next to hers, he shrugged. "I figured our first date was a reason for celebration."

She wanted to curse. "It is, but I can't wait any longer. This isn't the first time I've been pressed, but I didn't want to bother you with it before. I have the document for you to sign."

His gaze lingered on her for a moment. "I'll look it over now if you'd like," he said at last. "We can get this out of the way before we leave."

Her belly tightened. Would they be able to put the tension this was causing aside?

"Claude is picking us up at a quarter after seven so we

can make our reservation."

It was closing in on seven now, she knew. "I'll be right back."

She dashed upstairs, grabbed the paper and a Merriam pen, and ran back down. Breathless, she returned to find her aunt and uncle gazing quizzically in her direction. The new bottle of wine sat on the round table in the entryway, unopened. No one spoke, but Beau excused himself with a polite nod and crossed toward her. She made herself hand him the NDA.

From the corner of her eye, she saw her aunt and uncle quietly leave the room.

He set the document on the round table, right across from that bottle they should be drinking to celebrate their date, and he braced his hands on the wood, reading it. His finger traced the lines, and with each pass of his finger from left to right, she could detect a new feeling growing between them: caution. His shoulders were braced, and hers were up to her ears.

"I usually don't handle this sort of thing, but everything seems worded okay," he said.

Right. His mother did. Likely his lawyer too. For a moment, she regretted putting him on the spot, but better that she do so now than risk Quinn showing up to steamroll everything.

Beau extended his hand out, not looking at her, and it took her a moment to realize he was waiting for the pen in her hand. She thrust it out, and he grabbed it. The scratching sound of the pen against the paper grated on her nerves, as terrible as nails on a chalkboard. When he drew up and thrust the signed NDA back, his gaze was direct.

"Are you sure you still want to go on our date?"

His words made her heart pound. "Of course. That's not what this is about. I need you to understand that."

He looked off, tapping his thigh. "Right now it feels

like you don't trust me completely, and that feels downright rotten. Especially after everything we've shared."

She clenched her fists. "It feels rotten to me too, but this venture is the first one I get to lead as a Merriam, and there's a certain order to how we do things. I've bypassed some of those steps, trusting everything's going to fall into place. Because I know you." *Or think I do.* "Not everyone I work with and for understands that. So please don't put this on me. If it were up to me, we'd have had the contract signed and legalized when I first met you."

The tapping on his trousers wasn't near as fast as her heart rate, but still she felt its vibration. "I'd like to sign the contract, but I just can't yet. I told you that from the beginning."

"Yes, you did, and until today, I hadn't thought about asking for an NDA in lieu of the contract. Honestly, I didn't expect you to come here so soon. Beau, I know the timing looks bad, but these things are normally covered in the contract."

"Yet I keep coming back to trust. If you don't trust me, maybe we should call this off. I mean, I've trusted you with some deeply personal things about myself, and I didn't make you sign anything. Do you have any idea what kind of fodder that would be for the media given who I am?"

That he would remind her of his celebrity status only made the gap between them widen. Business. Pleasure. She could almost hear Quinn's voice reminding her they didn't mix.

She inhaled jaggedly, searching for the right word. "I know you trusted me with something very personal, and I can't tell you how much that means to me. But that's personal, and this is business. I want to trust you completely, but even you have to admit you're in the midst of a great transition. Beau, seeing you today, you look ready for a photoshoot for *GQ*, not *Southern Living*."

"Why can't I be on both magazine covers?" He closed the distance between them, his head inches from her face. "Why can't Beau Masters like wearing torn jeans and a T-shirt with his favorite boots and this kind of get-up?"

She went with honesty. "I don't know. Currently, it's not your image."

"Then my image needs changing. My *roots* need plucking. So let's circle back to the original question here. Do you still want to go out to dinner with me? And don't say yes unless you plan on kissing me like you did in the kitchen the other day because that's how I want this to go. This ain't no dinner for friends or business associates. This is for one man and one woman who fancy each other because dammit, Caitlyn Merriam, I fancy the hell out of you."

His drawl had gotten thicker, his voice louder. She stood trembling in her three-inch heels.

The loud bleating of a goat trickled through the air, forlorn and questing.

"Beau, that damn goat is back, crying for you," her uncle shouted from the other room. "You'd better take care of it before you and Caitlyn leave. I will not listen to that sad call while I'm eating dinner. It will give me indigestion."

"Yes, sir," Beau called out. "Excuse me a moment."

She followed slowly as he strode out the back, her mind a jumble of confusing thoughts. What was she really afraid of here?

A loud bleating reached her ears followed by some slow-drawl cursing. Beau Masters wore Italian shoes now and cursed. He even drank pink champagne. What had happened to the sweet, simple Beau she'd dreamed about, the one she'd wanted to help her sell her perfume?

Her feet carried her to the French doors. Beau had sunk down onto his knee in front of Chou-Chou, talking to the goat, rubbing him under those flappy little ears. The sight could have been in a movie, what with the fields of lavender behind them. A handsome man petting a goat, at home in a stylish European wardrobe.

It wasn't the scene she wanted for her new perfume. The businesswoman questioned whether it could make her perfume a success.

But did she still want the *man*? Was she interested enough in him to discover where all this change was leading? Time to move forward or bail, she realized.

The goat lowered its small head and butted Beau in the chest. He laughed, falling back onto his new gray trousers. He pushed Chou-Chou's head away from him playfully, but the moment brought clarity. A month ago, her tough-as-nails brother, Trevor, had been chased by a lovesick alpaca. Now, Trev could be a lot of things, but he'd never been an animal lover. And yet he'd become one, and not just with the alpaca lovingly called Buttercup. He'd embraced his new wife's cat and dog with equal aplomb. He'd *changed*, right before her eyes.

But not the core of him. He'd...

What was the word she was looking for? He'd expanded.

Perhaps that's what Beau was doing right before her eyes.

He stood, laughing, brushing the seat of his trousers off as if he didn't care that the baby goat had just gotten an expensive pair of pants dirty. The decision was easy, ultimately, the truth as clear in her mind as crystal.

She wanted *him*, the man.

Opening the French door, she started walking toward him. He looked over, and his laughter faded. In his blue eyes, she could see he expected her decision and was bracing himself for the possibility she might say no. He tucked his hands in his pockets, strolling to meet her halfway.

"I'd still like to go," she said, the hot breeze making her skin feel even tighter. "Do I need to apologize for earlier?"

He lifted a shoulder. "I was in the wrong too. Let's set it aside. Claude should be arriving any time now."

They walked companionably back toward the house, her aunt and uncle standing at the open French doors. Aunt Clara had topped off their champagne glasses, but they sat untouched in their hands.

"You know," Beau said, his drawl as spicy as the lavender, "I'd told myself I wanted us both to have the most romantic night of our lives tonight."

She felt her heart melt. "That's a tall order." But not surprising from the man who'd kissed her gently and walked her back to the house, hand in hand, after telling her about one of the worst discoveries of his life.

He took his hands out of his pockets and framed her face. "Someone at my label today asked if I'd come up with one of my signature love songs for the new album, and I thought of you. At the time, I wasn't sure what I would call it. Now I know."

She held her breath. This was the man she knew, the one her heart tripped for.

"'Sunshine in Her Eyes,'" he said, tucking her hair behind her ears. "I think it might be the best song I'm ever going to write."

Whoa! What did a girl say to that? "Thank you, but you'll still need to leave your goat at home tonight." Ibrahim's comment about her using humor in serious moments came to mind. She was doing it again.

"A goat wouldn't add romance?" He laughed, the sound loud and free. "Come on, honey. Our carriage awaits."

She reached for his hand, Chou-Chou calling for him sadly as they walked off. Waving to her aunt and uncle, she gathered her crazy emotions together.

She wanted this night to be the most romantic of their lives as much as he did.

***

"Clara, dear," Arthur said, watching the young couple walk off in the fading sunlight, "our romantic moment got interrupted by that darn goat." First, that crazy alpaca in Ireland and now this... "Next time we visit a Merriam, I am asking up front about farm animals."

She socked him in the arm, like she often did. "Oh, stop. At least it's cute. And the interruption was timely, it seems. Whatever Beau was signing seemed to cause a whole bunch of tension between them."

"Business papers, I imagine," Arthur said. "Trouble always comes when you mix love and money."

Picking up her champagne, she flounced—that was a good word for it—onto the leather sofa. He took his time sitting. Some people slid off Italian leather and ended up on the floor.

"I don't think we have much to worry about," Clara said. "They clearly like each other. I haven't seen that kind of a makeover in a man since George Michael went from being straight to out of the closet."

"I don't know who this George Michael fellow is, but after looking into Beau Masters more online, I can tell you one thing: whatever is troubling Beau isn't public yet." He'd spent the morning looking up everything he could about the singer. "A transformation like this is motivated by something. I mean, yesterday he looked like somebody from *Beverly Hillbillies* and today he could have been on *Lifestyles of the Rich and Famous*."

"And you don't know who George Michael is? *Oh, Arthur*." She lifted one of her legs on the sofa, the better to tantalize him. Until they'd reconnected, he hadn't thought a woman her age could have such great legs.

"Well, who is he?" If he didn't ask, she'd just pester him.

"He's deceased, but he was a British singer. Quite

the hottie in his 'Faith' days, let me tell you. The original bad boy in leather surrounded by models like Cindy Crawford and Naomi Campbell."

"Oh, pfft. You and your fashion, Clara."

"Only George got outed from the closet in a Beverly Hills bathroom by an undercover cop who caught him soliciting sex, and it didn't go so well after that. So sad."

"You think Beau is gay? Good Lord, Clara, sometimes I can't account for your thinking. That man is no more gay than I am."

She laughed. "Of course he's not gay. He wants to eat her up."

He put his hands over his ears. "Lalalala."

"Arthur, I only brought up the comparison because Beau's makeover was so drastic. Heavens, I'm going to need a gin and tonic after all this. Do you think they have the fixings?"

"The French hate the British and vice versa, so it's doubtful. Come on, we should eat. I'll probably end up waiting up for Caitlyn. Seeing her leave for a date reminded me of Jill and Meredith."

"Who are both happily married to good men and who've given you great-grandchildren. Oh, Arthur, sometimes I wish we could have had children together."

The wistfulness in her voice caught him by surprise. "We both led other lives, Clara." But while his other life had been happy, he knew hers had not.

"But you don't ever wonder?" she asked, sitting up and gazing at him steadily with those big blue eyes of hers.

The eighty-year-old in him wanted to give a snarky answer about being grateful he still got it up every day. That wasn't the man she needed to hear from now. "When we first met, when I was a young, handsome man, and you were an adorable beauty yet total brat—"

"Hah!"

Since she'd always loved his playful nickname, he

didn't apologize. "Back then, yes, I did wonder. I thought they'd be rather wonderful, those children."

She sighed and scooted closer to lay her head against his chest. "I do love you, Arthur Hale."

Another love match this late in life... Wasn't he the luckiest man alive? "And I you, dear Clara."

He kissed the top of her hair, and she wrapped her arms around him. Sunlight filled the main room, prisms dancing on the stone walls. He'd been reluctant to retire from the career he loved, but holding this woman in a French farmhouse surrounded by lavender? It wasn't a bad way to go...

"Come on," he said, pulling her up. "Let's go find Hargreaves and see if he's taken care of your gin and tonic fixings. Then we'll talk him into putting dinner on the table and joining us out on the portico. Someone needs to silence that darn goat." He could still hear it crying forlornly.

"Let's persuade Ibrahim to join us too. The man works way too much. Arthur, did you know he just lost his wife?"

"Loved her, did he?"

"Very much, Caitlyn says. I thought you might talk to him. Since you went through the same thing..."

When he'd lost his Harriet, he'd never expected to love like that again. Leave it to a Merriam to surprise him when he thought he was close to knowing it all.

"I thought perhaps seeing us," she said, reaching for his hand, "might give him some hope."

Love. Hope. Family. He didn't know much about perfume making, but situated as they were in the center of it, they seemed like the perfect base notes for one hell of a life.

CHAPTER 17

CAITLYN HAD HELD HIS HAND THROUGH THE ENTIRE CAR ride, but the tension between them hadn't diminished enough for his liking. He'd decided this would be the most romantic night of their lives, and he intended to ensure it was so.

Claude left them off in front of the restaurant ten minutes before their reservation. Perfect.

"Give me a moment," Beau said, kissing her cheek. He walked up to the service stand outside. "I'm Beau, Colette's friend."

"*Oui, monsieur*," the young woman said. "Paula has everything ready."

"We're a touch early," he said, smiling at her. "Would you happen to know if there's a flower stand close by? I forgot to give my lady friend the ones I'd bought in the town square earlier today, and she's still a mite vexed..."

The woman's brow wrinkled. "Vexed?"

"Upset," he finished. "Sorry, my English."

Her lips twitched. "But your English is very good, *monsieur*."

He laughed. "*Touché*."

"And your French is improving."

"I like you already," he said. "Are all Frenchwomen so wonderful? Colette isn't the exception?"

"Oh, she's exceptional to be sure, but we all have our own traits to commend ourselves. Since Colette spoke so highly of you, I will call the flower shop and have them bring an arrangement for you to give to your lady over there. Any preference?"

"I did think the wine-colored dahlias were bold. No roses, though, if they're out of the other."

"We will do our best, *monsieur*," the woman said.

"Thank you," he said, finally feeling like he could manage things in this foreign land although it was feeling less foreign every day. "What is your name, by the way?"

"I'm Bernadette," she said. "*Enchanté*. Good to meet you."

"You as well," he said. "Thank you, Bernadette. Just let me know how best to reimburse you."

"*Bien sur*," she said. "Bring your lady friend. I'll show you to your table."

He spanned the short distance to where Caitlyn stood waiting. "Everything worked out?" she asked.

"You bet. They have the table ready." He took her hand, eager to reestablish their connection.

A server showed them to the corner table under a blue awning. A candle was sputtering in a clear glass jar next to a short blue vase stuffed with wildflowers. He pulled Caitlyn's chair out, and when she sat, he indulged himself by touching a lock of her silky dark hair.

"You really do look beautiful," he said, taking the opposite chair. "I never get tired of looking at you. Although I told the hostess I thought you were still a mite vexed with me. Are you?"

She set down the drink menu she'd picked up and gazed at him, her green eyes searching his face. "When I look at you, it's like seeing someone else. Sometimes it makes me do a double take is all. There's been a lot more emotion on this trip than I expected. I'm feeling vulnerable. Not my comfort zone."

His mind circled back to their earlier discussion, the one causing the underlying tension between them. Ultimately, he understood her confusion. "What can I do to make it easier for you? It's important to me that we get to know each other, Caitlyn. I know attraction and after-dinner strolls can only take us so far, and honestly, I want to go as far down the road with you as I can."

"Maybe be a little patient with me too." She blew out a breath, but the server approached them to ask about wine. He fought off his impatience.

"Done." Beau asked, "How about some champagne? I noticed most people seem to have that, and it's one of your favorites."

"The French often have a glass of champagne to start dinner and then switch to wine," she told him. "I've always loved the idea. Seems to me it's like kicking off the celebration."

He liked that too. He'd never seen drinking as much of a celebration. Growing up, the glass of burning rot-gut Walt always had in hand had signified anger and bitterness. He'd been a messy, mean drunk. The French's approach to drinking was notably different, and he was starting to appreciate the new perspective. "Then let's follow suit. Since this is new to me, please select what sounds best to you. I'm out of my league there."

She ordered in French, and when the server left, he said, "Hearing the sound of your voice is as pleasing as wind chimes on a summer day. Maybe that line will go into the song I'm writing about you."

Leaning an elbow on the table, she rested her head against her palm. "It's a little funny, thinking about you writing a song about me."

The closer intimacy of her pose suited him, and he crowded the table with his big body, propping his elbows on the edge, and leaned toward her. "Honey, I've been writing a song about you from the moment you walked into my office."

"And you wonder why I'm feeling so emotional," she said, but with a smile. "Not every girl has a wonderful man write a song about her."

Seeing himself through her eyes helped settle him. "I'm still working on your song, but here are some of the lyrics so far. Don't poke fun, all right? It's still pretty rough, but it's taking shape." A flush of heat spread over his face as he gathered his breath, knowing he needed to sing the words to her.

"She was more than a breath of fresh air. She was a hurricane coming in off the Gulf.

The cloth of her sexy blue dress moved with her as if storm winds stirred around her.

She was young and beautiful, and she spoke with the full force of her heart.

She talked about women picking flowers, their babies resting on blankets beside them.

When she came out of her shoe and I bent down to help, her arch seemed like a long road I'd traveled, one I'd been on too long alone.

She's the one I've been waiting for my whole life.

My own kindred spirit.

When I look at her, I see sunshine in her eyes."

The light in those cat-like green eyes seemed to shower over him, and he sang softly, pitching his voice low: *"Sunshine in her eyes."*

He saw the tears in those sunshine eyes. Ignoring the heat in his cheeks, he reached for her hand—but she had already reached for him. Her fingers curled around his, squeezing hard in a way that told him she couldn't find any words to respond to him. That was okay. He wasn't sure he could speak right now either.

They were still holding hands when the server brought

their champagne. Not letting go of each other, they reached for their glasses at the same moment.

"My toast," he said, spellbound in a moment he knew he'd never forget. "To the woman who brings the sunshine, even in the darkest times. You make everything brighter. Caitlyn, it's no wonder I fell for you."

Her brows shot up to her hairline. "You're on a roll, but I love it. Beau, I'm falling too."

"Good. Hate to be alone here." Her laughter trickled out as he took that first sip, the bubbles tickling his lips gently in a pleasing way. Perhaps it was Ibrahim's influence, but when he tasted it, he smelled apple and pear and a fresh batch of yeast, almost like from baked bread. The notes reminded him of an expertly blended perfume. No one had ever told him this was possible with drink, and he was glad to have discovered it. It brought light into what had been a dark place for him growing up. He looked around at the other patrons, talking and laughing with their loved ones, sipping champagne, drinking wine.

No one was drunk. Caitlyn was right. Here was celebration.

"The French seem to know how to enjoy life," he said, taking one last look. "I didn't realize until this moment, but no one has their phones out."

She shook her head. "No, it's not like the States. People are present here. They have a phrase you may have heard. *Joie de vivre*. Joy of life."

Joy. He was finding his way to it, he realized, here in this sleepy little village sitting across from the woman he knew he could gaze at forever. "Earlier you said it's like doing a double take, seeing me like this. I'm doing the same each time I look in the mirror. When I saw this Frenchman walking in town today, he looked...comfortable in his own skin. I wanted to feel like that. In these clothes or ripped shirts and dirty jeans. Whatever I'm wearing." He ran a hand over his stubble. "And I'm done dithering. If I like something or want it, I'm going to reach for it. No waiting around or following some guidebook someone else gave me."

"Not all of the suggestions in that guidebook are wrong," she said, keeping her voice low. "I rather like the gentleman side of you, although I was going crazy waiting for you to kiss me."

"If I could go back, I'd ask you out when we were talking at the elevator after our first meeting."

Her lips twitched. "I wanted you to ask me out too. That's why I lingered."

Taking one of her hands, he raised it to his lips and kissed it. "Now I'm hoping to linger with you in a different way. Honey, I want to linger over every inch of you."

"You steal my breath when you talk like that," she whispered.

"I keep wondering how much quieter your voice can get," he teased. "Am I embarrassing you with this talk?"

She blushed a delicate pink. "A little."

"Good," he said, pressing her hand back down on the table. "I plan to do a lot more of it. Oh," he said, catching sight of a young man heading toward the restaurant with a bunch of those wine-colored dahlias, "get ready to blush again."

Sure enough, Bernadette took them from the messenger and brought them to their table, smiling brightly.

"A present from the gentleman," she said as Caitlyn pulled her hands away to take them.

Funny to hear that word—in English—all the way over here in France, so far from home. Although he'd decided to revise the rulebook he'd been given, he found he still identified with being a gentleman. Always would.

"Oh, goodness! These are gorgeous. I love dahlias! How did you know?"

He preened like a prize rooster at the state fair. "They're bold and beautiful like you, honey. Thanks, Bernadette."

"You're most welcome," she said. "When you're ready to order, Paula said to tell you the chef has something special prepared if you're willing to go with a tasting menu."

"I'd love that," Caitlyn said. "And thank you for the flowers, Beau. Oh, I'm flustered."

"Me too, honestly," he decided to say. "I forgot the other bouquet I bought earlier at the farmhouse."

She pressed them to her chest, inhaling them. "You can give them to me later then, and I'll act just as surprised and happy."

His heart turned over in his chest. *"That sunshine in her eyes can make the flowers grow."* Another perfect lyric to add to what he had so far.

Her green eyes were liquid pools when she looked up. Bernadette excused herself, but Beau barely heard her. All background noise faded. All he could hear was Caitlyn's soft breath and the steady beat of his own heart. God, he wanted to kiss her. He rose halfway out of his seat, thinking why not? She leaned forward, and the flowers tickled the underside of his jaw as his lips met hers, all soft and sweet.

When he resumed his seat, she smiled with the full force of that sun inside her. "Thank you, Beau."

"You're most welcome, honey," he said, liking that word as much as the honey he liked to put on a hot, buttered piece of toast.

He could feel the stirrings of a song, but he couldn't put his finger on the music or words yet. *Let them come.*

Like Rye had said, he couldn't bottle up his truth. This album was turning out to be the most honest he'd made, the songs chock full of truth, no sugar-coating.

Paula finally come over and introduced herself, saying she and Colette had known each other since they were children. They talked about Beau's fashion transformation. Colette had told the petite blond woman about his visit that day, how he'd come in wearing a torn shirt and jeans and cowboy boots. She said, "I wish I'd seen it. Colette is right. No one wears jeans like the Americans." Caitlyn barked out a laugh at that, and he found himself grinning as Paula told them about what their chef had in mind. His mouth salivated at her description of roasted beets with sea salt and goat cheese, a whole fish stuffed with citrus and *farigoule*—what Caitlyn translated as thyme since Paula couldn't remember the word in English. Everything he'd eaten so far had suited him, and he was eager to discover more.

Ibrahim had said not to rush the experimentation process. Beau was going to pull out a lawn chair and bask in the sun.

Caitlyn selected a rosé after consulting with Paula, and he sipped it with something akin to revelation. If someone had told him a month ago he'd start drinking one day, he'd have called them a liar. But if that person had said he'd enjoy drinking champagne and a pink-colored wine, he'd have laughed until he cried. But he liked the dance of the fruit and citrus on his tongue, much like he enjoyed the feel of the fine cotton shirt against his skin and the way he could run his finger over the velvet of his jacket and leave a mark.

If anyone had ever told him he'd fall for France and its people, he'd have laughed at that too. This land seemed fragrant with perfume, the bold colors, and the happy sounds of laughter.

The first course came, and he and Caitlyn got down to the business of eating, trading groans and moments of eye-closing silent enjoyment. When she leaned across the table and fed him some of her beets, he picked up his fork later and fed her some of his fish. She asked if he still liked to fish, and he told her he picked up a fishing pole every once in a while. Not as much as when he was a boy, trying his luck in the creeks with a makeshift pole from a hickory tree and earthworms from Mrs. Prentice's garden, which he'd sneak into in the hot humid mornings, plucking a tomato he'd eat on his way to catch something.

He'd forgotten about all that, he realized after finishing the tale. He'd stolen a tomato and technically the earthworms. More than once. His mama had never found out, and if Mrs. Prentice had seen him in the early morning light, she hadn't said a word. And had the sky fallen? No, he'd only been a lonely boy seeking the comfort of the creek, with all its redolent sounds, and the victory of a few rainbow trout for supper.

When the server brought a salad of simple greens after the fish, Caitlyn explained the French often had salad and cheese after the regular meal. He'd never been much for greens, and these windy, curly things were unrecognizable to him, but they tasted peppery yet sweet from the vinaigrette.

"So tell me why you really, *really* wanted to create this perfume?" he asked after the server had cleared their plates again, only to bring them a fig tart, the dark purple fruit encased in the most buttery crust he'd ever tasted. "Man, this is good."

"I love figs," she said. "We have them on our place in Napa. I used to love picking them with Michaela and my brothers and eating them warm off the trees."

She spoke softly about her family. Her eyes had even darkened when she'd mentioned her worry for Connor. He wondered if she knew.

"You read my proposal; it must be the kindred spirit thing that makes you know there's another reason." She pushed her empty plate to the side. "It's a little embarrassing."

Heat was already infusing her face. "More embarrassing than learning my mama lied about who my daddy was? Come on."

"That fact doesn't change who you are deep inside," she said, taking his hand, something they'd both been

doing from time to time as they ate. "A while back, I started dating a guy I thought was...a good guy. We went out
for a while, and he did all the good-guy things. You know...
He called me the next day after we went out. Brought me
flowers. Talked to me for hours late into the night when
one of us was traveling. Opened the door. Helped me with
my coat. Yada yada yada."

"He acted like a 'gentleman.'" He stroked her hand,
starting to understand her fears. "When did you find out
he wasn't a good guy?"

"I didn't see the signs before, but it smacked me in the
face when he offered to give me a boob job as a birthday
present."

Beau reeled back. "What? How could he— What in
the Sam Hill was wrong with him? You're perfect. Those
beauties—" He used his other hand to point at her chest.
"Are perfect. What an ass!" He could have let loose a
whole string of curses, but her face was already as red as
a hot poker.

"Need me to break his legs?" he asked when she remained quiet. "No, that's not good enough. A man who
says that to a woman deserves a few inches cut off his
dick. But wait. He probably didn't have that big of a dick
to start with." Usually he wasn't crass, but New Beau
thought it apt.

Her lips twitched then, and he knew she was putting
the crap behind her. "You're right about him not being
much of a man. When it came down to it, he thought he
was doing me a favor. He couldn't imagine I would be
happy with my boobs as they were. He clearly wasn't, but
he was nice enough not to say so. And that's what pissed
me off the most. He made the suggestion in such a way
that he could still tell himself he was a good guy after I
balked."

"A guy like that never thinks he's an asshole." Why
had no one ever told him how powerful it could feel to

use a hard word when the situation called for it? "So this perfume was your way of reminding yourself that you were good enough and that you mattered. To yourself. To someone." He remembered the words from her proposal. "You wanted to remember the core of you too."

"The roots of being a woman," she said. "It's not easy sometimes, feeling sexy or confident. I talk a good game, but I've got my feelings of inadequacy and doubts."

"Everyone does, honey," he said. "I expect even Ibrahim, our Perfume Jedi, does, and he's one of the wisest men I've met in some time."

She smiled, the candlelight flickering over her face. "I like that you called him ours. He's turned out to be so much more than a perfume master. This whole process... It's like a personal inventory, a life review. I mean, those questions he gives me, rolled up in those tiny scrolls, they've made me dig deep. I'm journaling about scents, which leads to memories."

"I'm loving it too," Beau said. "Making a perfume is like making a song. Ibrahim's encouraging me to search for my own truth, I guess. I figure coming here with you might be the best decision I've ever made since I picked up a guitar or wrote my first song."

"That's one of the sweetest things anyone has ever said to me," she said, her voice soft and hushed, and he leaned forward to better hear it.

"Even though you and me speak kinda different. You with your Yankee accent and me with my Southern one... I figure we speak the same language." He took her hand and put it on his chest. "We speak the language of the heart."

She stroked his chest, her fingers dipping between the buttons. His skin prickled at her touch. "We should tell Paula not to bring the cheese plate," she said.

He could feel the smile spread slowly over his mouth. "Eager to leave? Honey, we have a lot more romance to bring in tonight. In fact, if I could reach up and bring down one of those stars over our heads, I'd do that tonight even though they couldn't shine as bright as that sunshine in your eyes."

Another caress from those delicate fingertips made him edge even closer. She leaned into him, and he kissed her, using his lips to show her how much she mattered to him.

When they pulled apart, she said, "Beau, you've been romancing me for hours now. Until tonight, I thought romance was a bunch of gestures, but the way you talk to me. About me. I feel like I've never been romanced before."

"I find romancing you is one of the easiest things I've ever done," he said, the huskiness of his own voice reminding him of the low notes of musk.

She took his hand and kissed the back of it, her eyes radiating that golden sunlight.

"Honey, I just want to make sure I'm doing it enough to tell you all the things I can't seem to put words to."

"Then we should leave so you can show me," she whispered.

Her decision was in her voice, and it made his belly tighten. His heart throbbed once and settled. He was to become her lover tonight. Somehow the word struck him in a new way. Love. Her. The person who'd invented the word must have understood the act well.

He had to wait a while for the server to reappear. No one seemed to be pushing anyone out of their tables. He asked for the check, only to hear that yes, Paula did have a cheese plate coming. Caitlyn gave in, saying they would be delighted. Beau figured the kindness was enough to make them linger a while longer.

"It's a nice gesture," she said, shrugging. "You made friends today."

"I did, didn't I?" He shook his head. "How great is that?"

"Pretty great," she said. "When you receive true affection from the French, it's a special thing. But I'm not surprised. You treat people well. You listen to them."

He gazed at her, the candle sputtering on its last legs. "You mentioned liking that I listen to you. Were you not listened to much growing up? In a family with seven kids, I expect there was a lot of chatter."

"And not much time for one-on-one attention. You know, Ibrahim asked me why lavender. I finally remembered. My dad brought me lavender soaps from Provence for my sixteenth birthday. He always worked a lot, what with running the company. Unlike our generation, he didn't have any brothers or sisters to help him. So when he thought about me in the middle of a business trip..."

The light bulb went on. "You felt like you mattered to him. He wasn't just celebrating your birthday, he was celebrating you."

"Bingo. Does that make me sound silly?"

He blew out a rude noise. "Honey, you're talking to a man who had a breakdown over his father. Why wouldn't you want him to cherish you? He's your daddy. It's what he's supposed to do."

And not something Walt could ever have done. Perhaps some men might have been big enough to look past the events of his conception and eventual birth, but not many, he thought. He hadn't mattered to Walt Masters because he wasn't his son. Hell, he'd likely been a reminder of his wife stepping out on him.

"You're not here anymore," she said softly as the cheese plate arrived, followed by a glass of Paula's special pear brandy.

"I have a lot of thoughts these days about the past," he said. "Don't mind me."

She took the brandy and sipped, and he reached for his glass. He could smell the burn—the first note of scent reminding him of the hard liquor in Walt Masters'

Mason jar—mixed in with the pear and something like baking spices in a pie.

A deep breath in and out, and he took a sip.

"It's strong," he said, clearing his throat. "There's caramel to the flavor. Huh."

"Wine and spirits are a lot like perfume," she said, echoing his thought from earlier. "God, you should see the tasting notes for some wines. 'This rosé is a bold wine with fresh notes of ripe strawberry—why would you have it any other way?—a touch of orange finished off with hibiscus, clove for extra warmth.' Some of it is so pretentious."

He laughed. "I expect perfume can be the same. But yours won't be."

She was quiet a moment as she sipped her brandy. "No," she finally said, "*ours* won't be."

The warmth of the brandy mixed with the warmth in his chest. By the time they finally left the restaurant after the three-kiss send-off, he was feeling warm all over. The air was fragrant with the lingering notes of dinner and the pungent scent of flowers hanging from the walls enclosing them.

"Come, let's walk," he said, taking the hand not holding the dahlias. "I like that I can stroll around like a regular guy. If I were back home, I'd take you walking down my private path to Dare River. The fireflies would be out winking, and the cicadas would be singing their sad song."

The clock in the town square showed it was a quarter past twelve, and only a few couples sat under the bubbling fountain in the middle, kissing in passes like two dancers trying to find their rhythm.

Beau understood. He was still finding his rhythm with this woman, but like every song he'd written, he knew it would come, and it would be just right when it did. In the meantime, he kept breathing her in, feeling the warmth of her hand in his, and listening to the music of her voice.

His heart would tell him when they had it right, and then she'd be his for what he hoped might be forever.

CHAPTER 18

CAITLYN DIDN'T WANT THIS NIGHT TO END.

They walked hand in hand, navigating the meandering side streets of the quiet Provençal village with no destination in mind, content just to be together. Now and again, he'd comment on the quiet of the night, the unfamiliar French music playing softly from an open window, and she'd answer, or maybe just trail her fingers over his hand. With him, there was no impulse to digress. To fill the silence with unnecessary words. There was warmth there, and a connection so visible she realized they'd started to walk at the same pace.

Like one person.

Shivers rained down her spine, and she paused on the cobbled street. The soft golden light fell on Beau's chiseled face, and she traced his lips, wanting to kiss him. He leaned his head down to her, barely touching their mouths together. His hot breath sent another wave of shivers through her, and he pulled back and started to take off his jacket. Then he laid it over her shoulders, his scent enveloping her along with the warmth from his body.

"I wasn't cold," she said softly, stepping closer. "But I like that you thought to take care of it."

"I don't want my woman cold," he said, his drawl making her knees weak.

How many times had she heard Beau Masters sing about his woman and wonder: who is that lucky woman anyway? Now, to hear him say those words about her... "Am I your woman?"

He leveled back but lifted his hands to rest on her shoulders. "I'd like you to be. The question for you, I guess, is whether that suits you."

"Suits me?" She laughed. "Are you kidding?"

He cocked his head to the side. "Be sure you know it's me saying it—this man in the process of changing—and not the Beau of old."

She felt a tremble in her belly. "A fair point, but I feel... Oh, this sounds so corny."

He cupped her cheek. "No, tell me."

"There's this peace inside me," she said. "It's crazy really. Like I felt when we first met. Holding your hand. Walking through this town tonight. Simply talking. It's... easy."

"I always figured it was supposed to be, although I had no real models for it," he said, stroking her cheek. "It was just something I knew. In here."

He raised their joined hands to his chest. She felt the warmth there and the steady cadence of his heart. It reminded her of when he'd made this same gesture their first night on the farm. They'd come so far since then.

Gazing deeply into her eyes, he said, "I thought we might drive back to the farmhouse so we can let the driver get on home and then take a car out all by our lonesome. Find a private spot to listen to some music. Look at the stars. I...now I'll be corny. I've always wanted to do that with a girl on a date."

"Why didn't you ever?"

"Well, the girl I asked in high school said we'd get eaten alive by mosquitos, and she was probably right.

Still, I thought some bug spray might help. Truthfully, she thought I was too sensitive. Corny even. I stopped sharing those kinds of things with girls and put them into songs instead. They got a better audience that way. Ironic, isn't it?"

She wondered if the same was true of the twilight strolling. Had others poo-pooed it too? Crazy. "How in the world could anyone think that wasn't romantic? Let's call Claude right now and head home." *Home.* That word made her shiver again. She'd spent most of her life jet-setting, making her home wherever she went, and yet this felt natural.

It felt right.

"How could anyone suggest you're not absolutely perfect the way you are? I'm still upset about what that asshole said to you, by the way."

She wrapped her arms around him. "Forget both of them. You're not corny, and I'm..." *Say it.* "Perfect as I am."

He grimaced. "I can tell you're still working through that one, honey. Perhaps you'll let me help a little tonight when we're out under the stars. I...want you to know I've thought about the sleeping arrangements, what with you having relatives visiting and such. I don't want anyone to be uncomfortable. When you're ready to share yourself with me, we'll figure out a way to be private. I want you to feel comfortable." He laughed. "And I don't want to worry your aunt or uncle will take me to the woodshed for being friendly with you."

She'd thought about the full house too. "Aunt Clara would probably give you a blue ribbon. Not sure about Uncle Arthur yet. He's more crusty."

"So I noticed," he said, tapping her playfully on the nose. "Come on and call Claude. He prefers to speak French, I think."

"You did great today, setting everything up for our date." She kissed his cheek. "Thank you."

"Hargreaves and Colette did that. I only made a few suggestions. But the flowers and sitting in a car listening to music... That's all mine."

An hour later, they were doing just that, lounging on the back of the sedan, looking up at the constellations blinking light years away. He'd chosen Raï music, and its haunting, passionate blend seemed perfect for the warm night. Moonlight spilled over the lavender fields, casting the flowers in silver.

Maybe it was the music or the ongoing process of making this perfume—so much more than she'd bargained for—but Caitlyn found herself taking stock of her life. She was thirty-two and leading her first true Merriam business venture. A few months ago, she'd been reeling from Jace the Jerk's insult to her body. Tonight, everything inside her was as quiet as the land around them. No chatter inside her head to make her feel like she didn't have it all together. With her hand on Beau's warm thigh, she pretty much wanted to stay here forever.

"What are you thinking about?" he asked, turning toward her.

"Life. Right now everything feels...perfect. I want it to stay that way." She shifted to face him. "What about you?"

He made a sound filled with mystery. "I'm thinking about life too, I guess. How mad and betrayed I still feel. How I'm relieved—grateful even—that Walt Masters isn't my real father. I wonder who my real father is and if I'll ever find him. I'm hoping the geneticist will have a line on him, but the thought of reaching out to him scares me too."

His voice was hoarse, and she ran her hand down his chest in comfort. He grabbed it and held it against his heart. "I can't imagine how that must feel. So you would want to meet your real father?"

He sighed. "I suppose I might change my mind if I find out he's in jail or something, but some part of me needs, no, wants to face the man who helped give me life. He may not have done much to raise me, but I carry things from him with me. My looks, maybe even some of my mannerisms. When my geneticist gives me her full report, I hope to know a little more. It's amazing how they've figured out a process to gather information about you from simple things like hair or spit. Sorry, my language. Wait. Forget I said that. That's Old Beau. Nothing wrong with saying spit."

"Not in my world," she said, her lips twitching.

"I was also thinking how all the chaos inside me seems to settle when I'm with you," he said, running his fingers over the back of her hand where it still lay on his chest. "I've been sitting here, searching myself, I guess you could say, and I struck upon something. I'd been pondering whether I should say it, but I'm a new man, and I want to. Seems untruthful to do otherwise."

Her chest tightened, but then he lifted her hand to his mouth and placed a gentle kiss to it. He turned his head, the moonlight cascading over the sharp planes of his face, and she thought he was intentionally showing himself to her. His eyes shone, lit up by something more than moonlight. This was firelight, the kind that warmed the heart.

"I may still be working some things out, but I'm falling in love with you," he said, his voice tender and deep. "Whatever happens between us—personally I'm hoping for forever—I'll always be grateful for it. You've shown me what it really feels like to love a woman. I hope you'll let me show you what it feels like for a long time yet."

Her throat closed, so thick with an emotion she couldn't swallow. Oh, this man!

"I don't expect anything in return," he continued. "I certainly didn't say it to pressure you into feeling or saying anything. I only...tonight I found myself needing to tell you. That's all."

She cleared her throat, turning so the light fell over

her face too. "I know this is fast for both of us, but since I met you, I've been feeling things I've never felt before for anyone. They stir me up and also give me peace, and for a firecracker like me—that's what my family calls me sometimes—it's a big deal. You make me think it's okay to slow down. And when I'm with you, I feel warm in here."

She lifted his hand to the place between her breasts where a patch of soft skin peeked out.

"I'm falling in love with you too," she said. "The man I met in Nashville and this new one who's coming to the surface here." What would he look like when he finished the process? Would he still create these feelings inside her? God, she hoped so, but she realized a part of her was still scared. He didn't know what he was becoming, and she didn't either.

"Both men thank you," he said, leaning forward and kissing her cheek.

She turned her head a fraction so their lips were inches apart. "Maybe this is the perfect place for us to... make love." She'd never used those words before. With her three other boyfriends, the sex hadn't been as meaningful as her connection with Beau already felt.

He kissed her. Softly. Gently. Warmly. Her toes curled in her heels.

"I'd like that very much," he said, chuckling. "Problem is, I couldn't work up the courage to ask for Hargreaves' help with buying protection, and ordering it online seemed presumptuous. Maybe we should just fool around a little and tomorrow you can go to the village with me."

"On a sex shopping spree?" She poked at his chest, laughing herself. "First fashion and now this."

"Old Beau is dying here, honey," he said, shaking his head. His cheeks looked a little pink in the low light.

She couldn't help but tease him. "I don't know what the French word for 'protection' is. I might have to ask Hargreaves. Or Ibrahim."

"Now you're making fun," he said, pressing her back against the cool metal of the car. "Here I was, trying to be a good guy again."

"Protection shouldn't be a good guy or bad guy kinda thing. Oh, I'm sorry, I didn't realize this might upset you because of your...father situation."

He sat up straight. "It didn't cross my mind until now. I was only..."

She was an idiot. "I'm sorry. I shouldn't have teased you. I have a sick sense of humor sometimes. Beau, I'm on the pill. No more protection needed." She knew he'd be conscientious about his sexual health, but still she said, "I'm safe."

"Good, because so am I," he said, lowering her again and kissing the soft skin under her clavicle where she'd dotted her perfume earlier.

"Are you seriously planning on making love to me on top of this car? I never took you for a rap artist. They talk about doing things on their Escalades. Oh, but you country boys do them in the back of your pickup trucks, right? And here we only have a black sedan. So boring."

"Are you nervous? Is that what all this teasing is about?"

She gulped. "Probably. I'm always nervous in the beginning. My mind starts spinning. I mean, at least I have matching underwear on and shaved my legs. You know. The things a girl thinks about." She wouldn't tell him that dark voice in the back of her head was wondering if he'd be disappointed by what her breasts looked like without her bra. Damn Jace the Jerk.

He reached for her hand. "I'm a little nervous too, which I figure seems right. This is a big deal. You know I met a Frenchman today who told me one of the things that makes a man a man is how he makes love to a woman. Do you have any idea how much that blew my mind? I'd never given it much thought before. Bottom line. I plan to make love to you with everything I am and then some."

Her brain finished exploding from the litany—he'd met a Frenchman who'd said *that* and what was it about the part *and then some*. Good Lord, she was going to slide off this car in a second. "Well, in the interest of helping you with a song, how about I throw your jacket on the ground followed by your shirt and pants—you don't have an aversion to dirt, I've noticed—and we lie down here in the fields of lavender?"

His mouth twitched. "I could do that so long as I'm not the only one stripping here."

She inched off the car, her heels sinking into the warm earth. "I'd never let you do that all by yourself. But my dress stays away from the dirt. It's one of my favorites."

"It should be," he said, hefting himself off the car and standing next to her. "You look as pretty as a picture in it. I've been trying all night not to look at that open spot between your breasts, but I can't say I succeeded." He ran his finger down that bare patch of skin and then traced the edge of her neckline. "Did you put perfume here?"

When his head leaned down to that spot, she almost fell backward. Luckily his hands clasped her hips. She closed her eyes. "Yes, of course I put perfume there."

"Good," he said, inhaling deeply. "I want to take in all of your scents tonight."

He slid the jacket off her shoulders to the ground and started to unbutton his shirt. "In the interest of making you comfortable, I'll undress first."

"Don't be silly," she said. "I can do it too."

He caught her hands as she reached for the hem of her dress. "Let me help at least, honey. Seeing you undress the first time is something I plan to remember until my dying breath."

The words this man used. His hands slid up the backs of her legs, much like he'd done when he'd kissed her in the kitchen, leaving a trail of fire in their wake. He tugged her dress up and over her head, leaving her in the white lacy bralette she'd bought in Paris and her matching thong.

"My God," he said, running his hands over her hips before cupping them. "You're as perfect as a sunrise and as beautiful as a lake."

His shirt was partially unbuttoned, and she leaned forward and kissed the center of his chest, directly over his heart. "I love it when you talk to me like that." Her fingers took care of the rest of the buttons, and she let his shirt fall to the ground next to the bed they were making for their first time together. She already knew it was going to be one of the most powerful moments of her life.

He kissed the soft side of her neck, taking care of his pants. "I'm glad you like it. I hope you don't mind me taking my time. I want to savor every second with you."

Before she could chicken out, she unhooked her bra and stepped back to allow him to look at her in the silver light. She needed to reclaim a part of herself tonight. Beau's sharp intake soothed the nerves fizzing in her stomach.

"You're soft and round and beautiful here," he said, tracing the underside of her breasts with what Caitlyn could only feel was reverence. "Put any final lies to rest right now with me."

That he understood, that he cared...

She threaded her hands in his hair as he sank to a knee before her, taking one nipple into his mouth and softly sucking. She felt the weight of what she'd been carrying fall to the ground. Pleasure took its place, his mouth adding to her benediction.

"You're beautiful here," he said, releasing her and standing, cupping both her breasts. "Don't let me or any man ever make you feel different. That's truth, honey. God's honest truth."

Tears burned her eyes, and a place in the back of her throat grew tight, so she lifted up on her tiptoes to kiss him. Her shoes would have to go, but she wouldn't concern herself with that right now. All she wanted to do was kiss him and feel his warm, heavy body over hers.

His mouth opened, sensing her need, and his tongue met hers in perfect rhythm. A slow slide at first and then a playful tangle. He wrapped his arms around her hips, bringing them flush, and the force of his desire burned against her belly. Yes, she wanted him and then some. *And then some more*, she thought.

As if he sensed her thoughts, he slid his hand down until he cupped her butt and then rubbed himself against her. She let out a moan, the sound muted by the slow friction of their mouths mating. He tugged her thong down, making space to slide it off her body. His dark eyes lowered. He reached out to the V of her thighs, tracing it lightly with his hand.

"Beautiful here too," he said, lowering to both knees. "Lean back and let me love you."

She let him lower her to their makeshift bed on the ground. The land was still warm, the heat from the sunshine still palpable somehow. He opened her legs slowly, settling between them—and then his mouth was on her. The first soft touch of his lips sent her hips shooting off the ground. She was ready for him, ready for all of him. But she wanted this now, and as he slid his tongue inside her, she let herself take it.

She came in a flash of fire, the long line of her body arching off the ground in the moonlight. But still he took his fill of her, exploring her curves and textures, until she burned for him again.

"Now this would be a perfume for the ages," he said softly as she came back to herself. "But I rather like knowing it's mine and yours to share."

She inhaled the moment, wanting to bottle it in her

memory. Lavender. Earth. Musk. Sweat. And then something...a little metallic and a little floral. Her. In the arms of her lover.

"Come," she said, leaning up on an elbow and cupping his cheek. "Let's make another one together."

He slid up her body, trailing kisses along the way. She trailed her hand down the hard planes of his naked back, learning the texture of his skin and the way he responded to her touch. His muscles would tense and relax in her wake, but not until she touched the crown of his desire, eliciting a deep rumble of a groan, did she feel the full force of the power coursing between them. She sensed they both had the power to make each other become new.

Her touch transformed to benediction as she caressed her way across the geography of his body, this body he'd thought he knew but now seemed to pose so many questions. *Who am I? Who am I from?* Every bone, every feature needed her touch, so it could come back to its core truth.

He was simply Beau.

"You're your own man," she said, tracing his jaw, feeling the call to heal the parts of him weighed down with lies like he had done for her. "Don't let anyone ever make you believe differently."

He pressed his forehead to hers, struggling with emotions that had him tensing up for a different reason now. She felt the struggle and held him until he said, "Thank you, honey."

The only answer that was needed was the press of her lips to his. He met her then, his muscles relaxing. She felt as though the earth under them was absorbing everything into itself, almost like it was composting all the lies and wounds they'd carried and making room for something new and beautiful to grow.

"I want you inside me," she whispered when they broke apart, breathing hard.

It had to be now, with the moon bearing witness and the earth holding them in place. He brushed the most private part of her, and she shifted to give him entry. He seemed to know it because he whispered against her lips, "I love you," taking both her hands in his against the soft, warm earth and filling every inch of her with himself.

She heard the words in her heart before she spoke them. "I love you too." There was no denying the full truth of it now.

He stilled inside her, big and hot and full and ever so perfect. "God, Caitlyn. You. This. I've been waiting my whole life for you."

She believed him and felt her soul answer the call. Her eyes closed, white light peeking at the corners, as he started to thrust, first slow and languid before picking up the pace. He flowed into her like the tide, only to recede and then return. She opened herself up to his every movement, excitement filling her blood. They were merging now, becoming one in a way she'd only imagined was possible.

His breath was fast and hot against her ear, and she opened her eyes to see him poised above her, straining in the tide. "Come," she said, tilting her hips to give him deeper access.

She felt a force gathering inside her belly, swirling like the tide coming in and out of her, and then she was thrust forth into the sea of their own making. Crying out, she tensed around him and heard his answering shout followed by a primal, earthy groan.

"Oh, Christ," he rasped out, some of his weight coming down over her in the aftermath. "God, I never swear like this, but I can't seem to... Holy ever-loving Christ, Caitlyn. I never knew..."

She understood what he meant but couldn't say so. Her throat seemed to have gone dry. *This* is what sex was supposed to be like? Part of her wanted to laugh, rise to her feet, and throw her hands up to the sky with him. The other wanted to stay here with him inside her, their bodies replete from the rhythm they'd just danced.

Kissing his neck, she let herself soften even more under him. "I'd like to stay like this for a while longer."

"Forever if you'd like," he whispered back, his voice full of love and promise.

He gathered himself and lifted his head. Their eyes met, and this time it wasn't only moonlight she saw in his eyes.

She saw sunshine there too.

CHAPTER 19

ARTHUR KNEW A SATED COUPLE WHEN HE SAW ONE. Didn't he look in the mirror every morning after he and Clara showered? That beautiful woman who'd re-invigorated his life drank her coffee smugly next to him, and he waited for the elbow he knew was coming. The sharp jab to his ribs made him smile.

"Good morning, you two," he called out. Standing in the kitchen doorway with their hands on each other, they hadn't even noticed him and Clara sitting at the kitchen table by the window. Ah, *l'amour*...

"Uncle Arthur!" Caitlyn jumped apart from Beau, dropping her hands. "Aunt Clara. Didn't see you there."

"No kidding." He pulled off a piece of croissant. "How was your date?" Asking the obvious wasn't a bad thing. People liked to share happy times, and he liked to hear their stories.

The young couple gazed at each other, and Arthur could hear wedding bells. Well, that was fast. They'd been downright angsty before, but it seemed they'd come to a major understanding, one he knew went beyond sex. The physical couldn't make a person glow like Caitlyn was doing this morning, and Beau looked more transformed than he had after his shopping trip.

"The most romantic night of my life," Caitlyn breathed.

"Mine too," Beau said, his voice low, his hand brushing her hip in a quick caress.

"Sounds divine, my dears," Clara said, rising from the table. "How about some coffee?"

"That would be great," Caitlyn said, patting Beau's chest like she couldn't keep her hands off him. "You want some too?"

"Sure," he said, his eyes still on Caitlyn. "Thanks, Mrs. Hale."

Caitlyn walked over, glowing more with each step, and pressed a kiss to each of their cheeks.

"Clara, please," Clara said, her expression pleased as punch. "You might take a moment to see Chou-Chou when you can, Beau. I got him settled last night. He misses you terribly when you're gone."

Arthur couldn't make a goat joke. Last night, he'd realized Clara was channeling some of her frustrated mothering impulses into caring for it. So long as she didn't insist on taking it home with them, they'd be okay. He was terrified Hargreaves had some secret skill with goat's milk. Arthur was still getting used to his Indian food.

"I'll check on him," Beau said, finally letting his eyes rest on something other than Caitlyn. Arthur wouldn't be surprised if one of the young people ran into a door, what with the way they kept making eyes at each other. Still, when a person was in love, that's how it should be. Except at his age. Running into a door would make him need stitches in his noggin.

"Beau, I realized you might know a friend of ours, what with you being a country singer," Arthur said. "I saw online that you sang at Rye Crenshaw's annual concert to raise money for domestic violence. Have you met his good friend, Rhett Butler Blaylock? He's a poker player and lives in Dare Valley, our hometown."

His eyebrows shot to his hairline. "I've met him at Rye's

place a time or two. He wears a ten-gallon cowboy hat like nobody else. I didn't realize he lived in your hometown."

Clara gave him a look, and Arthur smiled. She knew he was fishing. He could call Rhett up and mention he'd just met someone Rhett knew and then pump him discreetly for information.

Caitlyn deserved the best, and Arthur wanted to make sure she was getting it. Sure, the man was looking at her like the sun rose and set on her, but he'd been a mess the past couple of days. Arthur had been studying human nature for decades, and he'd learned that a person had to wrestle with his troubles to kick them to the curb. Loving someone couldn't help you with that. Plus, being a journalist with black ink in his veins, Arthur was still curious about the cause of Beau's erratic behavior.

He sensed news when he saw it. Always would.

"It's a small world, isn't it?" Caitlyn caressed Beau's arm. "Has anyone seen Ibrahim today?"

"We had dinner with him last night," Arthur said. "He's hard at work creating your perfume."

"He asked if I'd be willing to visit his lab and do a smelling session with him," Clara said, beaming.

Arthur stood and crossed to where Clara was standing. "Ibrahim's wise enough to realize he needs input from a few beautiful women on this perfume of yours, Caitlyn."

The girl's squeal made Arthur's ears ring. "Oh, I should call my mom and Michaela! We could have a woman-only smelling session."

"What a great idea, dear," Clara said. "Maybe your father could come with Assumpta."

Arthur rubbed her back. Clara wanted so badly to reconnect with her brother, but the stubborn goat was still holding to his brick wall. Shawn *had* attended their wedding, and he'd been pleasant to them both there and at Trevor and Becca's wedding, but he hadn't spoken to Clara alone about the white elephant in the room. Maybe it was best. Some people couldn't fully set aside past grievances. Whatever the case, Arthur thought it best to stay out of the way. They needed to sort things out for themselves.

"I'll go call them right now," Caitlyn exclaimed. "Wait, what time is it in California?" She checked her watch. "Too early. But Michaela... Who knows where she is? I'll call her and see if she picks up." Her feet were already taking her to the doorway, like she was walking on a cloud. "Oh, I forgot." She ran back and kissed Beau on the lips.

Clara grinned while Arthur rolled his eyes.

"Good luck songwriting," she said, dancing out of Beau's reach.

"I think I've found my stride," Beau said, inclining his chin.

Good sex would do that to a man. "Well, Clara and I are going to head out for a walk before it gets too hot." Arthur took her arm and led her to the doorway where Caitlyn was standing. "We'll see you two later."

The moment they were out of range, Clara elbowed him again. "What was that whole thing about Rhett knowing Beau?"

"Caitlyn is in love with that man, Clara," he told her, walking them to the front door. "I owe it to her family to check him out. It's what a responsible matchmaker does."

The sun was blazing in the sky as they ambled across the lawn. His nostrils twitched at the smell of lavender. God, it smelled like a bubble bath every time he stepped outside. Would it still smell like that after the lavender was harvested? God, he hoped it wouldn't smell like pig shit or something worse. Sure, he hadn't embraced this whole perfume thing yet, but Ibrahim was fascinating, he had to admit. Maybe he would ask him more questions about perfume and discover what all the fuss was about.

"Hargreaves vouched for Beau to me," Clara told him

as that darn baby goat started running toward them.

"He's a good judge of character," Arthur said. "Now, Clara, we are not taking the goat home."

She lowered herself to one knee and hugged its spotted white and brown neck. Gosh, it was a cute thing, he had to admit, but still...

"Did I say anything about adopting him?" she asked, blinking those big blue eyes at him.

"No, but I'm only saying. Come on, let's walk."

She patted Chou-Chou one last time before linking arms with Arthur. "You know," she said, "I was thinking about taking a short overnight trip to see a few places a little farther afield. Nice. Marseilles. It's been ages since I've been in this part of France, and I'm remembering all the reasons I love it."

"And it will give Caitlyn and Beau more time alone," he said, shaking his head. Always plotting, his Clara. "Are you planning on inviting Ibrahim along?"

"I had thought about it, but he's working in his lab here." She released his arm so she could stretch in the sun, the sight making his mouth water. "I'll think of something."

"Keep stretching like that and *I'll* think of something." He turned and looked at her, letting her see how much he desired and loved her.

"That's what naps are for, my dear," she said, stopping and kissing him on the mouth. "I'll talk to Hargreaves when we get back."

Of course she would, but he didn't care where they went as long as she was by his side.

***

Beau's songwriting went like clockwork, and he filled the pages of his legal pad. When the sun was hot overhead, Chou-Chou trotted over to him and lay at his feet, bleating to the music of his guitar.

"Sometimes Country, Sometimes Confident" flowed out of him, the chorus scrawled in his chicken scratch.

I'm sometimes country, sometimes confident.
Let the soothing creek of my youth rise in me today.
Tomorrow let me put on city digs and have a rosé.
I'm the same man.
Sometimes country, sometimes confident.

He knew some people were going to laugh at the rosé part, but he didn't care. It was true. His truth. And he was tired of holding it in.

Setting all judgment aside, he let the bitter words he'd been storing up inside him spill out onto the paper. Eyes stinging, he dug the pen into the paper hard enough to tear through.

Damn her, those roots were false.
Like furniture nailed down to the floor.
She was afraid they'd topple over with a good whirl.

She was afraid I'd root them out.
Rip them up and throw them out.
I wasn't the man I thought I'd be.
But she can't root out the truth of me.

Her lies were but a mystery.
Damn her, those roots were false.

Have to find the truth of me.
Have to seek out the best in me.
Have to plant new roots.

I want to damn her.
I hope someday I can thank her.
But dammit, Mama...
Those roots were false.

The words blurred on the page when he finished, and

he broke down, emptying the pain to make room for something new, the fullness of being he was starting to feel with Caitlyn. Chou-Chou ambled up and laid his head against his chest, and he accepted the comfort.

"Oh, Mama," he whispered, letting the bone-deep pain sink into the ground.

When he was hollowed out, he fell back in the hot sun and let its rays soak into him, enliven him. The lavender spikes swayed in the breeze, not knowing their flowers would soon be harvested. Beau realized he was harvesting part of himself now. These songs were about turning his pain into something new. He was healing from the roots up.

"Sunshine in Her Eyes" came next. Most of the lyrics were already swirling around in his head. Like the rays pouring into him, he let his love for Caitlyn radiate out from his heart and onto the page. He had a new refrain after last night, and the power of it stole his breath.

But she isn't only sunshine.
She's moonlight.
And every kind of light in between.

She fills up all the dark places.
Helps me see the truth.
Her light has changed me.
And I hope it rains on me for the rest of my life.

He stared at the page, his handwriting calmer, easier to read for this song. Peace rolled through him like the breeze over the land, and he let it fill him. Gazing out across the fields, he could see himself coming out here with Caitlyn later, walking hand and hand in the moonlight. He hoped they'd be coming here for many years, and it didn't shock him to see an image in his mind of a little boy and girl running ahead of them in the fields. He didn't have all the answers. But he knew he wanted Caitlyn.

His phone rang, a harsh sound in the quiet, and he set his guitar aside and dug it out of his back pocket. It was Dr. Clarridge, and his chest turned into crushed metal. She had answers for him. Was he ready? He firmed his shoulders, put a hand on Chou-Chou, and answered.

"Dr. Clarridge," he said, his voice cracking, and for a singer that was something. "You have your findings already?"

"Yes, Beau," she said. "First, there were no DNA matches to your sample, I'm afraid. I thought it best to say that up front."

Disappointment hollowed out his stomach. He hadn't realized how much he'd let himself hope. "Thanks for trying, Dr. Clarridge."

"I'm sorry it didn't bear fruit. Now for the good news. I know you had concerns about Walt Masters' alcoholism, and I can assure you that your sample shows no trace of the genetic component of that disease."

"Good," he said, feeling an old shadow lift from him.

"I imagine the other health aspects aren't your highest priority right now. You can read about them in the report. Suffice it to say you have good genes, as we'd say in layman's terms."

"Great," he said. "But you're right, I'm more interested in what you learned about my ancestry, mostly on my father's side." His heart was tripping in his chest. He knew his mother's people were from Europe, but not much more than that.

"Beau, I took extra time to review your genetic profile, sifting out what you didn't think came from your mother. Without a sample from her, we're doing some speculating, sure, but I used what we know from mapping other people with similar genetic characteristics. In the end, it wasn't difficult to draw some conclusions.

Like you thought, your mother's ancestry is likely all northern European—Scottish, English, Irish, and a little Germanic. This is also in my report."

He held his breath. "And the rest?"

"Keep in mind this is what we call ethnicity estimation. Since I don't have a sample from your natural father, I can only go off of yours. Also, genetic tests aren't maps. They can't specifically tell us what country someone was from, but the sample you provided does give us a lead. Your genetic profile shows a strong ancestral influence from Spain and what we call indigenous areas. In the latter case, I'd postulate the people of what is now central America. Basically, you're half Spanish, Beau. Whether he's originally from Spain or Mexico or even Argentina, I just can't say."

He remembered Colette and her husband debating the possibility.

"This is...big news, Doc." His mama had insisted they were 'pure-blood' white when he'd asked what to pencil in as his ethnicity on a standardized test in school. She'd made a big deal out of it. Gotten so flustered her face had turned red. He'd known early on she was prejudiced, and he hadn't liked it. It made sense now. She was protecting her secret. Perhaps she was even ashamed. But that wasn't on him. He didn't judge people based on what language they spoke or the color of their skin, and frankly, he never had understood it.

"I don't know anything about that Spanish part of me," he said, running his hand through the loose dirt in the fields. "They have their own language and culture, and I don't know anything about it."

"Ethnicity is a strong influence, according to many social scientists, and even when someone doesn't know exactly where they are from or they weren't raised in that culture, it's common to feel like something is missing."

Had he? He certainly hadn't felt connected to Walt

Masters, but he'd always attributed it to him being a horrible father. God, he wanted answers. "Is there anything else that you found, Doc? Beyond what you'll send in the report."

"No, Beau, that's as far as this part of the science will take us. If your mother changes her mind, we can mine a little more information. I'll send the report over."

She wouldn't change it. She'd made that clear. Depression settled over him like a cloak.

"I understand that," he said. "Thank you, Doc."

"You're most welcome, Beau."

"I'm in France right now, Doc. Can you send it here?"

"Absolutely," she said. "I love France. What part are you in? Paris?"

"No, Provence. I'm sitting in a lavender field actually, writing songs."

"I need to get your job," she said, laughing. "I'm sitting in a lab without windows. Enjoy your songwriting. I know all your fans will be happy to hear the new album, me included."

"I didn't know you were a fan, Doc. I'll make sure to send something over to you for your kindness."

"It's my job, and I'm happy to help, but thank you all the same."

"See ya, Doc."

He dropped his phone and put his head in his hands. He was half Spanish—or Hispanic. Did it matter really? He found it did. Pulling out his phone, he began to research all things Spanish, and when he got bogged down in the history and geography, he turned to its music. He found an article about the flamenco guitar's classic, distinctive sound, accompanied by a picture. He remembered Hargreaves tuning in to that music in the car and mentioning he'd once played the instrument.

That was the place to start. He searched online until he found the perfect Spanish guitar and then had it shipped to the farmhouse. Would Hargreaves teach him? It wouldn't hurt to ask.

Beau picked up his equipment and headed back to the farmhouse. Chou-Chou followed him back to the house, and he bade the baby goat goodbye in the front yard. The temperature in the house was shades cooler, and Beau realized he'd been in the sun for hours. Hadn't he always tanned easily? People used to comment on his golden skin growing up, and his mama had always said he'd been blessed not to burn like she did. That was from his Spanish blood, he now knew. Anger burned in him, this new information adding fuel to an already raging fire. She'd lied about so much. Soon he would have to face her again, but not quite yet.

The house was quiet, and he cocked his ear for any chatter. Where was everybody? Caitlyn was probably working, and he wondered if he could interrupt her. No, he'd eat a snack first. Heading to the kitchen, he found Arthur Hale sitting at the table.

"You were out there so long I had to promise Clara I'd bring you some water if you went another hour," the older man said, setting aside the tablet he'd been reading on.

"With the lavender being harvested soon, I wanted to soak it all up," he said. "I never expected to love it this much. Where's the rest of the crew?"

"Clara talked Caitlyn into going to town. Shopping. Hargreaves has his nose in a book, I imagine. How did your songwriting go?"

He set his guitar on the ground and held up his legal pad. "Struck gold, I think. Got out of my own way finally." But he'd need to process this new information about his roots and consider how to work it into a song for his new album. "Do you know where Hargreaves is, sir?"

The refrigerator showered cool air on his hot face when he opened it and pulled out the ever-present cheese plate.

"He's probably reading in his room," Arthur said. "It's his favorite pastime. I'm still searching for my new one after retiring, but Clara is a good help. I like to tell her she's my new hobby." He laughed.

Beau plucked an apple out of the basket on the counter, biting into it as he selected a hunk of sharp cheese from the plate. "I expect she likes hearing that."

"She does," the man said. "You know I talked to my friend, Rhett Butler, earlier. He said you were a good guy to know. I'll admit I was happy to hear that. My niece is very taken with you, and I wanted to make sure she was in good company."

Beau studied the man before taking a seat at the table. "I'm glad you checked up on me. Despite current events, I'm usually a pretty stable guy. I'd like you to believe I'm good for Caitlyn because I'm in love with her."

"You know, I've been a journalist most of my adult life, and I've researched everything online about you for answers about this...lack of stability as you call it. Couldn't find anything."

Never say the old were rusty. This man was sharp as a tack. "It's not public. I only told Caitlyn a few days ago."

"I see," Arthur said, pulling off his reading glasses and setting them on the table. "You need any help with making it public, I'd be happy to write an article for you. Not to brag, but you've won Grammys, I've won Pulitzers. Since you matter to Caitlyn, you matter to me."

His offer of support echoed that of Hargreaves. Suddenly Beau couldn't swallow another bite of apple. "You don't even know me."

"Doesn't matter. I saw the way you look at each other. I figure that's when a couple needs to know they have people around them to help ground their relationship. In the beginning, it's nice to have one's family and friends on your side."

His mama wouldn't be on his side, Beau suddenly

realized, and he turned his head so Arthur wouldn't see the emotion in his eyes. "I appreciate that, sir. More than ever right now."

Arthur stood and patted him on the back. "I'm going up for a lie-down before Clara gets back. That woman would burn the candle at both ends if I let her. I'll send Hargreaves down if he's willing."

He was out of the kitchen before Beau could say anything. But honestly, he didn't know what to say. When Hargreaves appeared minutes later, he wasn't surprised.

"Master Arthur said you were looking for me, sir," he said, his hands folded calmly over his front.

"I'm receiving a flamenco guitar tomorrow, Hargreaves," he said, turning in his chair. "Since you heard me on the phone yesterday, I might as well tell you. I found out my real father is of Spanish ancestry; no idea what country, but I thought I might try to connect to my roots through music. Would you...teach me what you remember while I'm here?" Somehow it was easier to tell this man the truth because he didn't ask any questions. He knew without asking that Hargreaves would take any secrets he told him to the grave. He'd tell Caitlyn everything later when she returned.

Hargreaves' smile widened before falling back into its normal space. "I'd be honored, sir."

"Beau, please," he said, feeling indebted.

The man bowed and said, "Yes, sir."

Beau chuckled. "I'll bet I can out-sir you, Hargreaves. Being from the South, it's drilled into us at birth." Birth. His real father hadn't been at his. Did he even know Beau existed? The questions never ended.

"I'd be happy to see you try, sir," Hargreaves said. "I'll leave you to your repast."

He disappeared, and Beau took the opportunity to raise his arms up. In the midst of defeats, he'd received a victory. He was going to learn how to play Spanish guitar.

For the first time since he'd learned the truth, he felt more powerful. He remembered Ibrahim's question to him and he knew how to answer it, albeit partially.

A good man makes the best out of what he's given.

CHAPTER 20

CAITLYN OPENED HER BEDROOM DOOR TO LISTEN WHEN she heard the rapid strands of guitar. Hargreaves was giving Beau another lesson, like he had for the last four days. She couldn't put her gratitude for Aunt Clara's faithful butler into words. Since Beau had discovered his Spanish ancestry, he'd been laser-focused on three things: her, songwriting, and flamenco guitar. In that order.

During the day, he worked on his songs in his sitting spot in the fields. In the late afternoon, he returned and ate a snack before starting to practice with Hargreaves, who was really quite accomplished to her ears. Beau had confessed he had trouble believing Hargreaves hadn't played in many years. His technique was too precise.

Afterward, Beau would hold her hand and talk to her about flamenco guitar, everything from strumming patterns called *rasgueados* and rapid-fire fingerpicking called *picados*. The hurt he felt over his dead-end search for his father was carved into the harsh lines of his mouth, ones she did her best to tease into a smile.

Quinn hadn't texted her after she'd sent the NDA directly to Legal, and for that she was relieved. But she knew he would come back to her, and she had to tease herself to smile when she thought of it. She'd invited both Michaela—who was out of touch on a trek—and her mother, who'd talked about coming, to visit, but there were no definite plans. That wasn't surprising. Her family had a tendency to simply show up, something she normally loved about them. It might be good to have a little warning this time because she and Beau had moved in together, at the urging of Aunt Clara, who'd pulled Caitlyn aside on their shopping trip days ago to tell her to "take up" with Beau in the farmhouse. Uncle Arthur and she were of a continental mind about two consenting adults enjoying time together, after all. Caitlyn might have blushed a touch, delighting her aunt, but she'd appreciated the candor. Making love in the lavender fields was nice every once in a while—and time was ticking on that since the harvest was coming up—but she'd wanted Beau in her bed too, and it had been a joy to wake up with him every morning, the sun rising over the lavender fields outside their window.

She was in love and savoring every aspect about it, from the way their eyes met across the room to the brush of his hand across her back as he walked by. The sex continued to blow her mind—gentle at times, hot and sweaty at others.

She was floating on a cloud, and she knew it was nearing the time when she would need more balance. Ibrahim had been on a creative tear himself, saying he'd struck upon some more of the notes for their perfume. She'd left him alone. These creative types liked their space. When Beau was thinking about a song, she could see it on his face. He was off in another world, one she couldn't reach. That was okay with her. Songwriting was its own healing balm.

Still, she wanted to share her newfound feelings with someone. Flynn had texted her, asking if she was still being smart, and she'd replied, *of course*, leaving it at that. Beau might officially be her boyfriend, but she trusted he would be her celebrity spokesperson too. They would find a way to make the personal and the business work.

Her phone rang, and she grinned, seeing the caller.

"Michaela!" she said when she picked up on FaceTime. "I'm so glad you called. Where were you?"

"A quick trip to our goji berry farmers in Ningxia."

"Like I know where that is."

"North-Central China," Michaela said. "You look like a firecracker. I take it things are going well with Beau."

She wouldn't mention he'd found his feet these past few days. Sure, he was still wearing his cowboy hat and torn clothes for his mornings in the field with Chou-Chou, but he was also cleaning up and going into the village with her for a later dinner or a walk around town when no one was on the streets. She liked both styles, and he seemed pleased about that.

"I love him, Michaela! And he loves me. It's like a dream."

"What? You're kidding. I knew you *liked* him. Caitlyn, this is huge! I'm going to have to come and meet him ASAP. The perfume creating session will be a bonus."

"I was hoping you would," she said. "I want you to meet Beau. Michaela, I want him to meet everybody. Well, except for Quinn and Connor maybe."

Her sister snorted. "I understand that. They're scary. Okay, I just got back and don't know what time zone I'm in, but I'll fly over."

"I asked Mom to come for a perfume session, but she's not sure when she'll get away. She said Dad's helping in her herb garden." She could have fallen off her chair upon hearing that. "I told Mom I was really happy with Beau but told her not to say anything."

"Like she won't tell Dad. Have you told Flynn you're in love?"

She grimaced. "No, I—"

"Oh, my God, you're scared to tell Flynn! This is big. Caitlyn, he's going to be happy for you."

"He's concerned about the business/pleasure thing

and some of Beau's changes. I mean, I want him to be happy for me, but..."

"You're afraid he might not approve?" Michaela asked. "This is interesting. Why not?"

"It's complicated."

She pointed her finger at the screen. "Tell me or I'll call him."

"Beau wasn't acting himself then—for a good reason, mind you, but Flynn doesn't know what's going on with him. And Beau also hasn't signed a contract yet for the new perfume. Again, for a good reason." At least it had seemed like a good reason. With their new relationship, she was trying to tell herself it was still valid.

"Does Quinn know?" she asked.

"Of course not! I got Beau to sign an NDA, but I fibbed a little on the contract side. I'm not happy with myself about that."

Michaela whistled. "Do you remember how Quinn acted when he found out I hadn't asked my stupid then-boyfriend to sign a non-compete while interning at Merriam Labs?"

"Yes," she said, her stomach sinking. "But I under-stand why you didn't. You trusted Boyd." Caitlyn had liked Boyd McClellan a lot while the two were dating seriously. Two years older than Michaela—who'd graduated from high school at sixteen—they'd been in the same Ph.D. program in Food Science at the University of California at Davis.

"And where is Boyd at right now? With our top com-petitor. That's a FU if I've ever heard one."

Caitlyn still wasn't completely clear on the details of the split except that it had been over a grant Boyd had submitted for a super food he and Michaela had agreed to search for together. "You're telling me I need to get the contract signed."

"Yes. I know it's awkward. You have hot sex after wine

and pizza and ask, 'Hey, do you mind making this whole arrangement we've talked about legal?' It's worse than asking someone to move in with you. I didn't want to hurl when I asked Boyd *that*."

Michaela hadn't ever lived with another boyfriend, and they'd all thought he was her one and only. Shock had radiated through the family when she'd announced the breakup, the details clinical, much like how her mind worked.

"You're making me want to hurl now," Caitlyn said, "but I know you're right. It's such bad timing. We're only just getting to know each other."

"See if you can give it a few days, a week maybe." She shrugged. "Maybe it'll help if I meet him and can vouch for him with Quinn."

"Like you believe that." But it was sweet of her to say so.

"Do Uncle Arthur and Aunt Clara like him?" she asked.

"I think so. Uncle Arthur checked him out with someone in Dare Valley, and Aunt Clara has started to knit him a sweater to complement his new look."

"Wait! That's what you mean by changes? Tell me more."

Thank God for a sister who liked fashion. She recounted Beau's ongoing transformation—although not the reason for it. Beau was still chewing it all over, and he wasn't ready to go public.

"So what you're saying is that he's completely transformed his image," Michaela said slowly. "Are you sure he's still the best bet for the perfume? I mean, all your market research was for the country good guy image."

"And that was the one I pitched to Quinn," she said. "I know. I've had some concerns on that score too. But he's still Beau Masters, and these new changes have made him more...compelling." Did her voice crack a little? He was to her, but what about his fans? The world? Her prospective perfume buyers?

"That's been your selling point all along."

Her chest was tight. "Yes, it has. Besides, I think he might end up with a look that combines a little of the old with the new." Tomorrow he was going back to Colette and her husband's store with Hargreaves to ask the couple to help him do just that. "This might actually be good for us." She was going to continue to believe that.

"You'll know what to do," Michaela said. "See how things play out."

"Yes, but I need to make a decision soon."

"You'll make the right one," she said. "Expect me in a couple days. I have a report to write up, and I'm fried."

"I'll see you when I see you." She blew her a kiss. "Thanks, Mickey."

She growled but returned the air kiss. "You know I hate that. See you soon, Caity girl."

They hung up, and Caitlyn decided to check on Ibrahim before dinner. They were eating under the portico tonight, and Caitlyn couldn't wait to see if Beau convinced Hargreaves to join them. He was determined, and Aunt Clara thought his determination adorable, but she'd told him Hargreaves would never cave.

She found Beau in the entryway, his new guitar in his hand. "Hey! How was the lesson?" She didn't spy Hargreaves anywhere. They usually practiced in the library since Hargreaves loathed the sun, he'd said.

Beau took the stairs and met her halfway, kissing her soundly on the mouth. "Rough, but it's coming together. Slowly. I mean, I'm still getting used to the buzz in the tone and the speed, but I'm loving it. I've discovered so much new music here. First Raï, and now this. Caitlyn, you've changed my life. How am I going to repay you for that?"

Sign the contract. God, she couldn't say that. Love wasn't about repayment. He'd sign if and when he wanted to finalize their business agreement. He knew it was important to her. Maybe he didn't want to risk this little pocket they'd formed together, a paradise away from the rest of the world. In his mind, he had signed the NDA.

"You don't have to do anything, Beau. I'm happy you're happy."

"Getting there," he said. "When I see you, I've got no room for rage or questions." He traced her cheek. "I feel so damn lucky to love you."

She melted. "Me too." They kissed more slowly this time, and she angled close, not caring they were on the stairs.

"Where were you going?" he asked against her lips.

She could hear the desire in his words and in the heat of his body. They could go upstairs for a while. "I was going to see Ibrahim, but—"

"Come on, then," he said, taking her hand. "Let's go see him together. He's been creatively incubating, but he'll need some human interaction by now."

He'd declined to meet them every night for dinner, which she understood. This wasn't his family, and everyone needed their space. "We can still find some time together before dinner."

He raised her lips to his mouth, setting his guitar against the wall. "I was hoping for that. It's good we have other focuses because I'm not sure we'd ever leave the bedroom otherwise."

"Would that be such a bad thing?" She laughed. "We need a vacation. Alone. When we're in a good place with our work."

"Count on it," he said, and it was the first tangible agreement they'd made about the future, she noted.

They found Ibrahim listening to Maria Callas.

"Ibrahim, that woman sounds like an angel," Beau said. "Every time I find you in your lab, I hear something that makes my heart sing. Opera, right? I like it."

"Perhaps you'll play one of your new songs for us and make our hearts soar," Ibrahim suggested.

Beau shrugged. "If you like. How's your work going? I've been making music like crazy, so I get the impulse to creative binge."

"I think I've struck upon a few notes for the perfume, but I'm nowhere near finished. Caitlyn, I was hoping to have you smell them for me. Give me your impression. Beau, I'd love yours as well. Mind you, it's not the final formula, but they are notes that will play together. I like to start from the base and work my way up, like building the foundation of a house."

She liked the notion of the perfume as a living thing, the notes playing with one another. "Oh, I'm so excited."

He pulled out a small amber bottle and dipped in two smelling strips. Holding them out, he said, "Wave the strip a few inches from your nose."

She waved the strip much like she would have waved a princess wand from her childhood and inhaled slowly, taking care to measure her breath so she wouldn't saturate her olfactory senses. "Oh, that's yummy. Sorry, Ibrahim. That's not a very technical description."

He laughed. "But honest. What do you smell?"

Crap. She dreaded this part. "Lavender."

"I love how you always guess that," Ibrahim said.

"Ibrahim, we're in a lavender field." She almost rolled her eyes.

"But there *is* lavender in that sample," he said. "Beau?"

"Jasmine, I'd say," he said, waving the strip again. "I'm not clear on the other note, but it reminds me of cologne."

"Vetiver," Ibrahim said. "I've been thinking about women, the ones who really know themselves. They're well-rounded people. This perfume can't be purely floral or musky. That's too one-sided for a real woman. We want something that reflects all the facets of a woman. Strength. Mystery. Passion. Sensuality. Vulnerability. Caring. Love. I thought vetiver might convey the strength and mystery. It's known for smelling like newly tilled soil, which includes ground-up wood and leaves and other remnants. The scent also improves as it ages. Like women do in my experience."

"Like the wine in the bottle improving," she said. "Got it."

"I like the idea of newly tilled soil," Beau said. "It's an essential part of transformation, I think."

These two talked like poets when they got together.

"Jasmine always makes me think of passion and sensuality," Ibrahim continued. "It's one of the most prized flowers in perfumery, exotic and exquisite. Floral yet spicy and musky too. Every woman's sensuality is her own, but they are all exquisite."

She had to force herself not to look at Beau. Until making love with him, she hadn't understood words like "exotic" and "sensual." He was helping her uncover that part of herself, and he'd told her she was doing the same for him.

"I'll want to blend some more notes in," Ibrahim said, waving the smelling strip under his nose, "but this is part of my chorus, to use a music term."

She sniffed again. "I like this. A lot."

He smiled. "I'm glad. Of course, this could all change depending on what I choose next. A little less of this and a little more of that. We'll see. It's like substituting words in a chorus, Beau."

"At least I can cross out words. You have to upend the bottle and start again," Beau said, laughing.

"Every process has its peculiarities," Ibrahim said. "I'll do a little more investigating, but I'll look forward to seeing you at dinner. Clara came by earlier to press the invitation."

She was glad he was coming. "I'll put you two together so you can talk in riddles."

"Perhaps we can hear your work on the flamenco guitar," Ibrahim said.

Beau waved a hand. "Oh, that's not ready for public consumption. Do you know the music well?"

"I have a playlist," Ibrahim said, laughing. "I listen to it sometimes when dealing with the musks. It's passionate, powerful music."

"Yes, it is," Beau said. "Who knew I had so much passion and power inside me?"

"Anyone who's seen you sing, I imagine," Ibrahim said. "You're only plumbing the depths."

Caitlyn thought about sneaking out and leaving them alone. Would they notice?

"Speaking of depths," Ibrahim said, pulling out a drawer directly behind him. "I have new questions for you both."

More homework. She was still working on her best answers to his last questions. But she eagerly took the tiny roll of paper when he handed it to her.

"Unroll it after you leave," he said, his lips twitching. "Oh, we're doing some fine work here. I'll see you shortly."

She knew she was rushing to leave, if only to see the next question. As soon as she reached the hallway, she stopped and unrolled it.

What am I most afraid to say right now?

She veered back. What? Even if she knew, that sounded really scary.

Beau unrolled his scroll and chuckled. "The Perfume Jedi strikes again. I'm beginning to think he should meet Colette. They're both too wise by far."

"What does it say? Oh, is that too nosy?"

He put his arm around her as they walked out. "Honey, I'm sharing your bed and kissing and touching every inch of you. I think we're beyond nosy."

That reminded her of the "nap" they needed to get in before dinnertime. She increased her pace, pulling him along. "So what does it say?"

He handed it to her, and she unrolled it.

What have I waited my whole life to say?

"Wow! How do you answer something like that?" she asked, making him laugh.

"The crazy thing is that I think I'm getting pretty close," he said. "Come on, I'll race you back to the house."

"Is it terrible that I hope we won't run into my aunt and uncle just now?" she asked, running beside him.

"No," he answered. "I'm thinking about carrying you up the stairs like Prince Charming. I thought you might like that."

She considered it. "I would actually."

"See, I'm getting to know you. Every part of you."

When he lifted her into his arms, she looked into those blue-gray eyes of his, awash in love. So much had changed in both of their lives since that first powerful meeting at his office. What was she most afraid to say right now?

When you get to know all of me, don't stop loving me, Beau.

CHAPTER 21

As Beau looked at Caitlyn, sleeping soundly by his side, the sound of guitar, violin, and harmonica danced in his head, a morning symphony that flowed like the champagne they drank before dinner. He kissed her and left for his writing spot. The ache in his chest receded with each new song, and the day before the lavender harvest, he knew the answer to Ibrahim's question, one he'd only given him a short three days ago: *What have I waited my whole life to say?*

It came to him, accompanied with the haunting strains of flamenco guitar. *Boy, stop trying so hard.*

The rest of the song flowed out, unlocking another facet in him, and this time he recognized it as sweet forgiveness for Old Beau, the one who'd been propelled into the cocoon by Dr. Clarridge's revelation.

There's nothing more to prove.
His ghost is gone.
The shadow no more.
He wasn't the one haunting you.

You didn't trust.
You weren't sure of this heart.
You let people tell you who you should be.

You were good.
No one denies it.
But you don't have to try so hard.
You've got nothing more to prove.

So have yourself some fun.
See where the river runs.
Your life is your own.
No one else can boss you around.

Find love and keep it.
For you and the woman with sunshine in her eyes.
Settle down.

And some days perhaps raise a little hell.
Don't make you bad.
Boy, you've got nothing more to prove.

He sent the finished songs to Rye, knowing it would help his case to send them to his record label with his friend's thumbs-up. Then he went to find Caitlyn.

He found her with Clara, and his heart warmed up like a potbelly stove, seeing her knitting something in yellow. Was that for him? Clara had started making him a scarf, saying all well-styled men wore one, which had moved him something fierce. Was Caitlyn doing the same? The shape wasn't much more than a bunch of woven lines of yarn, but it touched him, this quiet, artistic side of her—a new facet.

"Hey!" Caitlyn glanced up, her hands continuing to move. "I'm finally getting more comfortable with this. Becca taught Clara and me when we were in Ireland. It's going to be a scarf for Flynn. The yellow is going to drive him nuts, but that's my evil plan."

He found he was oddly deflated. "That's awesome."

"Flynn is going to love it," Clara said, nudging her. "Anything made from your hands carries extra love."

And if that line wasn't enough to get the music playing

in his head again. "Clara, you're a genius. Can I use that for a song?"

She set her knitting project, one in a deep purple, down in her lap. *That* might be his. He was racking up a lot of purple these days, what with Colette and Étienne's help.

"Of course!" she exclaimed. "I've never collaborated on one of those. Arthur is never going to hear the end of it."

Humming it, he crossed to kiss Caitlyn. "Are you up for a night out? I just sent a batch of songs to Rye, and I feel really great about this album. I have a flamenco lesson with Hargreaves in a little while, but afterward, I'm yours if you want."

"I want," she said, beaming. "Michaela is coming late tonight—without Mom, unfortunately, who asked for a rain check. She just texted me. Decided to stop in Paris for a little shopping before heading down on the train."

He was excited to meet her sister. When he'd met Flynn, he'd been in a state. He hoped to make a better impression this time. "We should take the train to the city too sometime. It would be a shame not to see the Eiffel Tower while I'm here."

"Oh, that's a drop in the bucket," she said, resuming her knitting. "There are so many magical places. Right, Aunt Clara?"

"It's one of the most beautiful cities in the world," Clara said, sighing. "I'm going to get Arthur up there before we leave. We thought we'd wander a bit in the south and travel some, but we've... Never mind. I wonder where Arthur got along to. He left for a walk when I started to go on about buying more yarn and making him another sweater."

Caitlyn winked at him. "She's made him two already."

"He gets cold in Dare Valley," Clara said. "I'm only looking out for him, dear."

Beau glanced out the French doors. "I'll see if I can find him."

"He needs a snack," she said pointedly. "Thanks for looking for him, Beau."

"Be back in a bit," he said, letting himself out. Chou-Chou came running from his bed under the portico. "Hey, little fella. Have you seen Arthur? Come on. Let's find him."

He let his gaze roam but didn't see the silhouette of a lone man anywhere in the surrounding fields. He started for Ibrahim's house. Somehow he knew he was going to find the two men together. Sure enough, he heard laughter through the open windows.

"Hey y'all," he called out, opening the blue door at the back. "Coming in."

"We're in the lab, Beau," Ibrahim called.

The strands of classical opera were playing, indicating Ibrahim had been working on florals. He caught notes of jasmine and orange along with a base note of something musky and woodsy.

"If that's for the new perfume, I'm a fan," he said when he reached the doorway. "It smells incredible in here."

Ibrahim's brow lifted. "I'm getting closer. How's the songwriting going? Still pouring out of you?"

"Like a sieve," he said, taking a seat next to Arthur when Ibrahim gestured to the empty chair. "Clara was looking for you," he said with a nod. "Said you needed a snack."

"That woman worries too much," Arthur said. "I'm visiting with my new friend here."

Everyone had remarked how well Ibrahim and Arthur got along, speaking of everything from politics to culture. He'd never met two more learned men. Well, except for Hargreaves, but his new friend and flamenco mentor didn't talk much. Beau had come to appreciate his quiet presence.

"Ibrahim finally got me to do a little scent sampling," Arthur said, kicking out his feet and crossing his ankles. "Then we got onto discussing the merits of age and knowing yourself better. There's a lot to recommend youth, but I wouldn't trade my years for some less lived-in bones."

Now this was the kind of conversation he loved. "Tell me more."

Arthur laughed. "You're what? Just turned thirty, if I recall from my research."

He shifted in his seat. It was still a little weird to think about Arthur researching him. "Yep. Right now, I'm starting to feel like I have a better grip on things. The song I finished today was about having nothing more to prove."

"Then you're ahead of your years," Ibrahim said, his pencil-thin smile tipping up on the right. "I didn't realize that until my mid-forties."

Arthur patted his noggin. "I'm so old I can't tell you when I got that pearl. Heck, don't matter, I suppose. But you live differently as you age. Become your own man."

"Exactly," Beau said, folding his hands in his lap. He suddenly knew he was ready to share what he'd been going through with these two men. "I came here needing space. I'd just found out that the man I'd thought was my real father, Walt Masters, actually wasn't. To say it was a shock would be an understatement."

Arthur turned in his seat, his blue eyes ever sharp. "That would make anyone go on a bender. How did you find out, if you don't mind my asking?"

Ibrahim rose and came around his desk, pulling his chair with him, joining their circle. Beau coughed to clear his throat at the gesture. It was something a friend would do.

"Turning thirty got me to thinking about my roots. For my new album, I decided to have some genetic testing done on me and my daddy. Kinda my way of facing the ghosts I suspected were hiding in my very blood.

Alcoholism and the like. But the sample I gave for Walt showed he wasn't my father."

Ibrahim only gazed at him, his stillness a balm.

"Hell of a way to find out," Arthur said. "Did you ask your mother about it?"

He made a rude noise. "Of course. She was my first stop. She denied it until I told her about the sample. Then she refused to tell me who my real father was. I still don't know much of anything, except he's of Spanish and indigenous descent. Threw me for one hell of a loop."

Arthur made a clicking sound with his tongue. "No doubt."

"Hence the flamenco," Ibrahim said, nodding slowly.

"Yes," he said, coughing again. "It's not like the genetics can tell you what country your dad might be from originally. So I turned to music. I'll never be able to thank Hargreaves for his lessons."

"He's a man of many talents," Arthur said. "Never tell him I said so, but he's what we used to call a Renaissance man. Ibrahim is one of them too."

"As are you, my friend," Ibrahim said to Arthur with a smile. "You know one of the reasons why I love perfume so much? Every note is distinctly its own. A foul stench can't disguise a rose's smell. Did you know the most rotten smells always decay anyway? There's a reason, and it applies to your situation. Someone else's lie or secret can't change your truth. In perfume terms, we'd say essence. Beau, if you're born a rose, you're always a rose—no matter what anyone tells you."

Arthur patted him on the back. "Remember that, kid. Words of wisdom from the Perfume Jedi."

Ibrahim's brow shot up again. "I beg your pardon?"

"That's what Caitlyn and Beau and Clara call you,"

Arthur said with a snort. "You're lucky. I don't have a nickname."

"Not yet," Beau said, his throat still tight. "Thank you for saying that, Ibrahim."

Arthur stood, placing his hand on Beau's shoulder. "Masters or no Masters, you're still your own man, Beau. Keep the good. Leave the rest behind. It's all any of us can do. From my perch, you're doing pretty good after this dust-up. Well, I'm going to see what Clara's up to and have that snack. She still knitting? That woman will have me wrapped up in Irish sweaters all year long if I let her. See you two back at the farmhouse."

Beau was glad to have a moment with Ibrahim. "Those little questions you've been giving me have really helped. When I came here, I can't say I had any idea what all perfume making involved, but I'm very grateful to have been here for part of it. Once again, I want to ask if there's anything I can do as a way of saying thank you."

"Do your fans ask for ways to thank you for singing your songs?" Ibrahim asked.

"Some do," he mused, "but it's not why I do what I do."

Ibrahim rose. "It's not why I do this either, Beau. Perhaps you should ask yourself why you're always so eager to give back a kindness beyond saying thank you."

He blinked. "Why do I have a feeling you know?"

"I might postulate you're generous, but that would only be a surface answer. People who are abandoned by parents often feel they have to repay people for being kind to them."

Something tingled inside him, a bone-deep revelation sparked by Ibrahim's words.

"Or it's because my mama always made me give her something when she did something for me. I mean I know she started managing me when I was a teenager, but it started well before that. Bottom line: it's still trading for love." As a kid, he'd picked her flowers. When he'd gotten rich, he'd bought her a house. All because she'd done things for him and would sweetly say, *And how do you want to show Mama you love her and thank her for everything she's done for you?*

"You're finding love isn't about such checks and balances," Ibrahim said. "Love just is. Like the beautiful scent of the rose."

He made himself unclench his fists. "Thank God."

"Before you leave," he said, twisting another blue bottle open and dotting a smelling strip with it, "I was hoping you'd smell this base for the men's cologne. I haven't run it by Caitlyn yet, but I thought you might have strong feelings about it. Again, it's not complete. Only the base and middle notes."

Beau took the smelling strip Ibrahim presented to him. "I like it, but it's a complex base. I'm not sure I can distinguish it."

"Our bases are often complex," Ibrahim said. "Some call them foundations, you know. If you keep inhaling the fragrance, the truth of the notes will make themselves apparent with patience and perseverance."

More wisdom from their Perfume Jedi, and his mind was already blown. "You aren't going to tell me what the notes are?"

Ibrahim laughed. "What's the fun in that? Take the strip with you. See what your senses tell you over the next couple of days."

"You're thinking a couple of days, huh? I was thinking weeks, Ibrahim." He extended his hand to the man. "Thank you. For everything." Right now, in light of what his friend had told him, the words and a handshake seemed enough.

"We're far from done, Beau," Ibrahim said. "But we're all on the right track. I'll see you at dinner."

"Actually, I was thinking about taking Caitlyn to dinner in the village," he said. "To celebrate."

"You have much to celebrate together," Ibrahim said. "Tomorrow then."

As Beau was walking back to the house, his phone rang. It was Rye.

"Hey, man!" he answered. "That was fast."

"Once I read the line of the first song you sent, I was hooked. Bubba, it's some of your best stuff ever. I mean that song 'Damn Her' about slayed me in the best way possible. And 'Sunshine in Her Eyes?' Boy, you better marry that girl."

He stopped short. Yeah, he'd better. "Hope to. Meeting her sister later tonight."

"That's good. Family is important. Speaking of, I hear Boone crying, and I'm on solo baby duty, but before I go, I should say, I loved 'Sometimes Country, Sometimes Confident.' That lyric about the rosé? I about wet myself laughing. I'm sending over a case of some fancy rosé when you get back to Dare River."

He laughed. "Thanks, I guess. I'm not ashamed to like it."

"Who would have guessed?" Rye mused. "You tell Tommy Penders I think this is your best album yet. They can quote me on it. See ya, Bubba."

"Thanks again, Rye."

"It's what friends do," he said before ending the call.

Yes, it was what friends do, and he was adding more to his stable, so to speak, here in the south of France. Who would have guessed?

He picked up his pace and headed to the house. First, he would send the songs off, then he'd grab his new guitar.

He might not know much about his Spanish heritage, but one thing was certain.

Flamenco resonated with the contents of his soul.

CHAPTER 22

BEAU WAS TRANSFORMING RIGHT AND LEFT, EVERYTHING from clothing to enjoying a good rosé, and Caitlyn couldn't have been happier.

But she was grateful he'd suggested bringing her to meet Colette and Étienne before their shop closed for the night. The couple had been essential in helping him design his new look. Today he sported designer jeans, a simple white T-shirt under a deep purple velvet jacket, and his cowboy boots. It was a hot look.

The couple greeted Beau warmly, and she was surprised to see him so at ease with the traditional three-kiss greeting from Étienne as she started translating. Even Trevor, who'd spent a good amount of time in Europe, used to laugh about how weird it was to be greeted like that, but Beau was unfazed.

"His look is incredible, is it not?" Colette said, circling Beau with the eye of a woman sizing up her handiwork. "Étienne, *mon chéri*, if only you could wear jeans and cowboy boots like this one."

He laughed. "We would never leave our home, *chérie*, and then our store would close for good. It is better this way, I think."

They all laughed, and Beau opened his arms. "Colette, I know that look. What?"

She ran a finger over her mouth. "I have something for you, I think. It's a bit more daring than you would normally go, but I think it will be perfect. For a concert perhaps. Or perhaps your lady friend will be like me and wish you to wear it at home."

Caitlyn waggled her brows. "Now I'm really curious."

"It's Italian," she said, going around the counter and pulling out a box, "but we French forgive them because of their fashion. You don't have to take it, of course. It's only a suggestion."

"You haven't guided me wrong yet," he said, resting his elbow on the counter.

Colette held up a leather vest with ties, all in a deep plum. Caitlyn had to give the woman credit. Not only was it a beautiful piece of artistry, what with the tooled leather, but it would look good on Beau.

He took it from her. "What am I supposed to wear under it?"

She laughed, and Caitlyn had to bite her lip to keep from joining in. "*Chéri,* you wear nothing except that sun-kissed skin of yours. Am I right, Caitlyn?"

His mouth had parted, she saw, when he turned to face her. "Nothing?" he asked. "You've got to be kidding."

"How is this different from the torn clothes you've been wearing?" Caitlyn asked. "I love it."

"I wear those at home," he said. "I've never...shown my bare chest like this on stage."

Colette ran a teasing finger over his jacket, making Beau blush. "It wouldn't be all bare, and that's the point. Tell him, Étienne."

"She's right," he said, "but what do two French people in Provence know about country music?"

"We've been looking at videos on YouTube," Colette said. "You asked for an integrated look for Old and New Beau. This is my idea. Try it on before you decide."

His cheeks were red, but he let the woman usher him

into the changing room. Colette clapped her hands and turned to Caitlyn. "Hopefully he will see what I do."

When he came out, Caitlyn whistled, mostly to tease him like she would one of her brothers. Beau looked hot and reckless, and she got a little warm in the belly seeing his broad chest and carved arms. His flush deepened.

"It's hot," Caitlyn said. "That's 'Sometimes Country, Sometimes Confident' if I ever saw it." But she couldn't help but think of what Michaela had said to her on the phone the other day: *He's a sex symbol. Is this the look of a man who makes a woman feel like she matters? Is this the face of your perfume?*

He looked like a man you'd want to have sweep you off to bed.

Colette circled him again, yanking on the vest in the back until it was a solid line past the top of his jeans. "The choice is yours, Beau, but I think this is perfect for you."

He tugged on the ties of the vest. "This is pretty daring."

She could see the struggle and wanted to be helpful to him, the man she loved. "Do you like it? Sometimes when I really like something or know I need it, I buy it and wait until I'm ready to wear it."

"*Exactement,*" Colette said. "If you don't like it, you can always return it when you come back to France."

In the deep plum vest, his eyes were more gray than blue, and when they sought hers, she could see the question in them. When would he return to France? When they spoke of love, they talked about wanting forever, but those weren't details. He lived outside of Nashville in Dare River now, and she lived in New York when she wasn't traveling. These were practical considerations they would need to discuss.

"Let me change and then you can wrap it up," he said, heading back to the changing room. "There's no way I'm wearing that out to dinner. I'll be arrested."

"Or given a few euros," Colette said smartly, making Caitlyn choke out a laugh.

When Beau left to change, Caitlyn and Colette got down to some serious fashion talk until he emerged and paid for the vest.

"Beau, we have some more surprises coming in." Colette wrapped up the package with care, tying an artful silver ribbon around the box. "When are you leaving to go back home?"

Again, he looked at Caitlyn. "I don't rightly know."

She held her breath. His departure was inevitable, and yet, she'd done everything in her power not to think about it. Or the contract he still hadn't signed. Every day, Ibrahim was coming closer to the final formula for the perfume. She was trusting its completion would lead to the formal legal commitment between them.

"No matter," Colette said. "We will see you soon, Beau. Give me a couple of days to receive the next shipment. I am making some designers very happy, let me assure you."

He kissed her cheeks and then turned to Étienne. Caitlyn thought it downright touching how much affection they all shared for each other. She followed suit, and Colette squeezed her warmly when they embraced.

"Hold on to him," she whispered in Caitlyn's ear. "He is a wonderful man."

"I know," she whispered back. "Thank you."

After they left, Beau took her hand. "Aren't they terrific? I've never had anyone...consider my style and clothing with as much thought as those two. In some ways, they remind me of Ibrahim."

She nodded. "There's an artistry to crafting a good look for someone, something that fits them and their personality."

"You must see it all the time when you do your fashion stuff," he said. "Living in New York City, you must be at the very center of it."

The square was buzzing with people already enjoying a repast of snacks and champagne. A few glasses of cloudy pastis could be seen, mostly in front of well-dressed men. "The biggest difference from here to New York is how much people wear black. It sometimes drives me crazy. Other times I'm amazed how many clothing variations come in one color."

He smiled as they walked by an older couple, arms linked, looking like they'd been married sixty years. "Do you really think I could pull off the vest?"

She squeezed his arm, keeping her smile to herself. "Yes. That's a concert I'd love to see."

Again, the future loomed before them, but she'd purposely mentioned it, wanting him to know how she felt. He stopped and kissed her lightly, right on the street, one of his favorite things about France, he'd said many times. People were so much freer with their affection here. "I have a place backstage with your name on it, just say the word. Woman, I love you to pieces."

Her heart seemed to radiate in her chest. "I love you too," she said, and they shared a deeper kiss.

Breaking apart, they wandered around two more corners until they reached another restaurant Colette had recommended to Beau. After the hostess seated them, Caitlyn watched Beau pick up the menu with none of his earlier hesitation. He'd asked her how to say a few simple phrases in French, telling her he wanted to be able to treat her nicely. It made her feel like her vision for her perfume: that she mattered. When their server appeared, he ordered them *deux coupes de champagne*.

"Is that Beau Masters?" someone asked, loud enough to carry across the array of outside tables.

She turned her head, catching sight of a young American couple. The blond-haired woman in the paisley summer dress popped up from her table and rushed over to them. Caitlyn could almost hear Beau's wince, and she pasted a smile on her own face as the woman appeared at their table. She'd sat through moments like this with enough celebrities to know how to comport herself.

"Beau Masters, right?" The blond woman was clutching her phone in her hand, breathing hard, whether from nerves or her flight to their table, Caitlyn didn't know. Would he lie and say he was someone else, she wondered? Heck, if it were her, she'd be tempted to do just that. She couldn't imagine having her dinner interrupted or being stopped on the street. Then again, her career didn't depend on her being in the public eye.

"Funny you could guess that," Beau said, his smile a touch guarded. "What with this being France and all."

"Oh, I heard your voice," she said, "as my husband and I were walking to the restaurant. We were behind you. I thought it was you, but my husband said you were dressed all wrong. I'm the one who noticed your cowboy boots."

"Done in by cowboy boots," he said in his drawl. "Who would have thunk it?"

"Could I have a picture with you, Beau? I'm your biggest fan."

He looked at Caitlyn for a moment as if he were deciding something. "If you duck down next to me, ma'am, I'll have my lady friend take it. I'd stand, but I don't want to interrupt the other patrons' dinners. You understand."

"Oh, that's... Yes! Can my husband join us? He loves your music too. I mean, 'Country Boy Going Home' makes both of us tear up. He'd never admit it though."

"Thank you," Beau said. "If he can crouch down too. Again, I don't want to bother our fellow patrons here."

"Don't worry," she said, rushing off, nearly colliding with a waiter.

"Sorry about this," Beau said. "I should have left my cowboy boots at home."

"She caught your voice too," Caitlyn said, smiling as the waiter returned with their champagne.

Sure enough, the young couple rushed over, and because the tables were close together, the trio was squeezed into the space where Beau was sitting. Caitlyn caught the disgruntled looks of the other patrons and almost rolled her eyes when the blond woman asked her to take another picture, not liking how her hair was flying up in the breeze.

"Last one is always the best," Beau said as Caitlyn took another photo, his smile noticeably forced now.

When she handed the phone back to the woman, he said, "Thanks again for enjoying my music. Y'all have a good dinner."

"You too," the man said, holding his hand out for a handshake. "Beau Masters in freaking Provence. No one back home is going to believe it. I mean, I wouldn't recognize you. You sure do look different here. Makes me wonder..."

It hadn't been meant as a compliment, and Caitlyn took an instant dislike to the guy.

"Goodnight, folks," Beau said simply, holding up his hand. "Sorry, everybody." He looked around at the patrons who were staring at them. "Should we go?" he whispered to her.

"No," she said, picking up her champagne. "You took care of that. Now we're going to have fun."

"Again, I'm sorry." He extended his champagne. "To my new look and to Colette and Étienne. I don't care what that guy thinks. I like it."

So the barb had struck true. "And the vest. That's my favorite so far after your velvet jackets."

"You do like to rub against them like a cat might," he said. "That's why I like them too."

She laughed. "Wait until I show you what I want to do to you when you're wearing that vest." Her saucy smile had his brows lifting.

"Are you sure we still need to stay for dinner?" His

drawl was downright naughty, and she loved it. She was pretty sure Old Beau, as he referred to him, wouldn't have flirted like that.

"You'll be starving the minute we get back home," she said, "and besides, I'm starving right now."

"Of course," he said, sipping his champagne. "We'll eat fast then. Oh, wait. It's not possible. This is France."

"You're learning," she teased, opening her menu, but she was aware of the couple behind them. The feeling of being watched wasn't pleasant.

"My little anonymous bubble has disappeared, hasn't it?"

When she lowered her menu, he was gazing at her with an outstretched hand. She reached across and clasped it. He brought her hand to his lips and kissed the back of it.

"Let them look," he said, kissing her hand again. "We have nothing to be ashamed of. Just two people in love having a romantic dinner out."

Yes, they were.

CHAPTER 23

CLARA WAS GLAD SHE WASN'T SIPPING HER *CRÉMANT* WHEN Michaela came through the dining room doorway with Shawn.

Her brother zeroed in on her right away, and there wasn't a smile on his handsome face. They'd both gotten older during their estrangement, and it was still a shock to see his thick hair gray and the lines around his blue eyes. Clara hoped for his sake they were laugh lines. She hadn't laughed in the decades they'd been estranged, and that was on her. But he'd married a wonderful woman in Assumpta and had seven children she was quickly growing to love.

"Surprise!" Michaela called, holding out her hands. "Dad heard from Mom that I was coming this way, and he decided to jump on the plane with me after I met with Connor about biz stuff. Right, Dad? We even diverted going to Paris to get here right away."

Likely because Shawn hated shopping. Poor girl.

Her brother nodded, serious as an oak tree, in gray slacks, a white shirt, and tan jacket. Before retirement, he'd always opted for a three-piece suit. "I thought I'd see how Caitlyn's new enterprise was coming along. Assumpta decided to stay behind and enjoy having the house to herself."

Clara caught Michaela's eye roll. Yeah, she didn't buy

that either. Had Assumpta purposefully stayed back because she thought Shawn should come on his own?

Ibrahim rose from his seat, and Arthur, dear man,
took her by the arm and helped her up, giving her a com-
forting squeeze.

"Welcome," Ibrahim said, coming around the table to
shake Shawn's hand. "I'm Ibrahim Magdy, the perfumer.
It's been wonderful working with your daughter. Caitlyn
has a powerful vision for the world in her perfume and an
even greater heart."

"Shawn Merriam," her brother said, clasping Ibrahim's
hand. "This is our other daughter, Dr. Michaela Merriam."

Michaela made a face. "Dad, I hate it when you introduce me as a doctor. Hi, Ibrahim. Caitlyn has been
telling me so much about you. I can't wait to talk about
the plants your scents come from. I'm a plant fanatic."

"Caitlyn tells me you travel to interesting parts of the
world looking for rare plants for the health and beauty
lines in Merriam Enterprises. I believe your specialty is
super foods."

"Yes," she said, hugging Ibrahim briefly. "I can't help
myself. Caitlyn says you're totally cool. The Perfume
Jedi. It's an honor. Oh, this is so exciting."

Ibrahim's pencil-thin smile radiated out of his regal
bearing. "Your zest for life is a trait you share with your
sister, no doubt, and as refreshing as the most fragrant
jasmine."

"Flower compliments slay me." She put her hand
over her heart. "Jasmine is the crown jewel of flowers for
perfume—even though it's a genus from the olive tree
family, something I've always found fascinating. Did
you know it takes eight thousand flowers to make just
one gram of essential oil? Sorry we interrupted your dinner. Hey! Where are Caitlyn and Beau? Oh, Aunt Clara.
Uncle Arthur. I'm so out of it I forgot to say hello to you."

The young woman flew over to where Clara was

standing. She threw her arms around her, hugging her warmly, and whispered, "I'm so sorry about Dad! Mom totally set this up. I had no idea he was coming until last minute. He told me to keep it a surprise."

"Did he think I was going to flee?" she whispered back.

"God knows with Dad!" She finally released Clara and then turned to Arthur. "Oh, come here, you wonderful man."

"You're high as a kite," Arthur growled, but lovingly patted Michaela's long, curly brown hair. "Did you sniff glue on the airplane ride over?"

Michaela laughed. "Airplane fuel. I love that smell. Just kidding. Come over here, Dad. You're lurking like a ghoul."

Shawn's brow rose at being called out by his daughter, something Clara used to do when he was a boy, but he crossed to the table where they were standing. "Hello, Clara. Arthur. It's good to see you both."

She looked into his eyes. Did he mean it? "It's good to see you, Shawn," Clara said, years of breeding kicking in. "Did you have a pleasant flight?"

"Good God, they flew on a private plane, Clara," Arthur said. "Of course it was pleasant. Now, I'm about to put my nose into something, and I don't do it lightly. I'm going to take Michaela here to the kitchen and find her something to drink. Ibrahim, I expect you'll follow suit. *You two* say whatever you need to say and get it over with."

"Arthur!" She socked him.

"No, Clara, Shawn came here knowing you would be here, and I'm not going to dance around it. You're sorry, and you've missed him. If he's the man I think he is, he's going to admit his feelings. This farmhouse might have six bedrooms, but it's not big enough for you to two avoid each other. No one wants to walk on eggshells, and Shawn, I expect you to do your part with your sister, who loves you. Understand me?"

He kissed her sweetly on the cheek, looking at her with eyes full of love, then took Michaela's hand and left. Ibrahim gave Clara an encouraging smile before following them out. Silence radiated, making her aware of her body shaking with nerves. She looked at Shawn and noticed his mouth was still parted.

"Arthur does have a way, doesn't he?" She grabbed the back of the chair beside her. "Would you like to sit down a moment?"

He pulled her chair out, which made her heart lodge in her throat. She hadn't expected the kindness, and tears filled her eyes as he sat beside her.

"Oh, Shawn, I'm so sorry for everything. I was such a stubborn, stupid woman. Worse, I married probably the most worthless man on the planet. You can't know how deeply I regret his actions and my own, and then I got so mad at you for not..." Her voice broke. She finally understood Caitlyn's vision for the perfume. She hadn't felt like she mattered to her own brother at that time.

He turned his chair until he faced her, his head bowed. "I'm sorry too. Assumpta has told me, more than once, that I was a total fool for letting so many years pass without reaching out. She finally had enough of it—like Arthur, it seems. I suppose I needed a push after all these years. Clara, I know Reinhold was a jerk. I knew it the moment I met him. I'm sorry I didn't say anything, and I'm even sorrier I let him come between us all these years. Hearing J.T. had reached out to you—and that you helped him despite our differences—moved me...greatly. And I know how much you helped Trevor and Becca. You'll never know how much it meant to me, and Assumpta too."

"I love them, Shawn." She wiped a tear trailing down her face. "They're the most beautiful... I told Assumpta in Ireland you both did a bang-up job raising them. I wish... I wish I'd been around when they were younger, but I plan on making up for lost time. With them, and with Arthur..." She finally had the courage to look him in the eye again, and she didn't care that she was crying like a total ninny. "I feel like I have a second chance at life and family, and I'm not going to spoil it. I promise you... You don't ever need to worry about me being around them. If that's why you came here."

He patted her back. "Is that why you thought I'd come? Clara, I *wanted* to see you. Oh, dammit! It's hard to admit this, but I've been afraid to face you. Clara, you were right to be angry with me. I was angry with myself over how I treated you. But I couldn't let Reinhold into Merriam Enterprises."

Her tears were abating, thank God. "I knew that, but I didn't feel I had a choice. A wife is supposed to support her husband, or so I thought. I was newly married and desperate to make our marriage work. I thought...working with you at our family's company might...help Reinhold."

"Oh, Christ, Clara," Shawn said, shaking his head. "I didn't know that."

She used the napkin to wipe her nose. "It wouldn't have worked. Like the Irish say, you can't put lipstick on a pig, and you certainly couldn't have made Reinhold be less of a jackass. Still, I'm sorry we've gone all these years mad at each other. I'd hoped you'd reach out."

He sighed and patted her hand again. "I'd hoped that too. We Merriams can be stubborn. Assumpta tells me that all the time."

"She's wonderful, Shawn." She handed him a clean napkin when he sniffed. "You really got lucky with her."

"Don't I know it," he said. "Well, now that we've both cried over your supper like two stubborn old people, what do you say we start anew? I'd like you and Arthur to come visit us in Napa when you have time. Of course, I know our children are probably more fun to be around, but I've been known to show people a good time."

"I remember when you took me to see that artist's fair

in San Francisco when I visited you last." The day had been awash in vibrant paintings and the sweet thrill of an older sister spending time with a younger brother. "It was one of the happiest days of my life."

"Mine too," he said. "Do you remember the painting you encouraged me to buy that day?"

"Of course! The seaside one with the boat at full sail. It was beautiful."

"I have it in my office." He hung his head and sniffed again. "It was my way of remembering you."

Her heart clutched, simply clutched. "And I have the turquoise bracelet you bought me. I'm glad you came, Shawn."

"Me too. Haven't been this nervous since Assumpta went into labor with Connor." He laughed. "I was glad to hear you still have Hargreaves. The children have been telling me great stories about him. He seems not to have changed."

"I'll always have Hargreaves," she said, straightening her spine. "We couldn't manage without each other. Arthur won't admit it yet, but he's coming to enjoy having him around too."

"Michaela told me he's teaching Beau Masters to play flamenco guitar," Shawn said. "Is there anything the man can't do? Dad gave you a true gift when he said he'd give you a butler for your birthday. At the time, I thought he was crazy."

But somehow their father had known what she needed, and she would always be grateful for that. His gesture had made her feel she mattered to him. She'd have to tell Caitlyn later. "So, besides seeing me, are you here to check up on Caitlyn? You should know she's in love with Beau, and he's a good man. Has had a hard time for reasons he may or may not share with you, but don't be too concerned. He's won Arthur over, and that's no piece of cake."

"Don't I know it," Shawn said, chuckling. "I'm glad to see his no-bullshit policy is as cast iron as ever."

"It's one of the reasons I love him." She glanced toward the doorway. He was going to receive a lot of kisses tonight for his role in pushing her and Shawn into this overdue conversation.

"You're lucky too," Shawn said. "Finding Arthur again after so many years."

She snorted. "I can let go of my stubbornness too, it seems. Mostly. Of course, he did his part. But yes, I'm very lucky."

He stood. "Shall we join the others?"

When he held out his hand, she took it, tears blurring her eyes again. "Oh, darn it all, Shawn. I need to hug you."

She put her arms around him. For a moment, she could feel the shock run through his body, but then his arms banded around her in a tight hug, one reminiscent of the adoring younger brother he'd once been. They held each other for a long moment, and time seemed to merge between the happy young siblings they'd been to the mature adults they were now. Yes, she thought, everything was falling into place, like new parts in a treasured old watch, better oiled yet still familiar.

"Whatever are you thinking?" he asked as he patted her on the back one last time before letting her go.

She smiled, resisting the urge to pinch his cheek. "That we're a lot like an old watch."

He laughed and took her elbow, leading her to the doorway. "Speak for yourself. I'm not old. I'm seasoned."

"I'm happy to hear you don't believe you're old, Shawn." She slid her hand through the crook of his arm. "It's like I keep telling Arthur. I plan to live to one hundred or more, and he's going to match me and then some."

She stopped and faced him. He cocked his head to the side.

"Would you like to live that long too? Because I would

really like to spend a few decades getting to know my brother again."

His mouth tipped up. "Dammit, Clara. Yes, I sure as hell would."

She smiled, feeling lighter than she had in years. "Now all I have to do is convince Hargreaves."

That made Shawn laugh, and she joined in. My, how she had missed his baritone laughter, but that was all in the past now.

They were going to laugh their hearts out if she wasn't Clara Merriam Hale.

***

"Daddy!"

The word was out of Caitlyn's mouth before she could stop herself. When was the last time she'd called him that? But there he was, sitting between Aunt Clara and Michaela on the sofa in the main living room of the farmhouse with a brandy in his hand. Uncle Arthur and Ibrahim sat in adjoining chairs.

She glanced around for her mom, expecting her parents had come together, but there was no sign of her. What in the world?

Michaela ran over and hugged her. "Dad wanted to come and make it a surprise. And boy, it's been nothing but. Mom must be laughing at home because I know she stayed back on purpose."

And her mother hadn't said a word about any of it when they'd talked on the phone.

Michaela turned to Beau. "It's good to finally meet you. You'll forgive me if I have a bit of a moment. I love your music, so it's totally awesome that you're doing Caitlyn's perfume! Oh, and your new look?" She whistled, making everyone look over at them. "Where's the cowboy hat? 'Cause I have to see the cowboy hat. I'm Michaela, by the way."

Beau laughed, rubbing his cheek. "The hat is upstairs. Nice to meet you, Michaela. Your sister has told me a lot about you."

She shot Caitlyn a look. "All good, I'm sure. Come meet our dad. He up and jumped on the plane with me."

Her father rose from the sofa and was already extending his hand to Beau. "Shawn Merriam. It's good to meet you, Beau."

"You too, sir," he said, clearing his throat. "If we'd known you'd be here tonight, we'd have cut our evening short."

They'd lingered over dessert and then strolled through the quiet streets, the soft golden light washing over them. Of course, Beau had talked her into a shadowy side street, and they'd gotten to kissing. Mercy, it had been tempting to have sex right there on the street, but that was too racy for either of them, New Beau notwithstanding.

Her cheeks flamed. Sex! Beau! He'd moved into her room after her talk with Aunt Clara. But now her dad was here...

"Caitlyn," her dad said, pulling her into a hug. His embrace was warm and soft, completely unlike him. She glanced over at Aunt Clara, who was smiling from ear to ear. Had they finally reconciled? She needed to know what she was dealing with.

"Hi, Dad," she said when he finally released her. "What a wonderful surprise. You should have told me you were coming."

"I so rarely get to surprise any of you kids on my own, and your mother thought it a good idea," he said, unbuttoning his jacket and taking a good look at her and Beau. "Besides, I wanted to see your new enterprise up close and personal. From what Ibrahim tells me, you've been doing great work here."

She glanced over at the Perfume Jedi, and he lifted his brandy snifter in her direction. Nerves still raced through her, but she made her mouth form a smile. It struck her that the room-sharing situation wasn't the only problem. Quinn had been on her case about that contract from day one. Did her dad know about that somehow? And what exactly was her mom up to? "Yes, but mostly Ibrahim. He's the master here."

"Beau's last name is *Masters*," Michaela said, her mouth smirking. "How many masters does it take to change a lightbulb, do you think?"

"More than the brain cells you have firing right now, child," Uncle Arthur said. "Caitlyn, why don't you let Michaela show you what bottles we have open tonight? And take Beau with you since he's drinking now."

She knew a reprieve when she heard one. "Great idea! Come on, Mickey."

"Don't call me that," her sister said.

They walked to the kitchen, and Caitlyn pounced. "How could you not tell me he was coming? *Why* is he here?"

Her sister held out her hands. "I can't tell you with a hundred percent certainty, but he and Aunt Clara have made up. That might be one reason. You are likely the other. I doubt he came just to spend time with me. Do you have any idea how hard it was to spend hours alone with Dad? I didn't know what to talk about. I want to kill Mom."

"If this is his post-retirement reconnecting phase, we're all in trouble," Caitlyn breathed out. "Although I'm so happy to hear he and Aunt Clara made up."

"Uncle Arthur pretty much laid the law down and told them to work it out. I about fell out of my chair when they came out of the dining room smiling, arm in arm. Uncle Arthur has been smirking all night."

She caught Beau smiling at that. Dear Uncle Arthur. "So Quinn didn't send Dad to check up on me?"

Her sister's eyes narrowed. "No, I don't think so."

Relief swept through her, but they still had to deal with their living situation. One more to go. "Beau, we need to move you out of my room. My dad—"

"I was just thinking about that." He cleared his throat. "Give me—"

"No need to do that on my account," she heard her father say from the doorway. "And Caitlyn, I'm not your brother's messenger boy. I would have thought you knew me better than that. Appears your mother was right."

Looking up, she was sure her mouth was frozen in a silent scream. He'd heard all that? "Dad, you were supposed to stay..."

He snorted. "Like I didn't raise seven kids. I know a powwow when I see it. Clara suggested I come in and tell you there was no need to hustle Beau out of your room."

"I thought it might make you uncomfortable."

His crossed his arms. "No, honey, you're the one all nervous here. You kids are all adults now, something your mother has been telling me for years. We know you have relationships."

"Is that what we're calling Flynn's?" Michaela quipped. "Oh, excuse me. Dad, you were saying."

His lips twitched. "When you're finish talking, come back and join the party. We have a lot to celebrate. I suppose Mickey told you Clara and I have officially buried the hatchet."

"I didn't see one on the way in," Caitlyn said, making him laugh.

He waved a hand. "You're just like your mother. Always joking when you're nervous. Don't be long." With that, he turned and walked out.

Michaela whistled again, but this time it was more shrill. "Dad is even scarier now that he's retired. Do you think he heard what I said about spending time alone with him on the plane?"

She was in too much shock to do more than nod.

"Great. Mom must be falling over herself, knowing what this is doing to us."

Their mother did have a quirky sense of humor at times—apparently something they shared with her.

Beau shifted on his feet. "Ahem... We should probably pour ourselves a beverage and join the others. Unless you two need more time in here."

"Nope," Michaela said. "I'm good. Caitlyn?"

"Still in shock, I think, although that might never ease."

Beau walked over to the refrigerator and opened the door. After a moment, he pulled out the open bottle of champagne, a sterling silver spoon in the mouth—an old French technique that worked to keep the bubbles fresh. "Let's all settle down. You should be happy your daddy came to visit."

She looked over at him. "Of course I'm happy. It's just...a shock. Dad never does things like this without Mom."

"Mom is the best buffer in the world," Michaela said. "Dad can be pretty intimidating. Like Con and Quinn. Wait until you meet them, Beau."

But Dad wasn't acting intimidating *now*, Caitlyn realized. Not with her or Beau or their sharing a room situation. "Perhaps Dad *is* changing now that he's not working all the time. Maybe that's what Mom wants us to see." She couldn't imagine it though.

"I guess we'll find out," Michaela said, bringing over three champagne glasses. "It really is great to meet you, Beau. Would you sing for me sometime?"

He smiled. "I figure you and your dad's arrival is perfect for one of my new songs. If you'll pour the champagne and bring mine out, I'll grab my guitar."

When she and Michaela were alone, her sister grabbed her by the upper arms. "He's going to sing!"

Her excitement was contagious. He'd never performed

for anyone since arriving. Sure, he'd sing snatches of songs to her or sometimes play a little guitar, but this felt different. He was making a statement.

"Let's get out there then," she told Michaela, pouring the champagne herself.

"I want a front row seat," her sister said, following her back into the living room.

Conversation halted, and Caitlyn forced a smile. "Beau is going to play one of his new songs for us."

Michaela raised her glass, spilling some of her champagne in her exuberance. "I requested it."

"Come sit by me, Caitlyn," Aunt Clara said, holding out her hand.

"I'll sit on the floor," Michaela said, dropping into Lotus pose.

"Even if I could get my legs crossed like that, I wouldn't be able to feel them after a minute," Uncle Arthur said as Beau returned with his guitar. "Beau, grab your glass. We're going to have a toast before you sing."

Caitlyn realized she was still holding his champagne and walked over to him. His face was stained a bright red, so she knew whatever point he was making was important. "Thanks, honey," he said, soft enough so only she could hear.

"To family and new friends," her uncle said.

Everyone lifted their glasses, and Caitlyn clicked her glass with Beau's. It seemed appropriate that they should celebrate such a big moment. He'd just met more of her family, her father specifically. This was a big deal!

"Go on and sit," he told her after taking a sip and then setting his glass on one of the side tables. "This is one of my new songs, one I just finished yesterday. I was having all sorts of writer's block before I came here. But then everything opened, and it's because of that beautiful woman over there and this beautiful place we have here. It's called 'Sunshine in Her Eyes.' I hope you like it because it's dedicated to Caitlyn, who I owe so very much to."

Oh, Beau. Their eyes met, and his smile seemed to fill every chamber in her heart with sunlight. She knew why he'd chosen to play this song for her family. It was a public declaration of his love for her, much like the way he'd taken her hand in front of his fans at the restaurant, she realized. Her eyes filled, and she lowered her glass of champagne to her lap as he started to strum his guitar, the delicate opening chords changing to something more charged.

She was more than a breath of fresh air.
She was a hurricane coming in off the Gulf.
The cloth of her sexy blue dress moved with her,
As if storm winds stirred around her.

She was young and beautiful,
And she spoke with the full force of her heart.
She talked about women picking flowers,
Their babies resting on blankets beside them.

When she came out of her shoe,
And I bent down to help,
Her arch seemed like a long road I'd traveled,
One I'd been on too long alone.

She's the one I've been waiting for my whole life,
My very own kindred spirit.
When I look at her, I see sunshine in her eyes.
Sunshine in her eyes.

Even that sunshine in her eyes can make the flowers grow.
But she isn't only sunshine.
She's moonlight.
And every kind of light in between.

She fills up all the dark places.
Helps me see the truth.

Her light has changed me.
And I hope it rains on me for the rest of my life.

That girl with the dark brown hair,
The one with sunshine in her eyes.
Sunshine in her eyes.

When he finished, he simply stood there in front of her family. Caitlyn started to clap, and others joined in, but she couldn't look away from him. "I love you," she mouthed to him, wiping away the tears streaming down her face when he nodded, clearing his throat.

Someone grabbed hold of her hand. It was her dad, and she lifted her head. He was staring at her, and were those tears in his eyes?

"I'm so happy for you, Caity girl," her dad said. "I can't wait to tell your mother."

Someone whistled. Michaela, of course. "Bravo, Beau."

"You sure as hell seem to be done with writer's block, Beau," her uncle said as the clapping died down. "Nice song."

Michaela stood up, sipping her champagne. "I'd love it even if she wasn't my sister. What else do you have?"

Beau laughed. "Are you always this enthusiastic?"

"Yes!" Caitlyn and her dad cried out.

"Now I know why Chou-Chou follows you around everywhere, Beau," Aunt Clara said. "That baby goat loves a good love song."

"Baby goat?" her dad asked.

"You'll meet him tomorrow," her aunt said. "What does our Perfume Jedi think?"

Leave it to Aunt Clara to be straightforward about something like that.

"I'd say you have the perfect song," Ibrahim said. "I loved the line about truth."

"Like you said, Ibrahim," Beau said, "it's certainly the most prized quality in a perfume—or a song."

The perfumer gave him a mysterious smile. "Come visit me tomorrow in the lab. I have a new question for you."

Beau picked up his glass of champagne and lifted it in Ibrahim's direction. "I can't wait."

"Oh, can I get a question too?" Michaela asked. "Caitlyn's been telling me all about them. It sounds like a personal discovery seminar. I need something like that to counter my scientific mind."

"We need both passion and reason in life, Michaela." Ibrahim rose, closing his suit jacket, looking elegant and at ease.

Beau had asked Caitlyn if she thought he'd ever look so at home in himself. Tonight she thought it a certainty.

"I'm going to leave you," Ibrahim said. "We have the harvest tomorrow, and while I won't be the one picking the flowers, I will be walking the fields early."

"I've never seen lavender harvested," Michaela said. "I can't wait. The French are the only culture to use lavender in a cooking spice—*herbes de provence*—which is great thinking on their part because it has ton of natural benefits. Vitamin A for eye health, calcium for bones, and limonene for liver function."

"She's a walking encyclopedia," Caitlyn told Beau, who was grinning.

"You should go to bed, Michaela," her dad said. "You didn't sleep a wink on the plane even though you pretended to be so you wouldn't have to talk to me the whole way. My children seem to think I'm *intimidating*."

Aunt Clara laughed. "Of course you are, Shawn. Didn't anyone ever tell you that? Good thing I'm back in your life because there are some things only an older sister will tell you."

"Don't I know it," Michaela said with a groan. "Try being the youngest in this family."

Her dad kissed Caitlyn on the cheek before crossing to Michaela and pulling her into a half hug. "Oh, you have it so rough. Come on, kiddo. Let's draw straws for rooms."

"Hargreaves has your rooms ready," her aunt said. "I ran up and asked for his help after we broke from dinner."

Thank God for Aunt Clara. She was going to keep everyone and everything in line.

"We're off too," Uncle Arthur said. "I'm way too old to be staying up this late drinking brandy. Not that the company hasn't been great. Come on, Clara. This is a young person's game."

"I've applied for my young person's visa, thank you," she informed him as she stood up. "But I'll follow you because I still owe you a lot of kisses for your earlier interference."

"Good God, Clara, not in front of the children," her uncle scoffed, but he was smiling as she linked their arms. "Goodnight, everyone."

Soon Caitlyn and Beau were standing in the living room alone. It struck her as far from accidental that they'd been left to themselves. He set his guitar aside and reached for their champagne.

"I know why you sang that song," she whispered as he touched their glasses together, the sound as light as crystal.

"I'd been planning on singing it to you tonight at the restaurant, but then that couple came, and I wanted a more private moment."

"Good decision," she said, remembering how his fans had watched them all night.

"And sure, I figured it was a big move for your father to meet me—and then give his blessing for us to sleep in the same room." He lifted his shoulder. "I figured he should know much I love you. In his shoes, I'd want to be sure the man my daughter was with was good enough."

She touched his face. "You're more than good enough. You're perfect."

He kissed her lightly on the lips. "So are you, Sunshine. I think that might be my new nickname for you."

"Sunshine," she said, remembering the song. "I like it."

When they made love later, careful to keep their desire quiet in the full house, she realized she had a nickname for him too.

My man.

CHAPTER 24

THE HARVESTED FIELDS LOOKED LIKE A YOUNG BOY WHO'D gotten a summer buzz cut.

Beau missed the purple flowers swaying on their proud stalks in the warm breeze. Chou-Chou seemed none too happy either. The baby goat was bleating next to him as he and Caitlyn walked the fields, pausing from time to time to stick his nose in the sheared stumps still anchored in the chalky soil.

"It doesn't seem the same," he said to Caitlyn, whose hand he held. Who would have guessed harvesting would be so sad?

"Wait until you see the bunches of cut lavender in the distillery," she said. "Michaela and I wanted to jump on them like a pile of autumn leaves."

"I like the image," he said, raising her hand to his lips and kissing it. "We'll have to come earlier in the season next year. That is, if you'll have me."

The sky was as blue as a ribbon at the state fair when she turned to him. "I'm hoping that's what we're doing. Where we're going."

He put her hand on his heart. "I love you. I want to be with you. We have some figuring out to do, sure, but what we feel for each other is strong enough to make everything else slide into place."

Her cat-like green eyes studied him. "I hope so. My mom says the devil is in the details."

They resumed walking, and he let himself feel the give of the soil under his boots. They'd been planting things between them, eager to see what rose up come spring, and now it was time for them to cultivate the harvest. "I figure meeting some of your family is a big step."

She swung their hands playfully. "My dad likes you, and that was way easier than I'd ever imagined."

"For me too. I always thought getting a dad to like you was the hardest part, so it should only be easy sailing ahead. I want things to be permanent between us, Caitlyn. You must know I want you in my life. I'm not asking you to marry me just yet, but I'm going to want to." Nerves rolled through his belly. "How would that sit with you?"

She looked over with a soft smile. "That would sit with me just fine, assuming we're good on the details."

"Such as?"

"Where are we going to live? Don't take this the wrong way, but I'm not sure I can live in the South full-time. I like the West and East coasts. And Paris and here, of course."

"Before meeting you, I hadn't given much thought to living anywhere but Dare River, but I never imagined loving the south of France like this. I'm not a big fan of New York City, honestly. Too many people and too much noise."

"Then we'll have to figure out where we might be happy together," she said, swinging their linked hands into the air. "Oh, I'm suddenly so nervous talking about all this. I've never lived with anyone. My mom and dad made it look so easy."

"You're lucky for that," he said, spotting Michaela walking toward them. "It's going to be fine, honey. Come here and let me kiss you once before we have company. I figure your sister won't mind, being a huge fan and all."

She laughed, tilting her head up, and he took the silent invitation, sliding his hands in her hair and cupping her nape. "You're the best thing that's ever happened to me, Caitlyn Merriam, and damn if I don't love you to pieces."

Her hands settled on his waist. "I love you to pieces right back."

He kissed her softly on the lips, keeping his eyes open to gaze into hers. Yeah, he saw the sunshine in them and expected he always would.

"Oh, you two! You're so cute. Kissing in the fields and walking with that poor baby goat." Michaela reached down and nuzzled Chou-Chou under the ears as they broke apart. "But I have news. There are a bunch of photos of you two eating dinner in the village trending on social media. It's crazy! People are talking about your new look, Beau, and your new lady friend."

Caitlyn glanced at him. *That couple.*

He made a rude noise. "It happens. Not my favorite part of fame, but..."

"Some of the stuff people are saying is downright nasty. Wondering why you're in France in the first place, Beau, what with you being an all-American boy, and in a velvet jacket with a pocket square and such. I mean, it's ridiculous. Caitlyn, you're going to be pretty unhappy about some of the stuff they're saying about you too. Flynn called me and told me to warn you since he couldn't reach you by phone."

Beau didn't like the sound of that. They could say whatever they liked about him, but he hated the thought of anyone dragging Caitlyn over the coals.

"I left my phone at the house." Caitlyn took a deep breath. "What are they saying?"

Michaela rolled her eyes. "Someone figured out who you are, so they're saying you're all New York City and into fashion so you're changing him."

"Bullshit," Beau ground out, causing Chou-Chou to bleat.

"I know! They're saying you have cat-scratch fever, Beau. I'd never heard that before, but some moron journalist thought it was clever, what with Caitlyn being your new lady and it being part of her name."

He put his hand on Caitlyn's shoulder, noting her muscles were tense. What in the hell was he supposed to do to fix this? Maybe Rye would know. He'd certainly been a target of the tabloids back in the day. "I'm going to call a friend. See what he advises. Caitlyn, I don't want you to be upset about this. Anyone with enough sense to fill a thimble will know it's nonsense."

"Whatever you do, Caitlyn," Michaela said, rubbing her sister's back, "don't go online. Flynn is having all your calls redirected to a Merriam assistant at corporate."

"Why?" she asked.

"Because journalists are calling for interviews and quotes," Michaela said. "Beau Masters having a girlfriend is big news beyond all the changes he's got going on."

Terrific. He needed to call Rye stat. His publicist at the record label would be having fits. "Let's head back to the house."

When they returned, Shawn, Clara, and Arthur were waiting for them.

"It's the worst sort of journalism," Arthur spat out. "If you can even call it that."

Shawn looked him in the eye—measuring him again, Beau imagined—before putting a reassuring hand on Caitlyn's arm. "Flynn has things in hand with our PR people."

"I'm sorry about this, y'all," Beau said. "I can handle them saying things about me, but not her. I have a few calls I need to make. If you'll excuse me."

He cupped Caitlyn's face and kissed her softly. "It's going to be fine, Sunshine."

Her mouth tipped up, but her face was pale. As he strode up the stairs, he came across Hargreaves.

"I'm sorry about the media attention, sir," the butler said, his face somber. "I expect you'll want to postpone our guitar lesson."

Right. He'd forgotten. "Yes. Thank you."

"If I can be of any service, please let me know." He bowed and headed down the stairs.

When Beau reached the room he and Caitlyn shared, he picked up the phone he'd left on the bedside next to hers. There were a few missed calls and voicemails. One from Rye, the others from the switchboard phone number Rye's manager had set up.

Rye's voice was a balm to his nerves.

Nice threads, Bubba, and an even nicer lady friend. But it's causing a shitstorm. Give me a call, and we'll figure things out.

Damn, but he was a good friend.

Since he'd included the switchboard number with the songs, he wasn't surprised one of the voicemails was from Tommy Penders at his record label.

Beau, we've seen the photos of you in France and reviewed the songs you sent. Unfortunately, we've decided we don't like the direction you're going creatively, so we're releasing you from your contract. We've already informed your mama. I'm sorry it came to this.

He lowered the phone slowly. They'd cut him? And in a voicemail? He sank onto the bed, his gut sick. That was it? They didn't even want to talk about it? He'd heard about record labels being merciless, but he'd never expected it to happen to him. He'd been with them nearly fifteen years.

"Oh, God," he whispered, tears burning. All he'd ever wanted was to sing. How could they not have liked the songs? They were his best work ever.

He clicked on the last voicemail and jerked when his mama's voice began.

Tommy gave me this number after he told me he was dropping you. Dropping you! Dammit, Beau. I told you nothing good would come of this fancy French perfume with that Merriam girl. She's given you cat-scratch fever but good, what with those chichi clothes you're wearing and those new songs you sent Tommy. We'll have to talk about that song about me. That's not going to fly, but I'll forgive you for it. Don't worry. Mama's going to fix everything. We'll find a new label. Those bastards are going to rue the day they dropped my son, but boy, I need you back here. Now. Set aside the other stuff between us. Your career is in trouble, baby. Call me.

Oh, God. His mind was swirling. Fix it? What in the hell was she thinking of doing? He should call her. She shouldn't be making decisions for him. He replayed the message, and now that the shock had sunk in, rage blossomed in its wake. She'd forgive him? How big of her.

He called Rye first.

"Bubba, you are having a day," Rye said. "God knows, I've been there. Clayton and I have been talking about some options while we were waiting for you to call. Your mama needs to be stopped."

"I know." He pinched the bridge of his nose.

"So you know about the press release?"

He froze. "What?"

"She put out a press release on your behalf thirty minutes ago saying you're the new spokesperson for Ryan Williams' cologne, stressing the all-American angle," Rye said. "Knowing what I know, I figure you didn't authorize that."

"I sure as hell didn't." *Damn her.* "I can't be their spokesperson. I'm Caitlyn's." Oh, God. This was a disaster. His mama's betrayal cut open his guts. How could she have done this without talking to him? She knew how he felt, but that was the point, wasn't it? She was making a statement here, steering his ship in the direction *she* wanted, like she did whenever push came to shove. Not this time. "She does have power of attorney," Beau said. "Has since I was sixteen. We thought it was easier because she was my manager. That needs to stop."

"Clayton can draw up the paperwork and send it to you over your phone. You need to sign it and send it back. I hope to hell you have a printer out there in France, Bubba, because we need the real John Hancock."

"You'll have it." He walked over to the window, his throat aching. "Rye, my record label dropped me. Tommy left a voicemail. Said they didn't like the creative direction I was heading." Which meant they hated New Beau. His stomach quivered. Would his fans feel the same way? No, he would have to trust in them and himself, now more than ever.

"Peckerwoods," Rye said with a scoff. "Of all the stupid, short-sighted... Clayton, you aren't going to believe this."

Beau heard his friend talking under his breath, and the pause brought Beau into contact with the pain. His mama had up and betrayed him. Again. Caitlyn was going to be so upset. Rightfully so. He'd have to work it out.

"I'm putting you on speaker," Rye said. "Okay, Bubba, we both agree another label will pick you up. Don't worry about that now. What we need to do is stop your mama from doing more damage."

"Once you sign the papers I'm sending," Clayton said, "I'll deliver them myself and tell her she is no longer legally authorized to commit you to anything. Beau, I need to know whether you plan on firing her. I mean, she's your mama and she's been with you since the beginning, so I get it, but you need to decide what's best for you."

"How can I have her represent my interests after all this? I came here needing to clear my head, but after our last talk, I wasn't feeling sure we'd continue. Professionally or personally. This decided it."

"Do you want me to fire her for you? I hate to ask like this, but time is of the essence here."

He thought about it. It was something he needed to do. "No, I'll call and tell her myself. I owe her that much." His own label hadn't afforded him the personal courtesy, but he thought it fair. "I had a voicemail from her too. Tommy must have given her the switchboard number. She mentioned fixing things, but no details."

"She must have been talking to the Williams people right along. There's no way they could make a deal happen like that in a matter of hours."

Tommy had alluded to it when he'd asked about the songs, but Beau hadn't thought she'd make a deal without talking to him. She never had before. "I should have stopped her earlier."

"I'll have to look into how to break the Williams contract," Clayton said. "Might be tricky, but we'll figure something out. Now, lastly, in regard to your career. You might recall my mama, Georgia Belle Chandler, being Rye's manager before retiring. I called to see if she'd be willing to come out of retirement to get your career back on track. I'd love to do it myself, but Rye is a full-time job. She's agreed for an interim period until you find someone new. I'm not tooting her horn none when I say her name carries weight in Nashville."

He gripped the windowsill. "I don't rightly know what to say except thank you. I'm humbled by your help. I didn't expect any of this."

"We got ya, son," Rye said. "Plus, me and Jake Lassiter are going to be your backup singers on *The Morning Show* as soon as you can haul yourself back stateside. It's got the highest ratings for a morning TV program. We'll launch your new song, 'Sunshine In Your Eyes.' Maybe a few others. But we won't be wearing matching velvet jackets—not that I don't like me a little Elvis velvet. We need to get one of these new songs out and show the world Penders and your label screwed up big time."

"Great idea. I'll get right back. I don't have the music completely written down. It's in my head."

"You can walk Jake and me through it," Rye said. "We're quick studies. Clay, anything else?"

"Once you talk to your mama and give her the news about the change, you text me, and I'll take matters from there."

"Georgia will want to meet you," Rye said, "but she's not as scary as she looks."

"She managed to take you to the top," Clayton said, "when you were farting around."

"I'm a changed man," Rye said. "Beau, if you learn anything from the change in my image, it's this: fans like to see the true heart of a man. My fans enjoyed my bad boy ways, but now the very same people praise me for being a family man. You're not swinging as far from the left to the right as I did. We have some shoveling to do, but this is going to settle down pretty fast. Trust me on that."

"I do," he said, glad to hear his friends echo his earlier thoughts about the fans. "You're a good friend. Both of you."

"We got your back, Bubba. Now go call your mama and do what you've got to do."

Something slammed, and Beau glanced over sharply to see a dark-haired man in a suit standing in the doorway. The tailored suit and hard look in his green eyes, the same shade as Caitlyn's, told him he'd met Quinn Merriam.

"You'll need to cut that call short," the man said in a terse tone. "We have business."

Caitlyn appeared, her face stark white.

She knew about Ryan Williams. They both did.

His chest tightened. God, he'd never imagined hurting her like this. "Rye, I need to go. I'll take care of things and get back to you."

"We'll be waiting," Rye said.

Beau set the phone on the windowsill. "If this is about Ryan Williams—"

"You're damn right it is," the man ground out. "Let me introduce myself. I'm Quinn Merriam, and I'm going to sue the hell out of you for breach of contract, verbal or otherwise. And I'm going to break you in two for lying to my sister."

"Quinn—" Caitlyn grabbed his arm. "Beau, tell me it's not true. Was it your mom? I know you wouldn't do this."

Her faith moved him, never more so than in this moment.

"The hell he wouldn't," Quinn said. "He only signed an NDA, Caitlyn. That keeps his options open, right, Beau? What did they offer you? More money?"

Beau stalked across the room and faced the man down. "Look, man, I didn't authorize this. I'm fully committed to Caitlyn's perfume. My mama—my manager—acted without me. I was about to call and fire her before you stormed in."

"Quinn, I told you," Caitlyn said, grabbing his arm.

The man stared at him through narrowed eyes. "That doesn't begin to undo this clusterfuck. You promised *my sister* you would be the spokesperson for her perfume, and now people around the world know you've signed a contract with Ryan Williams. And after your cozy evening out with my sister, which is plastered all over social media."

Beau got in his face. "You're calling me a two-timing liar?"

"If the shoe fits," Quinn said.

"Quinn—"

"Out of respect for Caitlyn," Beau interrupted, "I'm not going to punch you for that. But you'd best watch your tone. I didn't lie."

"No? Well, the media is going to think maybe you did.

Some might say you've been playing with Caitlyn on the side while making a deal with our competitor. Or that my sister has been using her wiles to get you to sign with her. Do you understand our problem? And don't you dare tell me to watch my tone."

"You are so out of line, Quinn," Caitlyn said, her hands fisted at her sides.

"*Quinn*," Caitlyn's father said, coming into the room. "I'm not supposed to intercede in Merriam business anymore, but I heard you both shouting all the way downstairs. Given my impression of Beau—"

"You only met him last night, Dad," Quinn said.

"I taught you to take a man's measure in one look, one handshake. You need to hear me on this, son."

Quinn opened his suit jacket, laying his hands on his waist. "Fine, but we're in a serious predicament here, Dad. And that's not even considering how this will affect Caitlyn or her reputation."

"Stop speaking for me," she said, coming over to Beau and standing before him. "This is my project we're talking about. Beau, tell me what's going on. Start from the beginning."

He put his hands on her shoulders and gazed into her strained eyes. "I love you. That's first up and the most important."

Her brother scoffed, and Beau shot him a look.

"Second, I didn't authorize the Ryan Williams thing. My mama threatened me through a friend and my label about meeting with them, but I didn't think she'd go this far—not when she knew how I felt about your venture."

"What?" She stepped back from him. "You knew she was talking to them?"

"I didn't think she'd do anything. I hadn't even read their proposal. I didn't want to talk to her, so I..." Shit, this was on him. "I should have stopped her."

"Yes, you should have," Caitlyn said, staring at him.

"You were having problems with your manager, but you let her continue to act with legal authority on your behalf?" her brother asked. "I don't care if she's your mama. What kind of *idiot* are you?"

Beau closed the distance between them and shoved Quinn back a step. "I don't need to explain myself to you."

The man was in his face immediately. "You made a commitment to Merriam Enterprises verbally and in an NDA, and I'm the vice president, so you sure as hell do." He shoved him back.

"Quinn!" Caitlyn cried.

"Stop this!" Shawn shouted. "Both of you. We'll work this out like gentlemen. Squabbling isn't going to resolve anything. Beau, you should go ahead and make that call to your mama. Then I'd recommend calling your lawyer so they can talk to the Ryan Williams people and explain that she acted without your authorization. It will be embarrassing, perhaps, but we'll find a way to spin it for both of our camps."

Standing between her father and brother, Caitlyn seemed small, her shoulders stooped in pure dejection. Beau was going to have to fix this for her as much as him. "I was talking to people on just those points when you came in." He glared at Quinn. "You should know my record label just dropped me—"

"More good news," Quinn sneered.

What an asshole. "We're going to find me a new home. I'm signing with a new manager who has clout, but yes, right now my career is in trouble. There's one thing I do know. Caitlyn, if you'll trust me..."

"Oh, Beau, how could they drop you?" She shuffled forward and took his hands, searching his face.

Pain surged at her concern. He'd messed everything up, but she was worried about *him*. "They didn't like my new songs or creative direction. Caitlyn, they dumped me in a voicemail. After being with them for my whole career."

She put her arms around him. "I'm so sorry."

"Me too, Beau," Shawn said softly. "Quinn, let's leave them alone for a bit."

"Dad, we need to iron things out here and protect our interests," Quinn said. "Caitlyn, don't let him talk you into anything."

"Shut up, Quinn!" she said, making her brother reel back in shock. "I appreciate you showing up with your fiery sword on behalf of me and Merriam Enterprises, but I'm not a child. If it makes you feel any better to hear it, you were right. I was wrong not to insist on Beau signing a contract up front, but I know we're going to work this out."

"It's still going to look bad," Quinn said. "Caitlyn, I hate to do this, but it's my job. I green-lit your new perfume venture based on Beau Masters' media appeal. That seems to be in the tank right now. Are you sure you want him? Take your feelings out of the equation. We can find someone else to be your spokesman."

Caitlyn crossed her arms. "Just moments before you were spouting off about commitments, Quinn."

Her brother's gaze seemed to pick him apart. "That was before I knew about this. It's a serious matter, Caitlyn."

"I know it is." She turned and looked at him, her inspection like the pause between a chorus and refrain, and Beau held his breath. "Better than you, Quinn. Beau, I was at the restaurant last night and heard what that couple said. Do you believe your fans are going to embrace the new you?"

He met her gaze head on. This was the businesswoman talking. He knew the woman—his woman—embraced the new him. "I just got off the phone with Rye Crenshaw. We have a plan. If you know anything about Rye's history, you know he got even more popular after changing his image. If anyone knows how to turn negative press around, it's Rye." He realized he was the one doing the selling, and perhaps that wasn't a bad thing. Caitlyn's brother needed to hear it. He wasn't a man to go on blind faith.

"It's still risky," Quinn said, yanking on his tie. "I don't know anything about this Rye fellow, but having you as our spokesperson just became a liability. Might be better to cut ties altogether."

Beau held his breath.

"That's my decision to make," Caitlyn said, flicking her brother a hard glance. "If Beau says he's going to turn it around, I believe him. I also believe in this new direction. In the beginning, I was a little concerned he was moving so far away from the image I originally wanted, but in truth, he's more compelling now than he was then. I still think he's the right man for the job. Add in the power of Merriam Enterprises, and we'll get back on track."

He wanted to close the distance between them and kiss the heck out of her. Given the company, he settled instead for "thank you."

"That's settled then," Shawn said. "Like Caitlyn said, we'll put all our resources behind this. Come on, Quinn, let's find a bucket of water to put out your sword."

"Dad, I'm doing the job you asked of me," the man said, leaving with his father. "This situation—"

"I know, son," Beau heard, and then he and Caitlyn were alone together.

Needing to touch her, to claim her, he kissed her full on the lips before pulling back. "Thank you, Sunshine. You have no idea what that meant to me."

"My brother was out of line, but he was also forcing us to look at the business side of things. I'm still mad, but I'm glad he pushed it. Because this is business, Beau, and we swore to keep the personal and professional separate."

He nodded. "Speaking of, I need to call my mama,"

he said, the thought making his belly cramp. "Will you sit with me? I... It's not every day you fire your own mama. God, how did it come to this?"

Some of the good times flashed in his mind: celebrating at Outback Steakhouse after he signed his first record deal; presenting her with his first CMA award backstage; watching her cry when he played the first song he'd written about her, "Always in My Corner." He hung his head. Not all his memories were bad, but that didn't matter. She wasn't in his corner now, even though she probably thought otherwise.

Caitlyn patted his back as he dialed her number.

"Hello, Mama," he said when she answered.

"Boy, it's about time you called. Beau, we have one hell of a storm to weather, but we're going to do it. Tommy is going to rue the day he cut my son."

Even the outrage in her angry drawl didn't appease him none. "Mama, you were wrong to sign me to Ryan Williams. You knew I intended to do Caitlyn Merriam's perfume."

"It's bad for your image, but you wouldn't listen. That girl has you tied in knots, boy. I saw those pictures of you in that fancy Eurotrash suit, sipping pink champagne. Don't tell me what I know. You never dressed like a homo before you met that girl, and you sure as hell never drank. She's a bad influence, and your label dropping you is proof of that. Luckily the Ryan Williams people like your new look—classic Americana, they're calling it, even if it sounds like bullshit to me. They didn't drop you, which is why I put out that press release after talking to them. We needed a move, and after managing you all this time, I knew what had to be done. That you question it shows how messed up in the head you are."

He wondered how long ago she'd signed it. It hadn't been the last-ditch act of desperation he'd believed it to be. That made it easier to say what he needed to say, but it still didn't feel easy. "I'm not going to honor the contract, Mama. In fact, I'm calling to tell you... It's time we parted ways."

Silence hung heavily on the line, and then she burst out, "You're *firing* me? Your very own mama? The one who raised you and helped you become the man you are today? The famous singer you are today? No, sir. This isn't my Beau talking. I know you're mad at me right now, but you'd never do something this hurtful."

He clutched the phone. "Hurtful? Pot calling the kettle black, Mama. I never thought you'd lie or go behind my back. Mama, we're through." Discussing it further would be pointless. "Clayton Chandler will be serving you papers shortly on that score, and then Georgia Belle Chandler is gonna help me turn around things."

"Rye Crenshaw's old manager? That son of a bitch. I knew you were tight, but this is—"

"He's a good friend, Mama. I don't know what else there is to say. Maybe we'll speak of other things someday..."

"*Other things*," she said, her drawl turning from honey to battery acid. "You mean your real daddy. Isn't that why you're punishing me, Beau?"

He rubbed his jaw. "Mama, I'm not punishing you. I already asked you for the truth, and you refused to give it to me."

"But that's before you told your mama she was out." Her breathing was audible over the line. "What would you give me for your real daddy's name, Beau?"

Even he could hear the serpent's hiss in her voice. How he wanted that apple. "You offering a trade, Mama?"

She made a rude sound. "To keep my place at your side, you bet. You'll honor the Ryan Williams agreement. It will help your career. Besides, if you back out of this deal, your word will be shit. You know that, right, Beau?"

His jaw locked. Once a man lost his credibility, it was an uphill climb to get it back. "You've neatly boxed me in a corner."

"I know my son."

Yes, she did. He imagined she'd been planning this since the moment he'd left her house. "What else?"

"The new songs and this new Eurotrash look have to go. I'll figure out a way to get the Williams people on board."

His truth. She was asking him to give up his truth. He wouldn't do it. "No."

She was quiet, and he could almost hear the wheels in her mind turning. "I know every shade of your voice, son. Fine. The Williams' cologne only."

He couldn't believe he was still talking to her, let alone negotiating with her, and yet...how could he pass up the chance to learn his daddy's name? He had a plan to save his career, but this could be his only chance to learn the truth about himself.

"You're still out, Mama." That wasn't negotiable.

"So I save my son's career with this spokesperson gig, you walk into a new record deal, *and* you get your real daddy's name? Sounds like I'm getting the short stick."

But could he even count on his mama to be truthful?

"How will I know you're telling me the truth about my real daddy?" he asked.

A shudder ran through him, and Caitlyn met his gaze. Before, she'd had her head down, and he'd been too caught up in the conversation to discern what she was thinking. Would Caitlyn understand? Her brother probably still thought they should find another spokesman for her perfume. Surely they could. With Ibrahim as their perfumer, the product would sell itself.

"You can do that gene testing thing, can't you? Besides, he already knows about you. Has for years."

He almost folded over from the pain. "What do you mean my real daddy knows about me?"

"You met him when you were young, before I stopped him from seeing you behind my back."

He inhaled sharply. "What do you mean you *stopped* him? More betrayal, Mama?"

"Oh, you want his name so badly you can taste it. Let's finalize our deal. You keep paying me my salary."

Somehow he wasn't surprised the money was a consideration for her. "Fine." He had more money than he could spend in a lifetime, and despite everything, she was his mama. He couldn't let her be poor again.

"And you do the Williams thing. Then I'll give you your real father's name."

He glanced at the top of Caitlyn's brown hair. Could he really agree to this?

"Otherwise, I take it to my grave, Beau."

He could hear the steel in her voice. God help him, she meant it.

"He'd probably even want a father-son relationship with you." His heart thudded at the words. "After all, he's a real good man. Like you."

Her arrow struck hard and true. His mind filled with visions of meeting his daddy for the first time. He'd finally know the fullness of his roots. He'd finally understand where the other half of his features had come from. Maybe his daddy would come to his concerts. He could imagine grilling out back with him at the Dare River house, Caitlyn laughing with them as they all drank rosé together on the deck.

He squeezed his eyes shut. God, his mama was right. He wanted this so badly he could taste it. But he turned to the woman still resting her hand on his back in comfort. Could she understand this? She'd stood up to her brother for him, believed in him when it felt like no one did. But this was his daddy...

God, she had to understand.

"Okay, Mama, you win. The Williams deal and your full salary. Now, give me my daddy's name."

He felt Caitlyn tense against him. Watched as she stood before him, her narrowed eyes glued to his face.

I'm sorry, he mouthed, holding out his hand to her.

She shook her head slowly in disbelief and walked out of the room.

"Your real daddy is Carlos Garcia." Mama laughed shrilly as the shock rolled through him. "Remember him? He was the landscaper at your elementary school after Walt died."

"*Mr. Garcia?*" The quiet groundskeeper had been kind to him right after Walt had died, showing him how he cut the bushes around the school. Beau remembered helping him plant bright flowers in the big pots in the front of the school. Mr. Garcia had even let him sit on the riding mower when he'd mowed the soccer field and surrounding areas. He'd thought they were friends. But one day, he was simply gone. Beau had never known why, and the school representatives had told him he'd taken another job; they didn't know where or why. He'd kept looking for him around town, but he'd never seen him again.

"*What did you do, Mama?*"

"We met at a bar one night, and Carlos was real nice to me, nicer than those worthless rednecks who loitered around drunk every night. He didn't know I was married, and I never told him. He was new to town, just starting up his landscaping business. I stopped seeing him when I found out I was pregnant. Never told him about it or you."

All Beau could hear was his heart pounding in his chest.

"Somehow he found out about you, either because of the timing or your features. Heck, it was a small town.

When you came home from school one day talking about Mr. Garcia, I panicked. I told Carlos I would ruin him if he so much as came near you again. Told him I'd tell everyone he'd attacked me if he didn't leave town. I didn't want anyone to know you weren't Walt Masters' boy. I'd be ruined. You'd be called a bastard—a spic even—and treated even worse. You know small towns. You might not have looked like Walt much, but no one had the proof or the gall to say otherwise. See how you owe me, boy."

He realized he was gripping the duvet, his knuckles white. The threat she'd made was as ugly as they got. "Why didn't you tell me later? When I was older? I could have found him again."

"I couldn't make myself," she said, her voice cracking. "I...was afraid I'd see what I saw in your eyes the last day you came to my house. Your career was our ticket to everything I ever wanted for us, and I didn't want to lose you or hurt that. Beau, you've been my whole life."

Tears burned his eyes, his entire system flooding with grief. *Oh, Mama.* "Perhaps it shouldn't have been that way, but it's done now. I... Thank you for finally telling me." He couldn't handle what that had cost him right now, but he'd have to deal with it. She'd made him trade for his daddy's real name. A part of him still couldn't believe it. But he intended to honor his word. He needed to.

"And what about us, Beau? Where does this leave us? You can fire me, but I'm still your mama."

He sniffed and wiped away the tears leaking down his cheeks. "I don't rightly know right now. I love you, but I'm still really angry at you for what you've done. All of it. I'll... have to see."

Her sharp intake of breath seemed to drill in his skull. "You get that career back on track, ya hear? I know Georgia has one hell of a reputation, but if she messes up with you, she and I will have it out for sure. You tell her that."

He nodded, rubbing away more tears. "Goodbye, Mama."

"Bye, Beau."

When he hung up, the phone clattered to the floor. He put his head in his hands, the pain there throbbing, connecting to the pain in his heart. He sat there, praying it would abate some, and when he could stand, he walked to the door.

Now he had to explain what he'd done to Caitlyn.

CHAPTER 25

CAITLYN ASKED EVERYONE TO CLEAR THE HOUSE WHEN SHE came down the stairs.

Quinn stepped forward, his jaw hard. "What happened?"

She forced herself to say the words she still struggled to believe. "He's doing Ryan Williams."

"What?" Michaela, who'd been standing next to their dad in the main room, rushed over and hugged her. "He wouldn't! Caitlyn, he loves you."

"His mom made him a deal about something very personal." She glanced over to where Uncle Arthur and Aunt Clara were standing by the sofa. Everyone was on their feet, and no wonder. "She gave him the answer he wanted."

Uncle Arthur sighed. "Well, she knew how to get her way. He wanted that information badly."

"What answer?" Quinn locked his arms over his chest. "I thought everything was settled. Now, I'm going to have fun making him pay for hurting you and going back on his word."

"Enough, Quinn!" She marched over to him.

"I know you're upset, but I was coming down to help you counter the things they're saying against you in the press, by the way, because you're my sister. I only learned about the Williams press release when I checked my phone after landing."

"I can't...take this right now," she said. "I need you to arrange for Beau to leave on your plane. Right away." He would need to get back, and after what he'd done, she needed him gone.

Her father finally walked over and put his hand on her shoulder. "If you think that's best. Quinn, call your pilot."

"Caitlyn, are you sure?" Michaela asked.

She nodded, her throat thickening with emotion. She watched with a heavy heart as Quinn pulled out his phone and called his pilot.

"My car will take him when he's ready," her brother said. "The plane is being refueled now."

"Good." But it wasn't good. It was horrible. Unimaginable. His mother was an awful woman, but he'd let her manipulate him again. And after she'd stood up for him.

"Sorry situation all around," Uncle Arthur said. "For both of you."

"Oh, Caitlyn," Aunt Clara said. "It must have been a terrible choice for him. He does love you, but he's been haunted by that other matter the whole time he's been here."

She knew it. But she kept returning to the fact that he'd known about his mother's contact with Ryan Williams and done nothing to stop her... And while she understood why he'd traded his promise to her for his father's name, Beau had helped her grow confident enough in herself to know she deserved better than that. Even from him. But God, it hurt.

"I'm not leaving until I hear what's really going on here." Quinn planted his feet like a bull.

"It sounds like this is personal, Quinn," their dad said. "Come on. Let's leave her alone like she's asked." He kissed her cheek, and Quinn put his hand on her shoulder before following their father out. Michaela hugged her again with all her might, the sweetness of the gesture nearly making her cry.

"I'm so sorry," her sister said.

"Me too," she whispered.

Aunt Clara crossed to hug her warmly, her eyes filled with the tears. Uncle Arthur gazed at her, his face serious, before taking Aunt Clara's arm and leading her out.

The front door closed, and she let herself sink onto a chair in the main room. It was over. She'd known it when he'd mouthed *I'm sorry* to her. When she heard Beau's footsteps on the stairs, she walked into the entryway to face him.

He stopped on the last step. "I don't know what to say to you right now."

She found it hard to draw breath. "Me either."

"I didn't feel like I had a choice," he said, sitting on that last step and meeting her eyes. "You know how hard this was for me. Caitlyn, I've wanted to know who my real father is so badly, and then she told me that he'd probably want a relationship with me... I had to do it. Please understand. It was my only chance."

She pressed her hand to her heart. "Part of me understands but the other part... Beau, I trusted you. I put my faith in you. This perfume means so much to me. You mean so much to me, and I was excited for us to do this together."

His blue-gray eyes were wet. "Me too, that's why this is so hard."

"I know it's not on par with learning the real name of a parent, but if you'd just signed the contract like I wanted, this couldn't have happened."

"I wanted to—I was trying to buy more time," he said. "Caitlyn, my record label wasn't behind me doing it, but I planned to bring them on board after I left here. I didn't want to worry you."

"You never told me that," she said, her stomach

sinking to the ground.

"No, I didn't," he said. "I would have turned them around, but—"

"What else didn't you tell me? Because you sure as hell didn't tell me you that your mom told you about Ryan Williams."

"I have no excuses here," he said, standing slowly. "Caitlyn, I know I hurt you. I let you down. Tell me how to make things right."

Seeing him before her, his face haggard, his posture defeated, all she could do was shake her head again. "You can't, Beau. You said Old Beau let things slide, and I guess you were right. I can't be with someone who I can't trust when push comes to shove. The fact is: my perfume is in jeopardy, and you broke my heart."

He looked down for a moment before raising his eyes. "I know I did, and I'm sorry. The words aren't adequate. You put your trust in me, and I let you down."

She made herself say what needed saying. Then she could break down. "You need to get back to Nashville and put your career back on track. Quinn's driver will take you to Cannes as soon as you've packed. Our company pilot will fly you home. Since Merriam Enterprises brought you here, the least we can do is give you a return flight."

His throat moved as he swallowed. "What about you? What can I do to help *you*? I know how much this perfume means to you. I love it too. I don't want to be the cause of it failing. Maybe...I can ask Jake Lassiter to be the spokesperson. Or Rye Crenshaw. They're...good guys. Either of them would fit the bill."

Oh, she was going to lose it. He needed to leave. "I'll regroup. Figure something out. Thanks for the referrals though."

He made an agonized sound. "How do we go from talking about forever in the fields this morning to *this*?"

Pain slashed through her belly. Earlier, she'd

imagined their wedding taking place at the edge of the fields with the reception at the farmhouse where they'd fallen in love. Now those dreams had turned to dust.

"Quinn always says business shouldn't be mixed with other things," she said, her voice cracking. "I was wrong not to listen."

His face fell, but he stayed silent, gazing at her with red-rimmed blue eyes.

"You need to pack, and I need to see about some things. I'll say goodbye now. Good luck with everything, Beau."

His mouth pursed like he was fighting his words. Then he said, "You too, Sunshine. And thank you. For everything."

Her lips were trembling. She couldn't utter a reply, so she strode out the front door toward the fields. Usually the lavender soothed her, but only shorn plants remained.

The magic was gone.

CHAPTER 26

BEAU PACKED WITH A HEAVY HEART, HIS HANDS LINGERING over the coverlet of their bed when he finished. It smelled of them, and the thought nearly undid him.

They were done. Just like that. And his real last name was Garcia. Beau Garcia. He couldn't wrap his head around any of it.

He sank down, feeling the mattress give way. He still couldn't believe Carlos Garcia was his real father. As a boy, he'd thought him the kindest man, showing him things about the plants and grass and asking about his grades and school. His belly sliced open again. To think, his mama had threatened the man and forced him to leave town. He wanted to howl. All these years, his real dad had wanted to know him.

Well, he would find Mr. Garcia. His daddy. They would start over. Find new ground.

But Caitlyn? How was he supposed to walk away from this woman? He couldn't blame her for wanting him gone. He'd done wrong by her all the way, but he didn't see a clear path toward fixing it.

He picked up his bags and the flamenco guitar, his arms full, and walked to Hargreaves' door. Since he mostly kept to his room, there was a chance he'd be there. The rest of the house was silent. When he knocked, there was brief pause and the door opened.

Hargreaves stood there, his face somber. "Sir?"

He was getting choked up already. This man had helped him so much. "I wanted to say goodbye, Hargreaves, and thank you for everything."

The older man bowed formally. "Keep playing the flamenco guitar. You have talent. It was an honor to know you, sir."

"The honor was mine," he said, clearing his throat. Caitlyn's family—including this man—had been nothing but warm and supportive. Shame washed over him. "Please tell Arthur and Clara I'm sorry. They can explain what happened. I'll leave you now."

He nodded, and Beau made himself walk away. Downstairs, a driver was waiting in the entryway.

"I'll take your bags, sir," he said.

"I'll be a moment," Beau said, knowing he couldn't leave without trying to say goodbye to Ibrahim. The rest of Caitlyn's family might be gone—at her bidding likely—but Ibrahim would be in the lab, working on the perfume and cologne Beau would no longer help share with the world.

When he entered the other house, the lone call of a man's voice in French grabbed him by the throat. The singer sounded like he'd lost everything. He knew that kind of pain. It was odd how learning his real daddy's name hadn't lightened it none.

He rapped on the doorframe since Ibrahim was standing in front of his cabinets filled with fragrance notes. "You're listening to Raï again. I'll always be grateful you introduced me to it."

Ibrahim turned, cocking his head. "Whatever happened is grave. Your skin has lost all color, Beau."

He wasn't going to beat around the bush. Not with this man he respected. "I made some awful mistakes. My mother threatened to sign me with Ryan Williams' cologne if I didn't return to Nashville. I didn't take measures to stop her. I just learned she signed the contract in my name and the whole world knows."

Ibrahim's brows shot to his hairline. "That is serious."

"I was going to back out of it," he said, "but she dangled a powerful enticement in front of me."

"The name of your real father." He sighed deeply. "The truth at last."

He laughed, the sound harsh even to his ears. "What did you call it? The most prized of fragrances."

"Indeed," he said, gesturing to the chair and sitting down himself. "And this has no doubt harmed your personal relationship with Caitlyn."

"Yes. I love her, Ibrahim, but I had to know, especially after Mama told me I knew the man." He filled him in on the details and watched as his friend's face lost all color too.

"Your mother must feel a great deal of shame to go to such lengths to keep you and your father apart. I'm sorry for her. She was wrong to negotiate with you for something you had every right to know. The truth isn't a commodity."

"And yet she did, and I agreed to it. That's on me. The only thing is...I love Caitlyn with my heart and soul. I don't know how to make her trust me again. She said Old Beau got us into this situation, and she's not wrong."

"But you're not Old Beau anymore," Ibrahim said. "The man sitting in front of me is very different from the man who first arrived. I haven't explained the keystone in a fragrance yet, have I?"

His heart thudded in his chest. Somehow he knew this wisdom was going to hurt. "No."

"A keystone is the element that holds a perfume together. Your keystone is truth. It has been since the moment you learned of this betrayal."

He nodded. "I didn't think the truth would come at a cost."

Ibrahim's pencil-thin smile was sad this time. "You only feel the cost because you haven't brought Old and New Beau into balance. There's something we call an azeotropic mixture. This consists of two substances with different volatilities that reach an equilibrium and evaporate as one. When you find that equilibrium inside of yourself, there will be only Beau, not old, not new. Even cataclysmic occurrences, like learning your family's name, won't be able to shake who you are."

Gripping his knees, he stared at the man. "But how do I do *that*?"

The man smiled at him again as he took out the thick cream paper Beau recognized right away. "I have two more questions for you to answer."

Beau watched, mesmerized, as the Perfume Jedi wrote something on a sheet and rolled it up. He took it from him.

"You can read that one after you leave the room," he said, scrawling another note. He rolled it up and handed it to Beau. "This one should be read once you've returned to Nashville. If you answer the questions honestly, I think you'll find your own azeotropic mixture, and as such, the balance you've been seeking. Good luck with it, my friend."

Beau stood, his palms wrapped around the notes. "Is that it? You don't want to yell at me? It's your perfume I'm screwing over too. And the cologne."

Shaking his head, Ibrahim said, "No one person can ever hinder someone else's passion unless that person gives up. Caitlyn won't give up, and neither will I. This perfume will do everything she hopes it will do."

Beau felt his heart stop at that. Caitlyn wouldn't give up, and that somehow comforted him. Her perfume would go on. Like his music would. He only wished he could be a part of it all.

More than anything, he wished he could be part of her life.

"I didn't want it to be like this," he said. "End like this."

"Then don't end it here," Ibrahim said, flashing him a smile. "Goodbye for now, Beau."

As he left the lab, the haunting strands of a flamenco guitar filled his ears. Ibrahim must have changed the playlist. A final message? Beau didn't know. He couldn't breathe.

The driver was waiting for him, impatience stamped on his round face. Beau lifted his gaze to the second-floor window, the bedroom he'd shared with Caitlyn. They'd stood by that window after making love, arms wrapped around each other, looking out at the moonlit lavender. Pain shot through his heart. How was he supposed to walk away from her?

When he situated himself in the back seat, he realized he'd forgotten to say goodbye to Chou-Chou. "Stop the car."

The driver punched the gas.

"I said, 'Stop the car.'"

He jolted forward when the driver braked hard, but Beau barely noticed. He was already out of the car, leaving the door open in his wake. "Chou-Chou!" He kept calling the baby goat's name, running across the front lawn to the back of the house, tears filling his eyes.

He heard an answering bleating, and he sprinted to the portico. The baby goat was running toward him on his short, spindly little legs. He sank to his knees when he reached the little animal, wrapping his arms around his furry neck.

"Hey, buddy," he said, crying now. Hell, if anyone saw him, they'd think he was crazy, but he loved this little guy.

Chou-Chou nuzzled his neck, bleating softly. This goat was another thing Beau didn't want to leave behind. Who was going to take care of this little orphan when he was gone? Oh, hell.

"Thanks, buddy. For hanging out with me in the fields and helping me write the songs." He scratched him under the ears and made himself turn away.

Chou-Chou's cries followed him back to the car, and as he closed the door, he saw the goat running after them on the road as the driver punched the gas, sending dirt spraying in their wake.

The sky turned cloudy, and when he turned around, he couldn't see Chou-Chou anymore. Fear shot through him. He couldn't see the house. Or Caitlyn.

It was all gone as if it had never been.

He opened his right palm and unrolled the first paper from Ibrahim. The earth trembled as he read it:

When someone lies to me or makes me a party to their lies, I...

He crushed the paper against his heart, afraid to hear the answer, knowing it would change his course.

But a guitar sounded in his mind, and then he heard his own voice singing: *Damn her.*

Damn her, those roots were false.

Have to find the truth of me.
Have to seek out the best in me.
Have to plant new roots.

Beau had to find his new equilibrium, or the road ahead would always be cloudy.

CHAPTER 27

AFTER BEAU LEFT, CAITLYN PULLED HER CLOTHES OUT OF the chifforobe and hefted them over to Michaela's room. She couldn't stand smelling Beau everywhere.

Her sister wouldn't mind changing rooms. She'd been through a breakup.

She finally went online. Just like Michaela had warned her, the media had hazed her good. The papers were saying she'd enticed Beau Masters to be the spokesperson for her new perfume, and when the relationship had soured, he'd gotten his revenge by signing to do Ryan Williams' new cologne. They both looked like fools—even worse, petty lovers—but the impact would be worse for her because she was the woman. Who was going to buy her perfume? See her vision?

Everything seemed hopeless. Ibrahim deserved to know what was going on, and so she summoned the will to walk to the guesthouse.

The perfumer was sitting at his desk, listening to the poignant sounds of a Verdi opera, smelling strips on what looked to be a windmill. It made her think of *Don Quixote* and Beau and Chou-Chou sitting in the fields.

"Am I kidding myself, thinking we can still succeed without Beau as our spokesman?" she asked, sitting in the chair across from him. "People are saying some nasty things."

"Are we not still making one of the best perfumes out there?" he asked, inhaling as he spun the wheel. "One that will help every woman remember that she's important? One that will help her embrace her true essence and power?"

Those words—her words—had her hanging her head. "I don't feel any of that right now, and I hate it."

He reached into his pocket and pulled out a violet handkerchief, which only reminded her of the one Beau had given her. She'd stuffed it into the back of the chifforobe before she'd changed rooms.

"Best cry it out," he said. "The songs say love hurts, but I've found it's the loss of it that hurts the most."

She sniffed, the tears starting to fall. "I thought he loved me."

"Ah, *chérie*," Ibrahim said softy, gazing at her warmly from across his glass table. "He does, but he made some choices that have made you question it. The truth is, his actions don't diminish you in any way."

"You haven't seen what the media is saying," she said, sniffing.

"The media does not know the full story, do they? You still matter to Beau even though he chose to know his real father over doing this perfume."

She sat up straighter. "He told you that?"

"Before he left. He visited the poor baby goat too; I saw from my window. He seemed very upset to say good-bye to it. Not too many men could feel such love for a mere goat, but every life matters, does it not?"

Hearing he'd been torn up over leaving Chou-Chou warmed her heart. But rage wasn't far behind. "He didn't stop his mother or tell me his record label was against him doing this perfume. I don't want to be with someone like that. I mean, my brother Quinn can be tough—you'll meet him at dinner—but he flew here to help me combat the mess with the media. That's loyalty."

"So it's loyalty that tells you that you matter," Ibrahim said, spinning the wheel again. "Interesting."

"I know my family has my back when the chips are down. Why wouldn't I want the same in the man I love? I deserve that."

"Because sometimes a man's choice isn't about loyalty to this or that person," he said. "It's about love. Have you thought any more about the question I first asked you about what the foundation of a good woman is?"

She nodded. "If I had to answer today, I'd say it was the people who love her."

"I see," Ibrahim said, spinning the wheel. "You know, I think I have our perfume here. I was wondering just before you arrived, but now I'm sure of it. All along, my instincts told me to model it after you, and they are never wrong. You have been on the quest every woman must undertake—to embrace her true self, to know she matters. Come, inhale gently."

"You modeled it after me?" She pointed to herself in shock.

"But of course, *chérie*," he said, crooking his finger.

Standing, she bent over as he spun the wheel. She caught something woodsy and earthy, followed by an unmistakable hint of lavender, which made her think of her father. Then a top note burst through. "Is that grapefruit?"

"Very good. What did the lavender make you think of?"

"My dad," she said, inhaling again. "It's calming."

He made a soft sound. "You know there are many studies on the soothing effects of lavender, but the one I have found the most interesting and telling postulates that lavender helps build trust. In people and in oneself. If I were a betting man, I'd bet it's why you bought this lavender farm and why you want it to be in your perfume. It's also why you've been learning to trust yourself more. It's why Beau could find himself in the fields."

And why they'd chosen to make love for the first time with the lavender all around them, she thought, her heart tearing. She'd trusted him then. With everything she was.

"What else do you smell?" he asked. "Close your eyes."

She inhaled again, feeling the slight breeze from the wheel spinning. "I don't know what the note is, but it smells like Flynn."

"Who else?" he asked, his voice low.

She focused on the tip of her nose and inhaled softly. The earthy note made her think of Beau. Tears filled her eyes. "You know who."

"The name, please," he said, quietly yet firmly.

"Beau."

"What else?"

"There's something spicy with the grapefruit. I can't place it."

"Open your eyes and sit down." He folded his hands on the glass table. "Take a breath."

She inhaled raggedly until her chest eased. "This is intense, Ibrahim."

"It's because we're coming to the end of our journey with this perfume. When we first spoke, I understood how important family was to you. When I met Flynn, I smelled vetiver and clove at the base. He's the brother you're closest to, the one who always makes you feel you matter because you're important to him. Like a best friend, in fact."

Her mouth parted. "Yes, I guess you're right."

"Then there's the lavender symbolizing the kindness your father showed you by buying those soaps for you when you were a young woman, just beginning to discover yourself. It wasn't often he thought of you and you alone. That act told you that you mattered to him too, which is why it soothes you. We all want our parents to love and cherish us. They give us life, so to speak."

Daddy issues. "God, I'm a cliché."

"If that's true, we all are, Caitlyn." He spun the wheel again. "I added the notes I gave to Beau, ones he couldn't make out at the time. But they're like him. Earthy. Sandalwood. Cedar. And one housed in mystery, the facets of himself he was discovering while he stayed here: best described by myrrh, I thought. He made you feel you mattered too, like a lifetime partner should. Much like my wife made me feel every day we spent together."

She wasn't following, her heart tripping in her chest now. "But that's *them*. That's not me! And that's the whole problem, isn't it? I want to matter for me and me alone. I don't want to...need anyone to tell me I count."

He spun the wheel again. "Which is why the top notes are *you*. You see, the base and middle ones sometimes hold us up—like a foundation to a building, if you like. But the top note is all our own. Grapefruit for your zest for life, with a touch of cinnamon because you speak your mind and from your heart. Like every woman wishes for herself. Truth, Caitlyn. It's the most prized of fragrances."

Tears ran down her face, and she swiped at them. "Ibrahim, I had no idea when I hired you that making a perfume was going to be anything like this."

He laughed. "The perfume industry writ large has mostly lost its soul these past few decades, creating mass, synthetic scents that have no soul. It's no wonder so many people eschew perfume these days, saying it's unpleasant to the nose. What they are smelling are fakes, as crass as a false Monet. You hired me because you wanted a true perfume, one that meant something. Why wouldn't it be a process of great discovery? There's nothing more evocative, personal, or powerful than scent."

Hadn't she just moved out of the room she'd shared with Beau for that very reason? "Let me smell our perfume again."

"Spin the wheel," he said. "It's *your* perfume, Caitlyn,

one that will, I believe, resonate with every woman around the world."

She spun it with flourish, closing her eyes, savoring every note. "I love it, Ibrahim." This time her tears were for a different reason. "We women smell pretty great."

"Yes, you do," he said, smiling. "So again, at this final stage of our perfume journey, I ask you: what is the foundation of a great woman?"

She felt her heart open as if it had wings. *"Herself."*

"Brava" He clapped softly, the operatic music in the background a perfect accompaniment to his applause.

"We do need another spokesperson, however," she said.

"You'll find the right person," he said, reaching back and handing her a curved purple glass perfume bottle with a carved crystal top. "Here's the perfume. Now that we have the ingredients, I'll draw up the quantities we'll need to purchase."

"I'll talk to our bottle designer and finalize things," she said, enthusiasm cutting through her gloom. *"Thank you, Ibrahim."*

"You're most welcome," he said, "but really it's you who I need to thank. Without someone or something to inspire the master perfumer, there would be no perfume, and who would want to live in that scentless world? Not me."

"Come meet my brother tonight at dinner," she said. "You'll have to tell me what you think Quinn wears."

He turned and perused his glass cabinets before facing her again. "From what little you've told me, I'd say he'd be guided toward leather notes. And bergamot. But we'll see."

She stood, the perfume bottle tucked carefully in her hand. "I can't wait."

"Caitlyn, if I may..."

He ran his slender, well-manicured hands down his

suit. It struck her that this was the first time he'd ever seemed at a loss for words.

"I hesitate to say this, but I feel I'd be doing you and myself a disservice if I did not. While I've been here in the lavender, I've been asking myself questions much like the ones I've asked you and Beau. The one that stood out bears mention, for all of us. What is the single thing worth living for?"

The question startled her for a moment. Had he thought about not going on after his wife died?

"My answer remains unchanged. It's love. I had a great love, one I thought I could never replace. Here, I've come to see that my life is about discovering new people and passions. Our lives are but vehicles to find and feel more love. However things go in the next couple weeks and months of your own loss, I hope you'll remember that."

She nodded. "I will, Ibrahim, and if I forget, I'll have you roll up a piece of paper and hand it to me as a reminder."

"Count on it," he said, reaching for the violet handkerchief she'd left on the table. He dabbed it with a vial on the table and handed it to her. "Your scent, *chérie*. Wear it proudly."

She left with her head held high, her perfume bottle in one hand and the scented handkerchief in the other. The harvest was in. The perfume was done.

Time to bring it home like the businesswoman she was.

She searched the farmhouse for Quinn and found him with her father and Flynn at the kitchen table. They were all drinking wine, serious frowns on their faces.

"Flynn! When'd you get here?"

He was out of his chair and had his arms wrapped around her tightly. "I hopped on a flight as soon as I saw the headlines. I only wish I'd gotten here before that jerk left. I would have laid him flat. I filled Trev and J.T. in, and they feel the same way. No one messes with our sister."

She caught Quinn's eyes, and he nodded. "That goes for Con and me too."

"Can a father punch someone out and still be a good role model?" A smile rose briefly on his face.

"That's sweet of you guys," she said, "but unnecessary. Where's everyone else?"

"Arthur and Clara are in their room, and Michaela is sitting with Chou-Chou." Flynn made a face. "She's a softie. That darn goat was crying something fierce."

Missing Beau, she imagined, just like she was.

Her dad rose and put his arms around her. "Can I talk to you for a minute?"

Nerves danced in her belly. "Sure, Dad."

They walked into the hallway, and he tapped his thigh for a moment. Was he going to chew her out for bad business practices? Best head this off.

"I know I screwed up," she said.

He waved his hand. "Why would you think you needed to say that to me?" Something flashed in his eyes. "Damn, your mother was right. You kids are afraid of me."

She blinked. "Mom said that?"

"She's said it since Connor was born, but I wouldn't hear it. I guess I didn't want to believe it. I love you kids with everything I am."

Crap. She was going to cry again. "We know that, Dad."

"Do you? Caitlyn, when you texted to thank me for bringing you those lavender soaps from Provence when you were sixteen, I honestly didn't know what you were talking about. But your mother did, God love her. She's been the true north of my compass from the moment I met her. She told me it was the only gift I'd ever given you."

He started to pace while she stood there speechless. Her mother had said that?

"I told her that was crazy. I'd given you a lot of things.

Of course, I couldn't name any, and she laughed at me like she does whenever I don't want to admit she's onto something."

Go, Mom, she thought.

"It took me a few days to admit she was right. I worked a lot when you were kids, and I let her do most of the parenting. That included the gift giving. She did all that and more. I came here because...I wanted you to know I have a lot more to give you than a set of lavender soaps bought over fifteen years ago. You mom has been saying I need to spend more time with you kids—that I need to get to know the men and women you've become. That's why she didn't make this trip with me. When she's around...you gravitate to her. Makes sense, of course, but I need to forge a new path."

She bit her lip as he extended his hands to her before dropping them.

"I very much want to get to know you," he said, looking more unsure than she'd ever seen him. This wasn't the Shawn Merriam who ruled Merriam Enterprises for decades. This was a scared father, one made more approachable by his vulnerability.

"If you'll let me," he said, his mouth lifting briefly to form a smile. "If I'm not too late."

"Oh, Daddy," she said, crying softly to herself as she stepped forward and hugged him.

He cupped her head like he used to when she was little and curled her face into his neck. "*Thank you*, Caity girl."

"Everything all right in here— Whoa!" Flynn's face froze in place.

Caitlyn laughed, squeezing her father one last time and then stepping over to her brother. Flynn had come to save her, and that earned him his own hug.

"You'll have to tell me about that chat later," he whispered in her ear.

"You're not getting away so easily, son," her dad said when she and Flynn parted. "Come here, Flynn."

His eyes widened as their dad grabbed him and man-hugged him. "What the hell?" Flynn mouthed to her.

All she could do was smile in return.

"I hate to break up...whatever this is..." Quinn appeared in the hallway, shaking his head as if they were all crazy. He sidestepped when their father released Flynn and reached for him. "Leave us with a little dignity, please."

"Hugging is going to undo your dignity?" their dad asked.

"Yes, very much." Turning to Caitlyn, Quinn said, "I know things have been trying today, but we need to create a new plan of action."

"I know," she said, nodding. "But do you want to smell my perfume first? Ibrahim finished it today." She'd find Michaela in a second. Her sister couldn't hear an animal's cries without trying to comfort them.

There was a chorus of yeahs from everyone save Quinn, who just stood there with his arms crossed. God, he really did need a hug, but she wasn't going to force the issue. She handed Flynn the handkerchief first.

"I like it," he said after inhaling it. "Bold yet spicy and earthy. Fun yet complex. I know a few models who are going to love wearing this."

Quinn rolled his eyes. "Only a few? Here, let me smell it."

"You don't need to sound so touchy," she told him as Flynn passed the handkerchief.

He sniffed. "It's pleasant."

"Pleasant?" She wasn't surprised at his bland answer, but she still wanted to slap him silly. "You're a Neanderthal. Even the Perfume Jedi couldn't help you."

"What?" he asked.

"Oh, never mind," she said, grabbing it from him and passing it to her father.

He pressed the handkerchief to his nose, and her heart was too deeply lodged in her throat for her to tell him he didn't need to work that hard. He sniffed again. It was almost painful to watch.

"It's beautiful, honey," he said at last. "The most beautiful perfume I've ever smelled."

And with it, her heart took flight. Yes, she was ready to soar.

"What are you going to call it?" her dad asked.

She looked at the men who'd helped build her foundation and thought of Beau. Then she took the handkerchief and inhaled again, focusing on the grapefruit and cinnamon notes. Her. All women.

"*Cherish*," she said. "Every woman wants to feel cherished. By the ones she loves, but mostly by herself."

"I think we have a winner," Flynn said, lifting her up in the air like she was a champion.

With the scent of Cherish swirling around her, she felt like a champion. She felt like champagne bubbles rising in a glass.

Now it was time to share that feeling with the world.

CHAPTER 28

WHEN BEAU LANDED IN NASHVILLE, HE HAD A NEW SONG and a handle on Ibrahim's first question.

Still, he opened the man's final question to him with trepidation:

At the end of your life, what is the one thing you'll wish you'd done?

He reread the question. How was he supposed to answer that? He wasn't dying.

Not even close. Then it hit him. He wouldn't want there to be *one* thing. He'd want to go to his Maker with no regrets.

Caitlyn. He couldn't let her be a regret. She was supposed to be his present and future and everything in between. Somehow he had to win her back. He was hoping the new song he'd written would help, but he had other action items, the first of which was calling Arthur Hale via Michaela, who'd given him her phone number when she'd first arrived.

She picked up her phone at once, and he realized he hadn't thought to calculate the time. Clearly she was up. "I don't think I should be talking to you," she said without ceremony.

"I can understand that, and I'm not asking you to.

Would you put Arthur on, please? I need to ask him something."

"Everyone is packing up, getting ready to head off to our respective homes, except for me. I'm going to New York with Flynn and Caitlyn. I'm only telling you that in case you're not the douchebag my brothers think you are."

Her voice was a mixture of ire and hope—a relief. He'd have work to do with her brothers, but Michaela would forgive him if he proved himself. "Thanks for telling me. I'm working on turning this around."

"Work fast," she said. "Here's Uncle Arthur."

"You ready to talk turkey?" The older man huffed. "I can't imagine why else you'd be talking to me."

"Answer this question for me. I think I have it myself, but somehow I knew you would confirm it for me. What would you do if someone you loved lied to you or made you a party to their lie?"

"That's easy. I'd tell them to get their head out of their ass. Then I would hold them accountable. Untangle myself from their bullshit."

He got to his feet as the flight attendant took his bags off the plane. "That's what I thought." Difficult, but not impossible. "Michaela mentioned she's heading to New York. You might go as well. I'm going to send you some tickets to *The Morning Show*."

"Why would I want to go to a morning show? Takes me an hour to crawl out of bed these days. Oh, be quiet, Clara. That's not what I meant."

"I'm performing, and you might be interested in hearing it. Tell Hargreaves I'd like him there too if he would be willing." When he stepped outside, the humid air enveloped him in its stickiness. He welcomed it. It was good to be on familiar ground for what he needed to do next.

"Are you planning on making things right with Caitlyn? I won't lie and say it'll be easy. We're talking a serious magic act here."

"I know it," he said, stepping into the back of the car he'd arranged to meet him. "Lucky for me I know some pretty magical performers to back me up. See you soon, Arthur."

"Bah!" was all he heard before the call ended.

He headed straight to Rye's house like his friend had suggested via text. Jake, Clayton, and Georgia would join them for a powwow. Tory opened the door, a laughing Boone on her hip.

"Beau! Welcome. Rye thought it best for you to come here since you wouldn't have any food in your house. I made some smoked brisket and chocolate cake. Rye seems to think he has food cravings even though I'm the pregnant one."

"Baby!" Boone cried, poking his mama's still-flat belly.

"Yes, congratulations! Rye told me the great news."

"We're so excited. Aren't we, Boone? Maybe a baby sister to balance out all this tough-guy energy in the house. Come on, everyone is out back. Georgia can't wait to meet you. By the way, I like the new look personally. We can't all wear leather vests without shirts like Rye used to."

That remark got him laughing. "I actually have one of those now."

She blinked. "Really? I expect a lot of women are going to want to see that."

When he let himself out on the back patio, Rye let out a war cry. The rest of the group turned, Clayton looking like a country badass next to a petite woman with fiery red hair. Jake lifted his hand in greeting, his low-key persona the complete opposite of Rye, who came barreling toward him.

His friend bear-hugged him. "The man of the hour! Thank God you gained seven hours in all that time zone craziness. We're going to need it all, Bubba." He looked him straight in the eye. "You still doing okay?"

He nodded. "Getting more grounded by the minute. Hey, Clayton. Jake. And you must be the famous Georgia Belle. Thanks for stepping in and helping out."

The woman with the fiery red hair was eyeing him like Colette did, looking for angles only she could see. "I don't like anyone getting knocked down when it ain't his fault. Plus, I like your new look. I sure as hell love the new songs. Your old record label is going to be missing you something fierce. Bet your ass on that."

"We're booked on *The Morning Show* the day after tomorrow," Clayton said, shaking his hand. "I got you time for two songs and a joint interview. They want to talk to you, Rye, and Jake together, but they understand the focus is you."

"Jake is a man of few words anyway," Rye said, nudging the former soldier.

Beau shook his hand. "Thanks for volunteering to help turn things around."

"My pleasure," he said. "Besides, my wife, Susannah, is a big fan and so are her sisters."

"My wife too," Clayton said. "Now let's—"

"Before we get going on music, I want to talk about the Ryan Williams thing." He took a long, deep breath. He'd told Rye about his conversation with his mama, but not about the decision he'd made later. "I know I told my mama I would do it in exchange for the name of my father, but I just can't keep my word on this. I won't lose the woman I love over my mother's lie."

Thank God Ibrahim had phrased his moral dilemma clearly. He owed him a debt of gratitude for that and so much more.

"I told you that you'd better marry the woman you wrote the sunshine song for," Rye said, clapping him on the back. "I'm glad you found your way even though it's dicey."

He rubbed the back of his head, which was throbbing

after the hours he'd spent agonizing over this decision. "It's never easy to say bad things about your mama, but she was wrong to make me a party to her actions. The truth is: I don't want to do the Williams' cologne. I want to do Caitlyn's perfume. Even if I wasn't in love with her, I'd want to do it. I believe in it. Clayton, I know I might get dinged for breaking a contract, and I'm prepared to accept the consequences."

"I'd recommend hiring John Parker McGuiness as your lawyer to talk to the Williams people," Clayton said. "He's got a way about him. He'll find a way to settle this with minimal damage to your word or pocketbook."

"I don't care about the pocketbook none," he said. "But my word matters. People need to know it still does."

Georgia strolled toward him. "Your mama will get dinged too, you know."

Guilt wrapped iron bands around his belly, but he couldn't let this one slide. Mama might never understand why he'd broken his word to her, but she'd been wrong to ask him to uphold her lie to the Williams people in exchange for something she should have freely given him. "I know it. I can't help that. Since I plan on finding my real father and hope to get to know him, the truth of our split is probably going to come out anyway."

"Perhaps on *The Morning Show*?" Georgia's eyes were shrewd. "That would certainly help turn the tide."

He'd thought of that. "I want to meet my real father as soon as I can. When I learned he used to work at the school I went to..." He still couldn't put words to the way it made him feel.

"We'll ask Vander Montgomery to find him," Clayton said. "He's the best P.I. in town. Plus, he's basically family."

His heart seemed to lift, even though the winds were shaky. Mr. Garcia—Dad—had wanted to know him when he was seven. Did he still? Beau had agonized over that question, but deep down, he believed his daddy would want to be in his life. He planned to find out either way.

Georgia ran her blood-red nails over his velvet jacket. "Personally, I'm glad you're making your own decisions, Beau. It's hard for young singers, especially ones managed by family. I've seen it more times than I can count. Plus, it's high time for you to step out of that one-dimensional good ol' boy persona. I'm always skeptical of boys who are too good."

Beau choked out a laugh. "Glad you're on board."

"Never had that problem with me, did you, Georgia?" Rye said, putting his arm around her.

"True, but I never believed you were as bad as you said you were either. And I was right." She gave him a pointed look and glanced at the house. "You've got another baby on the way, honey. Makes my heart happy since my own son and daughter-in-law are still so focused on their careers."

Clayton sighed. "We're going to give you plenty of grandbabies, Mama. Don't worry. All right. Mama and I need to run with a few things. I'll call John Parker and get things moving with the Williams people. Jake here can talk to Vander. Mama, you're up on the social media front and putting out feelers to other record companies."

"That last part is a piece of cake," Georgia said, giving Beau a pat on the chest. "Especially after they hear you perform live in New York. I'm going to make sure every Nashville heavy has their TV turned on. The calls will start rolling in. Expect the biggest deal of your life, kid."

He hoped so, but he'd looked at the media coverage. They were making Caitlyn out to be both a temptress and a scorned woman. They had some major shoveling to do, but he was ready.

"I only want to sing what I want," he said. "My songs are my truth, and no one is gonna squelch that." His mama had tried to make him do that, and he wasn't sure he could forgive her. He still hadn't decided if he was going to keep paying her full salary or not. It wasn't about the money, which he could afford. It was about rewarding bad behavior. He wanted to come to the right decision free of all guilt or obligation to her.

"Speaking of," Clayton said, "y'all should start working on the music. Three country singers showing up together is news, but two of them backing up another headliner? They're already salivating in The Big Apple."

"Let's head to my studio," Rye said, pushing Beau toward the house. "I haven't seen Georgia and Clayton on a tear like this since my own media debacle. See how that turned out, Bubba? I got me the best wife and family a man could hope for out of that."

He thought about Caitlyn. He was hoping she'd keep her heart open to him and everything he planned to say and do in the next thirty-six hours. Either way, he would speak his truth. She deserved nothing less. "I hope you're ready to learn a new song. I'm swapping out 'Sunshine in Her Eyes.'"

Rye stopped short and looked over at Jake, who frowned. "Are you insane, Bubba?" Rye burst out. "That song is for your woman. It's perfect!"

Beau planted his feet, calling to mind the soft earth in the lavender fields. His gut was certain of this change. "She knows that song. I even performed it in front of her family. I wrote her another, one I hope and pray is going to turn the tide for good."

"What's it called?" Jake said.

He smiled, his heart quivering with uncertainty and hope. "'Love Among Lavender.'"

CHAPTER 29

MATCHMAKING HAD NEVER BEEN THIS DIFFICULT IN THE old days.

Certainly, it shouldn't involve subterfuge, and yet Arthur had joined Clara in insisting the entire family go out for breakfast at a restaurant right across the street of *The Morning Show*. Caution was part of matchmaking too, Clara had pointed out. Although Beau had followed through and sent them tickets, they didn't want to ambush Caitlyn without knowing what he planned on saying. If it was good—and it had better be prime—they wouldn't need to push the girl to cross the street.

Flynn had begrudgingly helped choose a restaurant with plenty of TVs, and Michaela had sweet-talked the manager into tuning it to the show Beau was headlining and cranking up the volume for her elderly uncle, God help him.

Sacrifices to his ego were also a part of matchmaking, it seemed. He'd have to keep those to a minimum going forward.

Hargreaves had even joined them, a silent vote of faith in whatever his flamenco student had planned. Clara kept giving Arthur knowing looks as he pushed around the worst oatmeal he'd ever tasted. If this was what New

Yorkers ate, no wonder they looked so stiff as they wove their way through the throng of people on the sidewalk outside the restaurant's windows. He didn't remember people being this rude, but then again, he hadn't lived here for some sixty years.

"Looks like *The Morning Show* is just starting," Michaela said, her hair damp from her shower.

Arthur glanced back at the TV. "Hold on to your butts," he muttered.

Michaela let out a nervous laugh. "You're quoting Samuel L. Jackson? Oh, that's so cool! Isn't it cool, Caitlyn?"

"Yep." Her monosyllabic answer was as clipped as her attitude. The poor girl looked like she'd cried her eyes out after showing them to their rooms.

Clara's elbow startled Arthur into dropping his spoon on the floor. It clattered as he heard a booming voice from the TV set announce: "Beau Masters is here with friends this morning. Grab your coffee. You don't want to miss this."

Caitlyn gasped, her gaze flying to the TV. Michaela had made sure her sister sat facing the TVs.

Sure enough, Beau filled the large-screen TV over the bar. The black velvet jacket, paired with a white shirt, jeans, and boots made him look like a country boy going to the Oscars, if you asked Arthur, but he knew some people liked the style.

"That's—"

"Beau," Clara finished, putting a hand on her niece's arm. "Yes, dear. Appears so."

"*He* doesn't look jet-lagged," Flynn growled. He was facing away from the TV, but he'd darted a look over his shoulder.

"He's a performer," Michaela said, resting her elbows on the table. "And my God! Is that Rye Crenshaw and Jake Lassiter too? I saw the show was advertising two other surprise guests."

The girl may have a Ph.D. in food stuffs, but she'd never earn one in subterfuge.

"I believe it is," Arthur said, following this insane script.

"Did you know about this?" Caitlyn stood and looked pointedly at all of them.

Arthur sighed. "The jig is up."

Clara patted his hand. "Shush. Caitlyn, he's making some important announcement."

Arthur rose and pushed her into his chair. "If he says something that makes you angry, you can throw red hots at the TV." He withdrew a few from his pocket and scattered the ammunition onto the table, making Hargreaves frown at him, likely because eating them now wouldn't be sanitary. "But maybe you'll like what he says."

The female host came on, beaming a smile as fake as her shiny white teeth, saying, "We're here with a man who's been making a lot of waves with his new look and a recent trip to France. Beau Masters is on our show this morning, and he's brought along two of his friends, Rye Crenshaw and Jake Lassiter. Welcome, gentlemen."

"This had better be good," Flynn ground out.

"Be quiet," Michaela said with a hiss.

The camera panned out to show the entire group. Rye and Jake were both wearing T-shirts under jackets, but Beau's velvet look stood out. They'd also positioned him in the center of the couch, which was no accident, Arthur knew. He was glad to see Caitlyn was riveted to the screen, just like the rest of them.

"This is quite a new look for you, Beau," the female commentator said, motioning to his attire. "Tell us what's prompted this change in your image."

Beau gave the woman his full attention and smiled, practically beaming star power, the kind Arthur had

seen in other great celebrities at showtime. After inter-
viewing people for decades, he recognized when they
turned it on, and Beau sure as hell had just turned it
on. This was a side of Beau he hadn't seen in France.

"Well, it's the darndest thing when you realize
you've been dressing the same way since you were a kid
in school. You know I started out in country music when
I was sixteen, and it's like I got trapped in some fashion
time warp. While I was in the countryside of France, I
came across this man who seemed so comfortable in
his skin. He wasn't wearing jeans and a button-down
shirt, like I was used to. Maybe men are different than
women, but I decided I wanted a makeover, something
new and different to better showcase the man I am
now. I was lucky to find a married couple who ran this
wonderful boutique. They helped me blend some new
threads with my normal look."

"I'm going to have to borrow that jacket sometime,
Bubba," Rye said with a determined wink. "My wife
likes the velvet."

"I couldn't pull it off in a million years," Jake added,
smiling.

The commentator laughed. Everyone smiled.
Arthur glanced at Caitlyn. *She* wasn't smiling. Yet.

"I have to agree with Rye's wife," the woman said.
"I like the velvet jacket too. And with the jeans and the
boots? Ladies, am I right? This is a *really* good look,
Beau."

Female cries and a shower of applause followed her
prompt, and the camera panned to the crowd.

"Y'all are going to make me blush," Beau said, waving his hand when the camera panned back to the interview. "But thank you kindly."

"Wait until you see his upcoming wardrobe change,"
Rye said. "I'd like to say he stole it from my closet, but
this was all his idea."

"Oh, we can't wait," the host said. "You'll all be performing two songs in just a minute, but we also wanted to talk about the new product you're promoting."

Beau nodded. "Yes, but it's not Ryan Williams' cologne like the press release said."

Caitlyn's mouth dropped open, and Michaela stood up and said, "Oh. My. God."

"Okay, I'm glad you dragged us all out of bed, Uncle Arthur," Flynn said, turning his chair around to face the TV. "Listen up, Caity girl."

"I'm listening," she whispered.

"That's been quite a boo-boo," the host said gently, but her eyes reminded Arthur of a hawk ready for some meat.

"Yes," he said, "it has. You see, my mama has been my manager since I first started my music career, and it's a tough thing for me to admit we've hit an impasse. I recently learned that Walt Masters wasn't my real father, and it put some pressure on our relationship. While I was away in France, she made the decision to sign with the Ryan Williams people without talking to me."

Caitlyn stood up next to Michaela, and Arthur smiled as he saw them reach for each other's hands.

"My goodness, that must have been terribly upsetting," the host said.

Arthur could tell the woman hadn't been briefed on this part of the interview because she fumbled her notes.

"It was, especially since I was in France with the owner of the perfume I still hope to promote. It's a new venture from Caitlyn Merriam, and it's called Cherish."

Caitlyn gasped. "How did he know—"

"I told him," Michaela said, looking at her sister. "I'll tell you about that later."

"Listen to the interview, Caitlyn," Arthur barked out. If he wasn't mistaken, Hargreaves' mouth twitched.

"I wanted to help share this perfume with y'all because

the message speaks to me. Caitlyn hopes to make women around the world realize they deserve to be cherished. Not just by the men in their lives, but by themselves. That's a concept I can get on board with. I figure women work really hard, and they need to be told more often how much we appreciate them."

Nicely done, Arthur thought. He took another look at Caitlyn. She had tears falling down her face. A good sign. He nudged Clara and noticed she had tears streaming down her cheeks too. Good God. No wonder the other patrons in the restaurant were staring at them.

"I'm guessing this wasn't just a business deal for you, Beau. The famous picture that blew up over the internet," the woman said. "That was of you and Caitlyn Merriam."

"Yes," he said, a smile touching his face. "I hadn't planned on falling completely in love with her. I mean, I loved her perfume proposal when I read it. We were like kindred spirits. Her heart was in her vision, much like I always try to put mine in my songs. She'd invited me to visit her farm in France, and I went there to clear my head and write some songs after finding out about my real father."

"It must have been a horrible shock to her when the press release went out about Ryan Williams," the woman said, her eyes narrowing.

He shook his head and his sigh gusted out. "Yes, and I can't blame her. Thankfully, the Williams people have been very understanding. I've parted ways with my mama as my manager over the incident. I can't have anyone speaking out of turn for me, not even my mama. Plus, they deserve someone who believes in their product as much as I do in Cherish."

"I can't wait to smell this perfume," the woman said. "It sounds like every woman needs it. We'll be back with one of Beau's new songs after the break."

Michaela fell back in her chair. "Caitlyn, you'd better get this perfume out fast. Everyone is going to want it."

She was staring at the TV. "I can't... I'm not..."

Arthur stood and patted her shoulder. "How about we cross the street and watch Beau perform? We have tickets."

Caitlyn gaped at him. "We do?"

"We figured if he said something good," Michaela said, "really good, you might be open to going. This is good, all right."

"I'd say," Flynn said, hauling himself out of his chair.

"He really loves me." Her big green eyes were shining, and she was all gooey now.

"Of course he does," Arthur said, pocketing the rest of the red hots before Clara swatted his hand away to stop him. "That was never in question. He just got tangled up with his mother's lies. This is when I tell you he called me from the plane and asked me a question, one I expect came from your Perfume Jedi."

"What did he ask?" she whispered.

He handed her his ever-ready handkerchief. "What do you do when someone you love lies to you or makes you a party to their lie? The thing is, I think he already knew the answer."

"He called his mom out on national TV," she said, blowing into the handkerchief.

"He should have. No one—not even blood—should ever get away with something so wrong. Come on. We have a show to catch."

Caitlyn took one last look at the TV before running to the front door, calling, "Hurry, everybody."

"I'll pay the bill and catch up," Arthur said, shooing the others from the table, including Hargreaves, who only gave him a bland look. Clearly, he didn't take to being shooed. Flynn wasn't all that biddable either—he pulled cash out of his wallet, insistent on paying, and took

Arthur's arm. So long as they were on their way, Arthur didn't much care.

Caitlyn and Beau's future was assured.

He whistled the whole way to the show's entrance, sure he could sweet-talk the producers into letting them backstage and keeping them out of sight until Beau was finished performing. Beau would likely turn into a tongue-tied moron upon seeing the woman he loved. Plus, the young couple deserved a fast exit so they could talk things out and kiss and make up. He was starting to like this gig.

Clara might call herself a budding matchmaker, but he was crowning himself with a new name after today.

He was the Matchmaker Jedi.

CHAPTER 30

BEAU STRUMMED HIS GUITAR IN ONE LAST BROAD STROKE to end the song.

The crowd was cheering, applause washing over them like a rainstorm. Rye strolled closer. "I'd say 'Sometimes Country, Sometimes Confident' is a sure-fire hit. Go change, Bubba. This next one is you alone."

"She's not here," he told Rye, scanning the rows of people again.

"Not yet. Keep up the faith."

He nodded and strode off stage to change outfits. God, he was shaking. All through the interview and performances he'd hoped and prayed this would change things between him and Caitlyn. But Arthur and Clara hadn't brought her. Well, he couldn't blame them. It had been a lot to ask.

He kept his hopes up. She'd hear about the interview. And his performances. If this didn't work, he'd try something else. He wouldn't give up so long as she loved him back.

Clayton appeared in his dressing room with Georgia in tow. "Your real dad wants to talk to you after the show. Vander called him first thing this morning. Told him about today's interview."

He fumbled with the ties on his leather vest, his heart knocking in his chest. "He did?"

"*Focus*," Georgia said, clapping her hands together. "Clayton, did I teach you nothing? You don't drop a bomb like that on a man before he performs. Beau, we have a minute to get you back out there."

"Sometimes performers need a kick," Clayton said with a drawl. "You're killing it out there, man."

"Yes, you are." Georgia pulled Beau by the vest for emphasis. "Okay, Rye has your other guitar. Go out and nail this."

He rushed out, the show's staff a blur as they counted down from commercial. Rye held out his new flamenco guitar and took up his position off camera alongside Jake.

The man behind the camera pointed to him, and he smiled at the tiny metal box. "My real father is from the land of flamenco guitar, and I wanted to honor that. This song is pretty special to me, and it's going out to the woman I call Sunshine."

He bent his head and let his fingers pick at the guitar, the melody playful yet haunting.

*I didn't expect to find
A love beyond all time.*

*Didn't know lavender was as blue as the sky.
Didn't know I'd yearn to hear a baby goat's cry.*

*The country was familiar in a way.
The earth chalky and sometimes gray.*

*The answers I sought were tough.
I figured I had it pretty rough.*

*But then I found love among lavender.
The purples and the blues wrapping around me and my woman.
The soil was warm when I laid her down,*

And loved her that first time.
Couldn't believe a love like this could be mine.

But the storm came in.
That blustering north wind.
And it tore at her hair and mine.

I felt her heart break.
Knew what was at stake.
Couldn't let her go.
I had to be the one to say no.
Tell the storm to go on its way.
With my heart, it would have no sway.

The image I hold dear.
Of her with me in those wild, spicy fields.
That baby goat crying.
The blue sky surrounding us.
Love among lavender.

He sang that last line one more time, his fingers picking at the strings. Opening his eyes, he let himself shrug, trying to come out of that deep place he went when he played. The cries and cheers from the audience washed over him.

Before he gathered himself enough to glance at Rye and Jake, he knew he'd nailed it. Then he froze. Caitlyn was standing beside Rye, who was smiling from ear to ear and pointing at the woman he loved.

The show's host came onto the stage as he stood on unsteady feet, his guitar slipping in his sweaty hands. "Wasn't that the most beautiful love song ever?" she asked the audience. "And we're all loving this leather vest and your new image. If you ask me, more men should show off their chests. Thank you, Beau, for sharing your new songs exclusively with us."

He could barely do more than nod and say, "Thanks for having us."

Then he was walking off stage, and Caitlyn was running to him.

***

Beau scooped her up off her feet and turned them in a circle.

"Thank God," she heard him utter three times in succession before he lowered her back down on the ground.

Since her head was already spinning from the mad dash to the show and his beautiful love song, she simply clutched his vest and said, "You went back on your word for me."

He cupped her face, his eyes a brilliant blue-gray. "No, I kept my word. To you."

"Way to go, Beau!" Michaela shouted, giving a shrill whistle.

She and Beau looked over. Flynn and Uncle Arthur and Aunt Clara were smiling like crazy, giving each other high fives as Michaela danced in place. Hargreaves gave her brother a pointed look, one eyebrow arched, when he held up his hand. She found herself laughing at the sight. Rye Crenshaw and Jake Lassiter waved at her, full smiles on their faces.

"Yeah," Rye called. "Go, Bubba!"

The whole crew started to applaud, and then Beau took her hand. "Will you come with me?"

She nodded, and he led her backstage down a hallway to an open door. God bless Uncle Arthur for outing her as Beau's "love among lavender" and convincing one of the crew to let them hide backstage until he finished performing.

"Georgia. Clayton. Can you give us a moment?" He drew her inside, past a red-haired older woman and a handsome man who looked to be their age. "We can make introductions later."

The red-haired woman only patted him on the chest

as they left. The younger man favored her around the eyes, and Caitlyn wondered if they were mother and son. Then Beau closed the door and held out his hands to her. She took them.

"Caitlyn, it wasn't right, what Mama did—or what I did in response. I couldn't lose you over it. I hope you can forgive me."

She shook her head. "After what you just did? On national television, no less. Beau, you're more than forgiven. I'm sorry too."

He drew her to him slowly. "If you're willing, let's agree to a clean slate. I'd hoped you'd come today, and I still plan on setting things right with the rest of your family, but there's something I wanted to talk about with you, and I find I can't pass up this moment."

Sinking to one knee, he pulled something out of his jeans pocket. It was a pink diamond, but in the light, it almost looked lavender to her. Being her kindred spirit, she somehow knew Beau had seen the lavender in the stone too and had selected it for that reason.

"I bought this yesterday with a lot of hope," he said, looking up at her. "Caitlyn Merriam, I love you and promise to cherish you every day we're together. Will you marry me?"

Cherish her. Exactly like her perfume. It was the sentiment she'd always wanted to feel for herself—and from the man she loved. "Yes, Beau Garcia. I'll marry you."

He pulled her down next to him on the floor, her arms banding around him. "You had to up and say my new name, didn't you?"

"Does knowing it make you feel cherished?" she asked, remembering how he'd looked talking about his real father in the interview.

"Yes, and it gives me peace and excitement too." He kissed her then, letting it linger until they were both breathing hard. "He wants to meet me, Caitlyn. I just heard."

She hugged him. "Oh, Beau, I'm so glad."

"Will you come with me, honey?" he asked.

An old vow came to her mind. "Where you go, I go."

His blue-gray eyes brightened and then he kissed her again. *"Yes."*

She wrapped her arms around him. "The perfume is ready," she said, her enthusiasm growing.

"So I heard from your sister. Is that what I'm smelling on you?" He kissed the side of her neck softly, inhaling gently, and continued a trail of kisses down to her collarbone. "I love it. Bold. Spicy. Then a little earthy. I'll dissect it later, after I've finished kissing you—something I can't imagine I'll ever be ready to do. But it's perfect. Like you. Nice name, by the way."

"I thought it apt," she said, her heart finding its way back to a steady beat now, not the wild hammering of before. "You'll be able to get a better sense of it from this." Pulling out the handkerchief she'd crazily tucked in her cleavage before leaving the house for breakfast, she held it out, the scents of grapefruit and cinnamon making her smile. Those were her scents, and she'd be forever proud of them.

"That's my handkerchief," he said, sitting back on his haunches.

She smiled. "No, it's mine. I couldn't leave it at the farmhouse, and I wasn't ready to give up that token from you yet. It was a reminder of a time I wanted to be grateful for, even if we weren't together anymore. I added perfume to remind myself I was complete nonetheless. Now it seems right I placed it against my heart. Beau, I love you."

"I love you too." He took her hand and raised it to his lips. "Well, damn... That makes me feel cherished and then some."

"Good," she said, fitting herself on his lap. "That's how we're both going to feel. For the rest of our lives."

"You bet, Sunshine." He kissed her again, lingering over her lips. "My initials are wrong, though."

"Details," she said, tilting her head to the side to give him better access.

"Aren't you the one who said the devil is in the details?" he asked.

"That's the old me," she said with a laugh. "Now I know all we need is love."

Woven in with a whole lot of cherishing, she thought, as his arms came around her.

EPILOGUE

CLARA SURVEYED THE PARTY IN FULL SWING AT HER brother's Napa estate.

The surrounding vineyards and fields were awash in purples and blues, so reminiscent of the farmhouse where Caitlyn and Beau had fallen in love.

"We pulled that match off by the hair of our chinny-chin-chins," Clara said to her husband, who was holding her hand rather sweetly.

"Too bad Becca and Trevor couldn't make the engagement party in person, but maybe someday," Arthur said. "At least they have other solutions to turn to while she's still being treated for her agoraphobia."

Flynn, ever the techie, had rigged up some high-tech hologram that had the couple literally standing and talking in the crowd even though they were at their home in Ireland. Freaky yet wonderful.

"I love it," Clara said. "Pretty soon we're going to punch a button and bilocate to another place like in *Star Trek*."

"I never took you for a sci-fan fan, Clara," he said, studying her.

She gave him a pout, saying, "There are still many things you have yet to discover about me, Mr. Hale."

Good God, she knew how to keep a man coming back for more. He leaned in and kissed her softly on the cheek, the better to smell her sexy perfume.

"It was good to see Ibrahim today," Arthur said, Clara's fragrance reminding him of the man they all called the Perfume Jedi. "He's working on the men's cologne now that Quinn has issued Caitlyn additional capital."

"As he should," she said with a regal nod of her head. "The wait list for Cherish is in the millions, Arthur. They've made a fortune, and it's not even out yet. You know, we should try and find the Perfume Jedi someone special. Maybe April?"

While he was fonder of his nephew's ex-wife than he was his nephew, and he'd be happy to see her matched with someone like Ibrahim, he still snorted. "He doesn't need any help in that department, my dear. Trust me. That man's got game. He'll find love again, if and when he's ready. Introductions could be made, however."

She grabbed his arm and led him to the makeshift dance floor in the middle of the lawn. She did love her Cole Porter. "So speaks the *Matchmaker Jedi*. I hate it that you have a nickname before I do."

"I've been quicker on my feet since you blew into my life," he said, turning her in a circle. "Speaking of which, I hear Michaela's ex-boyfriend has been calling her. Perhaps you should be the Terminator Jedi, beating any old loves who come out of the woodwork."

She poked him when he brought her back against him. "Not a chance, Arthur. Besides, Flynn tells me Boyd isn't all bad. He and Michaela had a huge misunderstanding. I have a feeling we might be helping Michaela next, what with her old beau coming back around."

Arthur scanned the crowd, looking for the woman in question. Michaela was talking animatedly with Caitlyn and Beau and Beau's real father and wife. Lovely people, the Garcias. Carlos had a flourishing landscaping business in a small town outside Nashville, and Beau had been bowled over to discover his father grew lavender in large pots all over his property, claiming the scent was calming to his animals, which included goats. He'd offered a home for Chou-Chou, so Beau could see the little guy whenever he'd like. After eighty years, Arthur well knew life could be wonderful and yet so weird.

"Since you're so cozy with Shawn these days," he said, turning her again, "maybe we'll stay a while longer in Napa and see if Michaela needs us. It would be nice to stay stateside for a while."

She swayed nicely in his arms but soon she pulled him into a turn. God, she was leading him. Of course, he let her. She was downright happy about it, the way her blue eyes were shining.

"Hargreaves said he was up for a more exotic adventure," she told him, "and I agree."

He could smell a trap coming. "It's that flamenco guitar Beau gifted to him that's giving him ideas, my dear."

She batted her eyelashes at him, continuing to feign innocence. "I know, maybe we should go with Michaela on one of her nature hunts."

When pigs flew. "You with no running water? I'd like to see the day."

She stepped back and did a little shimmy, running her hands down her front like Rita Hayworth back in her Gilda days. God, she was a bombshell.

"Like I said, there are a lot of things you don't know about me, Arthur Hale."

This time he was the one who spun her out. "I look forward to learning all of them, Mrs. Hale."

When Clara's brother appeared for the next dance, Arthur kissed his wife's cheek and headed for the young Merriam children. J.T. and Caroline were talking to Quinn and Connor, who still looked like they needed some serious time off. My goodness, had their Grandpa Emmits, his friend and mentor, ever looked so severe in a suit? They needed to learn to relax like their other siblings. If he had to, he'd help them along.

Oh, but he loved this new generation of Merriams. They sure knew how to party, and he knew another secret of age, one he'd divulge to Clara if she was especially nice to him.

Spend enough time around young people, and you'll feel younger too.

***

Michaela couldn't help but dance in place as she signed for the turquoise box wrapped in a sparkly white ribbon. It was pretty early for a delivery, just eight o'clock.

"Who could be sending me a present?" she mused aloud as she closed the slate gray door to her bungalow.

Man, it was good to be home. Caitlyn was heading back to Dare River with Beau to see his house in the country and get to know his friends better. Flynn was back to New York, but before too long he'd probably jet off to Europe to meet up with another model. J.T. and Caroline had gone back to Dare Valley to do museum stuff, and Quinn was probably making people cry in the conference room in London much like Connor did here at headquarters. Uncle Arthur and Aunt Clara were hanging around for a while, so she'd get to see them when she went over for one of her mother's home-cooked meals.

She rushed into the kitchen and set the box on the counter, untying the bow. Shame to ruin it given how perfectly it was tied. Excitement drummed through her as she opened it.

Tears burned in her eyes as she beheld the rarest flower in the world: Queen of the Night. She knew who'd sent the gift before she even opened the note. Boyd.

Bastard.

She'd ignored his calls for weeks now. Like she was

going to talk to him after what he'd done. But he'd never been one to take no for an answer, something she used to respect about him. Now it was like all his other qualities in her mind: questionable.

Only she knew the detailed planning required to get this large white fragrant flower to her. She'd bet this Queen of the Night was from the Arizona desert. It only flowered one night in the year, starting around eight p.m., so he must have had someone waiting to pick it at the penultimate moment and then rush it to her in California before the blooms faded. She had two hours to enjoy the flower before it died.

Seemed rather appropriate since that was what had happened to her love for him.

She studied the flower, her scientific mind kicking in. The white petals were a cluster of perfection, the yellow Orchid cactus from the genus Epiphyllum. The spines on the cactus stalks had been stripped. How kind. Like she'd forget how Boyd had turned from "The One" to a thorn in her side with his betrayal.

He'd given her gifts like this all the time in the year they'd spent together—a year she sometimes wished she could erase from the hundred billion brain cells in her skull. Rare vanilla from Madagascar. Large trumpet-shaped blue gentiana flowers from Tibet. Black turmeric from off the coast of the Bay of Bengal in India.

He wanted something. Badly.

This was too rare a gift for it to be a personal overture. This was about something else. Business. The very thing that had broken them apart seven months ago.

She opened the knife drawer and pulled out the only picture she'd allowed herself to keep after the relationship-burning ceremony she'd held with Caitlyn months ago. Usually she only allowed herself to look at it at two o'clock in the morning because if she were up at that hour, it was because he was still messing with her sleep.

Asshole. The knife drawer had seemed an appropriate place to keep this last piece of him. He'd cut her like no one ever had, and she needed to remember that.

His easy smile used to enliven her spirit. His dark brown eyes had seemed soulful as they'd gazed into hers while they were making love, often under the stars on one of their nature trips. She'd loved to run her hands through his shaggy brown hair. Being on the road so much, he'd always needed a haircut. And his scruff had felt so delicious against her soft skin.

Her phone rang.

Of course. He'd know she'd received his present. Correction. His bribe.

Well, forget him. She returned to the box. Should she enjoy his gift or toss it out? Keep it, she decided. It wasn't the plant's fault Boyd was trying to manipulate her. She pulled out the flower and picked up the turquoise card. She opened it with dread.

I need you. I think I found the Valley of Stars. Pick up the damn phone.

Her harsh gasp sounded in the silent kitchen. No, he couldn't have! For years, they'd heard whispers about a mythical valley deep in the African savannah that contained a rare flower supposedly capable of curing every disease. They'd scoured hundred-year-old travel journals, interviewed countless people. Like her love for him, it had remained a mystery.

Until now...

Could she believe him? Then she reminded herself his claim to need her was horseshit. If he'd found it, he certainly wouldn't want to share the find with her. His betrayal had proved his ruthlessness. No, this was a ruse of some sort, a game she wasn't going to play. He was her competitor these days, and competitors didn't share finds this epic.

The phone started to chime again, and she mercilessly

silenced it and put it on do not disturb. She tossed the card in the trash. Picked up his picture, fingering the edges, still able to feel his silky locks under her fingertips.

She looked at the garbage, ready to drop it in. But she couldn't make herself throw it away yet. Her rage grew.

Given the way he'd betrayed her and her family's business, she could never trust him again.

She was done with him for good.

Dear Reader,

How wonderful it was to be back with a hero who was a country music singer like Beau Masters. Never did I imagine I loved to write songs, but from the first moment with Rye Crenshaw in COUNTRY HEAVEN, I found it came from my soul. Beau, too, was a fabulous creative partner. Maybe it was me sitting in the fields with him alongside his trusty Chou-Chou. What a sight that would have been!

This book holds so many of the things I care about: family, truth, humor, love, personal discovery, and artistry. I never knew how artistic perfume was, and I was like a kid in a candy store researching and buying one essential oil after another and mixing them into magical potions as I wrote this story. To say our house was more fragrant was an understatement, and I know it will always be so from now on.

The Merriam family continues to inspire me, and I'm delighted to hear how much you love them too. Michaela will be going on a grand adventure in VALLEY OF STARS, and to check any games Boyd McClellan wants to play with her, she's bringing along Arthur and Clara but asking them to get their chaperone on (and leave their matchmaking hats at home). I just finished watching the classic movie, Romancing the Stone, again and I have to say, this next book is my own take on a fun adventure romp with my usual feel good threads of family, love, and personal discovery. It's going to be a fun time for us all.

Thanks again for being in our wonderful book family and continuing to embrace The Merriams.

Lots of love,

Ava

ABOUT THE AUTHOR

 International Bestselling Author Ava Miles joined the ranks of beloved storytellers with her powerful messages of healing, mystery, and magic. Millions of readers have discovered her fiction and nonfiction books, praised by *USA TODAY* and *Publisher's Weekly*. *Women's World Magazine* has selected a few of her novels for their book clubs while Southwest Airlines featured the #1 National Bestseller NORA ROBERTS LAND (the name used with Ms. Roberts' blessing) in its in-flight entertainment. Ava's books have been chosen as Best Books of the Year and Top Editor's Picks and are translated into multiple languages.

34918762R00208